Inner Lights

Michael Alan Shapiro

INNER LIGHTS

This work is dedicated
to my brother, Stephen.
May his soul be one with the Lord's.

Other Novels by Michael Shapiro

On Thunder Road

Femeron

Raman Shah

The Cross of Chorrillos

Chapter One
Rachel's Death

December 27th 1979

Driving on Highway 17 from San Jose to Santa Cruz, the winding mountain road climbs up, over and through coastal redwood forests. There are more than fifteen miles of banked S-turn after banked S-turn and I must admit I am one of the guys who enjoys racing over the course. I bought a Triumph TR6 and had a blast chasing Porsche Carreras through those banked S-turns. Today though I was taking a much more leisurely pace. I was driving with the top down and enjoying the sight and scent of the tall redwoods. Their thick brown bark and green branches cover the steep hillside and valleys and their sharp, sweet fragrance filled my car. I drove down off the mountain and entered into the little town of Santa Cruz. Exiting off of the highway and merging into light city traffic, I can see in the foreground, as if in a picture postcard, a white steepled Catholic Church. In the distance, there is a peek of the Pacific where waves crash dramatically onto brown cliff rocks. Through town and past a few lights and I'm up to the University of California. Empire Grade Road begins at the entrance to the university. From there the two lane, black asphalt road winds its way up the mountain going through open meadows and beneath stands of ancient redwood forests. On the left you can see a panoramic view of the rocky northern California coastline a thousand feet below. Twelve miles up Empire Grade, I turn right onto McGregor Path then a left at my driveway and through a meadow of wild grasses and sage to our single story, ranch house in Bonnie Doon.

I pulled into the driveway and came in through the back door by the kitchen. My wife, Mary and the kids, 10-year old Ava and 8-year old Noah were watching television together in the sunken living room. I waved to them and they acknowledged me but remained engrossed in the show. No big deal. I was that way myself. I went down the hall, past the kids' rooms and into the master bedroom. In a moment I was undressed and standing in the shower. I put my face up to the screen window and took a deep breath, filling my lungs with the strong, sweet aroma of sage from our meadow outside. I looked to the sunlit field where the tall grasses swayed in a gentle breeze. The water splashed over my body and I inhaled another breath of crisp mountain air. Suddenly, unexpected laughter shattered my enjoyment. What could make them laugh this loud? I opened the shower door and stuck my head out. That must be one funny tv show. I heard screaming from the living room. It was laughter, right? I mean it sounded like laughter but like screaming too. Okay, no that was screaming. I turned off the water and leaned out to listen closer. Damn, it was screaming! I could hear my wife, Mary and my daughter's voice become one great wail of sorrow.

I hurriedly pulled my jeans on and ran down the hallway in wet, bare feet. Mary was sitting at the breakfast bar between the living room and the kitchen. She held the phone with both hands to her ear. Her body shook as she sobbed. Ava stood several feet away crying. Noah stood next to Mary, silently watching them both.

"What's wrong? What's the matter?" I asked Mary.

Ava answered for her. "Rachel's dead."

"What happened? Rachel? Rachel Lyons?" I pictured Ava's classmate. They rode their ponies together on the old logging trails. "Did she have a riding accident?" I asked Mary.

"Rachel Eisner," Mary said looking up from the telephone. Her eyes were already puffy red and a flow of black mascara beginning to edge down her cheeks.

Chills ran up my spine. "Rachel Eisner? What happened?" My legs shook and tears clouded my vision.

"She was murdered," Mary sobbed.

I felt a flush of anger course through me body. "*No!*" I screamed and punched at God above my head. My scream echoed through the house. My anger turned to a feeling of helplessness and I leaned against the kitchen wall and sobbed.

The last time I saw Rachel she was keeping an eye on her younger brother, Mark while Mary and I finished dinner with her parents at a restaurant in Berkeley. She was eleven years old with raven black hair, dark eyes, a bright smile against olive skin. I recalled the first time I had ever seen her; she was six months old, in a crib looking up and laughing at me. Her coal black eyes and sharp chin a clear resemblance to her father. A toddler at 18 months who could unlock gates. At six she was spunky and mischievous, not afraid of dirt, or worms, beer or boys. She was the kid who made sure everyone got to play. Now in grammar school, she woke at 5am so she could be at school two hours early to practice gymnastics. After school she was off to music lessons or soccer practice. Rachel Eisner was a light in the world, now she was dead in Medford Oregon, two days after Christmas 1979.

Mary finished the call with Rachel's mother, Sarah, then redialed to make the plane and hotel reservations. I sat at the kitchen table, bleary eyed. There had never been a murder in either of our families. All the relatives we had lost, grandmothers, aunts and uncles had all been from illnesses. This violent taking of a young girl was shocking to my entire being. My hands trembled with anger as adrenaline raced through my blood. But I sensed a deeper feeling of blackness that I could not describe. Okay, I get it. I thought. We don't all live happily ever after. And tragedy is ready to crash down on us at any moment. But this brutality; I wasn't able to think or focus on my feelings.

I drank a cup of coffee and thought back to 1969 when Mary and I moved from New Jersey to Santa Cruz. David Eisner was doing his post graduate work in chemistry at UCSC. He and Sarah Eisner had come to Santa Cruz that same year from New York City. That was the year that I started junior college after returning from Vietnam. Both our families had six-month old baby daughters and we met at a yoga class and became fast friends. In the Aquarius days of Santa Cruz, we took acid trips together, smoked hashish and marijuana and generally shared the duties and joys of raising two little ones into the age of Flower Children.

In 1974 the Eisner family, now with a son, Mark, moved to Berkeley where David continued his research into the synthesis of opium, a project funded by the government but one which David categorized as corporate welfare. In 1977 he abandoned his chemistry career and moved his family to Oregon where he started a furniture business. His income dropped dramatically but he was pursuing his lifelong ambition to work with his hands and more importantly to him, to cause no damage to the environment or to society.

"I want to go too," Ava said while Mary spoke to the airline reservations.

"I don't think that would be a good idea," Mary answered after a moment's thought.

"Why not?" Ava asked.

"I think it would be very difficult for Sarah to see you right now."

Ava was quiet but Mary sensed she didn't understand.

"It would be very hard on Sarah because, Ava you would remind her so much of Rachel. Do you see how it might be very sad for her?"

"Yes," Ava said.

The next morning, Mary and I drove down Empire Grade Road past the steepled, white church on Mission Street then onto Highway 17 and over the Santa Cruz mountains to the San Jose airport. In Portland we rented a car and drove to Medford arriving at David and Sarah's home in the early afternoon. They lived in a quiet neighborhood, in a 40-year old, two story house that David had repainted a happy light blue with white trim. Potted ferns and geranium plants lined the porch. Sarah's mother answered our knock wearing no makeup and her eyes red and swollen. She let us into the living room where Sarah sat in a heap on the floor in front of the couch. Her long, wavy black hair with streaks of premature gray fell across her face and down her shoulders. She rose and hugged Mary and me then sat down on the couch and began to cry. Her face was pale with dark circles under her eyes. My lips trembled and before I started to sob, I walked out of the living room and into a hallway. There was a bedroom across from the kitchen and I went in there to compose myself. I took out my handkerchief and blew my nose. I noticed school books and watercolor paintings laying on the small desk next to the bed. Through the half opened closet door I saw Rachel's neatly pressed dresses. Her sneakers lay near the open closet, never to be worn again. I felt great sighs of despair rise uncontrollably up from my chest and I began to cry. David's mother came into the room.

"You must be strong," she said, placing a hand on my shoulder. She was tall and thin. "You'll make it harder for them this way."

"I'm sorry. I can't help it," I said." This is the worst thing that I've ever been through." I blew my nose again.

"For all of us," she said, "but we're all here to help Sarah and David."

"Yes, of course. I'm sorry. I'll do better."

She led me into the kitchen where Sarah and Mary sat at the oak dining room table drinking tea. The winter sunlight filtered through the yellow and white curtains above the double sink. I sat down with them at the table.

"We gave her a tennis racket for Christmas," Sarah said in a hoarse voice as Mary held her hand. "She called her friend, Lisa a couple of days later and the two of them went off to play tennis in the park. About 4:00 o'clock it was getting dark and they were late so I went out looking for them. I called for them all the way past the tennis courts in the school yard. It was dark when I came back home. I was hoping that they would already be in the house but they weren't so I called the police and they sent a car over. While I was talking to the policeman a second police car arrived. Someone had found Rachel's body at the football field. They drove us to the police station to identify her." Sarah's voice broke into sobs.

"Maybe you should take the sedative?" Mary suggested.

"No! I don't want to be numbed." She looked at Mary a moment then squeezed her hand, sighed and continued her story. "She had been beaten, raped then strangled to death."

I felt my hands and legs tremble. Head down, I tried not to sob. In my mind I saw Rachel's face and recalled her distinct way of speaking. She had an overbite which gave her speech pattern a childlike quality.

I recalled one time I was chopping firewood at our house; Rachel was visiting and she took a break from playing with Ava to watch me split the logs with a sledge ax.

"That wasn't too good," she said when I needed to chop three or four times, missing the heart of it on the first swing.

"Now that's the way," she said as I sliced one in two with a single blow.

I heard her voice now in my mind and saw her long black hair and bright eyes.

"They started to question us about whether Rachel smoked pot. 'She's eleven years old,' I said. 'We have to investigate all possibilities,' they said, but when they asked David to take a lie detector test, I screamed until they let us go home." Sarah stopped to take a sip of tea.

No one said anything. Sarah and Mary wept at the table and the house fell into a dark silence.

Afternoon turned slowly to dusk. To me each hour seemed like six. I thought about the killer, out enjoying the day. I imagined taking the killer's mother, cutting out her guts and draping her entrails over his head. I shook off the ghastly vision but not my anger. What kind of family raises a child who can grow up to do something like this? What did they do to him?

Maybe the killer would never be caught. What if he went free? What if they caught him and he didn't get the death sentence? I imagined myself killing the man in court. I had to shake that vision off too.

In the evening the phone rang and I heard Sarah break into fresh sobs. She explained that the police had found Lisa's nude body, wrapped in a blanket and dumped into a ditch off the side of a road. She had been repeatedly raped then smothered to death. The FBI was analyzing the blanket and road blocks had been set up along the California border.

Neighbors and friends brought food and the family ate without sitting down to dinner. Later that night Mary and I left the house and drove to a local motel. As I lay in bed and Mary washed in the bathroom, I heard the wind as it moaned outside our window.

"How could God let this happen?" I asked as Mary came into bed. "Every day little kids are tortured and raped; murdered by these beasts and where is God? Great job He did, creating a world like this!" I yelled and a gust of wind rattled the windows.

"Yelling at God is not going to help," Mary said as she came under the covers. She turned her back to me as she lay down beside me.

"It pisses me off."

"Everything pisses you off," Mary said without turning over.

"When will a defense attorney's child be raped and murdered by someone they defended?" I asked Mary. "When will the judge's grandchildren be destroyed by these animals? And the parole officials who let them loose on society, why is it their families never lose a child by a repeat offender? Man, I wish I had been there. I could have saved them. I would have killed him too. I may kill him yet."

"Can't you realize you don't matter in this?" Mary turned her head to speak over her shoulder. "You cursing God and wanting revenge doesn't bring them back. There's nothing any of us can do except be comforting to David and Sarah."

"Gee, I'm sorry I'm not handling this the way you think I should, boss. Excuse me for feeling angry and vengeful."

"Feel? The only thing you can feel is a rush from heroin or coke."

"Jesus, this is a great time to start on me."

"Paul, I want you to go get help. When we get back to Santa Cruz, I'm going to make an appointment for you. You've got to get sober. We're wasting our lives. Don't you see that? We can't waste another day."

"Why are you going crazy? I'm okay."

"You're okay? Paul, you're not okay. You get high every friggin' weekend."

"Wait a minute. You get high too."

"But I don't have to, you do. If you don't get stoned you mope around and withdraw. Paul, really, I'm not kidding, you have to get help, for the kids' sake. Please, we can't go on like this." She started to cry. I went to hold her but she pulled away. "I can't take it anymore," she sobbed, "not after this. I want real love, a real husband." She began to cry softly under the covers.

I pulled back from her. I went to argue with her but I felt a cold, creep on my skin as I realized she was right. I was empty inside. We had been together since high school, married at twenty and Ava born when we were just twenty-one. For years now I wanted to leave her but our lives were so intertwined I couldn't go. I stayed with her because I loved the children and wanted to be home with them in our house in the mountain meadows.

The wind swept across the roofs of the small town of Medford. It blew violently, howling, crying in anguish like a human voice. Under the covers I thought about the killer. I imagined him hearing this angry wind and knowing it was meant for him. Suddenly, lightning hit the power lines in the street right outside our window. There was an explosion of sound and white light. I jumped out of bed and looked through the window at the sparking power line as it danced around in the road outside the motel. I felt God's wrath unleashed. "You're too late, damn it," I shouted. Then in a whisper, "You're too late."

The next morning, I put on a dark blue suit and drove with Mary to the mortuary. Under a thick gray cloud cover, we walked in silence across the parking lot toward the single story, brick building. The sound of our shoes on the gravel driveway was dulled by the heavy morning air. The smell of rain and decaying leaves on the green lawn filled my nostrils as we walked up the steps and into the mortuary. Sarah and David were inside sitting in the mourners' room. I embraced them then looked out the windows at the cold, grey morning. The Oak trees stood motionless. Their naked, leafless branches covered with the night's dew.

"Would you witness the cremation with us?" Sarah asked. "Neither my parents nor David's want to."

"Yes, of course," I said and Mary agreed. A half hour later we walked into a room with yellow floor tiles. Two men in white coveralls rolled a steel sled with Rachel's wooden coffin into the incinerator chamber. One of the men pushed a button and the incinerator's thick iron doors slowly creaked shut. We held hands with Sarah and David.

The incinerator startled me with a loud pop. We watched through glass windows as the flames ignited the coffin. It burned white hot. Her body and the coffin were reduced to ashes in a matter of minutes. I wept. The meaning of the words eternity and finality struck me like a hammer. The flame went out and silence filled the mortuary room.

"Over," I said under my breath, feeling the finality of death. I wept, Sarah and Mary sobbed, David rocked back and forth, one foot to the other in what looked like a Tai Chi exercise.

I recalled my father's funeral eight years before. The cantor's voice sang mournfully as the congregation stood outside at the gravesite under dark skies. The smell of wet mowed lawn heavy in the spring air as the polished coffin was lowered into the ground. When the mourners dropped handfuls of dirt into the open hole, the sound of the dirt clods hitting the wooden coffin shot through to my heart, and through each nerve ending. The meaning of the words eternity and finality struck me.

Later in the day, at the memorial service Rachel's teacher played a guitar and led the audience in singing Rachel's favorite song, "You are my sunshine, my only sunshine. You make me happy when skies are gray..."

Next, a young Rabbi with a short, well-trimmed beard stood before the community of mourners and offered his benediction. "I ask only that we keep faith with the Lord our God. He has created all things for his own purposes. We are his children and we must trust in his infinite wisdom. We can have confidence in the knowledge that Rachel and Lisa are now at peace and are resting in the bosom of the Lord where they will be cherished and protected for all time. For it is written," he put his reading glasses on and read from a prayer book;

'Fear not death;
It is the lot of all flesh
Death is better than a bitter life;
And Eternal rest better than a ravaging sickness.
Set your heart aright and be steadfast,
And despair not in time of tribulation.
Be comforted in your sorrow;
Think not that the grave ends all.
Man's flesh links him to the animal,
But his spirit unites him with the Eternal.
Shall God who made life out of nothing
Be unable to turn what had life into higher life?
All things that are from the earth return to the earth,
And what is from on high returns on high.
All that is false and unjust is destroyed,
But that which is true abides forever.
The righteous live forever, and their reward is in
Thee, O Lord.'"

After the service Mary and I drove to the Eisner's house. We walked up the porch steps, stopping to wash our hands at the water dish put out for mourners. Later, sitting inside, greeting relatives and friends of the Eisners, I had a feeling that Rachel was okay, overlooking us now and in perfect peace. Not long afterwards, Sarah received a telephone call. She shared the news that the murderer had been caught. He was a 26-year old illegal immigrant who had been living in San Francisco. He was on parole after serving three years of a 10-year sentence for the kidnapping of a young girl. He had been caught then before he had had a chance to harm that little girl. I was happy for her but angry that they had ever let him out.

The killer had told the Medford police that he had lured Rachel and Lisa into the announcer's booth at the football stadium by telling them that he had found a puppy. When they were inside the booth, he tried to take off Rachel's clothes. She fought and scratched him. He punched her into submission then raped her. Even semi-conscious, she fought back. In the struggle, he strangled her to death. Lisa, witness to these horrors, did not resist as he raped her then took her to his car. He had her for the next four hours until he finally smothered her in a blanket and dumped her body off into a ditch on the side of the road.

The police told Sarah that the killer needed to vomit when he gave them his confession.

As I listened to the details, the anger came over me again. "I have to go for a walk," I said and got up and walked outside and stood on the porch. To my surprise the door opened behind me and Mary came out. I looked at her but didn't say anything. I walked down the front steps and she followed. I walked slowly so she could catch up. When she came along side me, I looked over at her. She kept her head down and walked in silence.

"And now with this creep," I finally said as we walked in the chill, autumn air. "Yet another defense attorney will try to find a technicality to get him off. People meeting this pig will treat him with kindness while others try to keep him out of the electric chair. Just once why isn't it one of those people's little girls? Maybe they would stop worrying about the criminals and more about the next little kid he'll get to."

Mary matched my rage with a cold silence until we turned to go back to the house. "What happened to you that you need rage to cover up your feelings?" she asked me, looking up into my face.

"Why are you analyzing me?" I asked.

"Why shouldn't I? Think about it. Your anger helps nobody, especially not you."

"No, I suppose not. But it's me, my anger. I'm not making it happen. It just happens. It's me. You've known me a long time, Mary. How come now, you don't like me? You don't like the way I act, what I feel, what I say."

She didn't answer me. We hardly talked at all the next day. I even tried to cheer her up. I didn't like this feeling, this divide between us. I also did not want to confront our problems. Mary hardly responded to my small talk. Not then or on the way to the airport or on the flight home. She finally broke her silence as we drove up Empire Grade Road in our blue Mazda station wagon. The car our children called, Blueberry.

"I don't think we should live together anymore," she suddenly said.

"What are you talking about?" I looked at her from the passenger seat.

"I'm wasting my life with you. You don't love me."

"I don't love you? Come on."

"You don't, be honest for once. We haven't been in love in years."

I sat silently, looking out at the majestic Santa Cruz mountain range. "It's not that I don't love you," I finally said. "I'm just messed up. There's no joy in my life. I'm empty inside. I love the kids and our house. Still it's not fun like when we were in high school."

"It will never be like that again but you can't walk around being depressed all week and then getting high every weekend. Don't you understand? I can't waste any more years with you like this."

I wasn't able to tell her my honest feelings; I did want to leave her. I did want to find someone new.

"But I have nowhere to go," I finally said.

"You can get an apartment in town. Maybe you can move in with George for a while. We have to do something. I can't go on like this."

"We can't afford for me to get an apartment and I don't want to live with George. I want to be home with the kids. Besides, it's my house. Why don't you move out?"

"I'd love to," Mary said. "Are you going to get the kids up each morning and make them breakfast before you go to work? Are you going to pick them from their friends'? Are you going to…"

"Okay, I get it. No, I can't do all the things you do for them. I don't have the time."

"I work and have the time though, right?"

"Give me a break, would you?"

"So, if I can't leave," she said, "that means you have to."

"No, it doesn't. I'm not going anywhere," I said. "It's my house."

"Do you know why I had the second abortion?" Mary asked after a long silence.

"What did you say?"

"I had the baby aborted because I was afraid there might be something physically or mentally wrong."

"What?"

"And I knew that if the baby wasn't perfect, that you wouldn't be strong enough to handle it."

I sat silent.

"You would run off into your drug world and hide, leaving me and the kids with all the work and all the pain."

"Let me out. I want to walk home," I said.

"You're staying. We're going to talk about our lives."

"You know, you have a monster in you, Mary," I said. "You talk like a man. You act like a man. Well, I want to be with a woman. Someone feminine and..."

"And I want to be with a *man,* she screamed. "Someone who doesn't run away."

"Let me out, god damn it, you flabby-tit, son-of-a-bitch."

Mary turned the steering wheel hard right, a boulder protruding out of the mountain wall scraped my door. I grabbed the steering wheel with one hand and turned the car left. Mary pulled it back into our lane then came to a stop.

"I'm going to walk home," I said.

"Wait, don't go. We have to talk," Mary said, her face white with fear.

"Maybe later, right now I just want to get away from you." I got out and walked up Empire Grade Road. She drove past me a few minutes later and I listened as the sound of the Mazda's tires hummed over the asphalt, through the tight turns then was gone. Silence returned to the mountain road. Sunlight streaked through the canopy of Redwood trees. The countryside was peaceful in stark contrast to my world.

What was I going to do? This couldn't go on. I had to find someone new, start a new life. I couldn't take her any more, everything I did was wrong. But how? How to do it quickly?

It took over an hour for me to walk the two miles up to the open meadow. I arrived home just before 3 o'clock. The winter sun had already lost its heat. It was a time of day that depressed me. I remembered the white front door in the house where I grew up. I would hear the sound of my father's key in the lock. This time of day, the hour before dusk. The merriment that had filled our home changed to solemn foreboding when we heard his car pull into the driveway. We could hear him pull down the garage door. My brother and sister and I waited for him to come through the front door. We could tell in a moment, from the look on his face if he was angry. If he was, the slightest provocation would give chance for his brooding to explode into yelling.

I walked up the back steps. Mary was in the kitchen making supper. "I'm sorry," she said as I closed the sliding glass door. "I think we should go see a counselor. Paul, we have to try something. Things have never been this bad."

"You go. You're the one who's crazy. I'm not paying for the repairs to Blueberry, either. That comes out of your check."

Mary started to cry. "The repairs? What difference does that make?"

"You could have killed me," I said.

"Paul, please. Please go with me to a counselor."

"I'll think about it." I went into the bedroom and changed into jeans then went out to the fenced-in back yard. Our Golden Retriever barked once from her pen, then waited for me, wagging her body in anticipation. I went over to the dog run and let her out.

"Hey, Brick. How you doing, girl?" She circled me, rubbed against my legs, her eyes half closed in bliss.

We walked together on the flat, sandy ground to the pump shed behind the house. I took a hose and watered the potted plants and shrubs around the house.

"Here they come, girl. I can hear the bus." I looked out across the blanket of tall yellow grasses in our meadow. I heard the school bus as it labored up the last bend of Empire Grade Road. Brick took off down the driveway; working the ground for telltale signs of neighborhood dogs. The yellow school bus pulled to the side of Empire Grade and six children of various ages and sizes got off. They shouted to their friends on the bus then split into groups to walk home. Ava and Noah came up the driveway with Brick leading the way.

"Hi, Dad." They both called out as they reached the front of the house.

"Hi. How was school?"

"Fine," Ava answered for them.

"Little League sign up is next week, Dad," Noah said, his young face excited at the thought.

"Oh yeah, already?"

"Are you going to coach again this year?" Ava asked me. She had her backpack on and had combed her hair for the bus ride home. Her green, hazel eyes and cheek bones had Mary's look.

"Noah will be in the big leagues this year," I said, "and they haven't asked me to coach but I'm sure I'll help out."

The children went into the house as I finished watering. Mary had set out snacks for them and smiled but they noticed her red eyes and felt a change in the atmosphere. There was a sadness in the silence between their parents and an air of foreboding that they could not name.

I didn't go to a marriage counselor with Mary. I hoped instead that we would either weather this storm as we had others, or that I would meet someone and would have a place to go. Rachel's death and Mary's new intolerance motivated me to stay sober but a few weeks later without my usual self-medication, the tension became unbearable. I woke up one morning unable to get out of bed.

"I can't move," I said as Mary dressed for work. "It feels like a steel rod is stuck in my neck." I winced when I tried to lift my head. "Call the paramedics. Please, oh Christ. Ow," I screamed in pain. "This really hurts. Please call someone, Mary."

"We haven't met the deductible yet," she said. "If you go to the hospital it will cost hundreds of dollars. Why don't you try and breathe deep and relax?" She sat down on the edge of the bed and I screamed.

"Oww! Christ, don't move the bed! God, this is bad. I'm paralyzed I'm telling you. Please call for help."

Mary leaned over and hissed into my face, "Look at you. You're not man enough to get up!" Her face was twisted in hatred and rage. It scared me to be so helpless and at her mercy.

"*HELP*!" I shouted. And again and again until finally she said.

"Okay, all right." I could see that she was embarrassed that the children could hear me. "Stop screaming. I'll call them for you."

Forty minutes later I heard voices at the front door then the sound of footsteps coming down the hallway. I remained motionless, staring at the ceiling, unable to turn my head.

"How are you doing?" One of the two paramedics, a young man with short blond hair and college good looks asked as he came into the bedroom.

"I can't move," I said still staring up at the ceiling. "It feels like a steel rod is in my neck."

"Can you feel this?" The other paramedic ran a metal coin across the bottom of my feet.

"Yes," I said.

"Good, that's good," the first paramedic said. "It looks like you may have a pinched nerve. We're going to isolate your back and neck, then take you down to the hospital. Okay?"

"I just want this pain gone."

"We know, hang in there."

The second paramedic placed a neck brace on me and they slid me onto a gurney, strapped me down and wheeled me outside. At the hospital I was rushed through the emergency room and started on an IV of Valium. The tranquilizer solution loosened my muscles and I slept.

17

Chapter Two
Saying Good-Bye

"Hi, how are you feeling?" Mary stood next to my hospital bed.

I opened my eyes and stared at her for a moment. "I never treated you like this," I said in a raspy voice.

Mary didn't answer right away. She sat down on a chair by the window and looked out at the lawn and afternoon traffic.

"I do love you, Paul but not our life together. You hate your work but refuse to look for something else. You love the kids and the house but rather than being satisfied with that, you get high or are thinking about getting high, or are coming down off a high."

"How could I quit my job? What would we do for money?"

She turned back to me from the window. "We'd be happier if you were happier."

"I wouldn't be happy being unemployed."

"You wouldn't be unemployed. You could go back to school. You could become a math teacher or music teacher."

"Teachers make twenty thousand a year," I said. "We couldn't keep the house; we'd have to rent again."

"You don't know that. Why don't you want to claim your life back?"

"So, you try to kill me with the car?"

"I'm sorry I did that," she said as she looked down at her hands. "I was frustrated. I don't know how to change things but I know I can't go on this way. I think we should try to go to a marriage counselor. We should try something, shouldn't we?"

"Okay, I'll go." I told her what she wanted to hear to stop the argument. Mary had changed. She wasn't the friend she had always been for me. My feelings for her had changed too. The realization that I no longer loved her felt like a massive cement block being dropped on me, nothing would change the outcome now.

I went back to work at the insurance agency the next day and before going to my cubicle, I stopped at the desk of one of the secretaries.

"Hi, Lydia," I said and she looked up. She had bleached blond hair and blue eyes. She was young and had a beautiful body.

"Hi, Paul, are you feeling better?" She smiled into my eyes. She had been flirting with me for weeks.

"Yeah, it was a pinched nerve or something, I don't know, but it's gone. Listen, would you like to go to lunch sometime?"

"Okay, that would be nice." She smiled and continued to look into my eyes.

"How about today?" I asked.

"Okay."

Her eyes told me everything I needed to know and we began to meet after work for an hour or two each night. Making love to someone new fulfilled more than a sexual drive in me, it gave me a sense of the world outside of my marriage. A world I gave up when I married at twenty. Touching a new woman, getting through the wall of a stranger to acceptance, to "yes", that was another of my addictions. I was attracted to every pretty woman I saw. I wanted to get to yes with every one of them.

"Where are you going?" Mary asked one evening as I shaved in the master bathroom.

"Out."

"No, you're not. Not without me."

"With you? What are you talking about?"

"You know damn well what I'm talking about. We haven't been out in months but now you think you're going to leave me at home to watch the kids?"

"I'm going to town for a drink."

"No, you're not. Stop lying to me. I know about her."

"About who?"

"About your little friend, you bastard."

"Okay, you know about her. Listen, I'm going out to have some fun. Is that okay, boss?" I went into the bedroom and took a shirt from the closet.

"Remember the time Patty and I went to Mexico?" Mary asked as she followed me.

"Last year? Yeah, I remember." I looked up from the edge of the bed as I tied my shoes.

"I never told you but Patty and I met a man at a night club in Rosarita Beach and we went back to his apartment in San Diego."

"You what?"

"We made love with him. Shall I describe it for you?"

"No."

"How about Alan, do you want to hear about him?"

I felt a knife of pain in my gut. Anger flushed across my face as I thought of her having intercourse with one of my friends and her experience in a ménage-a-trois with someone else.

Alan was a college friend. His wife left him with a 7-year old boy, Sean. Alan was in transition and Mary and I agreed to have Sean stay with us. We raised him for two years with our own children as Alan came and went. To think of him with Mary, betraying me. I was furious.

"I have to go for a walk." I felt my hands trembling. I started to leave but Mary blocked my way. "Please, let me walk this off," I said. "I'm coming back but right now I could kill you." I pushed her aside but she grabbed me by the shirt with both hands.

"You aren't going anywhere!" she shouted.

"Okay, I won't go to town." I looked up at the ceiling then into her eyes. "I need to walk, to get away from you. Let me out of here god-damn-it before I beat the shit out of you." I tried to pull back from her hold but she held me with both hands. Then she spit in my face.

I punched her in the jaw, knocking her to the floor. I bent over and hit her again. She screamed and Ava ran into the bedroom with a kitchen knife in her hand.

"Leave her alone or I'll kill you," Ava said. She held the knife as if she was going to stab me.

I grunted from surprise. The whole miserable scene sickened me. Vomit came into my mouth. I recalled a night when my father, in a rage swept the kitchen table with the back of his arm; the half-filled dinner plates and glasses went crashing against the walls and flying across the floor. It was a horrible scene and now I was horrible. I didn't want to play this part.

"I'm sorry," I said to Ava. "I lost control but she asked for it. I mean, I shouldn't have but... oh, you won't understand."

"Get out," Mary moaned from the floor.

"I'm sorry. Are you okay?"

"No, I'm not fucking okay? Just go away."

I felt sick to my stomach again. I left the house and drove my truck into town. I didn't know where to go or what to do. I felt dazed and ashamed. I should have sat down on the bed and withdrawn from her. Hitting her was a terrible mistake. Things had never been this bad. What were we going to do? I couldn't live with her now. I would have to get a place.

I drove around, dreading having to go home to face the kids and Mary but after midnight, tired and bleary eyed, I pulled up the long driveway. As the headlights lit the darkened house, I felt sadness sweep across my body. The house was dark and terribly quiet as I opened the door and walked down the hall into our bedroom. Mary was lying in bed. I saw her face in the dim light. She was black and blue from the beating.

"I'm sorry," I said. "I'm really sorry."

"If anyone ever hit me like that, you would kill them but you think you have the right."

"No, I don't have the right. I was wrong and I'm sorry."

"You beat me."

"So now I'm a wife beater too. Fine, but remember that you wouldn't let me leave and spitting in my face may have had something to do with it."

"You beat me. Look at my face."

"You had sex with one of my friends."

"And how many times have you cheated on me? And now you've beaten me."

My rage was gone, the sight of Mary's swollen face sapped all the energy from me.

"I want you to leave," Mary said.

"Okay. You're right, I'll find a place in town. We need some time off from this."

"Yes," Mary said sadly. Her voice betrayed a pang of fear at the prospect of a future without me.

I took a blanket and went to sleep on the couch. The next day at breakfast I tried to be cheerful with the kids but Ava wouldn't talk to me and Noah averted eye contact. I took the day off and went out to look for an apartment. After three tries I found one in Capitola that was okay and affordable.

On Saturday, when Mary and the children were purposely out shopping, I began to move my things. As I carried an armful of clothes through the silent house, I recalled my parents fighting. My mother had bought us new clothes for school one year but she had to hide the expense. Eventually though he found out what she had spent and his yelling echoed through the house. Then the silence; the buzzing silence that fills a sad place.

I finished loading my things into the truck and drove back to the apartment and called Lydia.

"We have a place now to be together," I said.

"I can't," Lydia spoke loud as her two-year old baby screamed in the background.

"Why not?"

"Paul, you're too depressing for me."

"Look I'm going through some shit," I said. "You know, there are a lot of things on my mind."

"Yeah, well I'm sorry for you but I'm too young to waste my time. You've got too many problems."

I didn't say anything.

"I've got to go now," Lydia finally said.

"If you change your mind, you'll call me?" I asked.

"Yeah sure, but don't call here anymore."

"Okay, I won't."

Desperate to meet a woman, on the following Friday I went to Santa Cruz's largest night club and sat at the bar as people screamed to be heard over the loud rock music. I put down my beer when I saw Mary come in. She was with her cousin, Maryanne and two tall, good looking men with slicked-back hair. Mary appeared engrossed by what her date was telling her. I could see by the look in her eyes that she liked him. Mary saw me and laughed, proudly displaying her triumph.

I left the Catalyst with a broken heart. A knife-like pain tore at my guts. The woman I had lived with for thirteen years, the person I had known since we were sixteen was gone. I had lost her love, my home and my children. This is what I deserved. I could see that clearly now; between the drugs and the affairs I had lost it all. I would never be going home. I would never be there when it rained, in the warm house with a fire going and the kids watching TV. Mary would never again look at me with loving eyes.

I left the Catalyst bar and found my truck in the parking lot. I couldn't drive at first, couldn't see through my tears. People walked by and noticed my sobbing. I pulled out so people wouldn't stare at me but it was too difficult to see the traffic so I parked in a Taco Bell. It hurt to listen to music on the radio, love songs tore me up. Finally making it to the apartment, I went in and had to lean against a wall to steady myself as I cried uncontrollably.

I hurt so bad I didn't sleep at all that night. The pain was the same pool of hurt where the pain of Rachel's death, my father's death and now where the death of Mary's love all lay inside my soul. The only thoughts that came through my mind were of all my miserable failures. On the verge of a nervous breakdown, death seemed a peaceful solution to the pain. I lay in bed filled with remorse. I imagined myself opening the top drawer of my dresser and taking out the pistol and putting the barrel to my head. It would be so easy to pull the trigger. I would be at peace. No more pain, no more feeling of emptiness. I could picture myself doing it and it made me tremble. I saw a vision of my father standing in the corner of the room. His hair was white.

He stood with his thumbs hooked humbly into the front pockets of his pants. "I love you, Paul." I heard his voice in my head. "Things will get better. Don't make this mistake, you'll only hurt the children more. Please, Paul, I love you."

I started to cry. I saw myself through my father's eyes. I knew how I would feel if my son was hurting like this. How I would feel if Noah had thoughts of suicide. I could see now that my father felt ashamed for the mistakes he had made as I was now for what I had done.

I got out of bed and called the Suicide Prevention Hotline and spoke to a middle-aged woman for a few minutes. She helped me to regain some composure. After the call, I dressed and left the apartment. It was late and all the shops were closed. I walked up West Cliff Drive. At the top of the road I stopped to watch the white capped waves pound into the rocks. Moonlight reflected on the dark sea; distant stars flickered in the black sky. The Universe seemed cold. My feelings were razor sharp pain. My hands and knees trembled. "Hang on. Just hang on until the morning." I told myself. This was the pain I had been avoiding with drugs since high school. This was the pain I covered over with my anger.

"Look where it's gotten me," I said into the cold night. "Look what I've done."

I remembered being a kid, everything was felt, really felt. Everything was experienced deeply. Everything had a thickness to it. Everything seen outside was felt inside. I remembered when I was eight and holding a telephone directory in my hands suddenly the thickness of the book went through me, my entire body felt thick. That was what it was like to feel, I could remember and compared it to the lack of feeling, the numbness I felt now. I was alert mentally, my mind didn't stop but inside, nothing. A thin line. But how do you get back feeling?

At sun up I returned to my apartment and showered, shaved and dressed for work. At the office I looked through my telephone messages and checked my appointment calendar, then rang the group secretary and canceled my appointments. I dialed the Santa Cruz free clinic as I lit a cigarette. I felt like I was in a fog.

"I would like to make an appointment with a counselor," I explained to the woman who answered.

"We have dependency counselors available but we don't take appointments. You can just come in."

"How long is the wait?"

"Usually a half hour."

"Okay, thanks."

I drove to a small cafe on Front Street and sat outside with a cup of coffee. Lit a cigarette and stared at the passing traffic. It was an ordinary day in the life of Santa Cruz. Street people smiled as they panhandled on the corner. Cars drove in and out of the Long's parking lot but my life wasn't normal any more. I'd lost my house and my family. I was sick, my nervous system shot from years of drug use.

I recalled a morning in Vietnam. I was sitting on a cot inside a barracks in Long Binh. Outside the sun began to bake the jungle. I loaded extra magazines into my green webbing. "C'mon, load'em up," I heard the first sergeant shout. The men in Charlie Company climbed into the back of waiting trucks. It was very hot outside in the intense Vietnam humidity. The trucks drove us to the gates of Long Binh. My platoon waited in the shade under trees at the edge of the tense jungle until an hour later when the word came down to move out. It was stifling hot and humid but we patrolled for an hour before they stopped us along the trail for a rest. We all kneeled down and I took out a bag of marijuana and lit up a pipe then passed it to Billy Mack.

"Good shit," Mack said blowing out blue smoke.

"It is good shit," I agreed. In a few moments I could feel the buzz from the weed. Vietnamese grass is strong and I got so intoxicated I thought I could hear ants as they walked over the leaf litter. I laughed out loud, then suddenly automatic weapons opened up, dit-dit, dit-dit-dit.

I started to get up but Mack yelled, "Stay DOWN!" and motioned to me with one hand. "Just where you are." Mack's bloodshot eyes were the only thing I could see clearly.

We heard men shouting from up the trail; "C'mon, let's go, let's go!" The soldiers ahead of us got up from the trail and ran towards the fire fight. I froze in terror.

"Mack, Mack," I yelled hoarsely, "I can't move! I'm so stoned I can't get up."

"C'mon, right by me. Ya got to, c'mon!" he shouted as he punched me in the shoulder. I got up then and followed behind him.

"Oh-Jesus," I said as we ran along the trail and the sounds of the firefight grew louder.

"You-okay?" Mack turned to check me out.

"No!"

"Alright, stay cool, stay cool."

We pushed our way through the brush along the narrow trail. My head was pounding, my vision was narrow. All I could see were my boots, my legs and the ground going by underneath me. Everything else was out of focus.

"Damn it!" I said out loud to myself. "This is it. This is where you die, you stupid fucking jerk."

At the edge of the jungle we hit the dirt. The firefight was off to their right where the trail opened up into a clearing. One at a time the squads on the trail got up and rushed out but before Mack and I had to join them the shooting stopped.

"They got 'em," Demery said. "C'mon." He was a tall, skinny soldier with coffee colored skin. He was standing at the edge of the clearing and he looked back and down at us with a quizzical look. "Let's go, now!"

"What do ya mean?" Mack asked.

"It's over," Demery said. "They're all killed."

I slowly followed Mack into the clearing. We saw men from November platoon combing the area. Serena and the men from Lima platoon stood over six dead Vietnamese bodies. They lay strewn around a large rocket launcher in the tall brown grass. Some of the men in Lima were patting Serena on the back.

"What the hell is that?" I pointed to the rocket launcher that was mounted on wheels so the North Vietnamese could roll it along the jungle trails.

"That's no RPG rocket," I said.

"I'm not sure," Sergeant Meyers answered as the men in Oscar Platoon gathered around the rocket launcher.

"It looks like a goddamn baby missile," I said. "Imagine them wheeling this bad boy through the jungle?"

"Yeah, well, this crew is done wheeling anything," Demery said as he pointed to the bodies of the six dead Vietnamese soldiers.

"These aren't kids," Sergeant Meyers said motioning with his chin. "Looks like Lima's taken out some valuable people."

A week later a special formation in Long Binh was called so that Kenny Serena could be awarded the Silver Star. After the formation was dismissed Mack and I with eight other friends sat around in the shade outside the barracks. In the background I heard the radio playing *Time Has Come Today* by the Chambers Brothers.

"I was walking point," Serena explained as we passed his medal and the marijuana pipe around. "I came out of the tree line into the clearing as the Vietcong crew were setting up the rocket. They were about to launch it when I shot and killed the gunner."

"I remember that," a red head named DeSousa said.

"Four of the others shot right back at me. One had his gun misfire and jam, the other three all missed! I heard the bullets hit the ground next to me and some go right by my head."

"Damn!" I said. "That wouldn't happen again in a hundred years, four automatic weapons missing from fifty yards!"

"I know," Serena shook his head. "Before they could adjust their fire, I hit the ground and the other guys from Lima joined in; drawing their fire away from me."

"We didn't have any casualties and all six of them were put down." DeSousa said.

"I've seen a whole lot braver shit than that," Serena said. "I just walked into it." We had been drinking and smoking grass and his emotions showed. "Look at all the shit we've been through, all the friends we lost and they give you a fucking piece of metal." Serena had tears in his eyes.

"Well, that's the way it goes," Mack said, shrugging and passing him the pipe.

"Yeah, right," Serena took a hit off of it then passed it to me.

"Shit, this feels awful," I mumbled as I exhaled. "My legs and hands feel as stiff as wood. This weed is bringing back the paranoia I felt out on that patrol."

"Here, try some of this." Mack cut a small piece from a two-inch Thai stick, put it into a pipe, lit it, and took a long hit then passed it to me.

The opium smoke gave me a strong buzz. I could feel my fingers again. There was a lightness in them and I felt what a fine classical guitarist's hands would feel like. My entire body relaxed and the tightness in my stomach changed to a feeling of tranquility. Freeing me from fear, the opium high seemed to me to be the best feeling I had had in a long time.

That afternoon I took a nap and woke up laughing, thinking of the strange, magical dreams the opium had brought on. "Dreams within dreams within dreams, all as real as real life," I said to Mack as we lay on our bunks listening to the music on the radio.

"Yeah, man, this is some good dope," Mack said. "Let's go smoke another stick out by the showers."

"We could get hooked on this stuff," I said.

"Yeah, and we could get killed tonight, too," Mack answered. "I'm gonna go smoke me some more." He searched through his rucksack for the black sticks.

I felt confused. I wanted to stop getting high. I was sick of the dope routine but Mack was right. What was I saving myself for? I may not have another day anyway and I didn't want to feel that fear anymore. That was the worst.

I took a sip of my coffee. That was the start. Somewhere during my year in Vietnam I lost control. When I got home, I still couldn't smoke marijuana and opium was hard to find but the dealer had heroin. I snorted it at first, then skin popped it, then learned to mainline it.

I shook my head in disgust as I put out my cigarette and got up to go into the free clinic. Before going in, I went next door to the adult education building and read through the list of evening classes. The oil painting class, three hours on Tuesday and Thursday nights sounded interesting. I signed up for it then went to the free clinic next door and sat in the waiting room on the second floor of an old office building. I felt out of place but there was also a certain feeling of satisfaction. I was finally doing something about getting better. I could see what it had cost me. I could see I was responsible for the whole mess my life was in.

A middle-aged man with long, shoulder length grey hair came into the waiting room. "Paul?" he asked.

"Yes," I answered and got up and shook his outstretched hand.

"Hi, I'm Allen Greenbaum." He was in his mid-forties, dressed in corduroy pants and a red plaid shirt opened at the collar. His handshake contained a vitality that said to me, I'm okay and I'm glad to meet you. His smile was sincere even as his eyes studied my face. He led the way into his office and I sat in a chair opposite his. The office was large with an entire wall of bookcases, dark wood floors with an old Persian carpet. His oak desk was in front of two tall, Victorian windows. I heard the traffic noise from Pacific Avenue outside filter up into the otherwise quiet building. Incense burned on a brass plate on the desk.

"How can I help you?" Greenbaum asked.

"I'm not doing too good. Last night I had to call suicide prevention."

"Did you hurt yourself?"

"No, but I thought about it."

"Why? What's going on?"

"I just separated from my wife." I paused, shrugged my shoulders. My lips began to tremble and I could not hold back a sob, "I saw her with her new boyfriend..." I began to cry. Greenbaum waited for me to gain control then asked.

"Perhaps you are jumping ahead of things. Did she ask for a divorce?"

"No, but I can tell."

"You assume."

"No, I saw the way she looked at him. You can tell everything by the look in a woman's eyes."

Greenbaum nodded. After a long moment of silence, he asked, "How did this happen?"

"It's a long story," I said, "but it comes down to my problem with drugs. Mary got tired of it."

"Do you want help to stop using?"

"Yes. I don't even want to get high now. I'm afraid to after last night."

"When was the first time you used drugs?" Greenbaum asked.

"I'm not sure," I said. "I smoked my first cigarette when I was ten. Then, I guess when I was about twelve the kids in the neighborhood started sniffing glue. And drinking, that started at about seventh grade. Wine and beer, mostly but also cough medicine with codeine. That was from thirteen or fourteen until I was...well nineteen and went into the army, then it was marijuana. When I got home from Vietnam I was addicted to opium." I hesitated, not sure I wanted to admit my level of drug use. I looked at Greenbaum and finally admitted, "I went from opium to heroin then to hallucinogenics."

"What exactly?" Greenbaum asked.

"LSD, Peyote, mushrooms, MDA, whatever I could get."

"How long did you use these heavy drugs?"

"All through college. It was Santa Cruz in the seventies, you know, everyone was tripping."

"Were you shooting up, main lining?"

Again, I hesitated, I didn't want to admit it and expose myself as being such a low life. "Yeah," I finally let it out.

"Was your wife using too?" Greenbaum turned in his chair.

"Yeah, she took everything I did, but not as much and not as often."

"It sounds like a lot of your relationship was based on getting high together?"

"I suppose. It's what we did for recreation along with the normal things like camping and school events with the kids. But yeah, when we put them to sleep, we'd take out the drugs and party. I never thought it would end up like this. I feel like I'm grieving over a death. I have a pain ripping at my guts."

"It is like a death," he said, "but shooting up was something I think your wife needed to end. If it meant throwing you out then she had to do it. Using needles and obtaining orgasmic ecstasy is ruinous for a relationship and could only lead to one thing; bottom. You're hitting bottom now." He let that sink in, still observing me closely he continued. "This is the conclusion to the path you started down the moment you sniffed your first bag of glue. Do you follow me? Do you agree?"

"Yeah, I see it," I said. "I made a lot of mistakes but I never thought it would lead to this."

"Some people hit bottom on the way to an emergency room," Greenbaum said. "For some it's the sound of the jail cell door locking. Eric Clapton was down to pawning his last guitar before he sought help. You're fortunate, some people don't quit until they die from an overdose and their body lies in the morgue." He paused then and tried to be positive. "Look, you still have your health. If you can make sobriety a way of life, you can get your wife and family back. We have two group meetings every day, this afternoon at four and again at eight in the evening. We can help you make it one day at a time." He looked into my face.

"Okay, sure. I'll be by tonight," I said. I felt dirty and embarrassed. I didn't meet his eye contact.

"Good. I think your wife will recognize this new attitude. Why don't you give it another try? Ask her to come with you to meet with me, either tomorrow or the day after."

"I'll ask her, but don't count on it. She's more into revenge right now than anything else."

"We'll use her anger, we'll use everything to help you stay sober," he said.

"Yeah, okay. That sounds good," I said

I went back to the apartment and slept through the afternoon. I felt strong enough that evening to call Mary.

"Hello?" she answered in a joyful voice. I thought I could hear her expecting the other man's call.

"Hi, it's me. How are you?"

She didn't answer right away. "The kids are driving me crazy but I'm fine. I need to get your check by the end of the week. Have you sent it yet?"

"I'll mail it tomorrow. I went to a dependency counselor today."

"Oh? Well, congratulations," Mary said.

"I thought maybe you... well, I would be willing to go to a marriage counselor with you."

"What for?" Mary asked.

"To sit and talk about things."

"I don't have the time."

I hesitated, confused by her attitude. "Now I'm willing to get help and you don't have the time?"

"That's right, you're a little too late."

"You're right. It is late and I'm sorry."

"You should be," Mary answered. "You've caused your children horrible pain and you're sorry? Not enough, not nearly enough."

"I feel terrible about what's happened. Please, give me another chance."

"You don't deserve another chance. I don't ever want to be with you again. I was born to hate you."

I felt my stomach tighten. My palms were perspiring.

"Well I wasn't born to hate anyone," I said. "I was born to love and be loved."

"Too bad you didn't show it."

"I didn't show it? I loved you and the kids. What are you talking about? I hardly recognize your voice, Mary."

"Well get used to it."

"We're still married," I said.

"No, we're not, not in my mind."

"Then I might as well file for a divorce and make it official."

"Well, don't let me stop you," she said with an attitude.

"Okay, I won't." I slammed the phone down hard.

The next day I called a divorce attorney and made an appointment. We filed the papers the end of that same week.

Four months later the divorce wasn't final, they said it would take a year, but the Judge ordered that our house be sold and that I was to get forty thousand dollars as my share of the equity. Despite the Judge's ruling, things weren't much better for me. My relationship with both children was strained. It was difficult emotionally for me to drive to the house to pick them up. I was homesick and the sight of the yard, the kids and the dog cut me deeply. Mary had lost ten pounds and had a new hair style. She looked good and flaunted her new found happiness as a single woman.

I stood at the front door hoping the kids would come right out and I wouldn't have to see her, or worse, the boyfriend but Mary answered my knock.

"Are they ready," I asked.

"They don't want to go."

"You have to make them." I said.

"No, I don't."

"What about my joint custody rights?"

"You don't have any *rights*, you left us," she raised her voice but was still smiling.

"I didn't leave you; you know that. We both agreed, we needed some space. Then your cousin came to live with you and you decided you liked being single. You wouldn't even let me come up to the house."

"That really got you."

"Yes, it did." I looked at her closely and saw her taking pleasure in my pain. "I don't even know who you are anymore, Mary. It's like I'm talking to a stranger."

She closed the door in my face and I rode back to town feeling frustrated. The divorce court didn't care what she did or whether my custody rights were observed. Mary was in control of the children. I had no say about anything in their lives. It hurt. I hated her for the way she did it to not only to me, but to Ava and Noah. They should have a father in their lives. It would be best for them. Mary didn't care now what was best for anyone but herself.

My only solace came from painting. I had taken several classes at adult education and painted now almost every day. I found in the oils the means to lose myself in concentration. The application of the smooth oil paints, placed thickly with a brush or palate knife transfixed me, bringing me into the moment. With a child's eye I saw the celestial light in the room where I painted. The golden light I remembered as a young boy. A peaceful, playful light illuminating the colorful oils and the entire room. It didn't matter if the painting was finely done, the oil itself was perfect. Its colors and textures always perfect. Seeing this forgiving nature of the medium, I strove not so much to be accurate as to be free with my brush strokes. I studied the Impressionists. Van Gogh became my inspiration; seeing in his bold, broad strokes the freedom oil painting can bring to the mind. During my painting sessions I caught sight of my own sanity. I could enjoy a moment without the rush of drugs. I could get satisfaction and feel a thickness to life. Painting to me was more than relaxing, it was transforming. I approached the easel each time with the expectancy of clearing my consciousness. I strove each time for this high, even if only for a few moments. When I finished a painting, I saw that those moments were now captured on my canvas.

At the next court appearance three months later, the judge ruled that the sales price of the house that Mary had set was too high. It would have to be reduced so that there would be a sale. The judge also ordered only half of what Mary had requested for child and spousal support.

Realizing she would lose the house; Mary came by my apartment that night to talk. "Can I come in?" she asked after I opened the door.

"No, we can talk here," I said, standing in the doorway.

"I want you to stop this, she said

"Can I come back home?" I asked.

"No, but I'll go with you to a marriage counselor."

"No? I can't come home? Why should I stop then?"

"We'll go to counseling then see how things go."

"You don't want me back. You only want time until you find a man that will marry you so you can keep the house."

"Don't you ever think about all the good times we had," Mary asked. "I'll never find anyone as good in bed as you were. Look, I brought you something."

"Yeah, what's that?"

Mary pulled out a vial of cocaine and two needles from her handbag.

"Let's get high and make love all night," she said.

"Great," I said sarcastically seeing the irony as I tried to keep hold of myself. "Just great, Mary. Thanks, but no thanks, I'm not interested. It's already cost me too much." I saw the sadness on her face as her ploy didn't go as planned. I guess I still loved her, deep down inside me because seeing her sadness melted my heart.

"Listen, Mary, I'm sorry for everything I've done. I hope you can see that it's better for the kids if you let me be a part of their lives."

"They don't want to see you."

"You could convince them. You could make it happen. I have to stay in their lives, I'm their dad."

"Why don't we go to a counselor to discuss all this?" Mary asked.

"Remember what you said when I told you I was filing for a divorce?" I waited for her to answer but she didn't say anything.

"'Don't let *me* stop you,'" I said it in a sarcastic high pitch voice imitating the meanness she had had in her tone. "Well nothing you say now *will* stop me. We are *over*, really over, you've shown me that. What I'm talking about now are the kids. You of all people should know that it's better for them to have me involved in their lives."

"If you loved them you wouldn't make us sell the house," Mary said.

"It's okay that I live in an apartment, have a mattress on the floor for a bed. That's okay, but now that you have to move to an apartment, now I'm supposed to help you out."

"Not me, the kids."

"I want you out of our house," my voice broke with anger. "I wasn't allowed to come inside. You brought strange men into my house. The kids seeing you with a strange man in my house. That's when you lost the house."

"You're on a power trip," she screamed.

"Yeah, that's right I am but you aren't going to live there, in *MY* house with someone else, no way."

"So, you would hurt the kids just to get back at me?"

"That's exactly what you've been doing," I said.

I finally closed the door on her but my heart was racing in my chest and my stomach was in a knot. The kids would be fine in a rental house. They wouldn't be up in the mountains of Bonnie Doon but down in Santa Cruz, not the worse place on earth to grow up.

Her attempt at delaying the divorce and the sale of the house having failed, Mary vowed to keep me from the children. I saw them only if I went to the grammar school playground at lunch time and then sometimes, they didn't come out to visit with me by the fence.

By the following spring the divorce was final. Mary's parents had given her $40,000 to pay me my half of the equity so she and the children could stay in the house. I had money but I was more miserable than ever. As I rode in my new blue MG over to the little league field to watch Noah play, I felt the tightness in my stomach at the thought of seeing Mary. I was having no luck at meeting anyone new and every time I saw her, she was with a different, younger man.

Mary was at the ballgame with one of her boyfriends and her cousin, Maryanne. They were sitting together up in the bleachers, laughing and talking to the other parents while I sat alone at the far end.

"Hey, Noah! Nice play," I called out as Noah fielded a ground ball at second and threw out the runner. Noah waved back. He was the cutest eleven-year old I ever saw but I could only watch half the game then had to leave. I was hurting inside and couldn't take the laughter I heard from Mary.

I went to my apartment and called my brother, Stephen in Los Angeles.

"Get the hell out of Dodge, man," Stephen said. "You're alone and that town ain't working for you. Quit your job, give'em notice at the apartment and in a month, I'll come up to get you. We'll rent a U-Haul and drive down to my place."

"You know, Steve, I'm going to do it. I don't want to be that far away from the kids but I don't get to see them here anyway. They don't want to spend any time with me."

"You'll call them every week and they'll come down here to see you. Things will get better once you're in a new situation."

"I hope," I said. "It can't get any worse than this."

Before I left, I was able to convince Ava and Noah to spend a weekend with me at my apartment in Capitola. It felt strange the three of us in my small place. Nothing was familiar to them and there was a lot of silence between us. Driving them back on Sunday afternoon I tried to find the words to say good bye.

"I'll call you every week and I'll write. I hope you'll call me too when something good happens, or something not so good." I said as I drove the MG up Empire Grade Road.

"We will," Noah said.

"I want you to know that I love you both and think of you all the time. You're always in my heart."

"We love you too, Dad." Noah said.

When we got out of the car at the house, Noah put his arms around my neck and kissed me and said, "I miss you, Dad."

Ava kissed me without saying anything and I drove away crying as the children walked up the long driveway through the open meadow. I felt our relationship die. It felt like Rachel's death. But it wasn't. They were alive and healthy. They had a good mother. My relationship with them would never be what it would have been, but they were alive.

Chapter Three
On 40th Street

June 1981

My brother, Stephen drove the rental U-Haul truck out of the driveway of my apartment house and worked his way through traffic. He found the on-ramp to Highway 1 outside Capitola and gunned the engine to bring us up to highway speed. The rental truck was loaded with cardboard boxes holding my worldly possessions and behind it we towed my blue MGB. The cab of the truck smelled of stale cigarettes. The red vinyl seats where dirty and stained and the dashboard dinged up from a thousand rides.

"I've past these places so many times," I said as I looked at the scenery along the coast. "I never imagined I would be leaving town like this."

Stephen concentrated on joining the flow of traffic. His brown hair bleached with golden highlights from the hours he spent at the beach. His tan face had premature wrinkles around his eyes.

"It may feel like you've lost," Stephen said as he looked to the left to check traffic, "but you've won your life back, Paul. Your marriage was over" he looked at me now. "How many people marry at twenty and stay together their entire lives?"

"Not many," I said, "but people stay together until their kids are grown."

"And you know how bad it would have gotten by then? Besides, Mary wasn't going to let it go on. She needed to find her next husband while she is still young enough to attract a man."

I felt the sharp edge of a knife in my gut. The thought that Mary was trying to attract another man turned the blade and I grimaced from the pain.

"Now you have your life back," Stephen went on. "It's a big world out there, with lots of great women and lots of great places. You're free to live your own life like you didn't get to do before."

"Do you realize mine is only the third divorce in our family?" I said, "Aunt Esther's, Cousin Eddie's and now mine. It just isn't supposed to happen."

"Forget that, Paul. It does happen. The question is where to from here?"

I thought for a moment, "I want to paint," I said, "stupid as that sounds. I'd like to be able to make a living by painting or writing."

"Okay, so take some time off and give it a try." Stephen smiled. He seemed pleased with my ambition. He and I both wanted to be writers. We each had written short stories and poetry but neither of us had ever sold anything.

"I'm going to," I said. "I have enough money saved so I don't have to work for a while. I expect to pay you rent, but pretty much I can lay back this summer and paint. Maybe I can sell something, who knows?"

"You know they have street fairs at the beach," Stephen said. "You can rent a booth and show your paintings there."

"Yeah? Okay, that's an idea. Now all I have to do is to paint something good enough."

Six hours after leaving my life in Santa Cruz, we drove along the ocean south of Playa del Rey. Surfers rode two-foot high waves as overhead, jetliners cleared the dunes of LAX. The sound from their jet engines wiped out our small talk for a mile. Up ahead, two tall smokestacks from a large electric facility spewed a column of white smoke into the sky. Despite the noise and smog, the beaches were crowded with people.

Five miles further south, the highway entered the section of Manhattan Beach known as El Porto. Stephen pulled off to the side of the road and we unhooked my blue MGB and I drove it behind him through town. Driving into Manhattan Beach along the main street, Highland Avenue, there are one and two-story buildings lining each side of the boulevard. Restaurants, bars, several laundromats, convenience stores, reality offices and apartment houses all crowd together. Stephen made a right down 40th street. It was steep and narrow and connected

Highland Avenue to the beach. He parked the rental truck in his driveway.

The houses along 40th Street, from Highland Avenue down to the Strand, were all different ages and architectural types. But they were similar in that they were all two or three stories high and except for one eight-unit apartment house, were all single-family homes. The houses ranged in age from Stephen's, which was built in the 1920s to several just now under construction. Beach properties with narrow lots, the buildings fairly scraped each other between alleyways. The houses in the neighborhood shared two other things in common; all were built to get every possible view of the beach and ocean. They used outside porches, upper story decks and wall length windows as each owner found a way to incorporate the beach life into their homes. The other thing they all shared was the noise from the continuous traffic of cars leaving the beach parking lot. Because of its steepness, the autos, trucks and motorcycles had to gun their engines to make it up the grade. The din of racing motors was a constant background noise for life on 40th Street.

Stephen rented a house a few hundred feet from the beach. The house was fifty years old and an unusual mix of Tudor and Spanish styles. The outside walls were natural stone. Two round dormer windows in the living room above the garage jutted out from each corner of the second story. They looked like parapets of an old castle. The weather-beaten front door opened to a very steep stairway. On the steps half way up, I saw a paint can with its lid off and a paint brush sticking out of it. The paint matched the color of the stucco walls but the paint in the can had long ago dried up. I surmised that two or three months ago, Stephen had taken on the task of painting the stairwell walls. Having finished, he just left the half empty paint can; went upstairs to get a cold beer out of the refrigerator and forgot about it. How he could walk by it every day for months without noticing it, well that was my brother's special talent. Charming and relaxed, few things and certainly not open paint cans, bothered him. At the top of the stairs a west facing window in the landing allowed bright sunlight into the living room. Turning right at the landing, I walked into the living room. A dozen plants hung in clay pots from the open beamed ceiling. Prints of sailboats and photographs of Native American Indians were on the white stucco walls. An old, beat up piano was along the left wall between the living room and kitchen. A brown couch along the far wall had a wooden coffee table in front of it. Stephen's bookcase and stereo system were opposite the couch. In the far-right and far-left corners of the room, the parapet's rounded windows let in a full view of the Strand and the Pacific Ocean a block away. In the right dormer corner, an antique wooden desk held stacks of unorganized papers.

I went through the living room into the hallway; to the right was the larger of the two bedrooms, to the left, the other bedroom and straight across the hall, the only bathroom.

I went to the bathroom, washed and tried to dry my hands with towels that hadn't been changed in a month. I opened a closet in the hallway and took out a fresh towel, wiped and went back downstairs. Stephen, his shirt off, had opened the U-Haul truck and was unloading my boxes out on the driveway. We carried my suitcases up the steep steps and into the smaller of the two bedrooms. Stephen went back downstairs for another load but I stayed and struggled to open the window. The room was airless. I managed to force the old window a third of the way open but was immediately stung by the odor of dog feces. Holding my hand over my nose, I leaned out the window and looked down into the fenced-in backyard. On what had once been a lawn, there lay the carcasses of three bicycles, rusted now and without seats or tires. A blue plastic tarpaulin covered over some other items and everywhere piles of dried up dog turds. I struggled to close the window. Finally getting it down, I went back to the truck to help Stephen. We stored my other boxes and a few pieces of furniture into the already overcrowded and disarranged garage.

"There's no parking anywhere along 40th Street," Stephen said. He pointed to my sports car parked along the curb. "You'll have to move until we return the truck and you can fit in the driveway. They'll tow you if you don't."

"Sure, okay," I said. I got my keys and went to get back into the MG but I had to catch my balance. The slope of the street was at least 60 degrees. Gravity pulled the door open and kept it open. In the driver's seat now, I leaned full out and slammed the door shut, started the engine and drove around the block until I found an empty meter on Highland. Walking down the hill back to the house on 40th Street, I heard loud, thumping rock music from several of the apartments. Surf boards and boogie boards lined some of the balconies and I smelled the strong pungent odor of marijuana. In the driveway two houses from Stephen's, a spray painted, multi-colored van had large iridescent balloon letters spelling LOVE painted on one side panel.

I recalled our summer vacations at the Jersey shore when we were kids. Stephen's lifestyle incorporated those care-free days. He worked in the teamsters' union of the motion picture industry. He was able to earn enough on a six-week movie, collecting overtime and meal penalties so he didn't have to work for the next eight weeks. It seemed right too, living as a Bohemian, that is. Both of us had been anti-establishment. Having fun was number one, and fun meant women and getting high.

The weather in L.A. was fine. The beach life was a vacation from the adult world. I felt free, sort of, but I felt too the ever-present yearning to see my children, Ava and little Noah. I wanted to talk to them but I knew I couldn't call them. I mean I could call them but telephone conversations with them were unsatisfactory; not immediate enough of an experience for a child. Talking on the phone was boring for them and frustrating for me. I could never find the words to explain what had happened to our family. They would never understand what I was going through. Then I thought, listen, I shouldn't worry about them. They're okay. They're kids and in the moment and having fun. That's their job. I was the lost one, even as I tried to enjoy a single day.

Stephen was sitting on the couch cursing as I reached the top of the stairs.

"What's the matter?" I asked.

"Pamela left a note for me on the bed." Stephen crumbled a piece of paper and threw it at the wastepaper basket by the desk. "She's moved across the street."

"Huh? I don't understand," I said.

"Me neither. She's moved in with Ken, the guy across the street."

"What? While you were gone two days to help me?"

Stephen didn't answer. He sat on the couch looking out the parapet window. "Was it because of me moving in with you?" I asked.

"No," he answered downcast. "No, it's not you." He looked up at me. "She's dumped me for him."

"Oh, geez. The guy across the street? Did you know this was going on?"

"I had no idea they were even seeing each other."

"Jesus, I'm sorry, Steve."

"Yeah, well she was being a jerk anyway. We were fighting over everything."

"You two were together for how long, what six months?"

"About that, yeah. Geez, this sucks. I mean I still have to see her right across the street. You'd think the two of them would have moved away."

I didn't say anything.

"How about some dinner," I asked after a few minutes. "Are you hungry?"

"Yeah, okay," Stephen said. "Let's go up to El Tarasco's and get some take out."

We walked up to Highland, made a right, walked two blocks to Rosecrans, crossed the street and stood in line at a small hole in the wall restaurant. The setting sun bathed us and the street in a golden hue.

We brought containers of burritos, enchiladas, rice and beans and drinks and carried it back to the house and unloaded it onto the kitchen table. The kitchen was ancient. Aged and yellowed linoleum floors, a fifties style chrome Formica table. The decrepit faucet dripped a constant flow of water into the once white porcelain sink. The gas stove was an old, old affair. At the far end of the kitchen, a shelved pantry led to the backdoor stairway. The smell of dog feces from the backyard made me nauseous.

"I can't eat here," I said. "That smell is too much." I brought my plate into the living room and put it on the coffee table and turned the television on. Stephen joined me. I noticed that he looked out the window each time he heard a car drive by. I couldn't tell if he felt relieved or disappointed when it wasn't Ken's car.

"We have to do something about the smell, Steve," I said. "It's disgusting."

"Yeah, I try to keep it clean but Abbey's shits are powerful."

"When was the last time you cleaned it up?"

"I don't know, six or seven months ago."

"Six or seven months! Man, no wonder it stinks." Abbey heard her name so she came over to be petted. "No offense, girl." I said as I scratched behind an ear for her.

After dinner, I sat on the desk looking out the parapet front window at the beach and the sunset. A dozen surfers rode the last waves before dark but everybody else was packing it up. The fragrance of saltwater was on the gentle ocean breeze that came through the screenless window. I leafed through Stephen's rolodex on top of the desk. There seemed to be no order to the cards. They weren't filed under the person's last or first name. "How do you find someone in here anyway?" I asked.

"I just know where they are," Stephen said from the couch where he was reading.

"You know where they are?" I looked over at him. "I don't understand. They're not filed by alphabet."

"Yeah they are."

"Michael Mulnar is in with the Jays," I said as I read one of the hand written cards.

"He's John Sima's friend," Stephen explained.

"Ah, I see," I nodded, "so it's by relationships."

"Pretty much." Stephen laughed.

The next day I went down the back steps and while wearing a bandanna over my nose and mouth that I soaked with a can of Coca-Cola, I filled three large trash cans with dog shit. I went back upstairs and dosed the bandana with a can of tomato juice. Refortified, I went back into the yard of dead dog shits and filled two large, black plastic trash bags and dragged them down the narrow alleyway to the curb for pick up. I needed a long, brisk shower after that mess so I went into the ancient bathroom and ran the shower. I wasn't surprised that the water flow from the showerhead was only slightly more powerful than the kitchen sink's dripping faucet.

After a very long shower, turning and turning my body under the dripping water, I dressed and went downstairs. I found a box with one of my blank canvas among the mess in the garage and I set up my easel at the large parapet window in the living room. I decided to paint Ken's yellow, one story house across the street. A warm sea breeze carried the scent of the ocean and sun tan lotion through the open window. An hour later, a white Ford van pulled into the driveway. Ken was in his twenties. He had long blond, curly hair. His face was puffy from a hangover but it didn't detract from his good looks. Pamela was a brunette. She wore a white short-sleeve blouse and white tennis skirt. She had long, tan, athletic legs. She noticed me in the window and waved. "I'll be right back." I heard her say to Ken as he carried their groceries into the yellow house. I watched her cross the street and without knocking, open the front door and walk up the steep stairs into the living room.

"Hi, I'm Pamela," she said as she came into the room. She was even prettier up close. Her thin nose and high cheekbones were shaped like a woman on a Grecian urn. Her mouth was wide with thin lips and sparkling white teeth set in her perfect, Hollywood tan face. Her dark brown eyes were intelligent and inquisitive. But it was her sensual, physical presence that filled the room. She was aware of it and she used it, flirting like a kitten.

"I'm Steve's brother, Paul," I said as I glanced at her chest. The three top buttons were unbuttoned.

"It's hot out," Pamela said feeling my stare. "Is Stephen home?"

"No, he's at the laundromat."

"Tell him I'd like to talk to him. Say, are you painting that?" She went past me and stood in front of the unfinished canvas. I didn't answer. "It's pretty good," she said. She rested her head on her hand and studied it. "It's kind of abstract," she said, turning toward me. "I mean the lines aren't very straight," she pointed to the outline of the yellow house, "and the shadows need to be worked, but I like it. I really do. It has an impressionistic feeling."

"Thanks, just practice," I said.

"Come by for a drink tonight," Pamela said as she turned again to face me. "You should meet Ken; he writes and paints too."

"Sure, if it's okay with Steve," I reminded her of the situation.

"Is he mad?" Pamela asked.

"Well, yeah, I guess you could say that. He didn't talk much about it except to say it was unexpected."

"God," she half laughed, half groaned. "We screamed and yelled at each other for two weeks and he says it's unexpected."

"I mean about moving in across the street with Ken," I said.

"Oh, well that just happened, nothing planned. I needed to get out of here."

"Okay, well, I'll tell him you came by," I said.

"Thanks. Nice to meet you."

I watched her walk away; her buttocks swinging discreetly but nicely. I had the feeling it was a practiced walk.

An hour later, I was still at the painting when I saw Stephen come down the street with Abbey. He carried a large laundry tub, overflowing with sheets, towels, jeans and shirts. Abbey had a long piece of beef jerky held like a trophy in her mouth.

"Pam was here," I said as Stephen lumbered up the steps and into the living room. He dropped the laundry basket and fell in a heap onto the couch.

"Oh yeah?" Stephen said as he gasped for air. "I saw Ken's van outside," he said, out of breath. "What'd she say?"

"She wants you to call her. She wants to talk."

"Okay, thanks," Stephen said. Abbey licked his face and Stephen closed his eyes and lifted his head back but not before Abbey got in a few good swipes. "Okay, knucklehead, that's enough," he said and pushed her away.

That Friday night I sat on the desk; dressed and waiting for Stephen. The ocean's rhythmic pounding filled the house. White capped waves reflected the bright moonlight. We had all the windows open and the cool ocean breeze swept through the living room. It was single's night all over America. I could feel that in the air too. Someone was going to get laid tonight and thousands were going to try. It had been years since I was single and I was new at the bar scene so I didn't expect any victories but Stephen convinced me I should go out with him.

"You can't score if you're not in the game." Is how he put it so we were on our way to McFly's in Santa Monica.

I drove the MG and Stephen directed me to Lincoln Boulevard, down Washington and over to Rose Avenue. We parked behind the club and went inside. A jazz trio played in the corner of the room. Stephen and I stood one deep from the bar and ordered beers. I sipped mine and surveyed the scene.

"I'm lost," I said. "I don't know who I am anymore. I'm so used to being married and doing everything with the kids and Mary."

"Well now you're free," Stephen said. "You'd better learn to enjoy it too. I'll tell you one thing though, Paul, nobody wants to be with a depressed person."

"No, I know but it's difficult, Steve. I don't think you can really understand how hard it is. You've never been married. You don't have two kids your heart is aching to see. I need to meet someone soon so I can start to feel good about myself."

"That's what I'm talking about, man," Stephen said shaking his head. "You've got to feel good about yourself first, even if you're only acting. Nobody wants to be around sad people."

"I'm not such a good actor," I said.

"No, you're not, but you'd better learn. I'm telling you, Paul, your sad face isn't going to attract anyone."

"Excuse me. Can my friend and I squeeze in to get a drink?" She was a tall brunette in a short red dress. Stephen flashed his charming smile.

"Sure," he said. "What are you drinking?"

"I'd like a gin and tonic, thanks."

"And your friend?"

"An iced tea, please." The friend was a shorter blond with a pixie nose and blue eyes.

"I'm Stephen. This is my brother, Paul."

"Jeanette, nice to meet ya." Jeanette squeezed closer, the crowd behind her pushed us all together.

"I'm Cat," the blond said. She shook Stephen's hand and smiled at me.

While Stephen and Jeanette talked, I noticed Cat looking around the room.

"Are you from Santa Monica?" I asked her.

"No, Venice," she said. "I hate these bars. The vibes in here are terrible. Look at them all trying to get laid, but acting cool. It's all so phony." She lifted her arms, held her hands, palms out towards the crowd, and let out a long, loud, high shrill note that came down octaves as her breath ran out. The bar was noisy but a few people stopped to stare at her. I stared at her too. "OOOOOOOoooooooooommmmmmm Tee – She - He."

"Well that cleaned the place up." I laughed as she came to the end and turned toward me. I toasted her with my beer and she laughed.

We exchange a few pleasantries, where are you from, what do you do but then she said, "C'mon, get me out of here."

"Sure," I said. "Where're we going?"

"Why don't we drive up the coast through Malibu?"

"I have my car," I said, "but Steve won't have a way home."

"We can take my car," she said. "I'll get you home."

"Sounds good." I nudged Stephen. "Here's a ten for our drinks and the keys to the MG. We're going to take a drive up the coast."

Stephen's eyes widened in disbelief.

I shrugged my shoulders and smiled. "It must have been my sad face."

"And quick too!" Stephen laughed.

Cat's yellow VW Bug was parked in a tow away zone behind McFly's.

"You're lucky they didn't haul you off," I said as I opened the door for her.

"Not lucky," she said. "I gave the car a good sonic clearing before I left."

"Well, it worked."

I pulled into traffic and took Pacific Coast Highway through Malibu. At Sunset Beach, I parked on the side of the road and took the blanket Cat kept in the back seat.

"Watch your step," I called back to her as we made our way over dark boulders. The pounding of the waves onto the sand filled the night with a roar of white sound.

I waited for her to catch up. "Here, this way," I said and chose a path across the boulders and she followed. Lights from passing headlights guided us down to the beach.

I spread the blanket on the sand and Cat took off her shoes and went to the surf line. The waves' white bubbles lapped over our feet then quickly disappeared as the water rushed back out to sea. I stood next to her and she leaned into me.

"This is much better," she said.

"It's poetic," I said.

"Poetic?" she asked.

"The waves are white," I said, "like ice cream. The huge, hard boulders behind us are a castle's walls."

"Or big chocolate chips." Cat laughed and held my hand. I turned to her. She came closer and we kissed. Our tongues touched. I felt her small, round breasts and put my hand under her dress. She felt my hard penis.

We made love on the blanket and I sat up after and wiped sand off of my arm and out of my hair.

"The only problem with the beach is it has too much sand," I said.

She laughed again. "Okay, so let's go back to my place and take a hot bath."

"Now that's a plan," I said.

We gathered the blanket and re-climbed the fortress boulders and I drove in the slow lane from Malibu south to Venice Beach. Cat lived in a detached cottage behind a house on a quiet side street two blocks from the Strand. She let us in the door and turned on one light by the couch. I relaxed in a bean bag chair with a glass of red wine while she filled the tub with steaming hot water and lit candles. I watched her through the open door as she stripped and went into the bubbles. I went in and sat on the side of the tub.

"Why don't you join me? The hot water is relaxing," Cat said.

I stripped and cautiously entered the steaming bath. The candles' filled the apartment with a gentle light and we made love again, Cat on top.

In the morning she dropped me off at Stephen's. I showered, filled a bag with socks, jeans and underwear; ate breakfast and returned to Cat's place in my MG. I parked in her driveway and walked to her front door. She left me a note on her door which read, "Paul, I'm on the beach at the end of the block."

I walked to the Strand, making my way through and around the traffic of bike riders, joggers and roller bladders. I stopped several times to watch jugglers, one-man-bands, limbo dancers and winos. Farther down, I saw Cat kneeling in the sand a few yards off the sidewalk. She was over a middle-aged woman lying on a blanket and I could hear her chanting even above the din of noise that was Venice Beach. Her "Om" was a long, drawn out song that lasted for minutes. As she sang it, she floated her open palms a few inches above the woman's body, starting at her feet and ending at the top of her head. The woman lay peacefully on her back with her eyes closed. A young man and his girlfriend waited for their turn. There was a hand-painted, brightly colored sign next to the blanket that advertised, "Sonic Cleansings".

"How much do you charge?" I asked Cat after she had finished the last two customers. She counted out her morning's take. "I don't have a set price. Some people leave a dollar, some leave twenty. It's whatever they want."

"Let's go out to Zuma Beach," she said as she put her money into a cloth purse and folded the blanket.

"Where is that?" I asked.

"Past Malibu, but let me change shoes first."

We went back to Cat's and she changed shoes and her clothes while I sat on a bean bag in the living room. She had a stick of patchouli incense burning. Sunshine flooded into the room through the windows. I felt relaxed. Cat's lifestyle reminded me of my hippie days in Santa Cruz. She came out of her bedroom in a red mini skirt and pink tank top.

"You look terrific, Cat," I said and she smiled.

I liked having her in the car with me. I drove the blue MG with the top down. We went north, past the pier at Santa Monica, past the houses along the Malibu corridor, past Sunset Beach to Zuma. I found a parking place at the far end of the parking lot and we climbed a well-worn trail up the steep sandstone cliff. The day was sunny and clear; a steady ocean breeze ruffled through our hair. White cumulus clouds sailed over the ocean. At the top of the cliff, we sat on boulders looking out at line after line of hypnotic surf.

"This is a poem too," Cat said.

"It is," I agreed.

"Describe it for me," she asked.

"On the cliffs above the beach," I said without thinking, "breaking waves, and white clouds in blue sky. The sea wind caresses us. How long has this been going on? How long will it be after we're gone?"

"I like that, Paul," Cat said. "Have you ever written your poems down?"

"I've written a few novels and books of poetry but no one is interested in publishing me."

"Is that what you really want to do?" she asked.

"I would like to create something that will last," I said. "Something, a painting or a novel that becomes a part of our culture. So far I haven't been good enough to produce anything of value." I turned back to look out at the far horizon. "Nothing that the world wants anyway."

"Your painting and your writing are important," she said. "Not because they may sell and make you famous but because you are alive and in touch with your feelings. You must be careful though, Paul, don' let the fame sickness take control."

I didn't answer.

"The richness of experience you describe," Cat went on, "and the joy in your paintings, they will bring you honor. Even if you are only acknowledged by a few; you must keep writing and painting because that's what you were meant to do."

"And you? What do you want to do in life?" I asked her.

"I'm here to help people experience bliss consciousness. I clean their vibrations; the colors around them that they've created with their thoughts."

"You can see auras?" I asked.

"Yes, and I can clean them with sound. You have a beautiful aura." She stood behind me and ran the palms of her hands along the outline of my shoulders and head. "But I see fear coming through, disrupting your vibration."

I started to protest but nodded, "Actually you're right," I said. "I'm always afraid. All the time; about money or about being alone for the rest of my life or about getting into a car wreck, about…"

"Close your eyes," she said as she rubbed my skull and chanted a low, soft, "Eeee-aaah-Oooom." She ran her hands down my back and repeated the phrase; "Moment by moment, breath by breath, in the Now, in Love, in God.

"Can you see the lights inside?" she asked.

I saw bright colors in my mind. They swirled then contracted into one beam of pure white light. It was brighter than the sun, but I could look directly into it. Was this my soul? I felt the Holy presence of Jesus Christ. Were these lights and colors coming from the center of the sun and from the center of me too? I felt divine, pure love sweep through my body and mind.

I had a realization that my consciousness was not from the physical atoms in my body, but from the emotions I felt. The Creator's emotion of Love; it had no mass and was not a part of my cells. I saw it and understood it, but I could not put it into words so that you would understand or see it too.

A soft, blushing red filled my consciousness. It condensed into an orange ball surrounded by black, empty space. I smiled to see it.

"What do you see?" Cat asked me.

"It was an orange ball but now it's changed into a beautiful white light with gold and silver along the edges."

"Good" Cat laughed. "I can prove to you that our consciousness survives death. These lights, how can you see them? You don't have eyes in your mind. And how can you hear your mind speaking? There isn't a mouth inside your brain. There aren't ears in your brain to hear with. There isn't anything vibrating, but you can hear yourself talking and you can see with your eyes closed. In your imagination you can picture anything you want."

"True enough," I said to myself. I heard the words in my mind.

"And after death," Cat said, "you will see and hear this same way, without a mouth, without eyes or ears. You will hear the angels calling and see God's perfect white light of love."

We sat for over an hour afterwards, neither of us speaking. We were together, a part of the beauty of the day. Later, when I drove her home, I was too tired to stay another night so I went back to Stephen's. That evening at home I set up my easel and began to paint the image of the orange planet I had imagined. I covered the canvas in thick, black paint then painted a round orange ball in the center. Stephen looked up when I had almost finished. "Hey, that looks like this photograph." He held up a Time magazine.

I was shocked to see a full-page photograph of an orange planet in a black sky. "What is that?" I asked.

"It's a photo from the Explorer mission. They just received these pictures back from millions of miles out in space. It's one of Jupiter's moons."

"That's the exact image I saw in my mind as Cat was rubbing my head and chanting to clear my aura."

"She what?"

"On the cliffs at Zuma Beach," I explained. "There was fear in my aura. It was disrupting my vibrations and she cleaned it up."

"I see," Stephen said.

"Yes, and after she cleaned my vibrations, I saw this vision in my mind. I can't believe it. It's exactly what I saw. Look." I put my canvas next to the magazine. The images were identical.

"Far out, man." Stephen said in a funny, mocking, Cheech and Chong acid-head voice.

Chapter Four
Not A Michelangelo

Stephen and I sat at the bar in Baxter's in Marina Del Rey watching Monday night football on the big screen. The place was packed and I watched as scores of bra-less, beach goddesses, in short shorts vamp in front of horny bachelors. Meanwhile, huge NFL linemen crashed across the big screens. It was hard to hear a word above the tin of conversations. The game wasn't important. I watched the real games play out at the bar.

I sipped my beer as Tony Dorsett went off right tackle; with a stagger step and head fake, he broke out of the hole; a sudden burst of speed and he scampered ahead for 12 yards and a first down.

Stephen leaned over and rubbed shoulders with me. "He's such a pleasure to watch, Frank."

"He sure is, Howard," I answered, half drunk. The experience muddled together in my mind; seven foot television screens, cold pitchers of yellow beer with tiny bubbles rising up through the yellow liquid to join millions of their bubble kind in the happy white foam; guys ya-hooing, tacos for a quarter, tits, tight-ass blue jeans, cowboy hats, bald heads, beards and

"Jesus Christ, welcome to America, y'all," I shouted out, drunk as hell.

"Thanks, Mate. Great to be here," the man sitting to my right said.

He offered me his hand and me being sociably drunk, shook it.

"I'm Allen Lewis," he shouted in my ear.

"Hello, there, Allen Lewis. Do I detect a British accent?"

"Yes, London. Born and raised as you Yanks like to say." He was about my height and build. He had dark curly hair too and all in all it was easy to see our resemblance.

"It's my first visit to the States and it's been a blast," he shouted into my ear, then pulled back with an ear to ear smile on his face.

"Good to hear," I shouted back.

He introduced himself to Stephen, who had to lean across me to hear him.

"We were just discussing how we're pretty much beat in here," I shouted into Allen's ear. "I'm five foot six in a six-foot world. I'm not ugly but I'm not good looking, charming or as easy going as these young sons. I don't have any lines, no come-ons. Like I said, pretty much beat in here."

Allen laughed and nodded his understanding.

"Yeah, me too," Stephen, also drunk, agreed.

"Damn, five inches," I bemoaned my fate. "That's all I needed. Just a lousy five more inches. A hundred and eighty-five pounds and five foot eleven and 'I could-a-been somebody'." I imitated Marlon Brando's *On the Waterfront*. Allen laughed.

I asked him about life in London. The women, friendly to Americans? That sort of thing but it was so loud in the bar, communications were difficult. Allen gave me his telephone number in London and I gave him Stephen's.

We laughed as we left the bar but personally, I was glad that the two-hour ordeal was over.

Abbey waited at the top of the stairs, woken from a glorious sleep on the forbidden couch. A sea breeze flapped the curtains as I closed the living room windows. Stephen turned on the cassette deck. *Let It Be* played and we sat on the couch with chips and beers. I leafed through a large book on *Dali* then through one on *Picasso*. I went further down the stack on the coffee table and rustled through the food stained paperbacks. I picked up Charles Bukowski's *Love is a Dog from Hell* and had to wince at the photo of Bukowski's pocked mark face on the cover. I turned the book face-down and inventoried the rest of the table. There was a coke mirror, a half bottle of White Horse Scotch, a lid of grass in an open zip lock bag, a box of Chips

Ahoy, a bag of potato chips and three empty glasses which had once been filled with milk. The glasses must have been on the table for days and now were glazed in a thick white crust.

Stephen, feet up on the coffee table, snored. I turned off the cassette player and looked out the window. The ocean was at low tide and the moon's light reflected across the surface. I could hear planes taking off from LAX. I searched my feelings and found nothing. I was numb and bored and a bit frightened. My future seemed to be an endless road of boring experiences. I wasn't looking forward to getting my own apartment but summer was nearly over and I wanted to move out. No, what I wanted was to go home but that wasn't going to happen. There didn't seem to be anything to look forward to, only fantasies of beautiful women and making money with my art. I remembered standing as a ten-year old in my back yard one summer night and my father explaining to me that the moon reflected the sun's light. The sun never really went down, it was only the earth that spun around turning away from it. It was a revelation and I remembered feeling the distance the light traveled from the sun's surface to the moon's surface and from the moon to the earth. I could feel the millions of miles of space; the distances that the light traveled were like a thickness inside me. Now, as an adult, I wanted nothing more than to feel the simple truth of the distances.

I called Cat. She told me two weeks ago that she was going to Seattle for a while and didn't know when she'd be back. I let the phone ring for a minute then hung up.

I called the kids next, but Mary answered. "Are they up?" I asked.

"I just sent them to bed," she said. "It's late. I'm still waiting for this month's check."

"Yeah, well I'm still waiting to talk to my children this month."

"It doesn't matter if you talk to them or not," Mary said, "you still have to pay child support."

"It may not matter to you or the courts," I said, "but it sure as hell matters to me so you either start making it happen or I don't pay."

"I'll let the District Attorney deal with you then," she said.

"That's just like you too," I said. "You're more interested in hurting me than having the children in my life."

She hung up on me.

I walked around the living room, angry at her controlling, masculine personality. It could be worse, I thought, I could still be there with her.

I opened my sketch pad and studied the charcoal portrait of a woman's face that I had drawn. I had to admit it wasn't very good. Her eyes were too big for her head and her nose was oddly distorted.

Stephen woke up and looked over my shoulder into the sketch pad, "The problem with your painting is you can't draw," he said.

"I know."

"These must be schools where they can teach you to draw. To do a nose right."

"There are, I'm sure."

"You should go."

"I'd love to," I said.

"Even then I'm afraid you'll never be a Michelangelo."

"No, few of us are." I looked at more of the drawings in my sketch pad. They all had a certain style, an imprint that I recognized as my own, as familiar to me as my signature.

"These aren't much but they're all mine," I said in my defense. "No one could copy them."

Stephen poured a scotch, "I don't think you have to worry about anyone copying them."

I drank my beer. "No, probably not."

It was quiet outside. There weren't any block parties going on and the usual stereos weren't blasting out. I could hear the pounding of the waves. A Volkswagen Beetle charged up the hill, full throttle; its little engine barely overcoming the force of gravity. Despite the occasional traffic noise, it was a quiet, late night on 40th street.

I listened to the sound of my shoes on the hardwood floors as I carried the empty glasses into the kitchen. Dirty dishes overflowed the sink, water dripped from the old faucet. I rinsed the glasses and put them on the countertop then went into the second bedroom and undressed. A feeling of loneliness gnawed at my gut. I finally went back out to the living room and fell asleep on the old brown couch.

We walked in silence across the parking lot. The smell of rain and decaying leaves on the green lawn filled my nostrils as we walked to the mortuary's front door. The trees in the front yard stood motionless, their naked, leafless branches covered with the night's dew.

"Would you witness the cremation with us?" Sarah asked. "Neither my parents or David's want to."

"Yes, of course," I said and Mary agreed and a half hour later we four held hands in a white room with yellow tiles. Two men in blue coveralls rolled a steel sled with Rachel's plain wooden coffin into the metal incinerator chamber. One of the men pushed a button and the incinerator's thick, iron doors creaked shut.

The incinerator startled me with a loud pop. We watched through glass windows as the flames ignited the coffin. It burned white hot. Her body and the coffin were reduced to ashes in a matter of minutes. I wept. The meaning of the words eternity and finality struck me like a hammer. The flame went out and silence filled the mortuary room.

Later in the day, at a memorial service Rachel's teacher played a guitar and led the audience in singing Rachel's favorite song, You Are My Sunshine.

The children's voices; sweet and clear. "You are my sunshine. My only sunshine. You make me happy when skies are gray..."

After the song, a young Rabbi offered his benediction. "At times like these, the worst life can dish out to us, the loss of a child, it is important for us keep faith with the Lord our God.

We must try to remember that He has created all things for his own purposes. We are his children and we must trust in his infinite wisdom. We can have confidence that Rachel and Lisa are now at peace; resting in the bosom of the Lord where they will be cherished and protected for all time. For it is written," he put his reading glasses on and read from a prayer book;

'*Fear not death;*
It is the lot of all flesh
Death is better than a bitter life;
And Eternal rest better than a ravaging sickness.
Set your heart aright and be steadfast,
And despair not in time of tribulation.
Be comforted in your sorrow;
Think not that the grave ends all.
Man's flesh links him to the earth,
But his spirit unites him with the Eternal.
Shall God who made life out of nothing
Be unable to turn what had life into higher life?
All things that are from the earth return to the earth,
And what is from on high returns on high.
All that is false and unjust is destroyed,
But that which is true abides forever.
The righteous live forever, and their reward is in
Thee, O'Lord.'"

I sat straight up with a short scream, "NO!"

Looking around and realizing where I was, I lay back down on the couch in the dark and listened to the soft, rhythmic sound of the surf as it echoed quietly in the living room.

The next morning, I rose early. The first light of sunrise came through the open windows and reflected onto the living room's walls. I had that nightmare every few weeks and I always woke from it sad and heavy hearted. I made myself get up and started work on a painting of the beach as seen through Stephen's living room window. I drank my morning coffee and stepped back after a while and studied the morning light. It made a white glare on the living room's hardwood floors. Do you lay down the brown paint first to get the color of the floor and then paint white on top to get the sun's glare or just the opposite? White first then the brown? These techniques must be worked out by trial and error.

A sea breeze gently blew through the open windows. I stopped to look out at the people on the beach. Why should I go right back to work? The summer was almost over, but if I found a job now, I'd be back in the grind and who knows if I'd ever get the chance again. The chance to do what?

A chance to travel and see masterworks, visit the great museums. A chance to find the one woman whose magic will make all these troubles worthwhile. I could go to New York or San Francisco but no, that would be more of the same. In Europe I would be out of my norm; everything would be different. Just counting foreign money would require my focus; enough concentration to get Mary out of my head and maybe get some relief from this knifelike pain in my stomach.

By late afternoon I had decided. I would buy a round trip, open ticket to Europe and take $3,000 in cash and Travelers checks. I began a list of things I wanted to pack. While I contemplated the list, Stephen pulled into the driveway and came upstairs.

"Hi, Steve. How was work?" I asked as he made the top of the stairs.

Abbey was spinning around in front of him and he leaned over and rubbed her back and head each revolution.

"Lousy kiss-ass bastards," Stephen muttered. "You gotta kiss-ass. Kiss-ass, that's what it's all about."

"So it's a kiss-ass kind of business, then?"

Stephen laughed but said seriously, "You have no idea what I have to put up with; the stars, the studio execs, the directors, all of 'em fuckin' ego maniacs. Just seven more weeks, then I can collect unemployment for a couple of months. How'd your day go?" he asked as he walked over to the couch.

"It was quiet," I said.

"What are you writing?" he leaned over the table to read from my pad.

"A list of things I'm taking to Europe."

"Oh yeah? Great idea. How long you going for?"

"I don't know. How long do you think three-grand will last me?"

"Depends where you stay and how you travel. I spend a month in Germany hitch hiking and back packing on three hundred bucks."

"I'm not going to Germany," I said, "and I'm not going to hitch hike. I was thinking instead of carrying a backpack and I'll buy a big trunk."

"Sure, that would work." Stephen opened a beer and sat on the couch rubbing Abbey's head. "If you stay out of the fancy hotels, you could make three grand last a couple of months at least."

"I'd like to find a place to stay and paint for a while."

"Really? That sounds great. When are you going?"

"I'll make reservations tomorrow to leave in a couple of weeks."

"Do you want to go out tonight?" Stephen asked.

"Sure, where to?"

"Let's try Tampico Tilly's."

I agreed and after a small supper, we drove to Santa Monica, first to Tampico Tilly's but the bar there was packed with men. I turned to Stephen and said, "Let's try Madame Wong's, okay? This place sucks."

"We just got here," Stephen objected.

"Yeah, I know. Humor me. I can't stand this place."

"Sometimes when you're down you got to act happy," he said.

"I know, you keep telling me."

"And it's true."

Despite his objections we left and as I drove down Lincoln Boulevard to Madame Wong's. Before we went in Stephen repeated his advice; I had to act happy.

"That's a tough one for me, Steve. I'm not a good actor."

"You have got to learn then."

"Okay, I'll learn," I said. I didn't want to hear it anymore.

"I'm just telling you this for your own good," Stephen said. "I only want to see you happy."

"Happiness is part of the neurosis," I said. "No, that's bullshit, but really I can't fake happy."

"Well, relaxed then."

"I'd love to be relaxed," I agreed.

"Well try then."

"I do. I try," I said.

He looked at me, thinking then said, "You know how many mornings you walk around saying, "Shit, damn, fuck!"

"Too many, I know," I said, "but I'm trying. Besides you walk around saying shit, damn, fuck, too."

"I'm not trying to get into egos with you," Stephen said.

"No? Then let's not."

Madame Wong's had a decent ratio of women. It was dark inside and we went upstairs to the nightclub. Stephen knew the bass player with the house band and we went back stage to meet him. Behind the stage curtain, Stephen pulled out a joint and passed it to the bass player. He was tall and skinny with blond hair and his eyes lit up as he exhaled the gray smoke.

"This is good stuff. Got any to sell?" he asked Stephen as he passed him back the joint.

"Sure do," Stephen said. "It's seventy a lid."

"That's a bit high, but okay, here." He pulled out the money and Stephen counted it.

"It's righteous," Stephen said, handing him a zip lock bag of green leaves and buds.

"There isn't a girl in here over 23," I said looking out to the dance floor.

"I'll tell you one thing," Stephen said, "one thing I really believe." Stephen pulled on the joint. "So help me God, a man must have young pussy."

The bass player and I looked at each other and nodded our consent to Stephen's hypothesis.

We three all looked around the room and took stock of the beauties. "I've been around the world," the bass player said, "and no place on earth can compare with Southern California.

Young pussy, hard, stand-up tits, flat stomachs, nice legs, hair, hair, hair and faces like goddesses. They're magic and in Southern California they're in number."

Two young women in tight, black stretch slacks walked by. They had perfect, round bottoms and wore high heel shoes.

"God bless the man who invented high heels," I said.

"The guy knew what he was doing alright," the bass player agreed. His voice sounded funny.

I looked into his blood-shot eyes. "You're stoned, right?" I asked him.

"I'm shit faced," he laughed.

We shook hands and he said he'd see us after the set.

Stephen and I hung out near the bar and as the band played, we watched the lovelies shake and dance. The night became torture. I spoke to no one. The young girls weren't interested in me and I got Stephen to leave after much discussion and advice from him. On the way home, driving along Pacific Highway through El Secondo he continued his criticism.

"You looked ridiculous with your sweater tucked in your pants," he said.

"Why do you have to do that?" I said. "I'm already feeling bad enough and you have to take a cheap shot. Fuck you, Steve." I put my foot down on the gas and downshifted. The MG went from thirty to seventy as I speed shifted through the gears; fish tailing all over the road. I took it to the brink, the very brink, asking and getting everything that little motor could give. Stephen froze in the passenger seat, inches from the guard rail.

Driving like an asshole, I leaned over the gear shift and looked into his eyes as the engine whined near redline.

"I've got a five-year old in me and I swear I'd die before I ever let anyone hurt him. You understand?"

"Yeah, I understand," Stephen shouted to be heard.

I brought the car down to a calm, very calm, thirty-five miles per hour. We had been a foot or two from disaster, now, in contrast as we drove along the beach, I could hear the surf peacefully striking the shoreline.

When we got back to Stephen's place, I finished the bottle of Amaretto on the coffee table then the couple of shots left in the Bailey's Crème bottle. Stephen had gone off to bed. Restless, I stood at the open window feeling the late-night breeze. I was on my way to Europe and I was nervous but excited too.

I laid down on the couch and fell asleep. I dreamed of Rachel and the old days in Santa Cruz; smoking marijuana with Mary and Sarah and Mark. Patchouli incense burned in the brass cistern and filled the old house with the scent of the Age of Aquarius. Sunlight streamed through the redwood trees and sitar music floated through the open windows out into the peaceful afternoon.

When I woke in the morning, I was in Stephen's living room on the couch. I still wore the clothes from the night before. I stumbled to the bathroom and washed my face in cold water and went to the kitchen and started a pot of coffee. Outside the kitchen window I could see a heavy morning fog. I sipped my coffee and listened to the waves' rhythmic pounding. For the first time in my life I felt what it would be like to live without a woman. Not for a month or a year, but for the rest of my life. Normally that realization would have saddened me but this morning it didn't hurt. To experience this room, this quiet beach morning; that was enough. "I wish I could keep this feeling; and have it any time I started to feel the loneliness crawl into my gut," I said to Abbey and she agreed, this morning was good.

Stephen slept most of the day. When he woke, we nodded to each other. It wasn't that we weren't talking, we just weren't bullshitting. I went out to shop for things for my trip. When I returned, Stephen was in the kitchen washing the dishes. Every dish in the house was in the two sinks and across the drain counters. I could hear him wash each plate very precisely. I knew that he was listening with pleasure to the click-clack sound of the dishes touching as he placed them on the drain board. The sound was good. It went perfectly with the gray afternoon and the cold ocean air coming in through the open windows.

It was quiet when Stephen finished. The sound of the high tide pounding on the beach filled the house like a beating heart. I scrubbed the coffee table while Stephen vacuumed the dark brown carpet.

I thought of our boyhood days; two children growing up in the school yard, playing baseball and football, stickball and horseshoes in the 1950s. Those were days of heaven but what had we become? Stephen worked six months a year as a teamster then hustled a few grand a year playing backgammon. He made another couple of thousand selling weed to the locals. I was a recovering addict, an unhappy man facing middle age as I dealt with emotional pain for the first time without medicating myself.

For right now I was crashed on my brother's couch in Manhattan Beach. It smelled from Abbey's doggy odor. Stephen was indifferent to the unpleasant smell. It bothered me to hell. I felt a silence inside myself. It reminded me of childhood days when the moments were timeless because I could feel. The light was special then because I wasn't worried. Everything I experienced was fresh; with no fantasy thoughts of yesterday or tomorrow, of women or fame. I questioned it all now; the odds of life on earth, the need to breath oxygen. I imagined golden hair vaginas and clits in silk panties.

I listened to a John Coltrane tune on the stereo, '*Why was I born?*'

Sometimes it seemed to me that our existence was a freak of nature. There was no reason why to anything, Mr. Coltrane.

I showered and went to get a shirt from Stephen's bedroom closet. He was still in bed but awake and looking out the window at the breakers.

"Mark called last night," I said.

"Oh yeah? What'd he say?" Stephen asked in a dull voice.

"He said he's been transferred to Torrance and would like you to keep an eye out for an apartment. Maybe when I move out, he could move in?"

"He's as depressing as you are," Stephen said.

"What do you mean, as I am?"

"Well, sometimes you're depressing," Stephen said from the bed where he lay with his head propped up on one elbow.

"Yeah and sometimes you're depressing," I said.

I borrowed a shirt from his closet. "I lived with Mary for over thirteen years," I said. "The last five years everything I said or did, she let me know didn't meet her standards and now you're doing it. Steve, I struggle each day to be positive about myself, the last thing I need is to be around someone who feeds me negative images; especially people I love and respect."

Stephen, looked up at me and paid attention.

"I miss my children," I said looking him in the eyes, "and my home but the children say they don't miss me. They told me they don't want me to come back home. Mary tells them that I don't love them. She told them that I've abandoned them. They don't know that my heart is breaking into a million pieces because I won't be there to see them grow up. Do you understand I'm in pain?'

"We're all in pain," Stephen said. "You have your broken relationships, I've got mine."

"How about a brother who thinks you're a jerk? You got one of them?" I asked.

"I don't think you're a jerk."

"No? You use every chance you get to take cheap shots at me."

"No, I don't."

"Yes, you do. You keep telling me about your terrific friends; like why can't you be like them. I can't take it, Steve. I just can't take it anymore. I want things to be like when we were young. I want to feel that feeling we had on summer vacation when we were buddies, partners like the Cisco Kid and Poncho. I want that feeling all the time. How do I get it back?"

"Man, I don't know and you just changed the subject. I do think you are terrific. Paul. I'm sorry if what I say sometimes feels like a dig. I'm having my own problems here, you know?"

"Yeah, I know."

I sat on the edge of his bed and looked out at the eternal Pacific Ocean.

"Why don't we play Frisbee with Abbey?" Stephen asked.

"Good idea," I said.

Outside, Stephen threw the Frisbee in front of the house while I sat on the front steps. Abbey chased the Frisbee up and down the steep street. She caught it every time. Her judgment was perfect; she could tell as soon as it left Stephen's hand where it was going to end up and how fast she'd have to go to get it on the run. She was a smooth, easy worker; pulling the Frisbee down in a leap, with all four paws leaving the ground. Then carrying it proudly back to him and putting it into his hand.

Suddenly raindrops pattered down.

"Hey, put my top up will ya?" Stephen called to me.

"Sure. Where are your keys?"

Stephen went inside and tossed his keys down to me. Abbey took off to sniff garbage cans and pee around her favorite spots. I got into Stephen's orange Fiat and put the roof up and attached it to the front windshield. I rolled up the windows and sat and listened to the sound of the light shower on the thin canvas roof. The streets were quiet, gray clouds rolled in from the ocean with a thick mist. I felt time, this passing moment in my life. I realized that it had been a long time since I had felt warmth from another human being, real warmth; the glow of a deep love. I'd been hated and scorned for years by Mary. Stephen's love was indirect. I longed for that love look; a look from a woman in love as she shined her eyes over my features, absorbed my moves, my style and loved everything about me. But here now, in this mellow, halfway place between awake and sleep; with my eyes closed and listening to the raindrops dance on the roof like drizzle on an umbrella, I felt peace. Still, I could recognize the hurt that was there in my gut at the thought of losing my children.

The rain became heavy, sweeping in sheets across the concrete street. I started the Fiat and pulled it into the garage and went upstairs and into the small second bedroom where my new silver trunk lay at the foot of the bed with its top open. Inside, jeans, plastic bags, books, shirts and assorted paraphernalia, all disarranged stared up at me telling me my story. I was on the move. A stable middle-class man without a home. A married man with no wife. A family man with no children. Suddenly each day was mine. I had my freedom but it contained a strong sense of exile. My relationship with my kids was gone forever, never to return. But there was a newness to my life too. An awareness that the now is always new, always giving. Could I bring joy into my story?

The next two weeks passed by slowly but finally it was time to go. I brought the last load of my things to storage and put the MG into a rented garage. The day was bright and clear. I looked down from the living room to the Strand and the beach. I had planned to swim one more time before leaving but I waited too long. The afternoon brought its daily film of brown plankton which I could see floating on the surface of the water.

Stephen had decided we should put wheels on my trunk and he walked across the street wearing last night's rumpled designer jeans, no shirt and a day-old beard. On his nose a white gauze patch covered the wound from recent skin cancer surgery. Despite the dangerous cancer, his body was burnt from constant sun bathing. Stephen unscrewed four castors from an old couch behind Pamela and Ken's yellow house and went back to his own garage and dug through piles of debris, miraculously finding screws and an electric drill.

Hearing him digging through the mess downstairs and worried about how the wheel job would turn out, I went down to supervise. Stephen tried but failed to screw the first sofa wheel into the bottom of the aluminum trunk. The trunk was three and a half feet long by two feet high by two wide and was difficult to handle. Stephen patiently but sloppily, screwed in the castor wheels.

I looked at my watch. It was 1:30 already! I raced upstairs and called Noah and Ava. A recording said, "four two six, seven six nine-nine, is no longer in service and there is no new number."

We had that telephone number for ten years. There must be some mistake. I dialed it again. Same recording. I called information but they had no new number. The truth hit me. Mary had gotten an unlisted number so I couldn't call the children.

Stephen yelled up to me from the front door. "Help me bring it up!" I heard the trunk banging against the stairwell walls; knocking stucco onto the tile steps. I went down to help him carry it up to my room and finished packing. Ready to go, I leaned out the front window and saw Stephen playing with some of the articles that had come out of the garage during his earlier search for tools. He swung an old tennis racket with broken strings.

"Stephen," I yelled from the window, "if the kids call, tell them if they ever need to reach me, to call you and you'll get a message to me."

"Sure," Stephen said.

"Flight number two, Laker Skytrain, departing 5:15pm LAX to Gatwick, on time," the recorded message said. I hung up. Ten hours flying then eight hours' time difference. I felt exhausted, dreading the thought of the cramped seats. I kneeled down and gave Abbey a pat good-bye. "You're a good dog, Abbey." She licked my face. "Watch over him, girl."

I struggled with the heavy trunk.

"Here, wait, let me help you," Stephen said as he came up the stairs to the top landing.

We carried it awkwardly down the steps, knocking more paint chips off the stairwell wall. Together we lifted it into tiny back seat of Stephen's orange Fiat. It was a short twenty-minute ride along the coast to LAX. Stephen pulled up to the front of the temporary international terminal and we got the trunk out of the back seat. I slung my backpack on and wheeled the trunk through the doors of the balloon structure.

"It's like walking into a wind tunnel," I called to Stephen. We lowered our heads and pushed forward.

It was cold inside. The authorities were keeping the balloon structure at a crisp 50 degrees. On the screen I found my flight and saw that it was delayed an hour and a half.

"I can't believe it," I said. "I just called and they said it was on-time. Geez."

"You could go home then come back," Stephen said.

"Nah, I think I'd rather just wait here."

"I'm gonna go then." Stephen hugged me. "I'm sorry about the hassles."

I smiled, "I've had fun. Thanks for everything, Steve."

"Don't think about anything," Stephen said. "You deserve this." We hugged again and Stephen left, turning once to wave good-bye.

I sat alone in the crowd at the gate on my way to Europe and the kids didn't even know. It felt strange to be this far out of their lives. I walked outside and watched the palm trees sway in a light breeze. The palm fronds rustled quietly overhead as I looked around and stood motionless; breathed in the exhaust fumes from the buses and autos and wondered what awaited me in Europe.

Chapter Five
London Bridges

September 1981

The Laker Skyway jet landed an hour and a half late at Gatwick. I filed out with everyone else and made my way through customs and immigration to the underground station where I boarded the first train to come by. While I tried to figure out the subway maps, the train went through London to the far outskirts of the city.

Without Mary's help, I was lost. I ran into obstacles and delays everywhere; nothing had gone right. Five hours after landing at Gatwick, I finally arrived at the hotel in central London where I had made reservations. The hotel manager, a fat man with a speech impediment was telling his wife out of the corner of his mouth that if I wanted a room, I must pay for two nights, not one night at a time. "Charge him for cashing his travelers check too," he said in a contorted British accent.

The woman seemed beyond despair. She half smiled at me and despite her husband's instructions at every turn, she was fair. I paid for just one night in advance. She took my travelers check and gave me the correct change without deducting a surcharge. She showed me to a tiny L shaped closet of a room on the second floor. The stained blue carpets and the old, dingy, peeling, wallpaper made it clear why the hotel owner wanted two nights paid upfront. I squeezed past the bed to get to the dresser drawers. Half the handles were missing and I had to pry the drawers open. The one tall window in the room overlooked a brick walled garden where several workmen repaired the walkway below. I stopped to listen to the sounds of their shovels. They worked in an unhurried but purposeful way and the sounds, random but methodical, mesmerized me. I was jet-lagged and the click-clack of their tools on the bricks and their shovels scrapping dirt, relaxed me and I sat on the bed for a half hour listening to them. I almost fell asleep but finally I was able to get up. I took two thin towels from behind the door and went to the communal bathroom to shower.

"How would normal size people fit in here?" I said as I bent my knees to get my head under the shower nozzle. Though uncomfortable, the experience was pleasant if for no other reason than making me aware that I was in another country and culture. I took a mental note though, that my travel guide had rated the place three stars. Only four stars from now on, I said as I negotiated with the part of me that was keeping track of the budget.

I dressed at six o'clock and although it was still early, I found myself staring into space as the jet lag creeped back into my mind. I sat on the old bed and realized I did not like the room or the hotel. I needed to find another. I went downstairs and with my European travel guide, *Europe on $25 A Day*, found "The Coronet: Nevern Square, Earl's Court Station. Clean premises, large rooms, and private bath in great neighborhood." And it was four stars, okay, budget director we're making a move.

I called from the payphone in the front hallway and made reservations for the next day. I called Allen Lewis next, the young Brit Stephen and I met at Baxter's bar a month ago.

"Listen, mate we're going to a great Guy Fawkes party tomorrow night." Allen said after the pleasantries. "A real dress soiree. Why don't you come along?"

"Sure, love to," I said. "What time?"

"I'll pick you up at seven."

"I'm at the Coronet Hotel"

"Yes, I'll find it. What about tonight? Would you like to get a bite to eat?"

"Thanks, Allen but I've been up for almost 48 hours. I'm bleary eyed. I can't even calculate how long I've been awake, not when I have to factor in the eight-hour time difference."

"I understand," Allen said. "See you tomorrow."

"Okay, see you tomorrow night then," I said.

I went back upstairs and whereas the tiny room would normally have kept me awake; sheer exhaustion put me into a black, dreamless sleep.

I was awake and up at seven, unable to sleep but still feeling the jet lag, I decided to go for a walk in the park across the street. On the other side of the park I found an open café and I stopped for coffee and toast. That helped, so it was back to the hotel and repack the trunk and check out, then out to the corner and wait for a cab to come by. It was a beautiful Saturday fall morning, 70 degrees and blue skies. A long, black handsome cab turned the corner and I hailed it. The cabbie and I loaded the trunk and bag into the "boot" and he drove to the Coronet Hotel.

My eyes glazed over as I watched the early morning Saturday traffic. Despite my jet lagged state, I picked up a good feeling for London. I felt a certain something emanating from the buildings. It wasn't just the old architecture as interesting as that was. There was something in the atmosphere that gave me a sense of history. Charles Dickens' London and wartime London, medieval London, the entire grand history of Great Britain hung in the air.

The cabbie pulled in front of the Coronet hotel and I paid him and brought my trunk and bag up the steps to the front door. It was locked. I rang the bell and watched through the front glass door as a woman in her early twenties came down the narrow, red carpeted hallway and unbolted the door.

"How do you do?" she asked, smiling.

"How do you do," I repeated. "I'm, Paul Gebhart."

"Bernadette, charmed."

I pulled the large trunk into the hallway. One of the front wheels had been badly damaged on my trip from Gatwick and now, after two steps, the trunk's black handle suddenly snapped off. The luggage thudded loudly onto the carpet and I laughed. "Wretched piece of crap," I said.

Bernadette laughed.

We deserted the trunk and I followed her down the hallway to the front desk.

"I'll explain the hotel's rules," she said as she went behind the counter.

"Rules?" I asked.

"Yes, the front door locks automatically, but we have a clerk at the desk 24 hours a day; ring the bell for entry. Breakfast is in the basement dining room, seven to nine."

"No exceptions for Americans?"

"Sorry, breakfast stops being served at nine, sharp, no exceptions. Your room is number twenty-six, on the second floor, upstairs on the street side."

"I sign here?" I pointed to the quest register.

"Yes, do, please."

I signed the book and went for my wallet.

"You can pay when you check out," Bernadette said.

"No deposit required?" I asked.

"No, that won't be necessary."

"Ah, trust. One human being trusting another. The basis of a civilized world."

Bernadette laughed as she came around the counter and led the way up the stairs to the second floor. I carried the trunk behind her. She opened the door to room twenty-six, went in and opened the balcony door. Sunlight streaked into the room and lit up the pink flowered wallpaper and yellow bedspread.

The room had fifteen-foot high ceilings. The balcony door opened up onto Nevern Square Road. I could see a small park across the street from my balcony.

"Enjoy your stay," Bernadette said as she left.

I unpacked and thought about a lady named, Carol that Stephen had mentioned to me. She was a woman he met in Jamaica several years ago. They had exchanged a few postcards since then and he thought she might be open to showing me around London. He said that she was quite well off and was looking for a husband. Maybe, I thought, just maybe she'll be the one. Stephen had given me her telephone number and I called her from the phone in the lobby. A gay, high pitched voice answered.

"Hi, Carol? I'm Stephen's brother, Paul Gebhart. From America?"

"Oh hi. Yes, of course I remember Stephen very well. It must have been two years ago and I only spent three days with him, but I remember it vividly because we fought for the entire three days!" Her laugh was genuine.

"Yes, well, Stephen can be difficult at times."

"Like morning, noon and tea time," Carol said.

"I hope you won't hold it against me."

"Of course not, darling. So how long are you here for?"

"A few days before going to France and Italy."

"Ah, the continent. I've only just returned from St. Tropez and Monte Carlo. You know what? I can't believe it! I sent Stephen a postcard from St. Tropez! How remarkable!"

"I'll say." I noted the fact that she made a point to drop the names of the expensive places.

"How long are you traveling for?" she asked.

"Well, I brought enough to last me for three months."

"That's exciting. Good for you."

"Yes, thank you. It was a now or never kind of thing. I'm in between jobs and coming out of a divorce."

"I see. Bravo, Paul. Listen, Love, I'm going to a private disco party at the Intercontinental tomorrow tonight. Why don't you meet me there?"

I thought for a moment; but sure, why not, I could make both parties. "Okay, that's very nice of you. What time?"

"Oh, say 10:30?"

"Fine, I'll be there. Meet you in the lobby. I'll have you paged."

"Good, okay then ta-ta, see you."

"Bye, Carol."

I called Allen and gave him the name of the new hotel and he came by at seven and we drove to his friend's apartment. We waited outside on the steps of the flat as the London traffic roared by. "These old taxis add an air of elegance," I said as several black, square taxis hurried down the street. "Seems like we're back in the 1940s," I said. "Well, except for the punks and skinheads." We watched as a group of teenagers crossed the road. The girls had loud, orange and green hair cut in a motley, chopped fashion. They wore black lipstick, white t-shirts, black leather jackets and black jeans, two sizes too big. The boys were dressed the same except that their heads were shaved bald.

"Charming group," I teased after they passed. "How come some of the autos only have their parking lights on?" I asked.

"That's all that's required," Allen said.

"Really? It looks strange to see cars with little yellow lights, not illuminating the roadway at all."

"We do several things different here in Britain."

"Yes, you do. And I think more than several."

Allen ignored my quip and explained, "Ted is a computer salesman and Susan is an art dealer. We're going to share a lift with them to the party."

I saw Ted and Susan come downstairs through the glass window of the front door. They came out onto the stoop and we shook hands and Ted unlocked his Peugeot parked curbside. Alan and I settled into the back seat and I was enjoying the London night scene but as we drove, the brakes squealed and Ted cursed each time they did. I became nauseous listening to the squealing brakes and then Ted's cursing.

"Ted, god damn it!" Susan finally shouted.

Ted stopped short, startled by her tone. "What is it?" he asked.

"Please shut up about the bloody brakes."

"The party is being given by old chums of mine," Allen said to me. "Three guys I grew up with and then lived with in college."

"I thought you said it was a 'dress up' party?" I said. "Look at you." Allen wore his Manhattan Beach garb; white shorts, thongs and a black T-shirt with 'Surf Punks' printed in iridescent letters.

"But I am formally dressed," Allen said. "Wait till you see the other customers."

Ted parked on a narrow street on the west side of London. The neighborhood was small, single family homes with no front yards and hardly an inch between properties. We walked up the front steps to one of the houses and Allen rang the bell. A tall gangly young man wearing a Royal Army uniform greeted us. "Hi, I'm Andy," he said as we shook hands. He gave Allen and Ted a hefty solute, then went into the dialogue from an old English war movie.

"The problem is, Andy," Allen said, "no one knows exactly which movie or what scene you're doing."

Andy laughed and let us in. I listened as he pulled the same routine with the next partiers to ring the bell. Allen and I walked through the living room, down a narrow hallway and into the kitchen. "Ah, there you are," Allen called to two young men in costumes. "Paul, this is John and Matt."

John was dressed in a red silk, Jester's costume. Matt had on a matching green one. Their faces painted in white grease paint and large, red clown mouths.

"Nice to meet you," I said. "I heard you were both mad men but I had no idea."

A pretty blond standing next to the refrigerator laughed. She wore a Nazi cap and a jacket with swastika patches on the shoulders. In place of pants, she had on black net stockings with high heels. Her white thighs showed above the garter belts. Only the half-buttoned jacket covered her bra and panties. Her blond hair was combed frizzy and stuck out from underneath the Nazi cap.

"What a delight!" I said. "And here I've always had such a bad feeling for the holocaust. Hi, I'm Paul." I shook hands with her and gave her my best smile.

"I'm Leslie," she said, also with a great smile.

Allen brought over two large glasses of brown ale and he and I wandered back into the hallway. I bumped into a woman wearing a plastic 'Super Drug' shopping bag over azure blue stockings. Her face painted white with blue stripes to match the plastic bag.

"I say, quite stylish," I imitated an upper-class Englishman.

She playfully slapped me on the shoulder.

The house was shaking from thumping, English rock music. I danced with the Super Drug woman while other guests squeezed past us. The small house was crammed with people by now. I saw Indian Chiefs, Boy and Girl scouts, waiters in white bibs with wine keys around their necks, Romans in togas, judges in long black gowns.

"Say, you don't suppose there's any kind of chemical entertainment available?" I asked Super Drug Woman between songs.

She gave me a knowing look, "How much did you want to buy?" she asked.

"Buy? Well, I only wanted a line or two if it was around," I said. I made a gesture with my thumb and forefinger to indicate a small line.

"Right. Let me see what's up."

She left, and returned with a young man dressed in jeans and vest. "This is Auberon," she introduced us and Auberon nodded for me to follow him upstairs. We went into a room on the second floor and Auberon took out a gram of white Persian H from his dresser. I bought a quid's worth and snorted it as Auberon smoked from a piece of tin foil. I bought another quid's worth and smoked it with him.

"Damn, I'm starting to rush," I said as I laid back into the armchair.

"You don't like it?" Auberon asked.

"Sure, I like it. I love it. That's the fucking problem."

"Yeah, it's tough. Nice stuff though, don't you think?"

"Yeah, sure, thanks."

Why was I getting stoned on heroin? What an asshole I am. And why? Why now? Why here? I recalled going to parties when I was a teenager. The young girls in make-up and tight dresses stood around talking and laughing as the music played. The boys stood around too, waiting for someone to show up with a bottle of cheap red wine. Outside, we passed it around and warm now inside, loose now in the mind, I could ask anyone to dance and I could dance.

I was in the arm chair by the window and Auberon on the bed. The room was dark except for the light from the upstairs hallway. I tried to get up but couldn't. I settled back and nodded off.

Later, I pulled myself out of the chair and went downstairs to join the party. I was really fucked up; people stared at me. Leslie the cute Nazi was in the corner of the living room making out with a tall, blond man in his twenties. Missed out again. Too old to be running around like this too. I was very nauseous. I could hardly see. I stumbled back upstairs and lay down on Auberon's bed. He had gone off somewhere. I wanted to leave, it was late and I had to meet Carol at the hotel but when I tried to sit up my stomach turned. I staggered downstairs to find Allen. The small house was jammed packed with people. The music played LOUD; the music, the laughter and the shouting joined together in a chaotic mess of sounds. I was pushed and shoved by bizarre people. I finally made it through the crush of sounds and people to the front porch. On the front sidewalk, I dry heaved. I went back through the crowded living room and through the packed hallway and into the kitchen. It took a physical effort to move through the crowded rooms. The noise was deafening, everyone had to scream to be heard. I found Allen.

"I'd like to leave." I yelled into his ear.

"In ten minutes." Allen shouted back in my ear.

"I'll be upstairs laying down."

"Right. Be right away. Go and lie down."

I squeezed my way out of the kitchen, through the hallway and up the narrow stairway. To the toilet, still couldn't puke. To bed and crash for another half hour then back downstairs to find Allen. This routine was repeated four times. The last time Ted followed me upstairs and sat on the bed.

"How are you feeling?" he asked.

"Terrible. I'm nauseous," I said, startled by Ted's presence.

"Did heroin, did ya?"

"What's it matter?"

"Oh nothing, it doesn't."

Fucker wants to know all the details like I was an American sideshow. 'Crazy bloke, fuck'n blind on her-o-in and all that.'

Allen finally came to help; he led me down the stairs; we passed several couples making out on the steps. A pretty red head had her blouse off. She moaned with pleasure and I stared at her tits.

"I never got to meet her," I said to Allen.

"With her boyfriend is probably why."

I nodded, "True."

At the bottom of the stairway I knocked over two drinks on a side table. I tried to save them but only managed to crash into a young woman standing next to the table.

"Christ! I'm really sick. I can't see three feet. Sorry," I said. She turned and studied my face. I looked at her through blurry vision. She was a short brunette with a pixie cut and blue-gray eyes. She wore designer jeans and heels with a white pullover knit sweater. She had small, straight tits, tight ass and very flat stomach. Even bleary eyed, stuff like that comes through.

"Sorry, I'm sorry," I said again as I tried to dry off the drink I spilt on her.

"It's okay, you don't... no, that's okay." She fended me off as I tried to dry her blouse.

"What's your name?" I shouted.

"Angela, Angela Coates."

"Hi, I'm, Paul. I'm not always this stupid. Really."

She laughed.

"I'm in London for a few days, and, well I was wondering if you'd like to go with me to the National Gallery?"

"Sure, why don't you ring me up tomorrow?" She wrote her number on a cocktail napkin and gave it to me.

Allen motioned with his head that we should leave as Ted and Susan were already in the car.

"I'll call you, have a good night," I said.

Angela laughed at me, "Can you make it?"

"Sure, I'm fine, fine." I turned and tripped into another woman. This one dressed in feathers.

"Sorry, I'm sorry," I said.

"Don't do anything!" she yelled.

"No, no, of course not," I said, trying not to sway. "Have a nice day."

Outside, finally, I found the car and got into the back seat.

"I don't think you should try the Intercontinental, Paul," Allen said.

"No? I look that bad, eh?"

Allen nodded.

Ted dropped me off two blocks from the Coronet Hotel and gave me directions on how to find it. It was 1:30 in the morning with not a car or soul on the streets. I couldn't see my feet, no less read street signs. I only understood one out of three or four words of Ted and Allen's British accent. "Street...half...right...down...left..."

I leaned against the car door and looked at their hands as they pointed this way, gestured a turn here, a turn down there.

I nodded my head, "Sure. Okay, right. Uh-huh, gotcha."

The Peugeot pulled away and I took three steps and vomited up against a red van.

Remarkably, I found the hotel with no problem. It being just where they said it would.

Sunday morning, I woke at six-thirty. I needed to pee but felt nauseous as I sat up. I made it to the John, watered but couldn't puke. I started to dress to go to breakfast but fell back on the bed and slept. Waking a second time, I looked at my watch. It was quarter to nine! Fifteen minutes before breakfast was over! No Exceptions!

I stumbled down to the dining room. Three other guests, sitting at one table, looked up at me as I bumped into the tea server. I found the closest empty seat and sat down.

"Eggs?" The waitress came to my white-clothed table. She spoke with a heavy, Italian accent.

"No eggs, juice," I said. I felt like I was chewing cotton balls.

"Jew-sa?" she asked.

"Yes, juice, orange juice."

"Oh, oran-a-jew-sa."

"Yes, and toast with jam."

"Toasta?" she asked.

"Yes, toast. You know, heated bread." I made a gesture to illustrate a piece of bread but the movements of my hands brought on waves of nausea. I wondered how hated I would be if I threw up on the table. I was just on the verge too. I rubbed his eyes and moaned in rhythm to the waves of nausea inside me.

"Okay, okay, coffee too," the waitress said. I had forgotten she was there. She went off towards the kitchen.

"Mind if I join you?"

"Huh?" I looked up at a neatly dressed, clean shaven Englishman.

"May I join you, sir?" He repeated in a bright tone.

"Yes, of course," I said. Couldn't he see the other seventeen empty tables?

My breakfast came; cereal, toast, juice, coffee and milk. I took a bite of toast and had to hold back the regurgitated first mouthful.

"Here on holiday? From America?" the man asked as I slowly re-swallowed the food. I nodded, yes.

"Where abouts? I've been there twice muhself, Chicago once in '67 then Pontiac, Michigan in, well, that must have been '74. No, no, it was the spring of '75."

"I'm really hungover, sick to my stomach," I said. "I've had a wretched night drinking 'bitters'."

"Bitter is a type of English beer," he corrected me. "Bitters is a liquor usually drunk as a cocktail. I'm not sure really which you are referring to."

"Whatever," I moaned. "The point is you see, I'm not feeling well, sorry to be rude, but I can't..." I belched. "talk right now."

"Ah well, it's good your enjoying your stay in London," he smiled. "I'm here for the jewelry trade show this morning at the Palladium. It should be quite an event. We expect..."

A loud burp erupted out of my belly. It was so loud that the other three people in the room almost dropped their forks. Even our happy friend looked warily and shut up.

I finished what I could of breakfast and went to leave but as I rose, I bumped into the table. This accident spilled the Englishman's tea and soaked the tablecloth and his dish of eggs as well.

"Oops. Sorry, really sorry," I said. "Well, luck at the convention and all that." I smiled, burped again and went back up to my room wondering if I may have tarnished the British/American 'special' relationship.

I lay in bed nude, falling in and out of dreams for an hour. I put on my jeans and went to the communal toilet down the hall and puked up breakfast. Back to bed but a half hour later I was up: put jeans on, to John, puke, jeans off, to bed. Jeans on, to John, puke up rice from deep down in small intestines, jeans off, back to bed.

I finally fell asleep but was startled awake when the Italian waitress suddenly unlocked my door. Always that Jewish modesty about me, I grunted loud enough to back her up as she entered the room.

"Sorry," she said, embarrassed, "I didn't know you were-a here." She held a bucket and rags and her vacuum cleaner sat behind her in the hallway. She was in her early twenties.

"It's okay. Wait just one minute," I said.

She closed the door and I put on my jeans and let her back in. "I'm Paul."

"Lucia," she said.

"Where are you from, Lucia? Not England."

"No, no," she laughed. "I'm from Milan." She looked closer into my face.

"I'm sick," I explained my sorry state, "hungover from last night.'

"Are you from America?" she asked.

"Yes, Los Angeles."

"You're-a here on business?"

"No, I quit my job. I'm just traveling for a few months."

"Not married?"

"No, divorced."

"Ah, I understand." Lucia said. She went to leave.

"No, no. It's okay," I stopped her. "You can straighten my room. I want to sleep and this way we'll both know it's been done."

"Okay," she said.

I went to the John to wash my face, when I returned Lucia was making the bed. I studied her from behind. She was in her early twenties with dyed blond hair and brown eyes. She wore a tight, yellow, button all the way down the front, dress. The first six buttons weren't and I could see her blue bra. I could see her blue panties too outlined against the tight yellow dress.

"Jesus, Lucia!" I said shaking my head.

"What?" she asked with a smile.

"Just, Jesus, you look terrific."

She blushed.

I sat on the second bed and watched her change the sheets and pillow cases.

"How is your hangover?" she asked.

"It's better. Lucia, are you married?"

"No."

"Have a boyfriend?"

"Yes, but no. Not like that. Why do you ask?" she half turned to look at me while she stuffed a pillow into its fresh white case.

"Because I wanted to ask you out to dinner and drinks."

"That would be nice."

"How about tonight?" I asked.

"No, I must sleep tonight. I was out until 3:00am and then working all day. I feel like-a you."

I laughed with her.

"Monday then?"

"No, I'm doing something. Tuesday would be okay."

"Tuesday? Umm, I'm not sure I'll still be in London. We'll see."

"Okay." She smiled.

After she finished the room, I fell back to sleep. At 1:00 I showered, dressed and went downstairs to call Angela Coates.

"So, we'll meet at the National Gallery?" I asked after the hellos and telling her where I was staying.

"No, I can come to the station at Earl's Court at 3:00," Angela said.

I looked at my watch. It was 2:00. "Okay, great I'll meet you at the ticket booth."

Around the corner at the Earl's Court station, I studied the people catching trains. Where were they all going? I tried to put myself inside their lives. I could see that Life was so big there was nothing small in it; underneath everything lay another layer and then another. Life would go on after me without missing a beat. I felt that now and the romance of being alive in London.

Angela arrived on time. She had on tight black slacks and a white lace blouse. She carried a black leather jacket on her arm. She was cute. Her face was small and she made the most of her looks with red lipstick and a touch of blue eye shadow. I put her in her mid-twenties, maybe even 27. She was trim, not thin, and I liked the curve of her butt and her perky tits. We took a subway to Trafalgar Square and walked to the National Gallery. She checked her handbag at the entrance way and we walked into the receiving hall. Skylights in the high ceiling overhead illuminated the room with a natural light. Sunshine streaked across the black mosaic floors. On the far side of the entry hall, a marble statue of a nude, winged woman stood in the middle of lush, green tropical plants. Beyond the statue, four brown marble pillars held up the archway leading into the gallery's long corridors. Through the open doorway beyond the brown pillars I saw Seurat's canvas of *The Bathers*. I walked quickly towards it but I turned before reaching it when I noticed Van Gough's *The Chair and Pipe*. I recognized the thickness of the paint, the raw undiluted color that could only be Van Gogh's work.

Two rooms of French Impressionists housed Renoir's *Boating Party*, several Monets, Van Gough's, *The Sun Flowers*, Picasso's, *Still Life of a Violin* and Gauguin's, *Still Life of Fruit and Flowers*. There were several wall-size Monet's including *The Pond,* layers of green, yellow, orange and lavender, gallons of paint applied without detail.

I took out my journal and sat on a couch in front of a Picasso and wrote. "Of all the works, Picasso's leaves me with the least inspiration, yet his paintings sell for the highest prices. Typical killer-world standards which I fail to meet. There is nothing special in these Picassos."

"What are you writing?" Angela asked.

"My journal. I'm impressed with these masterpieces."

"Will you read it to me?"

"Okay, sure," I said after a hesitant moment.

Angela listened and thought before commenting. "But why do you care how much Picasso's sell for?" she asked.

"I don't," I said, "but isn't it interesting that the world values his paintings so much more than these other artists." I pointed first to Picasso's then to Monet's. "From just looking at them, I'd say the Monet's are better, therefore should be worth more. Don't you agree?"

She thought for a moment. "No," she said. She looked into my eyes, "And I think it does matter to you. I think you are annoyed because the art world hasn't valued your work, so you're arguing with them."

I laughed. "How could you say that? You don't know me."

"I feel it. I see it in your intensity. You do paint, don't you?"

"Yes, I paint. And yes, I would like to have my paintings in a museum."

She waited for me to go on. I looked at her and nodded.

"That's quite intuitive, Angela," I finally said.

She smiled, "Living life is more important than being hung in a museum."

I looked into her eyes and nodded. "Yes, of course you're right."

I looked at the map of the gallery. "I want to find Titian's works. It's here." I pointed to the map.

"Yes," Angela agreed. She looked over my shoulder at the map. "Let's go."

On the way to find Titian, we stopped in each room we passed through. I was pulled over by one or more of the paintings, unable to resist the attraction of the masterworks.

"This is George Michele's, *Stormy Landscape*," I said looking closely at the painting. Through black storm clouds a streak of bright sunshine lighting the windblown landscape.

"Here's a Constable," Angela pointed to *The Hay Wain.*

"Ah, it's incredible," I said. I stared closely, within inches of the canvas. "Pictures within pictures within pictures," I said as I studied his brush strokes. "Each brick in the farmhouse's chimney, all the leaves on the trees have been painted individually. He has a fluidness that allows each to blend into the whole without distracting."

Angela pointed out a figure in the reeds. "Mr. Constable always painted himself into each of his pictures."

"I didn't know that," I said. I leaned in and studied the figure she was still pointing to. "I see," I said.

In room nine Titian's, *Portrait of a Man* attracted us. I went right up to it to see the brush strokes, and backed away then approached it again. After minutes of viewing the work in silence we went to leave, I glanced back one last time and gasped, "Look! It's coming out of the picture frame!"

Angela turned and was visibly frightened.

"I feel like I'm in the Twilight Zone," I said. "The figure seems to lean outside of the frame like he's leaning out of a window."

"It's magical," Angela agreed.

The next room contained masters of the Dutch school. I enjoyed the several Rembrandt's. "But this still life of fruit by Van Steenwick," I said in front of one of the 17th century works. "This is the most realistic painting that I've ever seen. I seems like I could reach in and take a piece of fruit off of the silver plate. The knives are so realistic, better than a photograph. I've never heard of Van Steenwick, nor seen any of his works in art books. How could that be? This is extraordinary stuff." I stopped and jotted notes into my journal. I was determined to research the life and works of Van Steenwick.

The afternoon turned to dusk. Angela and I went to dinner near the music halls, bought a bottle of wine and went back to my hotel room. We drank the wine and made out on the bed.

Angela was stiff but not resistant. The next hour of petting ended when she rose and straightened her hair.

"I've got to go," she said as she put her bra on. "Really, I have work tomorrow."

"I'll take you to the station," I said.

We walked through the quiet late-night London streets. It was chilly and Angela happily snuggled close when I put my arm around her waist. I waited with her until the train came. She kissed me and turned and ran into the car. I walked back to the hotel, the only soul on the empty, Sunday night streets.

Monday morning, I woke to the sound of tremendous hammer blows. The ceiling light in my room swayed. I put on jeans and walked out onto the balcony and leaned over the black wrought iron railing. In the thick morning fog, I could see a workman outside the basement apartment of the building next door. He was viciously tearing up the patio cement. He wore a yellow sweater and gray wool cap. Very sporty, I thought, especially with the overalls. I looked at my watch. It was 8:00am.

Across the street a black man rode by on a bicycle holding a white envelope in his mouth. The sound of the bicycle chain resonated through the cool, morning fog. I stretched and went back inside, put on a shirt and went down to breakfast. Bernadette was in the front hall vacuuming. The sunlight through the glass front door revealed her body underneath her pale green dress. As she vacuumed, her breasts swayed beautifully from side to side.

Downstairs, I sat in the crowded dining room. Lucia was dressed in the same yellow dress with the same open buttons as yesterday. She wore no makeup and her hair needed to be combed. Her face needed to be washed too but her small, round breasts stood straight and strong.

"Good morning, Lucia," I greeted her when she came to the table. She didn't smile but pulled out her pad and small yellow pencil and waited for my order.

"I'll have orange juice, toast and coffee with milk," I said.

"You should order a good breakfast," she said in a thick Italian accent.

"What's a good breakfast?" I asked.

"'Eggs and sausage."

"No thanks. Cereal is okay."

"Okay," she smiled.

A stocky man with black curly hair came into the room. He looked like me except he was 70 pounds heavier. No one else in the room met his glance and he sat alone by the window.

Be him. I said to myself. Be the stranger sitting alone by the window. Feel his life. He tied his shoes this morning to come down to breakfast just like you did. This is his world. It's his life that's important.

I suddenly felt my own feelings of loneliness, felt it deeply like a thickness in my body as I saw my own life; a single story, among billions of lives. This didn't make my life smaller, on the contrary, feeling the enormity of life made mine larger. This wasn't a fantasy or a dream, life went on without me. Everyday people died and life went on.

"Good morning," I smiled and said to the stranger when our eyes meet.

The man's face lit up, "Good morning," he said.

After breakfast I took my coffee back up to my room, admiring Bernadette bent over as I went past her again.

I turned on my portable tape player and finished my coffee listening to Randy Crawford singing *Rio di Janeiro Blues* and *You Might Need Somebody*. I thought about last night. I was disappointed that Angela hadn't stayed the night. I took out my journal and made entries for yesterday afternoon and the evening with Angela. Sometimes I enjoyed the re-telling of the events more than the original experience. My descriptions of the interactions, even the seemingly mundane ones allowed me to analyze my feelings. My feelings. That was it. This journal made my feelings paramount. The most important viewpoint, not Picasso's, not the Queen of England's, but mine. Mine were the most important feelings in the universe. I laughed. Why didn't everyone understand that?

Dressed in warmer clothes; I went out to the underground and took a train to Westminster Abbey. It began to drizzle as I walked bareheaded. The light rain felt good. The air was fresh and cold.

I toured the church then to the underground and waited for the subway car to go back to the hotel. I sat on a bench next to a young woman with a large suitcase and backpack.

"Just arriving?" I asked.

"Yes, I've just come from Australia," she said.

"Wow. Australia, that's quite a distance. It's nice to meet you. I'm Paul Gebhart."

"Anne Larkin," she smiled and we shook hands. Her strawberry blonde hair, green eyes and beautiful body enraptured me.

"You're American," she asked.

"Yes, California. Have you been there?"

"No, but I plan to get there, someday."

"One adventure at a time?"

"Yes, that's it. Right now, I'm trying to find the Australian hostel."

"Perhaps I can help you," I said. "Do you have the street address?"

"Yes, and a map." She brought out a small printed map of London from her backpack.

"Castletown Road, west of Kensington, I know that stop," I said. "May I take you there?"

"Certainly, that would be nice," she said.

I carried her suitcase onto the subway train and after getting off at Castletown Road, we walked outside into the London evening. Anne checked in at the hostel as I waited to take her to dinner. We went to a neighborhood pub where a stuffed African lion greeted us inside the front door.

"I'm impressed," I said as I stopped to touch the lion's beautiful, thick black mane. In my mind I saw him on the African savanna; then his last charge and the sudden explosion from an animal with a stick that threw out fire.

"Seems a friendly place," I said as I looked around and saw waiters laughing with the customers. We took a table near the bar and ordered dinner.

"Just a red wine for me," I told the waitress.

On a bar stool next to our table a loud, Scotsman took note of our arrival.

"My name's 'Spoon'," he said to me.

"Nice to meet ya, Spoon. I'm, Paul this is Anne." I reached up and shook his hand.

"American?" he asked.

"I am but Anne is from Australia."

"They don't like Australians here," Anne whispered.

"Not true!" Spoon said. He was in his forties with close cropped blonde hair. He was wearing jeans and a nice brown sport coat.

"The British are snobs, absolutely, but everyone's welcome from the colonies. I can't stand bigots!" Spoon spoke loud enough for the passerby's outside to hear. "I'm as black as anyone," he said, still too loud I thought. "And Jewish too for that matter and know you why? 'Cause I'm human first and a Scotsman second."

"I'm for the underdog, muhself," I imitated Spoon's Scottish brogue.

Spoon went on in a tyrant about something but I didn't get it.

"Can you understand him?" I asked Anne.

"Not very well," she said.

"And you're speaking English, is that right?" I asked Spoon when he took a breather.

"English?" he said. "Of course, it's English. The King's English, lad."

"And with a lot of furrrs and currrrs," I pointed out.

Anne rose to leave after she had finished her dinner. "You stay," she said. "I can find my way. I just want to sleep; this jet lag has really caught up with me."

"I understand," I said. "I'm only now getting over it myself."

She laid a five-pound note on the table.

"No, no." I handed her back the bill. "You can't do that," I said. "I'm buying."

"No, not tonight," Anne said. She placed the quid note back on the table.

"Okay," I smiled. "Tomorrow though, dinner is my treat."

"Okay, we'll see," she smiled. "Have a good night."

"Yes, good night, Anne."

I ordered a second bottle of wine and sat at the bar with Spoon. The waitress, Maura, came over when the place emptied out. She stood between us and spoke to the barmaid behind the bar. "I've just returned from New York City, Boston and Washington DC. Lord, what a trip. The states are great, really great!"

She told several funny stories of her escapades and the characters she had met in America. The other patrons laughed at her descriptions but I missed most of what she said because Spoon won't leave me alone.

"The grrreh-atest wrrrong dunn th's century was wen they rrreh-moo-v'd 'Soap' 'rom television," he said as he leaned into my shoulder.

"You mean the sitcom show, Soap? Hmmm, greatest wrong this century? I don't know, Spoon, but okay," I shrugged. "I guess you're right but personally I can't stand television except for NOVA or the nature shows."

"What? With them lions eating them sweet little an-ni-mols? Inhumane it is.

IN-HU-MANE!" He fairly screamed and I thought, how strange; he really doesn't know how loud he is.

"Inhumane? Huh? Well they are Lions and we all know how they can be. Besides they have cute little cubs that they have to feed."

I poured us both another glass of the red wine. We finished that and I knew I was pretty drunk because I couldn't see the other side of the room anymore. Spoon went into a small tirade about commercialism and television. I couldn't quite understand the finer points of his argument as his Scottish brogue got thicker by the drink.

"Are you really speaking English?" I asked again. "I can only make out a word or two of each sentence."

Spoon laughed, "English? Why of course I'm speaking English. Learned it in school as a little lad, I did."

"You're okay Spoon," I said, "but I gotta go. Take care of yourself."

"You too, my friend." Spoon patted me on the back. "Come and see us again."

I walked to the underground and caught the train for Earl's Court. London was very good. I liked it enough to stay. Maybe I could get a day job and write and paint here; share a flat with Angela or something.

In the morning I called Carol to apologize for not making the Intercontinental. She laughed, "A bit teetered?"

"Carol, I was bloody blind. Blind I'm tillin' ya," I used my best Spoon imitation and she laughed again.

"Paul, I know you're on a budget, and well I have a second bedroom here at my flat. You're welcome to stay with me, but you have to promise you'll behave."

"That is kind of you, Carol. I shall be on my honor."

Much obliged to Carol, I packed and checked out of the Coronet. I left my baggage behind the desk and headed to Pimlico and the Tate Gallery for the *Picasso's Picasso* exhibition. The trip there was a bad one. The men all had attitudes. That's the consequence of monogamy, uptight males ready to do battle. I hassled with everyone but one thought kept going through my mind; those men that push you aside on the sidewalk, let them be tougher. Those men that ignore you because they are richer, let them be richer. Those men that think they know it all, let them be holier. Let them be what they are or what they think they are. Let them. Don't judge them and stop competing with them.

After viewing paintings in the first hallway in the Tate, I stopped to write this in my journal.

"The Tate is a fine building but it should be visited first, before going to the National Gallery as it is a step down. As I walked in, I was immediately disappointed at the curators' ruinous decision to place glass in the picture frames. The glare from the electric lights made it difficult to study the paintings for any length of time."

In the next room, I stood before Turner's, *Frosty Morning*. I could feel the crisp morning in late autumn as the footsteps of the two men and the little girl sounded heavy through the chilled air. I recalled fishing from my father's boat at daybreak on a lake in New Jersey. The water was smooth as glass and a two-foot high blanket of fog lay across the surface. I remembered the peace I felt and the warmth of sharing the experience with my father and Stephen. Would my life ever be that good again?

In the next room, Van Gough's boldness again in, *Farms Near Auvers*. It was like a child's finger painting but so complete and therefore it left me with a completeness of feeling.

Monet's method of leaving parts of the canvas unused was very appealing to me. He exposed the truth that it was our own minds making sense out of these strokes of paint. The oil only suggested and our minds translate it into a reality. Likewise, the mind tries to identify the shapes and put meaning into abstract paintings. I think that is a mistake; a Rorschach ink-blot reaction to art. Yet we can use the mind's desire to label everything in order to free ourselves from its conclusions. Listen as your mind works through its process. Observe as our mind tries to identify and label. By being aware of it, we should be free from becoming attached to its conclusions. There is nothing represented in abstract art. They are colors and shapes, here in the now. The perfect light should become evident as we come into the moment. The only true moment in time is now. Not our memory of things past, nor a dream of the future. Children are the great artists of the world because they are in this celestial light. They are in the moment, in touch with their feelings.

I came to Picasso's works and sat on a couch and studied several of his large paintings. I was brought out of my concentration by the sound of an army of shoes as they came into the room. Thirty people quickly surrounded my couch. The group parted to let the guide through and she stood in front of the painting, *The Three Dancers.*

"There are several paintings in Picasso's life which represent different periods and the resultant, measurable changes to his style," she said. "*Three Dancers* is the most significant of those pivotal paintings. He painted it in 1925 but never sold it. It is one of very few works that he would not sell at any price. He donated it to the Tate Gallery in the 1960s. Almost forty years after painting it.

"*The Three Dancers* started off as a realistic composition. Picasso was working on it when he learned of the death of an old friend. The news brought back memories of when he had first moved to Paris. Another friend at that time had committed suicide over a lost lover. The woman he had lived with for years, left him and despondent, the man shot her then himself. Picasso's painting became a pictorial essay of Picasso's feelings towards these two people. His expression of bold, strong colors and line are what made Picasso an artist of such magnitude."

I scoffed. Why has the world made so much of Picasso's feelings? Weren't the feelings and these people now viewing his work of the same cosmic magnitude? Let them worship Picasso. Let them. Let them praise and glorify him. Let them.

It was 4:00pm when I left the Tate and took the underground back to the Coronet Hotel. Lucia was at the front desk.

"I'm going to the corner to flag a cab," I said. "I'll return to get my things."

"Okay," she said, "I'll watch them." She looked great, tight white knit dress with a little bouquet of flowers over her left breast.

"Should I call you for dinner?" I asked.

"No," she answered shyly.

"Okay. Well, you take care."

Lucia nodded without answering.

I brought the trunk outside and hailed a black cab. The cabby loaded it into the boot and we drove through rush hour London. Carol's flat was in a red brick apartment house in a very nice neighborhood on a quiet side street. She rang me in the front door and told me through the intercom to take the lift to the third floor. I rang her apartment doorbell.

"Hi Carol. Thanks for inviting me over," I said when she opened the front door.

"Sure, no problem," she said.

She was in her late twenties with golden blond hair worn to her shoulders. She had blue eyes and full mouth. She was chubby but not overly. We entered into a small entry way. I left my trunk there and walked across the white shag carpeting in the living room.

"Your room is just down this way," she said. "Need help with the trunk?"

"No, I can get it thanks. What I do need is to wash some clothes."

"The machine's here," she pointed to a door off the kitchen.

I unpacked in the guest room, sorted my dirty clothes into colors and started a load of wash in a machine that could hardly hold two pair of jeans.

We sat in the living room. Carol brought a chrome coffee pot and two coffee cups and placed them on the glass table.

She laughed nervously," I've never had a man stay over, not someone I don't know."

"I appreciate your generosity," I said. "London is expensive and this helps greatly, but can't I pay you something?"

"No, no," Carol held up both hands in gentle protest. "I wouldn't think of it."

"I'll buy the groceries then, okay?"

"That would be nice. I was thinking more about you, well, at night, you wouldn't come into my room? I'm a bit nervous."

"Of course not," I said. "Not unless I'm invited."

"I don't think we should be any more than friends," Carol said in a somewhat shaky voice. "You're leaving next week. I'm not into one-night stands."

"Well, technically it would be a three night stand."

She laughed. "Men. I never understood how they could just have sex. For me I need the emotional ties before I can get intimate."

"Well, that's how it is with all women," I said.

"All women?"

"Maybe there are a few nymphos," I said. "I never seem to meet them, but most women, okay? Most women, feel that way. The thing is though as moral and good as that sounds; especially when compared to the dog mentality we men have but what you don't understand, can't really ever understand, is that we're totally different. It's like men and women are two different species!"

Carol laughed again. "It does seem that way." She shook her head in bewilderment. "I could never understand, why do men always think about sex?"

"No woman can understand it," I agree. "You've never had a hard-on thumbing against your stomach in the middle of the night." I looked to see if my language shocked her. She laughed even as she blushed.

"Until they do," I went on, "no one can explain to them what a hard-on feels like and how it takes over your thoughts. The strangeness of women, their bodies, their scent, their high voices, it all brings blood rushing into the penis."

"Tell me about it," Carol laughed. "Really, it's very interesting, no one's ever quite explained it to me."

"It's that lack of understanding of how God made us and our hormones, which lead women to the erroneous conclusion that men should be monogamous. 'If only men were more moral,' they think but this flies in the face of the very nature of males."

Carol half bent over laughing and shook her head "yes".

"No woman gets it," I said "but until they do, "they'll continue to try and make a round peg fit into a square hole."

"It's not really square, but I see your point," Carol said.

Now I laughed. "What shall we do for dinner? I want to take you out."

"Quite nice of you. Actually, I was planning to have my friend, Darlene join us."

"Great. Is she single by chance?"

"Sorry, no. Her husband is quite wealthy. He owns two very good restaurants in London, Darlene's invited us to their Italian one. We're to go by her flat at eight."

"Mind if I invite a young lady I just met?"

"Not at all. What's her name, tell me about her."

"Her name's Anne. She's from Australia and she's, well, beautiful."

"How old is she?" Carol asked.

"I'd say in her early twenties."

"I see, robbing the cradle," Carol shook her finger at me with a smile.

"When they look like Anne, I do."

I took the telephone from its receiver to call Anne. The large, white English telephone felt strange in my hand. It was an instrument they would have used in the 1940s and its strange shape and weight put me in the moment as I asked the hostel's operator for Anne. She was in and agreed to meet us.

"And Darlene?" I asked after hanging up the phone, "What is she like?"

"She's very, very nice," Carol said. "Very well bred, but quite funny and relaxed."

We dressed and at 7:30 drove to Darlene's in Carol's Jaguar. Darlene had short blond hair with light blue eyes. Her eyes stood out like jewels in her tanned faced.

"You didn't get that tan in Britain," I said.

"No," Darlene laughed. "I've just came back from holiday in Bermuda."

Anne was outside the hostel when we pulled up. She slid into the back seat with me. Her long and straight strawberry blond hair lay luxurious against her shoulders and back. She wore a short, tight fitting black dress and heels.

We ordered 'G&T's' at Darlene's restaurant and I explained in a whisper to Anne when I could who Carol and Darlene were. She understood immediately that Darlene could find her work. She also understood that both women had been brought up with money.

I observed how the three women interacted. The Lady Anne was very sharp with lots of people sense. Darlene was humorous as was Carol, though Carol's humor was a bit rough.

"The first two things I want to know about a man before I date him," Carol said. "What do you do? And what's the balance in your checking account?" Darlene and Anne laughed.

"Well, I'm Jewish" Carol continued. "Paul's Jewish too, so he understands. You know, Paul," she said turning to face me, "I can prove that Jesus was Jewish. He lived at home until he was thirty, worked for his father and his mother thought he was God."

Dinner was good and the wine excellent and all of it on the house. I felt good except that Anne had all but ignored me. Darlene and Carol picked up on this as well. I resigned myself that it was another dead-end and would just as soon have dropped her off and gone on to the next one but in the car, Carol asked Anne if she would like to go back to her flat for coffee. When I had invited her a half hour before, Anne said she couldn't, now she was happy to accept Carol's invitation.

Once we were back at Carol's flat, she immediately excused herself and headed off to bed but not before whispering to me in the hallway, "Well, it was I who got her back here, the rest it up to you."

"Yes, I noticed that," I said, "and I'm not sure I'm grateful."

Carol kissed me on the cheek, "Goodnight, Love and luck."

Anne floated around reading book titles on the shelves in the living room. She looked through several of Carol's travel photo albums. I sat down on the red couch, bored, tired and wanting to call it a night. I took a pad and pen and drew a flower and wrote;

"Paul's feelings count.

He only wants to feel beautiful inside and to be with a woman who likes Paul."

I handed it to Anne and said in a quiet voice, "I wrote this because it's what I'm feeling."

"If someone likes me," I said when she had finished reading it. "They have to show it clearly so I know it isn't me making it up."

"Well that's what everyone wants. Isn't it, though?" Anne answered. I liked her Australian accent. I longed to touch her. She was a goddess is her black evening dress and high heels. Her breast full and firm, her legs shapely. A real ten plus.

"Everyone?" I said. "I don't know."

We sat quietly for a minute.

"I've always been a little drawn back when I first meet someone," Anne said. "I've had my face slapped a couple of times."

"I've been hurt too," I said. "And I promise I won't slap."

Anne laughed, and came over to the couch and sat next to me. "How old do you think I am?"

I looked into her green eyes. "Twenty-four or five. I guess."

"I'm twenty, just." She raised her eyebrow a tad.

"Really," I said. "I had no idea. You think I'm too old for you?"

"I don't know," she said. I touched her long hair; held a long strand of it away from her head. She looked me in the eye and I leaned over and kissed her, cupping my left hand behind her neck. She let me. I brushed her soft lips with mine, tasting her wetness. I kissed her again, lightly replacing the smooth saliva back onto her lips. Her skirt rose above her tan thighs as she shifted on the couch. I touched her shapely calf, the thin knee, then up to her silk smooth thighs. Her skin was a milk-smooth softness under my fingertips. I moved the tip of my tongue into her mouth and tasted her breath; loving it, swallowing it. Her strawberry-blond hair fell forward over her breasts. She pulled her hair back out of the way. I reached higher on her leg and touched her pink panties with my index finger. She moaned. I rubbed her softly with my knuckle. She was wet. I guided her back on the couch and caressed her legs with both hands. I slid my face down her flat stomach, pulled aside the panties and kissed her vagina. I smelled her stale, feminine freshness. I parted her blond bush and licked her with the tip of my tongue.

She moaned and opened her legs for me. Ah, yes. The lovely, 'Yes' of a woman accepting. I reached up and felt her round breasts. She unzipped her dress and pulled it over her head, then took off her bra. I looked up at her beautiful, round, firm breasts. I held one lightly in my right hand and felt the weight of it. I moved it slowly so she could feel the weight of it too. She started to hump on my mouth. I turned her over; on her knees and licked her vagina from the back. She gasped and stretched her body, arching her back in blissful relieve of tension.

I took off my pants and she licked me; swiping my penis with her tongue. She put me in her mouth and twisted her head, teasing me. I laid her back on the couch and mounted her so that my penis lay between her breasts. She put me in her mouth again. I humped between her beautiful breasts. I moaned. She looked up at me and smiled; her eyes flashed joy. She was happy to have me in her mouth. Her hair flowed over the pillows. I turned her over and entered her. Slowly, gently I penetrated her small vagina, centimeter by centimeter. Its wetness welcomed me into the gates of paradise.

A flush came over me. I recalled riding my bicycle when I was eleven. My best friend, Dennis Hood rode next to me. We had our gloves, bats and softballs and were headed to the game after school.

"My brother told me how they make babies," Dennis said as we rode.

"By kissing on the mouth, right?" I asked.

"No, by putting the man's dick in the woman's pussy," Dennis said.

I felt sick to my stomach, dizzy. I remembered seeing my mother stepping out of the shower when I was six. I pictured my father penetrating her and I was nauseous. I had to stop the bike and sit on the curb. Dennis laughed.

I went deeper into Anne.

"Paul, oh, please, Paul," she called out.

I pulled back but she leaned into me for more. She put me deeper inside her. I placed my right hand on her back and felt the passion dew of her perspiration. I stroked her round, perfect buttocks with my hand.

When I was ten my thirteen-year old cousin, Laura came into the bathroom at the house at the lake. We had just come up from the dock and were in wet bathing suits. She locked the bathroom door and took my suit off and touched my penis.

"It's pretty," she said. "Want to see my vagina?"

"Okay," I said.

She pulled her suit down and I saw her hairless vagina and felt flushed as blood rushed to my face. She played with my penis. To my amazement it grew. We took a shower together. I didn't come but my entire body blazed in sexual relief.

I came inside Anne as her moaning turned to gasping. She climaxed with me. Afterwards I gently withdrew and pushed her to her stomach. She laid on the couch with her eyes closed and I stretched out next to her.

"I have to go," she said in a few minutes.

"Okay," I said in hoarse, low voice. "I'll take you home."

"Let me up," she said. I moved over. She took her panties and bra and went into the bathroom where she quickly showered while I washed at the basin.

We walked to the Baker Street underground through quiet streets. People strolled the boulevard.

"It's a lovely night," I said. "Almost warm, quite nice, isn't it?"

"I keep feeling that everyone is staring at me," Anne said.

"They are," I said. "You are strikingly beautiful."

She was too. Five foot four, 39-24-35, 110 pounds. I wanted her very much but I had to be a realist, she was wonderful tonight but now as I walked her home, she was distant. When I went to kiss her, she turned her head and offered me her cheek instead. We stood on the sidewalk in front of the hostel.

"I'll call you," I said.

"No, I don't think you should," she said.

I was hurt and surprised.

"I have plans," she partly explained.

"Okay, well the next day then."

"No, I don't think you should."

On the top step, I stopped her and looked into her eyes. "Why not? You know I like you. I'll stay in London to be near you."

"It wouldn't work, Paul." She was being gentle but firm. I could tell her mind was made up. But where? When had she made this decision? It had been so good.

"Please, understand," she said, reading my mind. "Good night, good luck."

"Then why, why did you, tonight?" I asked before she could open the front door.

"You were nice, interesting, cute and I was horny but it was a mistake."

"No, it was wonderful," I said, holding her hand. I saw she wanted to leave. "I'll remember you," I said.

"Be safe, Paul." She kissed my cheek and went inside.

Back at Carol's I couldn't sleep. I wrote Ava and Noah a postcard.

"I'm sorry we never got to talk on the telephone the times I tried to reach you," I printed. "I miss you Ava. I miss you Noah, very much. If you ever want to reach me, call Uncle Steve. I'll be in touch with him every 2 weeks as I travel. Europe is very interesting. Perhaps someday you and I will tour it together. I think of you every day. Be good to each other.

Love Dad."

I felt guilty for not paying support. I needed them in my life. I wrote Mary a letter now too. I told her that I would pay her the arrears and keep current each month if she would give me their telephone number and encourage the children to have a relationship with me.

I fell into a restless sleep and was up a few hours later at daybreak. I made myself coffee and brought it back to the bedroom. I sat on the windowsill and looked down three stories to the back alley behind the apartments on Baker Street. I listened to the early morning traffic and thought about how I would paint the dawn's pink clouds and how I would block out the buildings, windows and fire escapes; how I would begin with the dark colors first, then add the lighter tones needed to capture the way the light struck everything.

"Coffee and toast?" Carol called me from the hall.

I went to the half-opened bedroom door and opened it and smiled back at Carol's shy but knowing smile.

"Good morning, Carol. Yes, it went well but with a sad ending. Coffee? Toast? Sure, sounds great."

At the kitchen table, Carol poured the coffee and said, "Want to tell me the sad part? I don't think I need to know about the good part, she was quite vocal you know. I've heard that about Australian women."

"Meow," I said and scratched at the air.

Carol laughed and went to get the toast from the toaster.

"Well, sadly," I said as she returned, placed two pieces on my dish and two on her own and sat down. She spread thick, orange marmalade across her toast, took a bite and looked into my eyes, signaling she was ready for the details.

"Anne thinks our age difference is just too great to give us any chance."

Carol nodded. "I think she's right."

"I don't. But what I think doesn't matter; except, Jesus, what could have been."

Carol was quiet. I think she was thinking of her own search for love and her dreams of a family and her fears of never finding it.

I called Angela after breakfast.

"Can we get together tonight?" I asked her after I told her I was staying at Carol's.

"Okay, where shall we meet?"

"I have the apartment for the evening," I said. "Carol is going out with some friends. Can you make it to the Baker Street station?"

"Sure, I'll be there at seven," she said.

I slept until 6:00 pm, showered, dressed and walked to the underground station to meet Angela. She was right on time and we went back to Carol's flat. I poured us each a glass of wine and we sat on the couch. Frank Sinatra played on the stereo. I put my arm around Angela and she snuggled up to me. I kissed her.

"Let's go into the bedroom and get comfortable," I said after a half hour of petting.

Angela followed me to the guest room and I took off my shoes and her top and kissed her.

"No. I can't," she said as I started to take her pants off. "I don't have any protection."

"It's okay, I have a vasectomy," I said.

"Sure," she said.

"No, really. I've had it since 1978," I said.

"You're just saying that."

"I'm not making it up."

"Why did you get a vasectomy?" she asked.

"It's a long story."

I could see she wanted to know the details.

"My wife was pregnant in 1976. She didn't want us to have another child, we already had two."

"You have children?"

"Yes, a boy and a girl. Anyway, she had an abortion. It was difficult for both of us, knowing that we would never know that child. Mary decided she never wanted to go through an abortion again so she had her tubes tied, then six months later she was pregnant again!"

"Really?"

"Yes, really. They said it was impossible. Her tubes weren't even connected any more. The egg had to somehow pass out of one tube, travel through her uterus, find the end of the other tube, and go in what should have been a sealed opening. It was a miracle and I told her we should have the child, and that we should name him, Hey-sus."

Angela laughed.

"Well, Mary went through a second abortion and it was harder than the first one. It's something we will both think about the rest of our lives. Afterwards she convinced me to have a vasectomy and I agreed."

Angela stared into my eyes. I reached over and kissed her. I felt her breasts. Her nipples were stiff and sensitive. I took off her pants and panties. She had a tight body.

After laying together for an hour, Angela dressed. "I have to go," she said.

"This early?"

"Yes, I'm sorry love but I have to transfer to the Piccadilly line then 50 minutes out to Hounslow and a drive home by car from there. I have to be up at 6:00am for work."

"I guess you really wanted to see me to go through all that twice in 3 hours."

Angela laughed. "Yes, I guess I really wanted to see you." She kissed me.

"Wait for me," I said. "I'll walk you."

We both washed up then went out into the London night.

At the underground I kissed her good night.

"How did you do it?" she asked while we still embraced.

"Do what?" I asked.

"Get me in bed? I made up my mind before I came over that we weren't going to make love."

I laughed then saw that she wanted an answer. "The turning point was when I put you on top of me. Remember? You have a masculine way sometimes, Angela. I saw it and as soon as I put you in the dominant position you got hot. All of a sudden you were moaning. Right there, Angela that was how and when."

She laughed, kissed me again, turned and ran down the stairs into the underground.

The next morning, I was up after Carol had gone to work. Sunlight streaked in through the bedroom window. I didn't want to sit around thinking of Anne or of Angela or about the kids or of Mary, God it never stopped did it?

I dressed and went to Oxford Street. I missed the train so I sat and studied the London underground and wrote in my journal. "There are thirteen lines, each named and color coded. Piccadilly for example is royal blue on the maps and signs. These thirteen lines stop at over 400 stations throughout London. At each station they connect with either the British rail system to get out of London or with the London bus system which itself has hundreds of separate lines and thousands of buses. The underground is safe. I've seen no fights, no arguments. It's also simple to figure out, even with jet lag it only takes a day to get it down. This is due to the fact that there are maps everywhere. On the walls in each station, inside each subway car and free maps to carry in your pocket.

"Some of the stations I've been to have wooden escalators left over from World War II. At the Leicester Square station there's a wooden escalator several hundred feet long traveling at a 45-degree angle. It was like a ride at an amusement park.

"The Covent Garden station doesn't have an escalator or even stairs. The way up and down to the trains is by elevator. Not a regular elevator but one the size of a large room. Amazing and romantic in a way, the entire room full of people goes down, then empties out onto the platforms when the doors reopen.

I'm also impressed at the lack of graffiti. In fact, only the Waterloo station on the south bank had any at all. Mostly religious statements like, "Skinheads Rule."

After a short subway ride, I went up the stairs at Trafalgar Square and into The National Portrait Gallery. I stopped in front of James Tissot's, *Captain Frederick Burnaby*. Burnaby posed in full military regalia laid back on a sofa. The colors black, red and white and the smoothness of the paint and the clarity of figure and objects; the realism all came together exquisitely. I read the plaque, "Captain Frederick Burnaby (1842-1885). Burnaby's exploits as a cavalry officer and explorer captured every school boy's imagination. Over six feet four inches tall, he was reported to be the strongest man in the British army. His books about his adventures including A Ride to Khia and On Horseback Through Asia were best sellers in 1888. He took part in the relief expedition to Khartoum in the Sudan and died from a spear wound in that battle."

Burnaby was probably killed by a native less than five feet tall, who was reputed to never have heard of Captain Frederick Burnaby. I could imagine Hemingway writing about the relief expedition and the death of Burnaby. I could also imagine Bukowski's version.

I returned to Carol's flat after 5:00 pm. She was sitting at the dining room table when I came in.

"Hi, Carol," I said.

"Hi, Paul. How was your day?"

"Very good, very good and yours?"

"Yes, rather pleasant. Allen Lewis called you."

"He did? Thank you, I'll call him now if you don't mind." I took my coat off and laid it on the white couch and dialed Allen's number.

"Hello, Allen."

"Ah, Paul. How are things?"

"Things are fine, and with you?"

"Fine here too. So, when are you leaving?"

"Yes, well, tomorrow actually. I'm sorry I didn't get to see you again."

"Hopefully we'll get together when you return to London."

"Absolutely," I said. "I'll be catching the hover craft tomorrow morning for France, then a long bus ride to Amsterdam."

"But you're okay?" Allen asked.

"Yes, fine. Sorry about getting so fucked up at the party. I hope I didn't embarrass you too much."

"Not to worry, we've all been wrecked. You missed a good party though."

"I had fun, and no, Allen, I didn't miss it. I just had a different perspective of it."

"Yes, that's right, a different prospective," he said with a laugh.

Chapter Six
Amsterdam

I lay in bed awake before dawn. Rain paddled softly against the window. A flash of lightning illuminated the guest bedroom and thunder rumbled over the sleeping neighborhood. I imagined the millions of souls in London who had just heard the thunder. I thought of all their separate stories and my own. The sound of the thunder clap, a shared physical experience, momentarily connected our lives. An experience in our lives soon forgot. And none of us thinking that one day we will be the ancient ones.

I had a dream before I woke. A large, white dog lay beside my bed. Its ears moved to each sound in the alley below. When there was a knock at the door, the dog raised its head and listened intently. The dream left me with the feeling of being watched over. Despite this security, I felt sad and empty. I wanted to be with my children. I wanted to be a part of their lives. This feeling of separation from them was never ending. Even when not thinking of them, the thought of them lay at the back of my mind. Where were they now? And I should be home with them.

I put on a pair of jeans and a sweater and opened the window not wanting to dwell on it anymore. I lit a cigarette and sat on the windowsill. The light from the street lamps lit the room with a dim, yellow cast. The rain had stopped and I heard a car drive slowly through the alley way. The sound of its tires on the wet cobblestones seemed to echo my loneliness. I dragged on the cigarette, the tip glowed red in the dark room. As I watched, daybreak absorbed the night. Colors returned to the buildings, overhead, dark, ominous clouds filled the sky.

I took a shower, shaved and packed my trunk. Carol was in the kitchen preparing breakfast when I came out of the guest bedroom.

"Up early, I see," she said.

"I wanted to say good-bye before you left for work."

"Right, well come sit down and have a bit of breakfast then."

"Sure, thanks." I sat at the small kitchen table and she handed me a cup of tea and plate of eggs.

"The eggs are a bit over-cooked and the toast burnt," Carol apologized, "but I think the tea came out okay. Anyway, I was always much better at supervising the staff."

"I understand," I said. I poked at the hard eggs with my fork; gave up and drank my tea.

"I wanted to thank you, Carol," I said, "for your hospitality. I hope I haven't been too much trouble."

"Not at all, Paul. I quite enjoyed it. I do wish you luck on finding that special someone."

"Or at least getting laid once a month," I interjected.

"That too," Carol giggled, embarrassed.

"Paul, I have an old friend living in Paris, Anne Fabian. She was my French tutor five summers ago."

I rinsed my plate in the sink. "That so?"

"I've written down her number for you. Here, please call her and tell her I send my regards."

"Thank you," I said. "I will."

"Do, and also I've written the name and address of the Hotel Vieux de Paree. It's a decent sort of place and I think you should try it. I do rather fear some of those flea traps in Paris."

I took the paper from her hand. "Carol, you're so kind to think of me. I'll call you when I get back to London."

"Ciao, Paul. Be safe." She walked me to the door and we touched cheeks and I left.

On the street, I hailed a cab in the wet morning fog. A large, broad faced English taxi driver stopped and loaded my trunk and bag into the boot of his black taxi.

"To the Royal National Hotel," I said.

It began to rain as the taxi pulled up to the hotel. I wheeled my trunk into the lobby, found the ticket counter, and went up to the window.

"The trip to Amsterdam is by coach from London to Dover," the ticket master explained as he handed me change and the ticket. "Then, hovercraft from Dover to Calais then coach again from Calais to Amsterdam. Total travel time is estimated at ten hours."

"Okay, thank you," I said.

I waited for the bus in the hotel lobby. My chair by the front windows overlooked the street and I watched the rain and morning traffic. Randy Crawford's *Rainy Night in Georgia* played over the lobby's intercom. The words seemed to fit the day, "I feel like it's raining all over the world."

I took the time to inspect the metal trunk. My repairs on the front wheel and black handle seemed to be holding up. The sound of it rolling along the sidewalk continued to cause a stir. I felt tension in my right eye caused by too many people staring at me. I tried to relax. I was safe and sound and had enjoyed London.

The bus to Dover was half empty when it left on time at 11:15am. The driver made his way through London traffic. The wet streets and overcast skies held the atmosphere thick with time and place. Black water marks and soot stains on the granite stone walls of the great old buildings seemed like tattoos of the history this ancient nation had endured.

The bus crossed over a bridge to the south bank of the Thames as river traffic sailed the waterway. The dismal morning light, filtered through thick gray skies, gave the green water of the Thames a cold pallor.

The sign on the seat in front of me read, "Mind your head." Very true, mind my thoughts now as depression and loneliness fill my soul. I'm a traveler far from home and family.

The bus arrived on time at the hovercraft terminal. I went into the lounge and sat by myself in a secluded part of the waiting area. I took off my money belt and discreetly counted it out. I was leaving England with $2,215 dollars. I had spent about $45 a day. Much too loosely, but then I made up for it by staying at Carol's for free. I'd have to be tighter from now on if I was to make what's left last two more months.

I boarded the ferry and found a place in the center, lower deck and settled in. The seats were oversized and comfortable. It seemed to me that I was sitting in an airplane rather than on a ship but this idea soon changed when the craft's engines whined to a start and it left the building and began to travel out over the rough seas.

"It fairly bounces across the channel," a middle-aged man seated next to me said.

"Pretty rough crossing," I agreed, shouting to be heard over the roar of the engines and the whacking of the boat's rubber hull against the waves. "It's supposed to ride a foot or two above the surface, isn't it?" I asked.

"Yes, but the swell's too high," the man explained.

"Uh-huh, I see, the swell's too high."

Farther out over the channel's dark waters, black foreboding storm clouds approached. A heavy rain soon began to pour down. I could see row after row of wind driven, white capped waves rising about us. The trip became a bone jarring, thumping ride as the airship's hull slammed into one white cap after another, fighting to make headway against the wind and waves.

The hovercraft battled the storm for two hours before finally reaching the safety of the port at Calais. Fatigued and my body aching from the rough ride, I left the hovercraft and walked through a light drizzle, past the terminal to the parking lot. The bus to Amsterdam was waiting with its motor running.

Peaches and Herb played on the stereo system of the sightseeing bus with large viewing windows. I found an empty seat towards the back. The music changed to a Rascals tune. Ah, good old American music, that's the thread between the U.S. and Western Europe.

It was raining heavily when I woke from a short nap. The bus was cold. I looked at my watch, it was 3:30pm. I turned on my cassette deck and played Randy Crawford's *Rio De Janeiro Blues* and *You Might Need Somebody*. The bus crossed over into the Netherlands where men sat under umbrellas fishing in the rain on the grass canal embankments. Some were alone, others had a child or a friend with them. A fat plow horse grazed in a field, oblivious to the rain. The superhighway traveled through countryside; flat, green, wet and peaceful. I lowered the volume on my tape player and thought back to my childhood. I remembered going by car with my parents and siblings to New York City to visit my aunts and uncles. I remembered too that New York City frightened me. The streets there were filled with strangers, odd men and women with less dignity, or more problems than normal people should have. But I knew that the excitement, the raw energy of New York proved concretely that life was bigger than my little world; bigger than my father's rules. I felt that again now. I saw the complexity of the lives in the world around me. I was lonely though and that loneliness was playing the blues inside my soul. "Use it. Use everything." I heard the voice of Al Greenbaum the Santa Cruz counselor in my mind.

It stopped raining outside of Antwerp. The sky was a thick overcast gray. I hadn't eaten anything since breakfast at 7:00am and I was starved. I also had to take a pee. The coach didn't have a lavatory. It was a good thing there weren't any children on board. They would never have made it.

The Netherlands looked very, very clean and modern, too much so. Here high-rise apartments, there a Quality Inn. The highway was wide with not a shred of litter along the manicured grass medians. I really did have to pee. Where's an obnoxious American when you need one? Someone to make this motherfucker pull over.

Reading my mind perhaps, the driver slowed then turned off the superhighway. He stopped in front of an orange and white, plastic restaurant called AC. After a mad dash for the toilets, I cashed a $10 traveler's check, ordered French fries, a hard roll with butter and a glass of apple juice. I carried my tray to a long table where a middle-aged man and woman sat across from me. I watched them out of the corner of my eye. They appeared to be only forty, but they looked much older. The man had on a wrinkled brown trench coat. His glasses needed to be wiped clean. His face was pallid white. Although the woman was drinking her tea and eating her piece of pie slowly, her husband was in a panic to get back on the bus. He either wanted his same seat or else was paranoid about being left behind. Either way he was neurotic; head and eyes darting about, his face just a few inches above his plate as he quickly and without joy, gulped his food. I became aware that I felt shitty about myself. Mary's words echoed in my ears, "You represent someone I was born to hate." I understood what she meant now. She saw me as I saw this Englishman.

I breathed deeply and tried to relax. All I wanted was to get Mary out of my mind so I could go on with my life. After fourteen years with one person it was hard. Her voice was a part of my inner psyche.

I felt better as the bus pulled back out onto the highway. The Netherlands were a bit too sterile for me. London was elegantly funky and I was sure Paris would follow suit but the Netherlands were way too German for my blood.

The coach arrived exactly on time and I took a cab to the Grand Hotel Krasna in downtown Amsterdam. A uniformed bellman came out and took my bags. The trunk's handle snapped off in his hands and the trunk thudded hard to the pavement.

"Piece of shit," I said. The bellman gave me a bad look. "Not you," I apologized. "I meant the trunk." I smiled but the bellman turned his back on me and walked into the lobby without answering. I checked in and another bellman led me up to my room on the 6th floor.

"There is sink only," he said in a thick accent, "but the toilets and showers are here." He pointed to a row of a half dozen doors in the hallway opposite my room.

"Thank you," I said tipping him.

I took a change of clothes and a bath towel and went out to the communal johns. A hefty woman housekeeper was in the hallway wringing out her mop. She stood erect, all 6 feet 200 pounds of her, and turned and looked at me, I had to smile. She had wide hips and thick forearms. Her white, starched maid's uniform was too tight for her. Her arms and legs fairly popped their seams. Her matching white starched hat was a bit too large; she'd pulled it down tightly leaving her red hair wildly extruding from underneath the cap.

"Hello, good day," I giggled, startled by her awkwardness. Her thick lips and round face made me laugh again and she frowned at my insult. I'd better watch out. She'd heave me about, mopping the floors with my ass.

I stepped around the cleaning lady's bucket and supplies and opened the first door and went into the white tiled bathroom. I surveyed the white porcelain pedestal sink, white porcelain toilet, white tiled shower, chrome fixtures and the thin metal mirror hung above the sink but one breath of the toilet's air and I flew back out the door.

"German sausage," I explained to the rotund one as I slammed the toilet's door behind me. "The air is thick with it." She frowned at me again. I went into the toilet that the housekeeper has just finished cleaning. I closed the door and tried to ignore the chemical odor permeating the air but I couldn't take it. Feeling like I was in a German death trap, I hurried out of toilet number two, this time not saying a word to Madame as I passed her on the way to toilet number three. I breathed in cautiously to test the atmosphere, and although the odor of disinfectant was strong now throughout the entire 6th floor, I was able to bear it long enough to take a quick shower, shave and dress.

I found the hotel's cashier downstairs and took $270 of traveler's checks from my money belt.

"Hello," I said to the young woman behind the cage. "I'd like to cash some checks, please." She looked back at me with disdain, took my checks and counted out Dutch florins and shoved them under the counter's guard rail.

I would have understood it if there were a crowd. I'd had to work under those kinds of pressures, but there was no one else around, no long lines. Why were these people so cold to strangers?

I left the hotel and walked through the neighborhood. There were porno shops on every street with signs flashing in neon lights, "Live Fucking Shows". I went by store fronts with large glass windows behind which young prostitutes sat in armchairs and on sofas, bidding the passing men to come in. A black man on the next corner came over to me and held out a small bag.

"I have Persian H. Just thirty dollars," he said.

"No thanks," I said and started to walk away.

"Cocaine? Hashish? Grass?" he called after me.

"No," I shook my head.

"You're American, aren't you?" the man called out.

I stopped and looked back at him. "Yeah. So?"

"Come on. Take a little taste. It's good stuff, man."

"You think every American wants to get loaded then laid?"

"They don't?" he asked.

"Yes, you're right, of course they do. But not today," I said.

Amsterdam was cancerous! Where was the light?

There were single men everywhere; men walking, men gawking. The bars were filled with men.

Where was the light?

The vibes were dirty. I planned to go the galleries tomorrow and Monday then get the hell out. Amsterdam is a wart on the rectum of a hundred-year old, syphilitic woman.

I ate dinner alone at a small restaurant then wondered through the red-light district then went back to the hotel, undressed and went to bed. The next morning after breakfast, I walked leisurely to the Ryks Museum, stopping by a canal to admire a small bronze statue of a young girl squatting down with both hands over her head, shielding herself. I felt that way too. Amsterdam had the most unfriendly, unhappy people I'd ever encountered. The "Friendly hotel staff" which will be "Happy to serve you in any way it can during your visit", wasn't. Where was the spiritual Amsterdam? Your church bells ring each hour of the day, beautiful sounds over your city but where is your inner beauty?

Continuing along the quiet morning streets, I made my way to the Ryks Museum and stood outside the building for a few minutes admiring the beautiful 18th Century architecture. Inside, I was happy to see that the curators had chosen to show the paintings without glass in the frames. I took a map from the lobby and went to work in my journal.

"Each room of the Ryks' gallery is filled with fine paintings. The 17th century Dutch painters have the most natural colors and expression of light. They mixed their paints to obtain the exact shades seen in life. My own talents would never produce anything of this quality, but it is good to see what is possible. For my work, my goal is to find the celestial light; like going back to kindergarten and finger painting. Let joy be experienced and let it shine through. That would be enough and I would count it as a success."

Rembrandt's *Self Portrait,* is it a characterization or a self-mockery? Did he always look like an idiot? I noticed the difference between this one with the dunce look and his other self-portraits. He did quite a few of the old mug but this one was distinctly different in clothes, hair style, all the more reason to wonder about it.

The Holy Family had the same effect on me as reading a Dickens Novel. The taciturn, boring daily routine, of which any moment was priceless but scarcely noticed. The picture was not of Jesus but rather a Dutch family in a room at night. There was a single source of light from a lamp behind the woman's back. The viewer doesn't see the actual source of this light but Rembrandt's way of spreading the rays across the wall is indescribably beautiful.

I went into a room full of Rembrandts. The sight of so many of the master's works sent a tingling sensation up my spine. He is the measure by which all who came after are judged. The *Dutch Masters*, used by the cigar company is really entitled, *The Sampling Officials of the Drapers Guild.* I sat in front of the original. A large canvas, at least 10'x10' but the room that it was in had so many other great works of Rembrandt's that The *Dutch Masters* was only one stop along the way. Rembrandt's style and ability actually progressed from this painting on. You can see the progression as you walk around this one room in the Ryks Museum and there are room after room of his works! In the next, I see four of the largest paintings ever done on canvas. Van de Hebt's, *Corporalschap Von Kapitan Roelof Brickeris* 10'x 40'! Govertflinck's, *Corporalschap Van Kapitan Albert Bas*

8'x20' and Rembrandt's, *Corporalschap of Kapitan Burning Cook* 12'x20'. All of them, though gigantic, have the detail work of a miniature.

I went into the gallery shop to purchase slides and several postcards. "I would like, Rembrandt's *Self Portrait*, please," I asked the old woman tending the counter.

"Nein," she answered me with a cold, hateful look.

"It's the one with the funny hair," I described the painting, thinking she must have it.

"Nein," she said. "They didn't make slides of that one."

"That seems odd. It's a very famous work."

"Buy things or getz outz," the old woman said.

"I understand," I said. I'm afraid with a touch of anger and sarcasm I continued in an imitation of a German accent. "Vee don like ourselves, do vee? Vell vee don likes yous either."

I went downstairs to the museum's coffee shop and sat at a table writing into my journal. At the table next to me a tall, thin man slowly drank a cup of tea. He hesitantly opened the conversation. "I imagine there's quite a bit to write about," he said in a quiet voice with a Scottish accent. "The art here is world class in every aspect."

"My favorite paintings are the impressionists," I said, "but Dutch realism is exquisite. Have you been to the Louvre?"

"Yes," he nodded and put his tea cup down and said, "I was in Paris two weeks ago, then to Den Haag. Den Haag is a much better city than Amsterdam, people-wise and money-wise."

"I'm sick of the Netherlands," I said. "I don't think I'm going to take the time to go there. I want to get to Paris."

"My name's Tom Skinner. I'm from Edinburgh." He reached over and we shook hands. He was dressed in slacks and a thick, natural wool, dark green pullover sweater. He had a slight build and keen blue eyes and appeared to be in his thirties.

"Nice to meet you, Tom. I'm Paul Gebhart. I'm from California."

"What do you do, Paul?"

"Well, I'm in between jobs right now, taking a couple of months off to travel after a nasty divorce, and you?"

"I'm on holiday too. I've been on the continent for three weeks."

"And what do you do back in Edinburgh?" I asked.

"I'm a stevedore."

"Really? Sorry, it's just that you don't look like a longshoreman."

"No? Well, I've been working on the docks since I was 17, so I must be a dock worker."

I laughed. "Yes, I guess you are."

"Impressionism is my favorite too," Skinner went on to say, "but really, the better impressionist paintings are not in the Louvre."

"No?"

"No. They're nearby at the museum called Jeu de Palmes."

"Better than what's exhibited in the Louvre?" I asked.

"Yes, and it's right near the Louvre. Ask for it at your hotel."

"Thanks, I'll be sure to find it. Tell me about Edinburgh. I would like to get up to Scotland one day."

"Do, it's a friendly place and plenty of art to see."

"Do you fish there?" I asked.

"Oh yes, there's some fine fishing all about. Here, take my address down, in case you do make it to Edinburgh, ring me up."

"Thanks, sure. That is kind of you. And here's my number in Los Angeles too. Be sure to call me if you get to the states."

"I have to be going, Tom," I said after I had finished my coffee and cake, "but it was a pleasure meeting you." I shook his hand feeling I had just met the best read, most sophisticated longshoreman in the world.

I waited in the autumn afternoon for my tram back to the hotel. The air was clean and brisk, the trees in the park and along the avenues had turned their autumn colors. I watched four-man crews row their fine wooden boats in the canals. White, billowing clouds floated overhead in an azure blue sky. Their reflection doubled again in the mirror of the canal's water. I felt filled up inside; not needing anything, not hungry, wanting neither to drink or smoke. I waited calmly for the tram, seeing everything with clarity. I recognized this peacefulness in myself.

Here at last was the serenity I sought after but which I only rarely experienced. I was happy to feel it now and knew that it came somehow from the great works of art I had just spent the day studying; slowly looking, waiting in front of each painting to get a connective feeling. It was the act of focusing in on the details of a painting, of seeing a single brush stroke which tied me to the work and in some cases, made me imagine that I stood in front of it applying the paint. The world around me seemed like a painting now. Amsterdam with its canals and old buildings looked at last a very beautiful city.

I went back to my hotel and napped until evening then dressed warmly and left the hotel and went out. I decided to take a tram anywhere it happened to go. The number nine street car came along outside the hotel and I rode for a mile or two then got off where the neighborhood looked interesting. I saw one porno movie house but only one, not six like on the streets near the hotel. There was a crowded bar farther down the block and I crossed the street and went inside and stood in line to order a glass of beer. Suddenly, I heard a woman shouting, 'I'm cold. I'm cold!' I turned around to look because it was quite warm in the restaurant and also, she seemed to be calling to me. As soon as I saw the woman's face, I knew that she was insane. Her scraggly blond hair was cut short and uneven. Her blue eyes were the color of water but there was fear in them, a wild look. Her face was grotesquely contorted. She looked directly into my eyes then lowered her voice and mumbled to herself.

I turned away but I knew immediately that this was a sign meant for me. I finished my beer and ignoring the warning; let my penis lead me outside and into the red-light district. I walked past a store front window where two young prostitutes sat, a brunette and the other with long auburn hair. I stood on the canal bridge across the street but I didn't have the nerve to go past the group of Japanese businessmen in front of their window. It started to rain; several flashes of lightning hit close by; loud thunder cracked through the night air. More signs that I shouldn't do this.

A petite brunette with a short blue dress and blue stockings walked up to me and smiled.

"Good evening," she said. She was cute. Her green eyes against the black hair was very attractive. She was young, in her early twenties and her skin was clean and fresh.

"How much?" I asked.

"Fifty florins," she answered in a quiet voice.

I calculated in my head that fifty florins was about $20.

"You want?" she asked.

"Where?'"

"My room is just over there," she pointed across the bridge. "Yes?"

"Okay," I said.

I walked with her over the canal bridge. It had started to rain and I held the umbrella and she walked under it with me. We went down a side street and she signaled for me to follow her inside one of the buildings. She led the way up a flight of stairs and into a small apartment. The single room had a bed, a couch, one chair and a sink with a small mirror.

"How do I know you're clean?" I asked her.

"I have to be or else I can't work," she said. "I have to go to the clinic twice a week, Friday and Mondays." She undressed as she talked.

"What's your name?" I asked.

"Oh, sorry, Maria and yours?"

"I'm Paul."

"Paul, you have to pay first."

"Do you have change of a hundred?" I took a hundred florin note from my pocket.

"No, put it on the dresser and we'll both get change when we're done."

I undressed and sat on the bed with her.

"How old are you?" I asked.

"I'm 22."

She had a small, square chin and a beautifully body. She lay back on the bed and we kissed but then she pulled away and went down on me. After a few minutes she stopped and said, "Do you want to come this way?"

"No," I said.

"Why not?"

"Because I don't."

"How then?"

"Fucking."

"Fucking costs 100 florin."

"No, you said fifty."

"Fifty is just sucking, fucking is 100."

"I'll pay 75, no more," I said aggravated at the hustle.

"I can't do that, it's 100 florins to fuck. If I do it for less then everyone will have to fuck for less. That will ruin it for all the girls."

"Well, I don't want to bring down the national economy or anything," I said, "but who would know we're fucking for 75 florins? I won't tell if you don't."

She went on like a TV commercial for a several minutes. I laughed at her bullshit then asked her, "Why didn't you explain all this outside when I asked you how much?"

"We always quote the lowest prices," she said. "If you want more there are additional charges."

I laughed again. "Jesus Christ, you should be in the insurance business, or car sales. Anyway, I've grown tired of the discussion and you, so I'm leaving."

"Pay me 50 florin first," she said.

"For what?"

"For the suck," she said becoming animated.

"No, that was a minute or two and I didn't come. I'm going."

"You can't leave until you pay me!"

I dressed slowly and calmly. "Call the police then." I answered her threat. "Call your pimp. I don't care."

Maria threw on her blouse and dress then called into the hallway. An old woman came into the room wearing a bathrobe over a dressing gown. She was plump and her gray hair was combed into waves in an attempt to cover balding spots.

Maria, with great gestures and in a loud voice told her the story. The old woman turned to me and asked me something in Dutch.

"Do you speak English?" I asked her.

"Nein," she said then asked me another question, in Dutch. Maria talked the entire time.

Maria walked over to the bed and pointed to it, explaining again the facts of her case. The woman asked me something in Dutch.

"I don't speak Dutch, remember?"

"NO!" she said, throwing her arms up, exasperated.

"Excuse me," I said and walked past the woman towards the door but Maria leaped in front of me blocking the exit. I smiled at her, turned and walked to the sink. I calmly splashed cold water on my face and combed my hair as I looked into the mirror and watched the two women behind my back. I saw that my nonchalance had unnerved the old Dutch woman. She leaned out into the hallway and called out for someone.

I steadied my nerves, thinking it was time for the big black pimp to join us. I was amazingly calm; my hands were steady and I felt relaxed. I turned around as another Dutch woman came into the room. She was skinner than the first one and had badly bleached, blonde hair. She was dressed in a shabby, long black dress.

"Vhat is de problem?" she asked me in broken English but before I could answer Maria launched into her story again. She walked around the room, shouting and waving her arms and pointing to the bed; pantomiming the entire scene for the second old woman. The two old women stood calmly by, as did I, all three of us following Maria's theatrics.

When she finally shut up, I softly explained, "Madame, she should have told me the prices outside, not after. When she did tell me how much she wanted, I stopped and said, no."

"I see, vell you are right I suppose," the second Dutch woman said.

Seeing that she agreed with me, Maria shook her finger, "You better pay me or you won't get out of the district. My boyfriend and his friends will see to that." She clenched her fist and shook it at me.

I turned to the second woman, "Please call the police," I said.

The first woman yelled something in Dutch at me and at Maria both. I didn't understand anything she was saying but saw that she had moved aside from the open door and I took this as a gesture that I could go.

I walked out of the room and down the narrow stairway onto the street. Maria was right behind me shouting the entire way. The first Dutch woman was behind Maria, speaking in Dutch to the second woman who was behind her. Out on the street Maria leaped past me and yelled something in Dutch. I walked slowly down the sidewalk. Whores, Japanese men in business suits, men and women coming home from work, the entire street full of people, watched as the dolce vita scene from my soon to be released movie, *Everyone's Life Is More Interesting Than Mine, Thank God*, played out.

I left the red-light district, turned the corner to my hotel when I realized I didn't have my glasses or wristwatch. Despite all common sense, I turned around and walked back to find Maria's apartment. I was nervous, as you might imagine especially since the last time I saw Maria she was running down the street shaking her fist at me and screaming, "You'll never make it out of the district. I'll get you!"

I recognized the apartment from the canal bridge and walked over and found Maria in the hallway.

"You have my watch and sunglasses," I said calmly.

"I have your glasses," she said, "but not your watch."

"Give them back to me, please," I said.

"You can have them for 50 florins," Maria said.

"I'll give you 10," I said. (I know I'm an idiot.)

The English speaking, thin Dutch woman was in the hallway too. "Will you take the ten florin and give him the damn glasses!" she shouted.

"No!" Maria shouted back.

"I'm going to go get the police," I said. I walked outside but couldn't find a policeman or anyone who knew how to get one.

I went into the corner bar and ordered a beer. The bar was very German and the strong odor of schnapps and sausage made me nauseous. I took two sips of my beer and walked back to the hotel and began to pack my bags. Tomorrow I would go to the Van Gogh museum, then get the hell out of Dodge.

The next morning, I rode the tram to the Van Gogh Museum. I got off at the right stop but then I didn't know which way to go.

"Excuse me," I asked a Dutch man in his late forties. "Could you direct me to the Van Gogh Museum?"

The white-haired man looked at me through shining blue eyes and smiled. "Of course, I can," he answered with a thick accent. I admired his appearance; he was perfectly clean shaven and wore an expensive gray suit which was impeccably smart. "I can walk you there in fact," the man said. "It's just over a few streets."

He and I walked together down the boulevard, busy with Monday morning traffic.

"It reminds me a bit of a chill early Monday morning in New York or London," I said. "The smell of the bus fumes and the people bustling off to work."

"That's it, everywhere the same," the man said.

We stopped in front of the museum.

"This was out of your way by a block or two," I said. "I appreciate your kindness."

"But I'm happy to do it," the man said. "And Van Gogh is pronounced G*ou*gh, rhymes with cough not with go."

"Ah, I didn't know that," I said. "Thank you."

The old man bowed his head, then walked off into his own life.

"Vincent Van Gogh, (rhymes with cough) born March 30th 1853 died July 18th, 1890." I wrote into my journal after entering the museum. "The museum in Amsterdam built to honor him, is of modern architecture on Museum Straat, several blocks behind the Ryks Museum. Well Vincent, this is a great place, the front door and entrance are very impressive. It's a little late but you'd be pleased to know that you've made the big-time kid, your own museum.

"The gallery takes the viewer up three levels, each one exhibiting Van Gogh's works in a chronological order, from the earliest on the ground floor to the third floor and his last days.

"*The Little Church at Numen* is a small painting of the church where Van Gogh's father preached.

Church Tower at Numen appeared to be just a step or two above my own efforts but next to it *The Potato Eaters* (1885) is much, much better. A real breakthrough and is regarded as Van Gogh's first masterpiece.

"I must learn to do figures," I wrote into my journal. "The human body, especially the face allows the widest range of artistic expression and is inherently interesting to the viewer."

"In his earlier painting, The *Avenue of Popselars,* Van Gogh left the woman's face one glob of color without any detail, then in October of 1885 in *The Potato Eaters,* he provides wonderful detail and a range of colors to suggest the shading on their faces. All his subsequent works display this level of excellence.

"It is interesting for me to note that Van Gogh's father died in October 1885 about the time Vincent made this major leap forward. Did his breakthrough come out of grief or relief? There is no doubt that from that month on, from the time his father died, his works are all masterpieces.

"Suddenly in 1888 another great change, more distinct than that of October 1885, for now Van Gogh's paintings drastically brighten and are done on larger canvases. *View From Montemarte*(1888) shows these changes in his style.

"*Still Life: Red Cabbages and Onions* (autumn 1887) is the quintessential Van Gogh. His dark slashes of red and maroon paint are offset by dull yellow. All his brush strokes are thick and wide with consummate confidence. Van Gogh never went back over a brush stroke, he never tried to better an application of his paint. I know from experience how difficult it is to not go back to try and fix some places, but Vincent applied the paint boldly, probably quickly and refused to "fix" anything.

"Self Portrait in Front of the Easel (1888), a dramatic picture and very intense. The museum notes that Van Gogh wrote about this self-portrait, "One seeks a deeper resemblance than the photographer's."

"The spring of 1888, in Paris, produced some of Van Gogh's most beautiful works. *The Pink Orchard* (March 1888) and *Orchard in Blossom* (April 1888), the latter of such gaiety and light that the viewer immediately remembers similar days in their own lives. The sky of happy blue, the tree, pink blossomed with dark maroon branches, all of it recalls an innocent day when the earth showed her love for us.

"The White Orchard (April 1888) another springtime delight but then in the autumn of 1888 comes another style change, suddenly the gaiety is gone. The sky darkens as shown in *House on the Place Lamartine*. But even with the brightness gone, Van Gogh's style is fun to view. *Bedroom in Arles* is a painting of which I've had a print in my office for several years and it is a reward to see the original. Solid, solid painting; childlike perhaps but Van Gogh's "just lay it out there" style gave all artists who came after him, his artistic heirs if you will, their freedom. Thank you, Vincent for your courage, though the struggle destroyed you, we have reaped your rewards.

"Boat on Beach at Les Saintes-Maries de La Mer (June 1888) is another painting of which I've had the print for years, now before the original I feel real joy.

"Harvest at La Vrau With Montmajor in the Background (June 1888), is a painting that stands out in the room and pulls me to it. I enjoy this physical attraction, then read on the plague that Van Gogh considered it his finest landscape and I agree.

"Bugler of the Zouave Regimet (June 1888) is a rare portrait painting from this year of landscapes. I stand a long time before it. The man's expression, the straight stare of his eyes, the coolness of his mouth. He has a story to tell; he has seen things and done things in his life; it's all inside of him now in his memories. He will share his experience now and then in a conversation with friends but he knows they will not understand how it really was.

"A year later his style changes again. *Pieta After Delacroix* (Sept. 1889), is an example. It reminds me of *The Potato Eaters* but what was happening inside Van Gogh? The struggle tightens, tensions increase. He seeks the answer to life's brutality, the paradox of a perfect God creating a cruel world. It takes a leap of faith, a leap made that much more difficult by the apparent failure of Van Gogh's efforts as the world is in no mad rush to buy his works. Hardly, he is all but totally ignored by the establishment and is broke. Only his brother's financial support keeps him from being homeless.

"*Undergrowth* (July 1889) and *Still Life: Vase With Irises Against Yellow Background* (May 1890) both are done with the heavy Van Gogh energy and they show a release of the inner tension through his application of thick, solid colors implanted, not painted but implanted on the canvas with force and vigor.

"*Crows in the Wheat Fields* (July 1890) shows the madness approaching. Beware the black crows, omen of darkness. Beware the awareness that life's answer may be no answer at all. There is no God. There is no logic in the chaotic chemical phenomenon; our thoughts and rationale merely a safety device, a buffer from the truth that we are freaks of nature, super-naturals in the natural world but no more important than the insects crushed beneath our feet.

"*Corner of the Garden of Daubigny* (June 1890), an oasis of calmness in the storm. An attempt to recapture the gaiety and the joy of the earlier days in Paris.

"Where is *Portrait of Pere Tanguy?* The Parisian shop owner who befriended Van Gogh and traded hand ground oils in exchange for Vincent's paintings.

I put my journal away and went downstairs to find the Pere Tanguy painting. I asked a uniformed guard about it but he didn't know. A middle aged, attractive Dutch woman who happened to be walking by overheard my question. She stopped and told me, "There are two Tan-gays, not Tan-guys. One is exhibited in Paris at the Jeu de Palmes, the other is in a private collection and cannot be viewed by the public."

"Oh? It's not here to see then?" I asked.

"It's in a private collection," she said. "Do you know what private means?"

"Yes," I laughed at her sarcasm, "I know what private means. Thank you for your help."

She was really quite intelligent this lovely lady. One of the few Dutch women who dressed in style; she wore a casual red pants suit with a mauve blouse. Her short, blond hair combed back on one side, hanging loose on the other.

I left the museum feeling a connection between myself and Van Gogh. This painting, Pere Tan-gay, which I so much wanted to see, was at the Jeu de Palme; a museum I never knew existed until by chance I met a Scotsman who not only made me aware of its existence but gave me directions to find it. A coincidence? In my view of the world, there is no father figure like the God of the Old Testament, but within each of us, there is a Holy of Holies. This is our soul and our connection to the mystery. We each have the subconscious power to influence the world so that our paths cross those of the people we must meet for our destiny toward that great unknown after-life. The tragedy is that our worldly egos do not recognize the same holy soul within other people. Everyone thinks they are better than everyone else; street beggars would like to give world leaders their opinions on how things should be run. The famous and the rich, spoiled into believing that they are the righteous and the blessed and that they have a duty to tell the rest of us how things should be done.

Personally, I don't think that God is selecting some and hurting others in some cosmic chess match. The mysterious Creator chose to have free will on Earth. HE/SHE/IT does not rape little children and toss their bodies on the side of the road. HE/SHE/IT does not make bad things happen. Free will is probably much more interesting to HE/SHE/IT than a manipulated creation. Everything is in balance and Life grows out of the chemical chaos. Life is going on in every living thing on earth, one not more important than the other and we have Our Times and Our Selves. The problem is we see our own life as the main story, the only story to some. When you are gone,

Life goes on, so you are not more important, nor are you *the* reason. Except we each *are* the reason, some way, somehow, we each are the reason for the Big Bang. For the formation of the stars and galaxies so we might evolve from the chemical chaos into emotional, humorous human beings.

I walked through central Amsterdam, turned off the main thoroughfare and down Canal Street. My stomach hurt from either too much coffee or not enough food but in the quiet crisp, autumn afternoon I listened to the sound of my shoes against the cobblestone sidewalks and felt calm and delight. The shops were bustling as the Amsterdam population on its way home from work, stopped to buy groceries. I noticed a man in his late twenties who looked like a university professor, carrying a leather briefcase. Filled with papers and books I imagined. His clothes were loose fitting, a wool sweater, baggy, thick corduroy trousers and brown leather shoes. His blond hair tossed about by the September breezes. He walked up a short flight of steps to my left and into an old building with green railings and a green wooden door with panels of clear glass window panes. As I walked past his apartment, I looked through the glass panels in the front door and saw posters and prints on the walls of a sparse but sophisticated apartment. I was happy for this man and admired his lifestyle.

As I walked further, I noticed that I was now in a black neighborhood. The vibes changed. There was litter in the street, hustlers were on every corner and prostitutes stood in front of apartment houses. The pain in my stomach increased as I looked down a side street and saw the whore, Maria. She was standing next to her boyfriend. I saw a look of recognition come across her face but she didn't point me out. I turned and walked away, went around a corner and found myself next to the railroad station.

I waited for a bus to the hotel; thinking back to the look on Maria's face. I don't care anymore about my watch, Maria. You have your life among the poor. Keep the glasses and the watch. Get the best you can for them. I only wish I had given you the

50 florins, you deserved it and I was being an ass. Forgive me someday, if you can.

I took a tram from in front of the railway station and found an Italian restaurant. The pain in my stomach was accompanied by a twitching in my right arm.

"I'll have an order of spaghetti with meat sauce and a glass of red wine," I said to the waitress after finding an empty booth. My arm was twitching like mad. I recognized that it was from fear. I was having a fear episode. This was something I had suffered from for years. It was the reason why I used drugs and alcohol, to numb the fear. I wanted relief from it now. It hurt and was maddening. My mind was clear and focused on my inner feelings. I tried breathing deeply but it didn't help. I thought of Al Greenbaum. "We'll use it. We'll use everything." It didn't help. I drank a glass of red wine, a little help. In a quiet voice I chanted, Ommm and it worked. The fear was gone and I sat relaxed; imagining how it would be if I ever grew out of these episodes and into days filled with serenity.

I finished dinner and walked back to the hotel but stopped on the way as I noticed a very large building which took up an entire city block. There were beautiful bronze statues on the roof, green now from the elements of time and weather. The central statute was a figure of Atlas holding the world on his back.

"Do you speak English?" I asked a gentleman in raincoat and hat.

"Yes," the man said and kept walking.

"Excuse me," I asked a woman carrying a package. "Could you tell me what this building is?" She walked off without looking up. I laughed at her rudeness.

"Do you know what building this is?" I asked another couple.

"Why, yes, that's the King's palace," the woman said as she took out a tour guide map and showed me where I was.

"Thank you," I said. "The King's Palace. Well it certainly looks like a palace."

I walked around the sides and back of it the building. Judging from the number of windows I believed it must have over 400 hundred rooms! I walked up the wide central walkway and tried the front door but it was locked. There wasn't much left to do but to go back to the hotel. There I stopped at the front desk and asked about the palace.

"The queen now lives in Den Haig," the desk clerk told me.

"Well, can't really blame her for that decision," I said.

"Where she has a country estate," the clerk ignored my remark. "The palace in Amsterdam is used for rare state visits, otherwise it remains closed. I was inside once; they allow the public into the outer rooms on Wednesdays and Sundays. Even the public rooms are quite splendid. They have beautiful natural wood panels, marble tiled floors and the statuary are very, very beautiful."

"Sorry I missed it," I said.

I went up to my room, packed and brought my trunk and bag downstairs and took a tram to the railroad station. I sat on a bench with my luggage among hundreds of other souls waiting for trains. There was a slow, steady, cold wind blowing. I put my yellow rain slicker on but the wind went right through it. My eyes hurt from writing without glasses in the dim light of dusk. I stopped writing and put the rain hood over my head and leaned back on the bench and smoked a cigarette. I looked out from under the rain hood. I felt good; mysterious and romantic.

Chapter Seven
Paris

I went back inside the train station in Amsterdam and walked through the crowded terminal pulling my trunk slowly along. Defused sunlight filtered through the high glass ceiling. People were coming and going, carrying bags and pushing carts. There were lines at the ticket booths and lines at the tobacco shop. Arriving and departing train times were shown in yellow lights on a black board overhead. The Paris train departure was 7:45pm on track 34. I rolled my trunk outside to the long, dimly lit platforms and sat on an empty bench under a light pole. The light reflected yellow off of the rain wet concrete. The steel and concrete world outside my skin was hard and certain while my hopes and dreams, wants and needs seemed to have little influence in this world. My soul told me there was a God. The world showed me there was gravity. And when you die, you're dead. What about the heavenly lights inside my head?

This world told me I wasn't good enough; not tall enough, not rich enough. Other men were tall, other men were rich and some men had talent, but me? I was mediocre. Everything I ever did was mediocre. I didn't win the state wrestling championship. I didn't play professional baseball. I can't sing or dance. I don't paint too good either. The only thing I was ever really world class at was getting high but I can't show anyone what I've seen; which means it doesn't count. I picked up a beautiful rock once when I was on LSD and I could see its molecular structure. In fact, I saw the molecular structure of everything around me. Fascinating, but since I can't describe it to you or show you, so no, that doesn't count. How about studying an orange when high on acid? I saw and understood that it was converted sun light. And when I took a bite, I was eating a part of the Sun's energy. Energy that had recently been on the surface of the Sun. But no, I can't describe the epiphany that brought me. No, it's got to be outside, not inside. You've got to show us; how big you are, how well you fly. Yeah, okay, I get it.

The train to Paris arrived at 8:05pm, without any public address announcement. The people on the platform gathered their belongings and I pulled my trunk and walked toward the front of the train, asking people as I went, "Is this the train for Paris? Is this the train to Paris?" No one answered me.

On the door of the first car I read a small 3 by 5 index card with the word, "Paree" neatly typed in small letters. I boarded the train and took a bed in the first empty compartment. The train had gone down the track only a few minutes before the conductor came through. He tilted his head back to read my ticket through his bifocals, then in French muttered under his breath, looked at me and said, also in French, "Your sleeper compartment is in one of the *last* two cars on the train. Not here, not here." He wagged his finger at me for trying to get over a fast one on him.

I wheeled my trunk down the hallway of the first car. At each connecting doorway I struggled to open the door, drag the heavy metal trunk between the cars then open the next car's door; then down the aisle of the next car to the rear door to repeat the process again and again. I finally found my sleeper compartment in the last car. There were six berths in it, three on a side. I matched the number on my ticket with the numbers on the bed frames, mine was on the lower left. A young man sat in the right bottom berth. "Je m'appel, Paul," I introduced myself.

"Mon nom est, Gabe." The young man shook my hand. He was in his late twenties with dark curly hair and a short and stocky build.

"Pardon," I said as I wheeled my trunk in and tried to place it under my berth. Gabe helped me with it.

"Parlez-vous Anglais?" I asked.

"Non," Gabe answered with a shrug of his shoulders. He lifted the bed frame and mattress and held it while I put the trunk underneath. The door opened behind us. A blond, blue eyed young man came in with a young woman companion.

"Pardon," I said trying to get out of their way. I sat down on my bunk and pulled my legs in for them to get by.

"Pardon moi." The young man smiled as he squeezed into the tiny room.

"Pardon, s'il vous plait." The young woman with him said but did not smile. They stored their luggage overhead then climbed into the two middle berths.

"Mon Nom est, Francis, et me ammi, Sabine," Francis said.

"Parlez vous, Anglais?" I asked him.

"Non, excusez moi."

"Et madame?" I asked.

"Non, triste," he said.

I lay back on my mattress, forgoing any thoughts of talking to my French roommates. We pulled out of Amsterdam and I dozed fitfully as the train swayed and bounced; the sound of the wheels clacking rhythmically beneath us. Finally falling asleep an hour later, I dreamed of walking over an arched bridge across a dark river. I was startled awake by the train's loud, screeching brakes. Bright lights from the station glared through the compartment's small windows. The sound of the public address system outside announced the arrival of the train to Paris. New passengers boarded and after a short layover the train lurched ahead, slowly building speed. I tossed and turned then fell asleep, only to be woken again an hour later at the next station.

Sometime after midnight I sat up and looked out through the pouring rain. The train had stopped at a station in the French countryside. I stared at the empty platform then to my watch, it was 1:30am. The trained pulled away but I was unable to go back to sleep; I sat up and watched as silver rain droplets ran sideways on the window pane. Their patterns combined and separated, always moving, all unnoticed and temporary. I was filled with the beauty of their light and shape and inside, my heart ached with loneliness.

It rained through the night but by morning had stopped and as the train pulled into Paris, the wet tile roofs of the buildings glistened in the morning light. The passengers emptied out onto the wide platforms under the glass and steel roof of the station.

The cement was wet with dew. The light through the glass roof reflected in small puddles of water. The air was crisp in the early autumn morning. I wheeled my trunk to the money exchange and cashed a traveler's check into French francs then went outside to the taxi stand.

"Hotel Vieux Paree, s'il vous plait," I asked the first cab driver, an Algerian man wearing a brown trench coat. His face was lined with age, his eyes sadder than any I had ever seen. The man shook his head. I showed him the note Carol had given me. He shook his head again and looked away, not interested in taking this fare.

I went to the next cabby, a Frenchman with light curly hair and yellow nicotine fingers. He hadn't heard of the Hotel Vieux Paree either and was altogether uninterested in my problem. Not one of the dozen cab drivers outside the station recognized Carol's hotel. I went back inside and to the Information Desk. Sitting on a stool behind the tall glass counter, a young man with a trimmed beard sat reading a novel.

"Parlez vous AngIais?" I asked him, smiling.

"Non," the information officer said looking up from his book.

"I can't find anyone who's heard of this hotel." I showed him Carol's note. The information man shrugged.

"Le Metro, le Metro." He pointed to a small map taped to the glass window of the information booth and indicated that I should go down into the Paris subway.

"Hotel Vieux Paree? In le Metro?" I asked, not understanding.

"Je ne sais pas, le Metro." ("I don't know, just go to the Metro") The man pointed to the Metro map again.

"Then what?" I asked him, shaking my head. The man ignored me and spoke to the next person in line.

I found two pay phones, neither had a phone book. I went into a tobacco shop. Using my French/English dictionary, I asked the old shopkeeper if he had a telephone book so I could look up the Hotel Vieux Paree's phone number. The shopkeeper spoke no English. I went back to a pay phone and called Carol in London.

"Carol? Hello? Carol?" I could hardly hear her on the decrepit old phone.

"Yes, this is she." She answered in her proper British accent.

"It's Paul." I screamed into the phone. "I'm sorry to call so early".

"Not a problem, Paul. I'm already up."

"Carol, no one here knows of this Hotel Vieux Paree. Do you have the address?"

"Yes, just a sec."

The sound of the pay phone's timer chimed off the seconds like a warning that life was passing me by. When the sound changed to a high pitch, I understood, time was running out on me so I added more coins.

"Ah yes, here it is," Carol said, "number nine Rue de le Couer."

"The cab drivers here never heard of this hotel. Are you sure this is the right name, Hotel Vieux Paree?"

"Ah, well you know, Parisian taxi drivers but yes, that's the name. There are other Americans and English tourists there I'm sure."

"It would be nice to hear English again," I said. "Okay, thanks for everything Carol."

"Ciao, Paul, good luck."

Outside, I showed the hotel's address to another six taxi drivers, none of them had ever heard of the street. Giving up, I took out my travel book and while keeping half an eye on my luggage, read the section on Paris. "The Hotel de Nantes is located just several blocks from the Le Opera House and is close to the Louvre. It cost 12 dollars a night which includes breakfast. This one has, friendly service."

Yes, but this was the same guide book that told me the Hotel Krasna in Amsterdam had friendly service. I showed the address of the Hotel de Nantes to a taxi driver. The cabby knew it and we loaded my trunk into his tiny Fiat. A mile from the train station we stopped in front of a hotel that was wedged in among stores and shops on a busy side street in central Paris. I carried my trunk and bag into the dimly lit lobby. Behind an elevated counter, a middle aged, overweight Frenchman looked down on me. He watched with interest but without smiling as I hauled my heavy trunk through the door.

"Oui, we have a room. How many nights?" he asked.

"Four I think." I was happy to hear English.

"The room won't be ready until ten o'clock but you can leave your things here in my office."

"Merci," I said.

The man came around the desk front and unlocked a storage closet in the hallway. He was about five feet tall and I understood how he must enjoy looking down on people from his elevated platform.

Taking my backpack and trusting that my luggage was safe, I went to a café around the corner and ordered coffee. I sat outside at a table reading through my French/English dictionary. I began to practice a few phrases but the animated, fast patter of the Parisian workers in the coffee shop interrupted my concentration. I listened to their voices and then put my dictionary away. It was a hopeless task. I drank my coffee and listened, not understanding a word but still enjoying the sound of the French language. Its nasal sounds and how they smooth out their consonants; very romantic this French. It can be felt as well as heard.

I looked out the window at the shops and buildings along the avenue. Street merchants sold everything from magazines to nylon stockings on the sidewalks. In the middle of the intersection, an old fountain with a weathered bronze statue, dripped droplets of water over the edge of its marble bowl into a pool. I enjoyed the feel of Paris.

It was drizzling as I walked back to the hotel. I paid for four nights in advance and went to my room. The hotel was very old and very Parisian funky. The water stains on the wallpaper and the eighty-year old carpets were a bit depressing but I unpacked my clothes and placed them into the drawers of an old, fragile dresser. The smell from fifty years of visitors was only slightly less offensive then the odor from the tiny toilet in the decrepit bathroom. I finished unpacking and left the room to walk again along the Parisian streets. The gray sky was like a ceiling above the roofs of the buildings.

At the corner a city bus came by and stopped. I boarded and not knowing how much the fare was, I held out a hand full of francs to the driver. The driver, a middle-aged man with a dirty shirt and bloodshot eyes, spoke rapid French asking me for the exact fare. I held out my hand again and smiled, "I don't speak French," I said. "I don't know how much you want, here, take what you need from this." But the driver only repeated the amount, then finally waved me off the bus with the back of his hand and a look of disdain. No one on the bus tried to translate or help.

I walked along the boulevard and four blocks later I saw an optometrist's shop. I went in and managed to get fitted for and order new glasses then do a load of wash at a laundromat around the corner. I was exhausted when I returned back to the hotel in the early evening. The language barrier had been very difficult to penetrate. I felt like an idiot all day, smiling with a dumb, "I don't understand you" look on my face. It made for the loneliest day in Europe without human contact.

I sat at the little desk by the window and turned on the radio and watched people go by below. Every ten minutes it seemed I heard the harsh blare of Parisian police sirens go by outside.

I listened to a Bach fugue followed by a Bossa Nova, followed by a heavy metal tune. I tried several other stations but they were all the same, none of them seemed to have a specific format. I kept searching the dial for the right music. It was either that or change moods every two minutes to some French programmer's diabolical taste.

I thought about the Parisian women. They were the prettiest I had seen in Europe but even with fluent French it would be tough to get through to them. I didn't speak fluent French; I was beat here too. Thinking of this, I remembered Mary telling me during the divorce, "There isn't anyone for you." Maybe her curse was true. My whole life alone? I shuttered at the thought and tears came to my eyes. I was exhausted and my nerves ragged from the long train trip. Tonight, I wouldn't do anything; to bed early and a full night's sleep then I'd have a new outlook in the morning.

Paris is a city to visit with someone, to share the trials and tribulations with, not to mention the incredible beauty. This last thought had been with me all day. I missed Mary, missed the kids too. I had shared so much of my life with her and now this trip to Europe was lonely without her. My heart ached too at every dark-haired young boy I saw. They reminded me of Noah and today was the day for young, curly headed French boys to be out and about.

After a nap, I walked to an outdoor café and ordered a beer. The cafes were loaded with men but no women. A disappointing ratio of 80,000 to 1. I took out two postcards and high on the French beer wrote.

"Dear Ava and Noah,
"Paris is the most beautiful, sophisticated, cultured city in the world but very lonely when you don't speak French. I think of you both and miss you. I hope school is okay and you have teachers you like who like you. I love you Ava. I love you Noah."

"Dear Stephen,
"I'm drunk. It's late. I hear you telling me how I should handle things. I don't. Paris is overwhelming. I feel I'm the only American in town. Really, there aren't ten other American tourists in Paris this time of year and the other nine I feel sure are off together somewhere laughing and having fun. Still, I am enchanted by the feel of Paris. I hope things are going well for you. I'm okay. Love Paul."

Next morning, rested, breakfasted, showered and shaved, I headed off to the Louvre. As I waited on the underground platform, I recalled my dream; finches and doves flew into a tree to be near me. Then several beautiful, delicate ones flew down to perch on my fingers. I recalled feeling that I was worthy of love, worthy of trust.

At Le Musee du Louvre; I am duly impressed. It covers twenty city blocks and would take many rolls of film to photograph all of the outside. The line to get in was quite long and the crowd maddening. Electricity is in the air as everyone anticipates the greatness promised within. Once at the front door, the crush became horrific, little children and nuns being run over by the mob.

I paid for my entrance ticket and received a four-page map of the exhibits. I went first to the Egyptian exhibit and relaxed in peace and studied the museum map. My goal was easy, the Mona Lisa located at the very center of the museum. My intent was to go directly there but as I strolled through the first room, I walked by fifteen masterpieces including Whistler's Mother, which I had to stop and admire and study. Next, I walked through a room of impressionist works; several Monets and a Renoir. I had to stop in every room, *drawn* to one or two of the thousands of paintings. The ultimate goal, the Mona Lisa seemed further away.

I saw a man my age in front of one work, writing into his journal. I wouldn't be able to describe a fraction of what I was seeing and feeling. It was just too much. I was in awe of the building itself. I read where it took 300 hundred years to complete. Every room being made by crews of master craftsmen who tirelessly pursued perfection. I could imagine that James Michner would write a 6,000-page novel on how the Louvre was built. He hasn't written one, even Michner knows his limits, but if he did, I'm sure he would start out by describing the formation of the Alps and the special glacier that 500 million years ago created the marble and granite from which the Louvre is constructed. Michner would then describe the life of one of the Parisian laborers who spends ten years working along with scores of his brethren on only two rooms. That's the building, the art work hanging on its walls are the treasures of western civilization.

In a room so large it held thirty of the world's largest paintings with room to spare, one in particular pulled me over. Girodet-Trioson's, *Atala Portee Au Tombiau*. The sunlight showed through the man's right ear lobe, the delicacy of the pierced earring, the absolute perfection of their forms; the expression of grief at the death of a beautiful woman were all so wonderful done. I had never heard of Trioson and I hadn't seen any of Michelangelo's works yet. I was on my way to see DaVinci's Mona Lisa. I had seen Turner, Constable, Rembrandt, Picasso and Titian but none exceeded Trioson's ability. She was a rare woman painter in the 18th century but she had been gifted with the ultimate talent that a human being could ever be blessed with.

It took me two hours to go directly to the Mona Lisa. As I walked up to the open doorway and looked in, I saw that the room overflowed with people moving in a continuous, circulating action. Those patrons coming into the room edging towards the painting. Those who had gotten to within one, two or three rows of it, depending on their luck and aggressiveness, melting outward, allowing others to squeeze closer. This circulating dance took about fifteen minutes until I was close enough to view the painting in detail. The woman next to me gasped in awe when she saw it. I laughed spontaneously. The canvas was magical. I noticed the right sleeve of her dress and the way the light reflected off of the high points of its folds. But it was her mouth and forehead that gave Mona Lisa her magical air. There was something about the way the corners of her mouth are turned up and the tension that creates that makes us ready for her to smile at any moment. A smile that would show us her teeth and wrinkle her forehead and eyes. This understanding that our minds anticipate a full smile if it is given certain other body language, was DaVinci's secret. With this knowledge, he made the Mona Lisa psychedelic in the sense that she seemed to be changing expression right before our eyes.

Her forehead and temple and the way her hair is combed, I have seen many women who have that look. They are feminine but something about the outline of their skull and face, making them look like a man. Mary looked that way with her make up off. I saw her now in my memory and recalled the times I really studied her until there was a oneness between us. A soul recognizing themselves in another being.

What was Mona Lisa like? She appeared to have had a wonderful grace. Yet now, after thinking of Mary and the similarities between their faces, I could see a real bitchiness in Mona Lisa too!

Back upstairs again, working my way to Michelangelo's, *The Captive* and other sculptures, I passed through a Roman sculpture garden where the French had placed a complete Roman temple; the original walls and columns into a room in the Louvre. There they reassembled stone walls, ancient statues and fountains. The ceiling, all glass, goes up 250 feet.

I stopped in front of *Venus di Milo*. She stood tragically looking back to men and times long gone. The transitory nature of human life being brought into clear focus by these ancient masterpieces surviving their creators and their worlds.

Down the wide, granite stairs to the basement where sunlight comes through high windows. Here two statues, works of Michelangelo, each entitled, *Esclave*, (Slave). The room is spacious and quiet, off from the main flow of gallery traffic. While I am there, several people come in, stroll about, view the sculptures from 360 degrees, talking quietly to each other and stroll back out. The guard is standing inconspicuously behind a granite column. He does not notice me and I reach out and feel the calves, feet and toes of the sculptures. Their feet especially interest me. Michelangelo has the weight of the statues forced down onto them and the tension this creates, through the ankle and tendons, is the basis for much of the upper work, especially as it relates to the other tension created by the strap across the chest of the first *Esclave.*

This first statue is roughly finished. A sculpture of a man with his hands behind him; his entire body frozen within the marble. His face strains from the struggle to be free of the stone. The second *Esclave* done a year later is finished much smoother and is complete as to skin tone. This figure does not struggle to be freed but rather has his head back and his eyes closed. There is an expression of physical comfort, passion really, on his face. His hands caress his own breast, fingertips brushing lightly over his right rib and pectoral.

Michelangelo did both of these sculptures within a year. He gave them the same title and obviously meant for them to be exhibited together, yet they have two completely different messages. Certainly, one gets the idea of his homosexuality from both of them but the first *Esclave* is more than that; as he struggles to be released from the rock, from the forces that have shaped his life. We recognize this battle inside our own psyche; events which cannot be undone, in a culture we cannot control. These forces have forged our lives and Michelangelo sculpted this; showing us man's struggle to be free from the consequences.

I left the Louvre tired but satisfied. On the way back to the hotel I stopped to look at doorways of several old Parisian buildings. Their hand carved doors were weathered but beautifully made. One was of bronze and had scenes of the French countryside hammered out in the metal in great delicate detail. Paris is doorways on side streets and gray tiled roofs, lighted monuments, odors of garlic and onions cooking and the sound of your shoes on the cobblestone streets.

I called Carol's old French teacher from the pay phone at the front desk.

"Parlez-vous Anglais?" I asked when a woman answered.

"Yes, I speak English," she said.

"Wonderful. I'm Paul Gebhart, Carol in London gave me your telephone number."

"Oh, Paul, yes, she called us. I'm Anne. Carol told us to expect your call and to feel safe with you, that you were a charming American."

"Ah, well, Carol is kind. If you aren't busy, perhaps you would have time to meet with me. What are you doing tomorrow?" I asked.

"I work and my cousin Montaigne does too but we would like to invite you to our home for dinner. What are you doing tonight?"

"Tonight? Nothing, sure I'd love to come by."

Back in my funky room hotel, I sat by the window listening to the Los Angeles Philharmonic playing Mahler. I looked out at the Paris landscape and was aware of a feeling of serenity. I remembered this is what I felt like when I was a child. It was probably the way I was always supposed to feel but I'd lost it along the way. I was surprised and thankful whenever this feeling of serenity came back over me.

I brushed my teeth and dressed then walked to the Paris Metro and took a subway to Anne's stop. I was early so I strolled Ave Demousil and found a liquor store and bought a bottle of wine. The city of Paris was inside me, its rhythms, its ancient history, I felt all of it inside. I watched people on the street and felt what it was like to be this man carrying a loaf of bread home on an autumn evening in Paris.

I found Anne's apartment in an old brown stone building across from a small park. I climbed the five floors of worn stairs to their apartment and knocked. Anne answered and let me in. Her cousin, Montaigne stood in the living room, smiling. We shook hands and touched cheeks. Both women were in their late twenties, both were plump with plain features and short hair.

"Hello, Paul," Anne said. "Right on time. Welcome." She spoke fluent English.

"I brought a bottle of tinta at the corner," I said, handing her the paper bag and bottle.

"Thank you, shall I open it now?"

"Yes, that would be nice, but allow me," I said, taking the bottle back from her.

Anne went into her small kitchen and I followed. I looked quickly at the knickknacks on the bookshelves as I passed through the living room.

She handed me the cork screw and I stood by the kitchen sink. Her apartment overlooked the playground of a grammar school and I heard the shouts of school children coming in through the window above the sink. I twisted the cork free and poured three glasses.

"A votre sante," I said clicking glasses with both ladies.

"You speak French quite well," Montaigne said.

"I wish. No-no. No one understands a word I say except 'thank you', 'please' and 'good-bye'."

I noticed several framed newspaper articles on the wall in the hallway near the kitchen door. The by-lines were Anne's. "You're a journalist?" I asked her.

"I work in the administration Division of Reuter's news agency but I have done a few articles."

"How interesting," I said, "being in the center of the news I mean."

"I like my work," Anne said, "but I want to progress. I've begun to study law."

"Where have you been on your trip?" Montaigne changed the subject. She was the quieter of the two women but I noticed her intent, sober, observing eye. I had nothing to hide from her and so welcomed her scrutiny.

"London, then Amsterdam, now Paris," I said.

"How long will you be traveling?" she asked as she leaned against the kitchen counter.

"I think I have enough money for two months, perhaps three if I budget."

"And Paris, have you enjoyed you visit here?" Anne asked.

"Paris? I love it and hate it. It sounds such a cliché but it's true. It's been the worst and best almost at the same moment."

"Allow me to apologize for France's treatment of its visitors," Anne said seriously. "It isn't just with visitors though. I spent two weeks in Portugal on vacation last month and at the hotel I noticed that the English said hello. The Americans loved to meet people and talk about everything. Even the cold, reserved Germans said hello. It was only the French people who never said hello, not even to their own countrymen. I'm really quite disgusted with the French personality."

"Despite the rumor that Europeans all speak some English," I said, "the French do not, nor do they care to. Their attitude is,

'Come back when you know how to talk, too busy to play with you now.' That and a down right dislike for Americans."

"The Parisians feel that French is the superior language of a superior culture," Anne explained. "And you're right, the French people in general do not like Americans, English, Germans, Spaniards, Italians, Algerians..."

"No one!" Montaigne added and we laughed.

"Too bad," I said. "But you know, there are great people everywhere and jerks too."

"That's true," Anne said. "People are people. We're from Bordeaux and until we picked up the Parisian dialect, few people here would even talk to us."

"Then you can imagine what I've been going through," I said.

"Mais oui, Paul but you must not take it personally. These people have a fabulous pride but are no longer a world power so they despise everyone," Montaigne said.

"You don't know how hard it can be here," Anne finished for her. "It's very difficult for a single woman. At the discos no one dances, no one talks to strangers. They just drink. They've really a problem." Anne quietly looked down, feeling she'd said too much.

"Come let us eat," Montaigne said.

There was hardly room for the plates and glasses at the small kitchen table but we laughed and squeezed together. Montaigne served a Portuguese dish of fish, shrimp and rice. It was a delicious meal and I ate it with gusto; smiling, closing my eyes in delight and wiping my mouth between sips of the very nice red, table wine.

"What do you do?" I asked Montaigne.

"I write about Third World causes for a Parisian magazine, before that I lived in Brazil for six years. I've only just returned to Paris this spring."

"I'm afraid we are both feminists and socialists," Anne said with a smile.

"Militant?" I asked and both women laughed.

"Hardly militant," Anne answered.

I sipped from my second glass of wine. "The Louvre was an experience I'll never forget, simply the greatest art in the world," I said, recalling the fabulous museum.

"Carol said you were an artist," Montaigne said.

"An artist? Not professionally, no, but I paint; abstracts and sometimes a still life."

"Would you like to see some of Montaigne's work?" Anne asked.

"Yes, of course, please," I said.

"Come, we'll go into the living room," Anne said.

I followed them into the comfortable but small living room. Montaigne brought her portfolio to the couch and opened it on the coffee table. She sat next to me as I slowly studied each drawing. There were dozens of lovely Paris street scenes done in pencil. Her shading and attention to detail in the drawings was incredible.

"She is submitting ten of her best pencil drawings to the art university in Paris," Anne said from the chair alongside the sofa.

"If they think I have potential, I will be selected to attend," Montaigne explained.

"Potential? Montaigne, these are wonderful. I love them."

"Merci, Paul."

"You must be selected. Who could they choose over this kind of work?"

"I'm afraid it is very competitive, very selective," Montaigne said.

"Yes, of course, I understand," I said. "But damn them if they don't recognize the loveliness of your art. You must paint these in oil so that people may enjoy them forever."

"Thank you, Paul. You are most kind," Montaigne blushed.

"I'm also not a bullshit artist. I mean every word of it."

"How long will you be in Paris?" Anne asked.

"Well, I think just a day or two more," I said. I turned to her still ready to argue the merits of Montaigne's work. "Paris is very expensive and I have to be careful or I'll have to go home in two weeks instead of two months."

"Perhaps, Paul you would like to stay here with us, that would save you hotel costs," Montaigne suggested.

"That is very kind of you. Very kind, thank you but no, I think I want to get out of Paris. I'll go to Nice, then to Italy."

"We have friends in Rome, here let me write down Dominique's number." Anne got up and looked through a desk drawer for her address book. "And if you do get to Portugal, I'll write a few names and numbers there as well," she said over her shoulder.

"Will you return to Paris?" Montaigne asked.

"I don't know," I said. "Maybe now that I've met you two I will. I had half decided not to come back but maybe. Besides once I'm out of Paris and look back on it, I may see it differently. I may remember the absolute beauty and charm of its streets and fountains. Of course, its galleries will always call me back, but I would love to find a place in Spain where I can live cheaply among other artists and just paint and write for six months."

"I hope you find what you are looking for," Montaigne said.

"Paul, if you have problems in Paris you must call us so we can help," Anne said as she came over and handed me the yellow paper she had written the names and numbers on.

"Thank you, Anne. I shall. Merci Madames. Merci beau coup."

They laughed at my French.

"You see," I said with a wave of my hand, "I speak French, but with a *slight* New Jersey accent."

"Ah, but not a Parisian accent," Anne said, waving her finger at me like a school teacher.

"That's my problem all right, I'm a Jersey guy in a Parisian world."

The next morning, I went to the corner bistro. "Cafe au lait, s'il vous plait." I ordered my breakfast from a short, older man with gray, frizzy hair and day-old beard.

"Can you tell me how to get to the Jeu de Palme?" I asked the waiter when he returned.

"Le musee Jeu de Palme? Oui, le autobus soixante-douze." The waiter pointed to the next corner.

"Number 72, thank you, merci," I said.

After breakfast, I walked to the corner where the number 72 bus did come by only a few minutes later. I watched as it stopped down the block right in front of my hotel, then went by me without stopping. I walked back to the hotel and waited for the next Number 72 bus. Forty minutes later, I paid the woman driver the exact fare and asked her, "S'il vous plait, le musee Jeu de Palme." But after sitting on the bus for twenty minutes, the passenger in front of me turned and said, "Jeu de Palme," pointing to a white building at the end of the tree lined park we had just passed.

"Le gallery, Jeu de Palme?" I asked him.

"Oui, Jeu de Palme," the man said again pointing back to the building. I went to the exit door in the rear of the bus and pulled the cord. I heard the buzzer ring at the front but the driver ignored it. At the next stop the woman driver looked at me in her rear-view mirror but continued on without opening the rear door.

"Madame, s'il vous plait," I called out. She ignored me. I kicked the exit door hard, BANG BANG BANG and she stopped at the next corner.

"I don't think I'm going to come back to Paris," I muttered to myself as I started back the ten blocks to the museum. "It's just no good alone. I'm sick of the Parisians. Fuck the French. Their greatness was two hundred years ago. What have they done lately? They're an elitist, racist society. You destroyed your own Monarchy and now you worship it. Fuckers!" I cursed them quietly as I walked through a beautiful park now in autumn colors. I slowed down to enjoy the cool, clear day and the smell of the grass and decaying gold and red leaves lying on the sidewalk. I recalled a painting by Renoir of this very same day.

Before entering the museum, a man standing next to a black Citroen parked in the street, called to me in a thick Italian accent.

"eh-Scusa me, eh-scusa me, my friend," he said to get my attention. "I want to make you a gift." He reached into the trunk of the Citroen and took out a long fur coat. "These are-a thousand-a- dollar elk-a jackets and all I want-ta is enough-a money for-a gas a-back-a to Roma."

"How much is that?" I asked.

"A hundred dollars."

"Let me try one on first."

"It's your size." He stepped up to the sidewalk and held out the jacket.

"How do you know it's my size?"

"I know, I know. You're a perfect 46."

"I'm a perfect 40 short."

"Well in Roma a 46 is the same as-a U.S-a 40."

I tried on several of the coats. Each time I put one, on the Italian shouted, "Perfect!" gesturing with his hands. "You look-a terrific. Beautiful! Wonderful." He said as he helped me on with the jackets which were all three sizes too large, my fingertips barely showed out of the sleeves.

"They're all too big and this isn't real elk," I said as I examined the fur closer. "And they're poorly made."

"No, no, no my friend, there all-a good-a coats, all-a one hundred-a percent-a real-a Elk-ka."

I handed him back the coat and walked away with the man still calling to me, "Hey, come-a back! I give you a gift, a present. Hey. Hey! Help me just-a enough to get-a back-a to Roma."

I didn't turn around. I found the entrance to Jeu de Palme on the edge of the park and squeezed in with the crowd. Inside there were no chairs or couches to sit on and it was so crowded as to be almost impossible to stand near the paintings for any length of time as people pushed and shoved to get closer. I was saddened too that the curators at the Jeu de Palme put the paintings behind glass, creating a glare which not only destroyed the viewing quality but gave the viewers a headache as they must squint past the reflected light to see any detail. Unhappy at all that, I still was joyful as I viewed the great impressionists.

Edgar Degas, the master of facial expressions as shown in, *Pagans et Auguste* and *La Classe de Dance.* Then his signature masterpiece, *Les Repasseuses.* It is a portrait of two women ironing. One is yawning, the other presses on, absorbed, thinking about the argument she had with her husband the night before.

Edourd Manet, *Fleures dans un Vase Crystal* is gently done. Standing in front of it, I put myself inside Manet's mind and body as he stood in front of the canvas capturing a single moment, a single glance, the multitude of which comprise all our lives.

The gallery Jeu de Palme to my surprise is only five or six rooms which is deceiving because from the outside the building looked quite large. The exhibition portion takes up less than half of it. I wondered what was in the other, off limits rooms? "Yes, I know what private means." I recalled the woman at the Van Gogh museum. And where was that Pierre Tangay?

I found more enchanting paintings; Gustave Carllebotte's *The Floor Scrappers* is the best painting at the Jeu de Palmes! Not impressionist but like Latour's realism in the Dutch tradition. It is a very impressive work as is Latour's, *Un Coin de Table.*

Pierre Auguste Renoir's, *Torse de Femme au Soeil* pulled me over. Sunlight filtering through trees, mmm, onto a beautiful nude woman, mmm-mmm. Again and again in both, *Le Moulin de la Galette* and *La Balancoire.* Both paintings have a warm, summertime, relaxed feeling.

I returned to my hotel, my feet hurt, my soul hurt and my body was exhausted. I showered, shaved and lay down for a nap. Lying on the old, caved in mattress with yellowed bedspread, I took a bite of a peach, looked at it as I chewed and saw a worm wiggle inside.

"God!" I shouted and spit out the peach. I leaned down and picked it up and examined it closer. "I didn't swallow any of it. Man, shit." I threw the peach out the window. "Disgusting. Enough of Paris. I'm looking forward to a couple of days in Nice, lying on the beach and swimming in the Mediterranean."

Unable to sleep, I went to the post office to call Stephen. I made change and stood in line until it was my turn to use one of the wooden and glass telephone booths. I dropped the coins in and they made a thick chime sound in the receiver.

"Hi Steve, it's me," I said when he answered. In the back ground, every second a chime sounded, advising me of the passing time.

"Paul! It's good to hear your voice. How are you?"

"I'm okay, I'm in Paris…" The line went dead. I realized I had forgot to keep adding coins.

"The French telephones suck them up quickly on a long-distance call," I said to Stephen after re-dialing. "I have to add one every 3 seconds, It's crazy here."

"Europe is different okay," Stephen said.

We had a lousy connection now and I had to shout to be heard over the static. "Did the kids call?"

"No."

"Did Mary call?"

"No."

"Did the D.A. call?"

"No."

"Did you get my present?"

"No, not yet."

"Well it's coming. Did you get my postcards?"

"One from London. Did you see Carol?"

"Yes. I stayed with her for four days."

"She's nice, huh?" Stephen asked.

"Yes, a very nice lady," I said.

"Where are you headed next?"

"Nice."

"Oh, Nice. It's very expensive there. Don't stay too long."

"No, just a couple of days then on to Florence."

"Oh, you'll love Florence. Be sure to go to the…gallery."

"The what gallery?" I asked, not having understood as the telephone connection was getting worse.

"To the…gallery. It's on…street. And Michelangelo's David."

"Yes, I'm going to see that. Look, I'll call you in a couple of weeks from Italy, or maybe Madrid. I'm okay. How about you?"

"I had the last of my melanoma surgery done," Stephen said.

"How does it look?" I asked.

"Well, only ten stitches now. It's not too bad."

"Good, stay out of the sun, will you?"

"Sure. When are you coming back?"

"I may not make it back by the end of October," I said.

"Okay, you shouldn't rush," Stephen said. "Take your time."

"I have the garage rented for the car until October 26th," I said. "Maybe you can speak to someone on the block about renting another garage after that?"

"Okay, I will. I'll take care of things here, you just enjoy," Stephen said.

"I will."

"I love you, Paul. Don't worry about anything."

"Thanks Steve. Okay, I won't."

We were cut off at that point and I was out of coins. It was a nine-dollar call but worth every penny to me as the sound of someone familiar, someone who cared about me, warmed me inside.

Back at the hotel I lay in bed listening to the Paris Symphony on the radio and drinking wine. I lit a cigarette, then a second one. I was always, neurotically, putting things into my mouth; trying in vain to fill the emptiness inside. After food it was a cigarette or cigar smoke. Then chew on gum, but it didn't help, only touching a woman's body filled the void. Would I ever not be neurotic?

I went outside and walked to the metro. My feet swept through the fallen leaves. I felt their beauty and life's poetry. It didn't dissolve the terror or the emptiness but it helped for the moment.

A sadness overcame me. I still couldn't believe what had happened to my family. Why couldn't I get over it? The kids had; Mary had. They all told me so. They've all showed me that they've accepted it. Gladly it seemed, they went on with their lives. Why did I still relate everything I experience back to Mary and the kids? People told me there would be ups and downs in the next several years getting over the divorce. What I felt now was only a tenth of the pain of a year ago but how did they do it so quickly? Mary's cousin, Maryanne moving in with them? New boyfriends? Why did I have to be alone? Why couldn't I be happy and feel complete inside?

I took the metro to the American Center. The building was dark but I walked up the steps to the front door anyway. I had to cup a hand over my eyes to defeat the glare in the window and peered into the deserted lobby. A sign read, "American Center Closed Due To Special Benefit Staring Gene Kelly."

I began to daydream. I was singing and dancing on the front steps of the American Center, dancing like Gene Kelly in "An American in Paris." I was in my California garb; jeans, bright shirt and comfortable walking shoes. I danced up and down the marble steps in a tea for two kind of way as I sang an ad lib song in an American/French accent like Maurice Chevalier at times, at other times in my own Jersey City accent.

"Oh zee French are assholes, oui, s'il vous plait. Little assholes of zee world. Oh yes, oh oui-oui, the French got no heart. Oh oui, may-oui, zee French got no heart and got no soul. The French they are fucked, oui - oui, merci. Zee French are bigots, racists, oh oui-oui, lit-tle assholes of zee world." Tap-tap, shuffle-shuffle and so forth. People walked by as I sang and danced, some stopped to watch, not understanding a word. Some were embarrassed as people do become, others smiled.

I walked aimlessly through Paris, stopping several times to admire wooden doors carved by long dead craftsmen. Their beautiful, intricate work impressed me. It showed the kind of quality that brought, even to a passerby, a sense of time and dignity.

I walked on Le Raspail which I saw was a better part of town. I went by an outdoor café and heard three or four middle aged couples speaking English. I found a table in the corner back from the street. A glass of red wine warmed my body and soul. I thought about the Renoir paintings I had seen earlier in the day. The background of defused colors of the table cloth against the clear form of my hand, made me smile. I laughed drunkenly as I saw my own hand through Renoir's perspective. I looked at the cafe scene, seeing it too as a Renoir painting.

Back to the hotel after midnight, drunk and amazed I found the place. I woke late in the morning. The travel clock on the old wooden night table next to the bed read 10:15am. I heard a light rain fall against the window pane.

I dressed and went out. Along a narrow cobblestoned side street, a group of third graders came out of a schoolyard. They walked double file undisturbed by the drizzle. I stopped to watch them parade by, holding hands and chatting with each other. Their teacher, a handsome man over six feet tall with curly blond hair, wore a blue warm-up suit and sneakers. He spoke with the children in an easy, non-controlling way.

I remembered being in third grade and walking with my friends like this. We too held hands, boys with boys, girls with girls, all friends and innocent. We too had open faces and clear eyes.

I felt good for these children, growing up in Paris and having this handsome, friendly teacher. I knew that they would remember this day for its beauty. The city was not depressing for those with young hearts.

I stood behind four French women at the pastry shop and waited to be served by a redhead shop clerk. She took the orders from the women, each of them buying their daily bread; long loaves and twisted loaves and round loaves while I looked at the redhead's full breasts and slim body. She wore a tight white jump suit opened to the third button. She had blue eyes and a beautiful face. She noticed me watching and looked into my eyes. I didn't look away. When my turn came, I ordered coffee and an apple croissant. She smiled and charged me half price.

"Merci," I smiled. "Parlez vous Anglais?"

"No, triste," she said shyly.

I sat outside with my coffee; another path crossed but not walked.

I sat at a table under a canopy listening to the car tires driving through the puddles on the cobblestone street. The slate roof tops of the apartment houses glistened in the rain. This heavy, dull atmosphere, this thick weather, the Paris monuments and streets were inside me now. Lonely and blue as I was, I felt unhurried and alive in the moment.

After breakfast I took a bus to Notre Dame. I went inside and walked up to the tower floor and stood on the observation deck. The rain had stopped but there was a gray mist between the buildings. The River Seine wrapped dark silver through Paris.

A young mulatto guide interrupted my daydream.

"Next group, please. S'il vous plait, Madame. We are going to the bell tower, but you must stay in line, Cheri." The guide wore a blue uniform. He had short hair and green eyes. His lips were perfectly formed as were his eyebrows and nose. A gold earring pierced his right ear. When the group arrived at the top of the medieval, twisting wrought iron winding stairs, the guide explained in French, then English; "The bell weighs 15,000 kilograms. It's made of brass and bronze." He lightly struck the bell with a short metal rod and it sounded a perfect A. The guide hit octaves, thirds and fifths on the bell, singing in harmony to the ringing bell, "ahh, aahh, aaaahh."

"For centuries, eight men were used to ring the bell, then in 1934, an electric motor was installed. If we were here in the tower when the bell was being rung, that is the 2,000-kilogram pistol hitting the 13,000-kilogram bell, the vibrations would knock us to the ground."

The group of tourists I was with took turns touching the bell and taking pictures in front of it.

"Here, let me take one of you," the guide said to me, reaching for my camera when he noticed that I was alone. I handed it to him. He was very handsome and I thought probably gay. Suddenly my stomach turned. I was homophobic to the core.

"Thanks," I said uncomfortable. The guide aimed the camera, then stopped and looked over it at me. "It's okay, don't smile," he said. He looked through the lens to line up the shot again. "It's much more real just like you are."

It rained as I left the cathedral. I opened my black umbrella and strolled down the street along the Seine. Back at my hotel,

I lie in bed listening to slow French love ballads on the radio and reading a book as my mind drifted into fantasy. I was making love this afternoon while it rained outside. Enjoying and being enjoyed by the young French woman from the pastry shop. We were playing, snuggling, teasing with soft fingers, getting hot, making out; the sights, sounds and smells of love, then climaxing and laying back listening to the rain and the Paris traffic. I masturbated into the sheets then fell asleep.

The sun came out in the late afternoon and I dressed and packed my trunk. "Bon soir," I said to the room. "Au'voir," I answered, enjoying the rhyme.

At 8:30pm I was at Le Gare de Lyon station, sitting on platform 13 waiting for the "Blue Train", the express to Nice. I had the cold, cement blues. The rejection blues. The never going home again; don't know what's going to happen to me, cold-cement blues. I wanted to paint this pain, this anguish. I would draw a man howling in pain, screaming torment from his soul. I needed to find a place where I could settle for a few weeks or a month and paint this howling man. I could picture it clearly in my mind; the man sitting on the edge of a bed, arms extended, palms up, looking at the viewer and pleading for mercy and love.

It had threatened to rain all evening but didn't. There was a chill in the air but I was at the train station two hours early because I really wanted to get out of Paris. Track number thirteen was lined now with people waiting for the train to Marseilles. I had heard that Marseilles was a bad town, looking at the characters getting on the train, I knew it was true. I made a mental note to scratch that from the places I want to visit list.

I couldn't help but wonder what Mary and the kids were doing. Sunday dinner, baths then TV. I pictured the house in the meadow. Doves calling quietly at dusk outside; the long driveway up to the house, the garden and flowers. It hurt and hurt even more to remember how she did it to me. "Don't come around here anymore. This is *my* house," she said even before I had filed for divorce. She needed her privacy for her boyfriends. I would like to think someday it will be the other way around.

She'll have the loneliness and the sense of loss. But I doubted it. She'll marry someone and live happily ever after. I knew it didn't matter anymore. What mattered was my own life. Either finding someone or learning to enjoy being alone.

Chapter Eight
Nice

Lying on the beach in Nice is actually to lie on a pile of rocks. Large granite pebbles poked my back through the thin hotel towel. I sat up and looked out at the Mediterranean Sea. It was calm and a beautiful aquamarine. I was lying next to Sandy from South Bend, Indiana. She thought I was listening to her when in reality I was focused on the tits of the topless women around us. It seemed to make up for the lousy stones.

After an uneventful train ride from Paris, I had dragged my broken trunk up two flights of stairs at the station in Nice and found a pay phone and called a hotel out of my European travel guide.

"Do you have any rooms, si vous plais," I asked.

"All of the hotels in Nice are full," the woman said and hung up on me.

A brunette with long slim legs and attractive face stood at the other pay phone.

"Do you speak English?" I asked her. She looked at me and smiled. Her eyes said "I wish I did." But she shook her head no and before I could try my weak French, a young, heavy set woman jumped up from a bench and said,

"I do! My name's Sandy. Hi I'm from South Bend." She reached out and we shook hands.

"I'm, Paul Gebhart, Los Angeles. You just getting into town?"

"No, actually I'm looking for another hotel. The one I'm in now is too expensive and the operators are very uptight."

"How unlike the French," I said.

"I have a list." Sandy took a torn telephone page from her purse and she used the phone to call several places. One, the Hotel Mimosa on Rue de la Buffa had rooms available.

It was a short taxi ride from the train station to the hotel district. The cabbie pulled up along a row of three-star hotels.

"The fare is thirty francs plus ten francs because of the trunk," the driver said.

"To go two miles?" I asked.

"Oui, monsieur."

I paid him with a fifty franc note and the driver handed me back the change.

"Wait a minute," I said, "this isn't a ten-franc coin."

"Oui, monsieur, ten francs."

"The bastard is trying to pass off a ten-cent piece as a ten-franc coin," I said to Sandy.

"Non, non." Sandy waved her finger at him.

"Okay, okay," the cabbie said as he studied the coin then gave me a ten-franc bill.

We walked up a long flight of stone stairs in a stairwell lit with a single 40-watt bulb. The hotel operator showed us to a single room then a double room.

"We should share a double room for sixty-five francs," Sandy said, "rather than two singles at forty-five francs each."

"Personally," I said looking her in the eye, "I think it's worth the thirteen francs to have our own rooms."

Sandy looked disappointed.

"We don't really know each other," I explained, "and besides I may want to bring another woman back to the room, where would you wait?"

"I understand," she said, "and I may want to bring another man back."

"See, there you go, so two rooms it is then."

I unpacked, showered and shaved in the communal bath in the hallway then walked with Sandy to the beach a few blocks away. She was talking now to three Americans lying next to us on the rock beach. The women were all in their early twenties. Betsy was the cutest of the three. She had short, dirty blond hair and a beautiful smile. She was cute and with a rock-hard body. Her friends, Susan and Gail were both a little on the plumb side, both were brunettes. I tried talking to Betsy but Susan kept interrupting me. Gail and Sandy talked non-stop. Susan and Betsy were from Boston. Gail was from New Jersey. I gave up on Betsy when I learned they were leaving tomorrow for Munich and the Octoberfest.

I could tell by that that it wouldn't have worked.

Why wasn't it the beautiful girl at the train station who wanted to share a room with me? Oh well, at least I was in Nice and felt better than I did in Paris.

I went back to the hotel and took a nap. In the evening I went with Sandy and the girls to the train station where we caught the 8:00 o'clock express to Monte Carlo. Betsy wore a tight red skirt with rope belt. She had one of the best walks I'd ever seen, albeit a bit too fast. All of them walked too fast for that matter. They fairly ran up the hill from the train station through Monte Carlo to the casino.

"Le Casino was designed by the same architect who designed L'Opera in Paris," Sandy advised us as we went up the front stairs.

"We need a plan," Betsy said.

"Let's have a drink," Gail suggested.

"There's a plan," I said and I led the way to the bar. I ordered a gin and tonic to cool off from the 5k in from the train station.

The drinks arrived and the women relapsed into a long discussion about men. Unable to take it, I excused myself and walked into the casino. It was a very small room and overcrowded. There were nine black jack tables but the operators used only three for the 25franc minimum. There was one table for the 100-franc minimum and one for the 200-franc minimum. Five tables were closed down even though at the three 25Franc tables, people stood four-deep to get a seat. Only one person played at the 100 Franc table and no one at the 200franc table.

After losing 50 francs at craps, I went outside to be alone. It was a balmy evening and very clear. The moon and stars shone brightly above the mountains. I took a table at an outdoor cafe across the street from the casino and ordered an ice cream. While I waited, I watched the Monte Carlo police hassle cars that stopped to let people off in front of the casino. They didn't hassle any of the Rolls Royces or Mercedes Benzes that stopped but any other make was fair game. There was a distinct pecking order in France that the men spend a lot of energy to keep up. I could feel my place in that order too. I wasn't a 200-franc player. I wasn't a powerful man. What did these other men have that I didn't? I was from a middle class, working Jewish family. No real estate holdings other than the house I grew up in. It wasn't in the best section of town either and because of its location, I went from grammar school into a half-black junior high. Most of the other Jewish kids attended the all-white school on the other side of town.

I recalled those days. That's when I changed from a funny, peaceful boy into an angry man. Those three years at Burnet Junior High, worrying each day which black kid would try to steal my lunch or hold me up for money or wait outside after school to fight. I had joined a white gang for mutual protection. We drank wine and sniffed glue.

I had learned to fight then and I learned that I was dangerous. I could lose my temper and frighten people. In shop class, I once ran after a black kid with a claw hammer. I really wanted to pound his skull with it. I would have too but I couldn't catch him and the shop teacher and three others tackled me and held me down.

The more times I raged out like that, the fewer times I had to. My reputation preceded me.

My mother and father saw these changes in me but they didn't know what to do about them. They didn't realize that they had to get me out of that junior high school and how could they have anyway? They didn't have the money for a new house in a better neighborhood.

So now, here in Monte Carlo, I'm not a 200-franc player, I am not an equal to the industrialists whose yachts floated peacefully in the harbor below. What was I then? Not a normal tourist. I was an artist. Uncelebrated, unknown but feeling like an artist. That took the sting out of my failures; my many long and miserable failures. To think of myself as an artist gave me the latitude to look on the scene without having to compare my fortunes with others.

Now, sitting eating ice cream, I sought comfort in the sweet sugar milk. Like a kid without worries, just watch it unfold and make it fun. Make it art.

The girls walked over from the casino. They ordered beers and talked and drank until we all decided to try the bar at the Hotel de Paris, the swank hotel on the corner next to the casino. Inside the hotel bar, the women drank and talked, always getting back to the French and their attitudes.

"Let's each put in ten francs and play a slot machine together," I suggested to change things up and get out of the bar talk.

"No," Sandy immediately responded.

"Yes, it is a good idea," Gail who had the strongest personality of the four women agreed with me.

Back into the casino, we walked down a row of slot machines.

"You can't just sit at the first machine you come to," I said. "You have to feel the vibes."

"Feel the vibes?" Betsy asked.

"Yes. It's very important; stand in front of this one a few seconds. Do you feel good? Are you lucky? How about compared to the one next to it?"

"It's this one," Sandy said from two machines down.

I went over and stood in front of it. "I thinks she's right," I said. "I really do think she's got it. Do you feel it, Betsy?"

"Oh absolutely. No question about it," she said. "Why I just tingle with good vibes."

"There you go," I said. "But be careful, good vibes often lead to sexual tingles even possible orgasm."

She giggled breaking the sour mood.

We took turns deciding how many francs we would play and who would put the money in and who would pull the handle. We had pocketed a cool twenty dollars in an hour's time; which seemed very suspicious to the tuxedoed casino honcho that the bosses had sent over to keep a close eye on us. What fucking assholes.

The next afternoon, hungover and still tired from the late night, I sat on a mattress at a private beach. I had paid five dollars for the privilege of laying on a mattress and being able to walk down a wooden pathway to get in and out of the water without having to walk across the tortuous, stones and pebbles.

Laying on my belly, the sun whited out my vision but I could hear the beach boy leading people to the mattresses next to me. I shaded my eyes as two young women walked down the wooden path. They both had rings through their noses, multiple pierced earrings and bracelets on their wrists and ankles. They were also both topless.

I waited until they got settled, then asked the prettier one, "Do you have the time?"

"One fifty," she answered in English and showed me her watch dial.

"Thank you. Are you from Nice?" I asked.

"No, Sweden."

"Oh? What part?"

"Stockholm."

"Ah, so very beautiful," I said, never having been there. "You're on vacation then?"

"Yes," she said.

"I'm Paul Gebhart. Nice to meet you."

"I'm Lotta," she said.

I nodded hello and looked at the other girl. But she didn't respond.

"And this is Maria," Lotta answered for her.

They both laid down and ignored me. End of conversation. They didn't want to meet me. I went back to writing in my journal. I was describing last night at the casino but I had to stop because I hurt inside. I was tired of rejection; tired of feeling I wasn't handsome enough, wasn't tall enough. Why cross their paths with mine then have it go like this? Why keep doing this to me?

I thought of Cat. Everyone thought she was crazy because she talked to spirits and made high pitched sonic noises. I was crazy too then because she made sense to me. Maybe we were both running away from the truth. There weren't any spirit guides. There wasn't a divine intelligence. It was all a mental fantasy to hide behind; to protect ourselves from the terror of life. I wanted to believe that God existed. I'd seen Jesus' vibrations when I was stoned on acid and good weed. I felt that Jesus was observing my life with compassion. The problem was God gave everyone a freewill; His leaving it up to me to choose my own path was a mistake though because I was a sinner plain and simple. I wanted to make love with every pretty woman I saw. But freewill made it so much more interesting with infinitely more possibilities. That must be how the Creator wanted it to be and He added faith into the mix to create yet even more dimensions. God was not boring.

I hoped Jesus would appear to me now. That I could feel His presence in my daily life. That was the journey or the bullshit, depending on who you talked to. Meanwhile I felt like shit right now. I was the total sum of negative thoughts and feelings that I'd ever received in my life. I wanted to feel better and to be positive but these disappointments only fed into more negative thoughts.

I put down my pen. The Swedish girls both looked over at me, both smiled and said, "Hi".

Thank you, Jesus.

"So how is it in Sweden?" I asked Maria. She was closest to me but it was Lotta who answered.

"It's cold and rainy. Where are you from?"

"Los Angeles."

"And how is it in Los Angeles?" Lotta asked.

"It's warm and rainy," I said and she laughed.

"What work do you do?" Again, I asked Maria, but she ignored me. Lotta, seeing this, answered for them.

"I work at a Disco; Maria is a sales assistant at an auto store."

"An auto store? Oh, a dealership."

"And what do you do?" Lotta asked me.

"Right now, nothing. I'm here in Europe to find a place to live for a while and paint and write."

In order to hear me better Lotta, nude except for the briefest of bottoms, leaned over Maria's naked body. Her tits lay unselfconsciously on Maria's back. They both had dynamite, thin bodies and I was high on the smell of their suntan lotions and I swear, their vaginas. It gave me a hard-on and I had to lay on my stomach. I needed to pee too but I couldn't get up. I had an erection that could be seen 100 feet away.

Finally, I managed to lose the Johnson. We all three got up, the girls put on their tiny tops, helping each other tie their straps and we walked up the board walk to the beach restaurant. We sat at one of the dozen white plastic tables under a blue and green umbrella. "I have no idea what to get," I said, looking at the two-page menu. "I am very poor in French."

"What do you like, meat or fish?" Lotta asked me.

"Fish, yes and a salad, please."

She ordered for herself and me, Maria ordered for herself and we handed the menus back to the young waitress and sat looking out from behind our sunglasses at the blue Mediterranean. Children playing in the surf, yelled in delight. The smell and feel of suntan lotion left me feeling relaxed and at ease.

I think the girls sensed this and they relaxed too.

"Bon appetite," I said when our food came.

We clinked glasses of Avion.

"So, you paint. What style?" Lotta asked.

"Nude women," I said. "The feminine body is the most wonderful of all God's creations. Don't you think? I will spend my lifetime trying to capture its sensual energy and beauty."

Lotta said something in Swedish to Maria and they both laughed. I smiled. I wasn't sure what they said but I realized that Maria was shy because she didn't speak English as well as Lotta.

During lunch, we exchanged addresses and telephone numbers. I asked them if they would like to go to dinner but Lotta said they were busy doing washing.

"How about for a drink then?" I asked.

She spoke to Maria, then nodded her head and said, "Well, yes, okay. But Maria must come too."

"Yes, of course," I said. "That will be fun."

Lotta looked into my eyes. There was something there, a thought, an idea, a plan. I didn't know what, except that she was thinking something.

"We have a rental car," she said. "We'll pick you up at your hotel at nine. Where do you stay?"

"At the Hotel Mimosa on Rue de la Buffa."

"I'll find it," she said. "We must be going right after lunch. We leave tomorrow for home and have a week's worth of clothes to wash." And so, after lunch, they both kissed me ciao on both cheeks and walked off the beach. I watched them go. God, what bodies. Clean and perfect.

Lotta and Maria, picked me up in front of the hotel right on time in their rented Peugeot.

"We'll go to the Old City if you like," Lotta said after we touched cheeks.

Weaving through traffic like a true French maniac, she parked on a main street downtown.

"We have to walk now, just 6 blocks or so," she said.

Once we made it to the old quarter, there were crowds of people walking the narrow streets but no autos. It was quiet and I could hear the sound of our shoes on the cobblestones and the soft voices of people passing by. We walked unhurried and there was a sense of peace in the night air.

Maria wore a yellow dress with belt and high heels. Her brown hair with blond highlights hung down over her shoulders. She had lovely eyes. Lotta wore shorts and a see through top. Her long legs attracted attention from every male we passed. She had high cheekbones and full eyebrows which added to her natural allure. She wore just a touch of lipstick and powder. Her blue eyes were set off in her tan face.

We turned off the narrow street and entered a courtyard restaurant. There were perhaps twenty outdoor tables with aluminum gas heaters, one for every four tables. We sat down and a waiter dressed in starched whites came over. I chose a French chardonnay and showed the menu to Lotta.

"I thought we were just going to have a drink," Maria said.

"You can order, if you like," I said. "Or we can just drink the wine. Whichever you prefer." I smiled and raised my glass in a toast, "Saluda."

We clinked glasses and the girls seemed to relax. Lotta ordered hor d'oevres. Her French was quite good.

"We must be up early and to the airport in the afternoon," she said after we toasted.

"Don't talk of leaving," I said, "not now."

"You're right." Lotta smiled and raised her glass to toast again. "Here's to an evening in Nice."

"Cheers," I said and we three laughed.

The waiter brought the plate of appetizers and we enjoyed a lovely tray of fish and fried potatoes. The light fragrance from the ladies' perfume mixed in the warm, night air with the fragrances of the food. We could smell the delicious aroma of the food with onions and garlic cooking from the kitchen. Outside the courtyard, people passed by on the cobblestone street.

"What are your plans, Paul?" Lotta asked me.

"I want to find an apartment where I can begin to paint," I said.

"Paint the nude women?" Maria added with a smile.

"Yes, of course," I said. "The nude women and the landscapes."

"In Ville Franche," Lotta said. "That's where I've heard there's an artists' colony. Perhaps that would be worth looking into."

"How far is it?" I asked.

"Oh, not far at all, maybe ten kilometers east of Nice. There is a small boat harbor there and nice restaurants."

"Yes, I should try there."

"Why don't we go there after dinner?" Lotta asked.

"That would be terrific," I toasted her decision.

After dinner Lotta drove east along the coast to the little village of Ville Franche. We went past a 17th century castle near the harbor, then by the church on the hill. She drove quickly up the winding, twisting side streets until the way was too narrow for cars so we parked and began to walk up the steep, cobble stoned street. The apartments and homes were all interesting architecture and carefully landscaped.

"There are Americans, English, Germans and French here. Monet lived in Ville Franche when he was developing impressionism," Lotta said.

"I'm not sure he was a part of developing Impressionism but it is an interesting town," I said as I admired the private homes.

"A flat here would be about 500 francs a month, food and living expense another 500," Maria said.

"Two hundred dollars per month for rent? Really? Even if you're way off, I could live here for four to five hundred dollars a month?"

I looked down the hill to the lights on the boats in the small harbor. "Do you think I could meet some of the fishermen in the seaport and get to fish with them?"

"Sure, why not?" Maria answered with an assuring wave of her hand.

"Let's take a ride," Lotta said.

"That sounds good." I was happy that she didn't want to end the evening. We drove into the hills and parked at a spot overlooking Antibes Bay. I put Michael Frank's *Sleeping Gypsy* tape into the car's cassette player and we sat outside on a bench at a scenic turn out. It was a balmy Mediterranean night. The lights of Nice sparkled below us. Only the screeching tires and exhaust of an occasional car along the winding mountain road disturbed the peace of the forest.

Maria took out a joint and lit it and passed it to Lotta, who passed it to me.

We smoked it quietly, each of us enjoying the evening. Maria finally stomping the tiny roach under her heel.

Michael Franks played sensually from the car's radio. The red wine warmed my blood.

"Why do you sit so far away?" I asked Lotta. "Come closer so I can touch you."

She looked at me a moment, "I'm a bit slow," she finally said. "Here sit between Maria and me."

Maria and I changed places on the bench. The fragrance from her perfume and the lingering marijuana smoke heightened my sensations of their femininity.

"Now you have the two of us," Lotta smiled.

"Two against one," I said. "I like that."

We laughed and Lotta leaned over and we kissed.

"You mustn't forget, Maria," Lotta said.

I turned and looked at Maria. She was beautiful in the star light.

She looked at me and smiled. I put my hand under her long hair, on the nape of her neck, and pulled her to me. We kissed. Lotta was at my pants fly and I felt myself throbbing. I helped her pull my penis from my pants. They both took turns sucking me as I played with their small, pointed breasts.

"I like you." Maria looked up into my face and I leaned near to her and kissed her soft lips.

"I can just picture us in bed in my apartment in Ville Franche," I said, "drinking red wine in the middle of the day. That's the way I want to learn French."

Lotta laughed, "Yes it sounds good." Her eyes were alive.

Maria sucked me harder. She really did like me.

"How will you come?" Lotta asked, as I moaned with pleasure.

"Inside you," I said.

"No, not tonight," Lotta said. "In my mouth."

She and Maria worked me very well and they happily took my summation into their mouths.

There is something very releasing in that act. Call it total submission to the male desire. But why? I think it is the fact that in this, a man feels he is King. He isn't of course and the world lets him know that every day, but this act, this brief act is about saying; Yes, I am king.

We drove back to Nice. It was late and the streets quiet. Lotta dropped me off in front of the pension and I kissed them each goodnight.

"I'll call you in the morning," Lotta said. "We will go with you to find the apartment in Ville Franche."

"Thank you, I'll be up. Ciao." I said and closed the door.

I walked up the long, stone stairwell and down the wooden paneled hall to my room. I undressed and brushed my teeth then lay in bed thinking. I was living a dream; how could I make them stay with me. I wanted them both, every day.

In the morning, I went out and had an early coffee and croissant at the corner bakery. The girls came by right on time and Lotta drove us down the coast and into Ville Franche. We stopped at a tobacco shop and picked up the local paper and while sitting at an outside table drinking coffee; Lotta went through the rent ads, marking them with a pen. I sat across from her and next to Maria. Maria ignored me and the conversation about the apartments. She stared out at the calm Mediterranean. I could never tell what she was thinking or feeling. She came from very stoic, Norse blood.

"I think we have three here that are worth looking at," Lotta said. She folded the paper and we walked back to the car across the park. A woman walking a dog and two old men; all stopped to look at us and wonder; could it be, two beautiful girls and he?

Lotta found the first apartment up the street past the church. It was of modern design with pleasant landscaping. I rang the buzzer of the manager's apartment. An old woman came to the front door and led us through the apartment that was for rent. It was okay, but not 200 or 300 francs but 700 per month. Not anywhere close and as we left and walked down the front steps, Lotta said, "Well I think we have not enough time to see the other places. Here, try them another time. We have to get to the airport." She handed me the newspaper and we got back in the car and drove back into Nice. They dropped me off at the hotel. When I went to kiss them on the lips, I was offered a cheek. That kind of stung, but I was still on a buzz from last night and thanked them and wished them a safe trip and watched them pull away.

I put my dirty clothes in a shopping bag and went out to find a laundromat. As I walked on the side streets of Nice, I studied the faces of the shopkeepers, the children and the old people. Outside an empty store, a man sat on a chair with his head in his hands. He stared blankly at the sidewalk. I looked closely at him and his posture. What problems was he having? It was a ten second stare but I saw an entire novel left untold.

I stopped several times to ask for directions to a laundromat. The six people I asked each gave me six different directions. But as they all seemed to be indicating the same general direction, I kept going. Finally, further down the street, a shopkeeper took me outside and pointed; one down, first right.

"Okay, merci, merci beau coup," I said.

I understood too that I could learn more about a city and its people by taking a load of wash to the laundry then by visiting all its galleries and museums.

It took several hours at the laundromat to do two loads of wash and to dry them in the old machines. I wrote postcards while I waited for the decrepit machines to finish. After the postcards were out of the way, I sat and watched others doing their daily routines. I couldn't take this loneliness. I decided that I needed to get out of Nice and over to Florence and to the statue of David. Then down to Rome.

I returned to the hotel before dark and called Rome from the pay phone in the lobby. I reached Anne's friend Dominique. Her English was not good so she put her husband, Sergio on the line and he spoke less English than her. I hung up and asked the hotel keeper, Madame Adie to help me call them. When she hung up, she told me that Anne had called and told them about me. They invited me to stay at their home in Rome for one or two days. I was to call them from Florence.

The next day I went to see an exhibition of Monet and Picasso. The exhibition gallery was very ornate with chandeliers and sculptured ceilings but the paintings exhibited were not of the same caliber as in London or Paris. Eighty percent of the works were by artists I'd never heard of. There were only six Picasso's, five were from his cubist years. There was only one

Monet despite the fact that red and gold banners hanging all over Nice advertised the exhibition as "*Monet and Picasso*".

I left the museum and took a bus to a park overlooking Nice. Along pathways lined with tropical ferns, I washed my hands at a marble fountain. The cool water reminded me of Rachel's funeral. We had come back to the house after her cremation; the vision of the white flames and the sound of the furnace still vivid in my mind. A bowl of water and towels for the mourners had been placed on the porch steps. I sprinkled water on my hands and rubbed them together in a ceremonial washing. Ron's brother, William walked by the bowl and up the porch steps to go into the house.

"Wait, Bill," I called to him. "Wash before you enter the house."

Bill came back down the porch steps and washed his hands. He began to cry and walked away so I wouldn't see his face, then turned and said, "All we have is the moment."

"Yes," I nodded.

Back in Nice, it began to rain. I crossed the road seeking shelter under a covered patio of an outdoor restaurant. The restaurant was closed so I wiped away leaves from a chair and looked out from under the patio's canvas roof. Dark rain clouds swept across the sky and collided into the mountains above Nice. I heard a church bell ringing. I took a deep breath, pulling in the aroma of the decaying leaves.

Several couples came in out of the rain, two young women dressed in jeans and black raincoats, ate green apples and looked out at the panorama. A middle-aged woman wearing a designer quality dress, sat with a middle-aged man, writing postcards while another young couple sat at an adjoining table. The young woman was quite beautiful. Her tight-fitting jeans and a white T-shirt showed off a fine, supple body. Her brown, straight hair flowed sensually down to her waist. She took a book from her purse to read and the young man played with his expensive camera. I ached inside. I wanted to meet her.

The rain tapped out a rhythm on the canvas roof above our heads. Suddenly a loud peel of thunder exploded in the air, pigeons flew up against the wind and leaves fluttered down from the trees. Another flash of lightning left an electric, ionized odor in the atmosphere. The wind picked up, driving the rain under the canvas protection and onto the slate floor of the restaurant's patio. I sketched my hand and the young woman turned and glanced at me. I looked into her eyes but she looked quickly away.

It rained harder and she and the young man got up and moved closer to the restaurant and sat together, holding each other against the cold, wet wind. I moved away from the driving rain as well. As I walked by the two girls in black raincoats, I asked them, "Do you speak English?"

"Yes," one answered with a British accent. Her blond hair was chopped short. She wore purple lipstick, garishly loud against her pale, white skin. The other young woman wore her short black hair stiff with hair spray.

"Do you know if I can walk back to the hotel district this way, or do I have to go down to the right?" I pointed to the road.

"I'm not sure actually." The blond girl responded. The other young woman took a map from her purse and I sat down at their table.

"You have a map, great." I smiled at the brunette but she flipped the map on the table with a bad vibe. As I opened it the blond said, "We came up on the number 18 bus. It goes right to the train station."

I closed the map and tossed it back on the table. "That's all I needed to know, thanks." I went to leave but the blond asked, "Did you walk up here?"

"No, I took a bus but I didn't think to note what number it was. I was thinking about the paintings at the Monet-Picasso exhibit. Did you see it?"

"Yes, this morning."

"I thought it was quite poor actually, just the one Monet."

The brunette interrupted, "Well the Picasso's alone were worth it."

"Hmm... No, I don't know think so. The Tate gallery had much better Picassos, hundreds and hundreds of his works."

"Well, *The Pipe, Bike and Violin* is his best painting ever."

"His best painting ever?" I looked her in the eye. "That's rather subjective. Don't you think?"

"It's his best painting, that's a generally accepted fact," she insisted.

"I like his other works more," I said.

"It's his best cubist work," she said.

"Best cubist work? Really? Well okay, possibly, but his cubist works are almost hysterical at times. Wouldn't you agree?"

We sat in silence after that remark and finally I said, "Well, thank you for your help. Enjoy."

I went back to my table and looked out at the boring rain on what had become a boring day. I wanted to get back to the hotel but I would get soaked standing in my T-shirt and shorts at the bus stop. I waited, sketching the young lovers with their backs to me but then I saw a bus coming up the hill. I grabbed my things and ran out into the rain, reaching the bus stop in time to get on as the driver opened the doors.

I rode back to town but got soaked anyway walking the last four blocks from the bus station to the hotel. When I finally got back to my room, I changed out of my wet clothes and went to bed.

It poured all night except for an hour which I used to go out for dinner. When I returned I called Dominique in Rome. Our conversation was a mixture of Spanish, Italian and English. Where there had been tension and raw energy in our voices on the first call, now I heard peace in her tone and I felt relaxed speaking to her.

I slept on and off until seven-thirty the next morning, had an early breakfast of cappuccino, sweet roll and a large glass of pear juice then wandered through Nice. I preferred the side streets, admiring the homes with courtyards holding ancient marble statues. Many shops and homes had beautifully carved front doors.

On the corner of one street, I heard flute and violin music playing from inside a small church. I crossed the street and went inside. Going in through beautiful bronze doors, I looked up to the vaulted ceilings. At the front of the church, under a dome ceiling the brown marble altar was surrounded by four brown and white marble columns. It was the most beautiful little church I'd ever seen.

I lit candles for my grandmother, father and Rachel then spent some time walking around the church. I admired the detail of construction and the artwork in the side altar rooms.

Leaving the church, I found a good restaurant across the street. I walked through its tall, iron gates and pass the outdoor tables and went inside. Feathered Guinea hens hung from wooden ceiling beams. I ordered Lasagna and a bottle of local wine.

The white jacketed waiter poured the wine into my crystal glass and the ruby red color somehow reminded me of Mary. This was her kind of place; she'd love it here.

I closed my eyes but instead of seeing Mary's face, I saw the face of the statue Venus di Milo. I smiled and toasted her. A toast to you, Venus mi amour.

Chapter Nine
Florence

Sunshine streamed through the old yellowed, wooden blinds in my funky pension room in Nice. Shafts of white light squeezed through the blinds and hit the floor and bed covers. A fine day to travel but first breakfast. I rose and went to the corner for coffee and an apple croissant then brought my breakfast across the street and sat in a park. Women walked their dogs in the cool morning air. Their Poodles strutted on the park's sidewalks, proud to be French on such a fine day. I went back to the hotel and packed then took a cab to the train station. When the train arrived I pulled my trunk down the narrow hallway until I found my compartment. There were six seats inside, three facing three. I put the trunk under a seat then sorted through my tapes. A young man with short, wavy blond hair and steel rimmed glasses came into the car.

"Nice to meet you," I leaned forward in my seat and shook his hand. "I'm Paul Gebhart.

"Hi," he said. "I'm Peter."

"Your accent, Canadian?"

"Yes, Ontario but I live in Connecticut."

Another young man came to the open doorway as Peter put his large backpack under the seat opposite mine.

"Libra?" the young man pointed to the seat next to me.

"No, Pisces." I said, then smiled. "Yes, yes it's free."

"You're American?" He said in fluent English.

"I didn't mean to be sarcastic and yes, you're right, I'm an American but you won't hold it against an entire nation."

"Possibly," he smiled. "My name is Jean Pierre." He put his backpack under the third seat. He had straight black hair, brown eyes and a very handsome face including a classic square chin with dimple.

"I'm, Paul Gebhart," I said and reached out to shake his hand after he was seated.

"And I'm Peter," Peter reached over and shook his hand.

"Ah, Peter and Paul," Jean said. "What a pleasure to meet you both at last."

"I hadn't thought, yes I suppose we are a holy pair," Peter said.

"Where are you from, Jean Pierre?" I asked.

"Bordeaux, and you?"

"California, Los ...."

"Ontario," Peter interrupted me, "but I'm living in Connecticut."

"Touring Europe then, for how long?"

"Just a week's vacation to visit friends in Italy."

"I see, and you, Paul?"

"I'm in Europe, perhaps for a few months."

"That's quite a while."

"Yes, well I quit my job and am taking some time for myself."

"I see. It' quite warm in here. You will please excuse me. I need some air." Jean Pierre went into the hall and stood by an open window.

The train pulled out of Nice a half hour late, then stopped at every station along the French coast on its way to the Italian frontier. At one small station an hour later, I went into the hallway and looked out the window, down the rugged hillside to the shoreline several hundred feet below. Strong winds churned up white-capped waves in the green Mediterranean.

Back in the car, I asked Jean Pierre a question. "If Paris is Paree, Rome is Roma and Florence is Firenze, why don't American maps have the correct spelling and pronunciation of the European cities?"

"Where you purchase the map, that will determine which language is being used," Peter explained.

"Okay, fine I understand that but the question is why are the names different? Paris should be Paree, pronounced Par-ree with no s at the end. That's how the French spell it. Rome should be Roma, with an a at the end. That's how the Italians spell it."

Peter began to answer but then turned away and rolled his eyes.

"It's a good question and I don't know the answer," Jean Pierre laughed.

"No, apparently no one does," I sighed.

After the train crossed the frontier into Italy, it stopped at a small station between Genoa and Florence. The railroad yard was next to a school. It was two o'clock in the afternoon and I could hear children playing on the other side of the school's stone wall. Their shouts echoed off the concrete and wafted through the train's open windows. The engine had shut down so that the children's' joyous voices hung in the air. I went into the hallway and leaned out the window. It was hot and humid and I day-dreamed of grammar school. We played softball on days like this and our voices sang out with shrieks of joy. Our calls echoed just this same way; our excitement and laughter sounded exactly as from these boys and girls now.

I remembered looking up from the game one day and seeing adults stopping on their way home to watch us play. They looked bored and sad. I told my friends, "I'm never growing up. I don't want to look like that. Life is fun. Why can't they see it and be happy? I'm staying young, forever. I don't want to be old."

Now I'm in my thirties and I know my face carries the wounds of hurt from my experiences. When I look in the mirror these days, I see sadness in my eyes. My smile is gone. I've learned you grow old whether you want to or not. We change in response to our experiences. For me, the death of my best friend, Gene O'Connell killed in Vietnam and my grandmother dying from diabetes after having had one leg amputated, my father dying when he was only fifty-two years old. And Rachel's death, brutally beaten, raped and strangled. All my life experiences have left their marks on me.

I was the only one I had now. Right or wrong, I was going to sell my car and stay in Europe and paint. I may never sell one or even paint one worthy of notice, but I was going to paint and if it meant not working and not sending child support, well too bad. Maybe Mary and the children will realize that they needed me in their lives. Maybe they shouldn't take my support for granted. Maybe they would show me some kindness and attention. The train started again and pulled slowly out of the station.

We arrived in Florence at five o'clock and I went into the hallway and looked out the window as we rolled through the neighborhoods. The train's wheels, clack-clacked as the light from the setting sun reflected a warm golden-orange against the buildings and trees. Dust particles hung in the air like a luminous cloud between the buildings. The homes and apartments were painted in soft yellows and cream colors; contrasting beautifully with their red tiled roofs. I could see lush vegetation growing in gardens behind long stone walls. The train passed a large mansion with a backyard filled with palm trees.

"I had no idea Florence was so tropical. I just saw a banana tree," I said to Jean Pierre.

Peter overheard the remark as he was coming to join us in the hallway, "Florence is on the same latitude with New York City."

"How could that be?" I asked. "I don't have a map to show you, but you're wrong, Peter," I said. "New York is equal to Amsterdam or Paris but not Florence."

"No, no it is you who is wrong, *again*. They're on the same latitude."

"No way, New York isn't tropical like this at the end of September."

"I wish we had a map."

"So do I," Peter said with an attitude.

"Well here we are," Jean Pierre said trying to break up the bad vibes.

The train pulled into the old station downtown and I wheeled my trunk outside where I stood for a moment and watched the hordes of young tourists crowding the narrow streets. It seemed everyone was bent on finding a room for the night at one of the cheap pensions nearby. I went into the first hotel. They were booked up but the young clerk said I could leave my trunk behind his desk while I looked for a room elsewhere. I thanked him and taking my backpack I went outside to the corner. I saw Jean Pierre and Peter with their backpacks on. Peter had a street map of Florence open in one hand.

"We've just come from two pensions, no luck," Peter said.

"Me neither," I said.

"Let's try here," Jean Pierre pointed up a side street. We walked through throngs of tourists and went inside an old, rundown building. The lobby was dark. An old red sofa and chair sat in the small lobby in front of windows half blackened with soot. The man at the desk read a newspaper but looked up to as we entered.

"Yes, we have rooms," he said in Italian. Jean Pierre interpreted for us. "You can share, four in a room."

"How much?" I asked.

"Six dollars each," the desk man said.

"I don't think we have a choice," I said.

"And for once I think you're right," Peter mocked.

"It's number 710 on the 7th floor," the old man said as we each paid him.

"Where's the elevator?" I asked, looking around the lobby.

"No, no elevator," he wagged his index finger then pointed to the stairwell.

Jean Pierre raised his eyebrow as he interpreted.

"No elevator? Great, fine, stairs," I said, "I need the exercise."

I went back to the first pension for my trunk then lugged it through the crowded sidewalks. Jean Pierre had waited for me in the lobby and he helped me carry it up the seven flights of stairs.

"This rug smells a couple of hundred years old," I said as we went up the first landing. He sneezed from the dusty stairwell.

"Two more fucking flights," I gasped, having to stop on the 5th floor landing to sit down.

"Just two more," Jean Pierre said reaching for the trunk after a minute's rest.

"Yeah, two more," I groaned as I lifted the other end and we started up the stairs again.

Room 710 had four beds and four dressers stuffed into a small, dormitory style room. I went to the communal bathroom where I waited for the water to run hot. To my dismay it never became warmer than room temperature and I had to take a cold shower.

"We're going to dinner," Jean Pierre said when I came back into the room.

"Thanks, not me. I'm going to look for a better hotel. Do you think our things will be safe here?"

"Did you lock your trunk?" Jean Pierre asked.

"Yes."

"Then no problem, we'll lock up the room."

We split up and I walked on the side streets until I saw the Atlantico Hotel. I went in and spoke in bad French to the clerk. He answered me in pigeon English. A single room was $20 a night he told me and, yes, they had an elevator and hot water. I decided I would stay the first night at the old pension then tomorrow move to the Atlantico.

I found a restaurant on the same quiet street and ate dinner alone; a consume soup with bread, spaghetti and red wine, all for three dollars. It was a nice meal but it didn't help my depression. I couldn't get my young son, Noah out of my mind. I felt bad inside. I was going to miss so many days, so many little experiences that make up a father and son's relationship. How do you get over that loss? I felt like shit and ate and smoked continuously and though my stomach was full, I felt only emptiness inside.

It was a warm, humid night as I walked back to the pension. A light drizzle cleaned the air of the car fumes. I stopped and sat on the marble steps of the Il Doumo. Florence was the dirtiest city I had been to since Newark. The ancient statues were coated with a black soot. The streets crowded with lonely old men sitting on steps watching the hundreds of beautiful American and European girls go by. It must be worse in summertime; hot, muggy and filled to the point of madness.

I climbed the seven floors of stairs in the old pension and got into bed but not ten minutes later fleas began biting me. I scratched and tossed all night and then finally falling asleep, I was woken when Peter came in and turned on the lights. I didn't fall into a heavy sleep until five-thirty, only to be jolted awake at seven when the hotel operator began to argue with someone in the hallway. The old man's loud voice woke us all up.

"This has been the worst night I've had in Europe," I said. "I'm getting out of here." It was only seven-thirty but I dressed and carried my trunk and bag down the stairs and to the Hotel Atlantico. They let me check in early and I wheeled my trunk down the lobby's carpeted hallway to their solitary, black, wrought iron elevator. It was from the beginning of the century; the kind you see in movies. I could see through the wrought iron grill of the car as it lifted me up. I was looking down into the lobby when the car shook to a sudden stop, stuck between the second and third floors.

"Is okay, no worry, no worry, we fix." The young desk clerk called up to me.

"Okay, sure. I'll just wait here until you do," I yelled back.

The maintenance man played with the fuses in the fuse box on the ground floor and the elevator kicked back in. If the ride up to my room made me think twice about my choice of hotels; it was dispelled when I opened the door on the 5th floor. The room had high ceilings, a wooden dresser and a four-poster bed. It was spacious with double doors leading out onto a balcony. My room overlooked rows of Renaissance buildings and had a lovely view of the church six blocks away. On the distant green hills beyond the city, country villas dotted the landscape.

I showered in the communal bathroom and washed away the scuzzy feeling of fleas and the mental thickness I was feeling from lack of sleep. Revived from the shower and pleased with my new accommodations, I dressed in shorts and a collarless, white shirt and went downstairs and purchased a map from the hotel front desk. I was on my way to find Michelangelo's David.

The gallery was easy to locate and I stopped across the street to have coffee and a pastry for breakfast. Feeling revived with the small breakfast, I walked across the street and paid to enter into the large, vaulted, central room where the statue stood alone. I took out my journal and began to take notes of my impression and feelings of this wonderful work of art. It was quiet and uncrowded, peaceful in the gallery. I walked around David, deliberately stopping at different angles for several minutes. The perfection of Michelangelo's sculpting somehow filled me with both pleasure and a peaceful feeling. My life was somehow more complete for having experienced this masterpiece.

In an ante room there were several other sculptures. These later works by Michelangelo he chose to not finish with the same, perfect smoothness as he did his famous, David or The Pieta. His contemporaries thought he had gone mad, but Michelangelo was free from their opinions. Actually, walking around them and imagining myself working with chisel and hammer, I liked them as much as David. These sculptures in his later style show more of man's struggle, more tension then any of the 'finished' pieces."

I left the gallery and walked to Giardino Dei Semplici, The Gardens of Peace but found the gates to the garden locked. An old man approached on the sidewalk. He had a full head of silver-gray hair which grew down to his shoulders. He had a handsome face with a thin, gray mustache and very brown, smooth tanned skin. His eyes were a unique shade of light blue. Using a cane to steady himself, he slowly walked up to me. His brown tattered suit somehow went well with his wrinkled blue shirt, coconut tanned face and silver hair.

The old man took a 100-lira coin from his pocket. I held out my hand and said, "Okay, grazie".

The old man closed his hand around the coin and shook his head, no. He began to explain in Italian that it was he who wanted a coin from me. I laughed and the old man saw the joke and smiled. His eyes had a peacefulness that I admired.

"How can I get into the garden?" I asked him in pidgin Italian. I pointed and indicated with gestures that I wanted to get past the high, black iron fence. The old man shrugged; he didn't know how. He held out the coin again and I nodded yes and took the only coin I had, a 100-lira piece from my pocket and gave it to him.

"Grazie," the old man said.

I gently squeezed his wrist with affection as I handed him the coin and we both moved on, neither of us turning back, both of us smiling.

I walked to Il Duomo where I saw Jean Pierre sitting on the steps in front of the tall, magnificent bronze front doors. We sat together watching tourists going in and out of the church. I began to chant "OM" and Jean Pierre stared then laughed at me; a mocking snort. It began to drizzle but we remained seated on the steps until a loud thunder clap burst overhead and it began to pour. We ran across the street to the 13th century church known as Battistero. I was wearing rubber, flip-flop sandals and slipped on the slick sidewalks and wet marble steps. I almost fell but caught my balance before cracking my skull open. Sliding into the church; laughing at the excitement of the run through the rain, my laughter quickly turned to silent admiration of the golden frescos painted on the masonry walls of this 16th century church. The dome extended several hundred feet above our heads. The church was illuminated without any electric lights; only the light filtering through the round window in the center of the dome above and through small, colored glass windows over the golden frescoes. This filtered sunlight light and the light from hundreds of candles lit the entire building.

There were dozens of people inside the church waiting out the storm. Their quiet conversations echoed through the large chapel. In one corner I noticed a pattern laid into the white mosaic floor. Alternating tiles of brown and white marble formed circles within circles. I counted nine circles out from the center to the edge. I stood in the center of the design and as I moved my head, the mosaic pattern began to rotate and spin beneath my feet. Some mosaic circles turned to the left, other circles to the right. I took out my journal and knelt down to copy the pattern.

"What are you doing, Paul?" Jean Pierre asked.

"Stand there in the center of the circles." I pointed to the center of the concentric pattern. "Stand there," I pointed again but Jean Pierre didn't move. People were looking at us. I felt their gaze too but ignored them and went back to counting the circles and copying it all down. Jean Pierre stepped into the center of the mosaic pattern.

"That's something, huh? It whirls around like a carnival ride. Doesn't it?"

Jean Pierre didn't answer.

"Pretty psychedelic for the 13th century, don't you think?"

He still didn't answer.

I shook my head; I could see that Jean Pierre thought me equally mad about the floor spinning as he had about me chanting OM.

I went to leave the church and felt a flush came over my face and felt a flash of deja-vu. I realized that I was meant to be delayed here until I noticed and sketched this magical, mosaic floor.

I left Jean Pierre at the church and took a bus that wound its way up the hills overlooking Florence. I got off at a park in the foothills. A twenty-foot bronze replica of David was placed center stage in the gardens. I walked along sidewalks lined with ferns looking down at the valley below where orange tiled roofs and Renaissance buildings sprawled across the landscape as the Arno River wound like a serpent across the countryside.

I sat down on a bench alone and of course began thinking of Mary and the kids.

Chapter Ten
Rome

I woke early, paid my hotel bill at the Atlantico and pulling my trunk, went across the street for breakfast. After coffee and a pastry, I ordered a bottle of a local Tuscany red and sat for an hour watching the spectacle of tourists coming and going along the street. I left the restaurant a little too high on the vino and walked for quite a while before it occurred to me that I didn't know where I was. I looked around. I had never seen this part of Florence. It was too clean to be near the train station. I looked at my map and was shocked to see that I had wandered miles out of my way. It was nine-forty, my train for Rome left at eleven. If I missed that train, I'd have to return to the hotel and try again the next day. I hurried back towards the station half blind. The alcohol had narrowed my field of vision and I could only see my feet and the sidewalk. Even so, I reached the station with time to purchase my ticket and find the correct platform to Rome.

The train was forty-five minutes late. One hundred people got off and five hundred got on. I lugged my trunk and bag up the steps and into the closest car. Inside there were rows of seats down both sides of the car separated by a narrow aisle down the middle. I couldn't find an empty seat and people crammed the aisle. I squeezed my way through the car with my trunk and bag. "Excuse moi. Excuse me, si vous plais." I apologized all the way down the crowded aisle for the annoyance I was causing. It took me a while but I inched my way to the door at the far end of the car and went outside and stood in the space between the two cars. When I closed the door, I saw the only English sign I'd seen in all of France or Italy. It read; "It is forbidden to stand in the gangway."

I left my trunk and bag in the gangway and squeezed into the aisle of the next car. I made a space for myself, to everyone's further annoyance and stood swaying as the train rocked and clattered down the tracks.

We made a stop at every station along the route. After several stations, when people got off and before a new crowd could make their way on, I found an empty seat and placed my bag and camera on it to save it, and went into the hallway to mind my trunk until the train had once again departed. When I returned to my seat, I looked out the window to the Italian landscape. It was humid inside the train. The seats were sticky. I checked the train schedule and realized that we didn't arrive into Rome for another six hours. Not sure how I was going to bear it, I stared out the window and my mind drifted to Mary.

I could imagine her parked along West Cliff Drive. She would be sitting alone in her car watching the breakers pound into the cliffs; sending surf spraying twenty feet into the air then sliding off as white foam from the wet boulders. Monterey Bay would be wind tossed, choppy black with white capped waves and she would be thinking about her appointment that morning with the District Attorney. The postcard I mailed the children from London would be in her lap and in her mind, she would be telling me:

You haven't made a child support payment since you left Santa Cruz in June. I would have lost the house except that my parents loaned me the money to pay the mortgage payments. You know both my parents are in their sixties and it is their retirement savings they're loaning me. I didn't want to take it from them, but you forced me to. I am so pissed-off at you, Paul. God, I hate you! My friends tell me I should try talking to you but I can't. I won't! I don't have to ask you for support. The divorce decree ordered you to pay me five hundred dollars a month, not enough, not nearly half of what it takes to keep the kids in their home, but you were ordered to pay it. I shouldn't have to negotiate with you any further. It isn't my fault that the children don't want to see you or talk to you. That's your problem, not mine.

I had to turn the case over to the Family Support Unit today. They'll catch you, Paul and attach your wages, you'll see. But when? They can't do anything until you get back from

Europe and get a job. When are you coming back? I hate you. I hate you more than I can even express.

As this played out in my mind, the train stopped again, this time in a larger city and hundreds more Italians boarded. A plump Italian woman and her 8-year old son came into the car. As it happened, two seats next to me were vacant and she and the boy put their bags down. The woman struggled to lift her suitcase onto the luggage rack, I got up and helped her put her things overhead.

"Grazie," she thanked me then motioned for me to be seated. She took cheese and salami from her large cloth sack and passed them to me with a knife.

"Mange, mange," she said taking out a bottle of homemade wine and passing me that too. Her son brought paper cups from another bag and he poured wine for everyone. I turned on my tape player and played Marvin Gay and Aretha. The thumping bass lines livened up the car.

We had changed conductors at the last stop and a new Italian conductor, an Al Pacino look-alike wearing a pucca bead necklace came in to punch our tickets. He bounced to the rhythm of the music and the old woman poured him a glass of wine too.

The train arrived in Rome at six-thirty. As we rolled slowly through the neighborhoods, the light from the setting sun glowed orange against the walls of the buildings. It was beautiful; I didn't realize that Rome was so tropical. The train emptied and enjoying the warm breeze, I wheeled my trunk along the platform and into the station. I found the bar where I was to meet Sergio. It was closed, lights out but I waited by the front door and in a few minutes a man approached. Sergio was of medium height, skinny, with shoulder length brown hair and a long, bushy mustache. He wore jeans and a blue checkered shirt.

"Sergio?" I asked as he walked up to me.

"Si".

"So good to meet you." We shook hands.

Sergio explained in Italian that he didn't live in Rome but in a suburb some thirty kilometers away. He didn't have a car so we would have to take a bus. He also thought that we would have big communications problems because he, Sergio, didn't speak a word of English.

"No?" I asked.

Sergio held up his thumb and index finger in a zero.

"For me, no problem." I pointed to Sergio, "For you?"

"No, no problem."

"Okay?" I asked again, sensing that Sergio was having second thoughts about my visit.

"Okay," Sergio said.

I'm pretty certain he was thinking that Dominique was looking forward to the visit by the American. He didn't want me to stay in their apartment but he didn't want problems with her either.

We walked to the bus stop and got on an old, green commuter bus. Lugging my trunk to the back down the narrow aisle, we sat together as the bus rattled through Rome. I didn't have the energy to try to speak broken Italian. I looked out at the streets lit up in evening lights. The ancient city was awash with people and traffic. The bus drove by beautiful fountains and ancient columns before leaving the dramatic lights of Rome and going down a dark two-lane highway lined with tall trees. Forty minutes later the bus stopped in a parking lot outside the town of Mentana. Sergio motioned that this was our stop and we hauled my luggage off the bus and loaded it into his white, four door Fiat.

Mentana has a high stone wall around it from medieval times and cobblestone streets too narrow for all but the smallest of cars. We rode past the central market, then left the little village through the southern gates. Sergio parked on a rural, quiet street behind a group of isolated apartment buildings. His apartment was part of a six-plex with a common garden in the back. A wooden fence protected grape vines, old olive trees and patches of lettuce and vegetables. Dominique called to us and waved hello from their third-floor balcony. Sergio helped me to carry the trunk up three flights of stairs and Dominique met us at the door. She kissed Sergio, then me on both cheeks. She had long, auburn hair, hazel eyes and beautiful lips. Her smile was warm and genuine.

"I feel like I'm in an Italian movie," I said as we toured their two-bedroom apartment. "Your place is classic; Italian funk with marble floors and French doors leading out to balconies from every room. Just great."

Sergio and Dominique looked at me, not having understood my rapid English.

"Nice, very nice." I indicated their apartment with my hands and they both smiled. The apartment's large kitchen had old wooden cabinets, light cream-colored marble floors and gray counter tops.

Sergio prepared spaghetti with tomato sauce, fried pork chops, green salad and toasted garlic bread. Dominique and I sat at the table drinking a red wine that Sergio had made last year. We talked as he cooked, each of us taking turns looking up words in the Italian-English dictionary. I told them about my travels in London, Amsterdam, Paris and Nice. My stories reminded them of their own travels and museum tours.

As we ate dinner, an old Sophia Loren movie, "Judith" played on the black and white television set. Outside, looking through the open French doors, I could see the lights from the village.

For desert Dominique brought out cherry and apple pies. We drank coffee and talked more about our lives and our families. The communication was slow but we understood each other surprising well. Dominique was French but also spoke Italian and Spanish. Sergio was from Napoli and spoke only Italian. I was from Newark and spoke English with a New Jersey accent. Our saving grace was the fact that Dominique and I each spoke a little Spanish.

We sat at the dining room table drinking wine and smoking cigarettes. Dominique explained that right before I called them from Nice, she had just hung up the telephone with Anne in Paris. Anne had called to see if I had been in contact with them.

"Quite a coincidence, no?"

"Si," I said. "Anne is very intuitive."

"She really is," Dominique nodded. "It isn't the first time she's called me at exactly the right moment."

Tired from the wine and the task of finding words in a dictionary, we went to bed at eleven. I unpacked my trunk into the top three drawers of an armoire in the spare bedroom. I slept well and woke refreshed. The Saturday morning Roman sun shined through the slats of the shutters on the balcony doors. Nearby, geese honked and dogs barked. The sounds echoed between the apartment houses. I went out onto the balcony where Sergio's wooden easel was set up. I looked out, surveying the neighborhood. There were four, six-unit apartment houses but they were well spread out with a field or garden or orchard between each building. Past the apartment houses lay hill country with old farmhouses. Their red tiled roofs glistened in the morning sunshine.

Sergio and Dominique were up and I joined them in the kitchen for expresso, bread and homemade marmalade. Sergio was on his way to his studio in Monte-Rotondo, another medieval walled town near Mentana.

I used my Italian-English dictionary to write them a note, "I want to buy the groceries."

Sergio hesitated, then passed Dominique the note.

"Bien, bien," she said but Sergio wouldn't take my 10,000-lira bill.

"Later," he held up his hand, refusing the money.

Dominique wrote their address and telephone number in Italian then had me practice in Italian, "The second stop in Mentana, please."

"Seconda fermata in Mentana per favore." I diligently repeated.

"Very good, molto biene, Paul," Dominique laughed and patted me on the shoulder.

I drove with Sergio to the bus station where he waited with me until the bus to Rome pulled in. He motioned to the bus, we shook hands and I took my pack back and went aboard. It was an old, old bus and I sat in a window seat as it slowly, loudly, pulled out onto the highway. I closed my eyes, and as the trees and telephone poles sped across the path of the sunlight, I saw flashing lights in my mind; red then white then red. Flash, flash, flash, each time going deeper and deeper inside my consciousness. I followed the experience back into my mind. How was I seeing these inner lights? Where was the source of my consciousness? More inner lights as they turned red then purple then brilliant white. Watching them brought a smile to my face. I received no answers to my questions but the experience put me deeper into myself. When I opened my eyes, I was looking out onto the world from deep inside my skull.

The bus drove through Rome passing classical monuments; the Tomb of the Unknown Soldier then past The Arco di Contantino; an arch to commemorate Constantine's victory over Maxentitius in 315 A.D. The Chiesa di S. Pietro in Vincoli is a monument erected to preserve St. Peter's chains. Michelangelo sculpted the famous statue of Moses outside the tomb. Then past the Trevi Fountain which dates from 1453. It has a large sculpture of a chariot pulled by Seahorses. Later, to the right, Palazzo Farnese, the most beautiful 16th century palace in Rome; begun in 1514 and one in which Michelangelo was employed to paint frescos on the walls.

The bus drove by The Spanish Steps, then past the panoramic square with the Sallustan Obelisk. This is one of Rome's most picturesque settings. Then by Pincio, a terrace overlooking Piazza del Popolo with the dome of St. Peter's in the background. Then past Marcello, the impressive remains of a Roman amphitheater dedicated by Augustus in the 1st century B.C.

The bus stopped at the Vatican and I got out and walked up the long marble steps. Inside I took the tour of the Sistine Chapel. In the Chapel of the Virgin Mary, one fresco depicted a woman chopping the head off a man. Another panel showed a woman driving an iron spike into the head of another man. The symbolism was not lost on me. Overlooking all of these grisly scenes was the Virgin Mary and next to her, Christ. He is pointing to her, indicating that we should look at her sitting in tranquility next to God.

In the Egyptian museum I puzzled over why they had mummies in the Vatican? It didn't feel very Christian. One mummy still had skin, fingernails and eyelids. While I was writing in my journal, a dozen German tourists wearing black coats and bow ties suddenly came through the museum. Like Gestapo storm troopers, bumping and shoving people out of their way they walked among the ghastly exhibition.

After seeing the wonderful *Pieta* statue by Michelangelo and touring the main altar room, I left the Vatican and took the number 64 bus to Plaza Venecia and walked from there through the Roman ruins towards the coliseum. As I walked down the ancient roadbed and through the Roman Forum I wandered among the fallen columns and statues. I got the strong feeling that I had been there before and I understood why they called Rome the eternal city. These solid marble buildings, ancient roads and monuments have been seen by millions of souls over thousands of years. This city of stone is the eternal and we humans only temporary flesh passing through. On our way to what?

I walked past the ruins of an ancient Roman apartment house. I climbed unnoticed up a small embankment and went into one of the apartments. Inside the cave entrance, I walked down the dark passageway towards the rooms in the rear. As I went further in, I felt nervous; on-the-look-out for snakes and bugs but there were none. The walls were damp and the air musty. The dim light from the sunshine outside illuminated the inside of the rooms. I could feel the spirits of people who had once lived there, a boy of sixteen and his mother, in her forties. The city outside was bathed in bright sunshine. Two thousand years ago residents of this apartment house came out and saw the pillars ablaze in sunlight just as they were today.

I found a small shard of clay jar on the ground at the entrance to the apartment and put it in my pocket then came out of the apartments and walked towards the Coliseum. The sun light struck the Coliseum bathing it in an orange hue. I could hear the roar of the crowd and someone saying to me, "Prepare yourself. Today you die."

It was the same sunlight, the same moment now as then. Only time had crumbled the buildings.

After touring the Coliseum, I walked to the bus stop and waited for the bus to Mentana. I found a window seat and looked out as we made our way out of Rome and into the countryside. The sunlight painted the trees yellow in the orchards. It was Saturday afternoon when I arrived back in Mentana. As I walked through town, I passed old men sitting outside the restaurants drinking wine, talking and playing cards and dominos. Women carried their cloth shopping bags over their shoulders and young girls walked arm in arm while teenage boys rode Vespa motor scooters and shouted out to everyone but especially to the girls.

I recognized Sergio at a stall in the market. I waved and Sergio nodded hello. We shopped together and despite Sergio's protest, I paid for the groceries. On our way home, I explained as best I could what I had seen in Rome. We carried the packages upstairs as Dominique's piano playing floated through the hallway. The slow, minor chords of a nocturne she was playing were poetry in tempo to the setting sun. The village lights flickered in a blue lilac evening.

I showered and changed, wrote a postcard to Ava and Noah then sat on the balcony and listened to the piano. Children played in the courtyard below. The sounds of Sergio's footsteps on the marble floors echoed in the kitchen. I was at peace. I could feel myself as one of the children downstairs. And what it was like to be Sergio cooking supper in the kitchen.

Dominique stopped playing. She and Sergio were preparing potatoes and eggs as I came into the kitchen.

"Is there something I can do?" I asked.

"No, it's okay, sit," Dominique smiled over her shoulder from the sink.

We ate and drank wine until all three of us needed a break from the strain of the language barrier. It didn't help matters that Sergio was fighting with Dominique. They seemed to be fighting more and more each hour of my stay. I couldn't tell what it was about. Sergio kept correcting Dominique, interrupting her and making rude gestures with his hand. I had spent time with both of them alone, Dominique laughed easily, Sergio only occasionally. I knew the scene. I'd lived through it and seen it in a hundred homes. It was the same story, the sex gets boring, the job kills, there are things to buy and not enough money.

The next morning was Sunday and Sergio dressed and went off to his studio in Mentana while Dominique and I sat drinking coffee on the balcony.

"You paint too?" she asked, pointing to Sergio's easel.

"Yes, I try."

"You can paint here."

"No. Thank you but I don't feel it."

"Do you play the piano?"

"No, not really. I play the sax, a little."

"Ah, the saxophone, I want to learn it."

"It's easier than the piano."

"Can you teach me to play the blues?" she asked.

"The blues? Well, I know the chord progressions."

"Show me, please," Dominique's eyes studied my face. She smiled and placed her hand on my arm.

We went into the living room and sat together on the piano bench. I showed her that the blues chords were very simple.

"Let's play in A minor. The twelve bars blues would be; A minor for four bars." I hammered out a back-beat rhythm counting to four in each bar. "Then it moves to the fourth, or D major for two measures." I played the same rhythm in the higher chord. "Then back to A minor for two...then up to the fifth for one measure, that's E in this case, then down to the fourth again, remember that is D for one bar, and home again to the A minor for two. Then it starts all over again."

Even though I was obviously not a piano player, the pattern I played, and being in rhythm, excited her. "That's wonderful!" she laughed.

"You try it." I moved over to let her play. She wasn't wearing perfume but I could smell her feminine, fresh and lovely scent. She played very poorly but still at times it was real blues in that she enjoyed the sound enough to hold it and let it ring out.

"There is also an 8-bar blues for rock and roll but really the next thing for you to learn is the substitution of chords in the progression." I played the A minor pattern again for four bars but instead of going to the D major I hit a different chord.

"I substituted a B minor. Do you hear the difference? The feeling changes, yes?"

"Yes, yes this is wonderful. I must practice it."

I went out onto the balcony and sat in the sun listening to her as I wrote in my journal. Several times she called me in to show her more. I played right hand melodies as she played the left-hand chord changes. Sitting next to her, her side and leg touching mine, the look of love in her eyes, I had to stop.

"Let's go for a walk," I said, standing up before I kissed her.

She looked into my face for a moment then nodded, "Okay, I'll get my jacket."

We walked through town on cobblestone streets.

"Let's sit inside." Dominique gestured to me. She pointed to a small restaurant where old men were playing cards in the patio outside. The wood floors inside had a layer of sawdust. Dominique ordered lunch for us from a short man with gray beard and red checkered apron. It started to drizzle and the old men came in, glancing at Dominique as they found tables to resume their games. I wondered what stories would be going through the village. Dominique tapped her fingertips on the tabletop, wanting to tell me something, then thought better of it and sipped at her cappuccino instead.

The small restaurant was cozy with the soft rain dripping from the awning. The smell of fresh baked bread and pasta sauce floated through the air and became the atmosphere.

After a good lunch and glasses of local red wine, we left the restaurant. The rain had stopped and we walked down the wet sidewalks for several blocks. Dominique turned up an alleyway and knocked on the door of an old apartment building. A young woman answered the door.

"Hi, Silvia. This is, Paul," Dominique introduced us.

"Hello," Silvia said, kissing Dominique. I shook her hand but she leaned over and kissed me on both cheeks. She had bleached blond hair, a thin face with a small mouth and friendly brown eyes.

She led us down the hallway and into the kitchen. I noticed a trapeze hanging from the ceiling in a small bedroom off of the living room.

"How can you use a trapeze in so small a room?" I asked Silvia.

"Very carefully," she answered.

The kitchen floors were marble. A large, antique wooden table and chairs filled the center of the room. A brick fireplace was built into the corner wall opposite the sink. It was an old apartment house but it was obvious that someone had done a lot of work remodeling it. There were new doors, new glass in the windows, new shelves and cabinets.

We sat in the kitchen as the rain started again. It beat against the windows as I walked around the kitchen admiring the quality of the construction.

"This is quite well done," I said, Dominique interpreting for me.

"My husband, Franco did the work."

"It really is dramatic. I love the feeling."

"Thank you," Franco said as he came into the kitchen. We shook hands.

"Franco is an actor, not a carpenter," Dominique explained.

"Yes?" I said, "Of course. I can see a resemblance to Omar Shariff."

"Oof, thank you, thank you. You are too kind," Franco replied in English. "You may speak English with me. It's been awhile but I will understand what you say." He smiled and patted me on the shoulder in warm welcome. "Dominique tells me you are from California?"

"Yes."

"I've not been there but perhaps someday. And why have you come to Europe?" He paused to think of the right English words. "Are you on business?"

"No, I'm traveling for a few months," I said.

"A few months? I see, this must involve a woman."

"My wife... ex-wife, yes," I laughed.

They waited for an explanation, "I went through a divorce, quit my job and came to Europe," I smiled as I gave them the short version.

"Pain, in the stomach?" Franco asked.

"It feels like a knife sometimes," I agreed with the diagnosis.

"Of course, my friend. I understand. A love gone bad is exactly the same in any country. And you have children?"

"Yes, two," I said.

"I see," Franco nodded. "It is difficult. Love that's ended, very difficult. But it can lead to good too. It takes courage to start again and to travel alone. Good for you. I wish you well my friend."

"Thank you," I smiled. "And for you too. Do you really use the trapeze?"

"Ah, only when Silvia is in the mood," Franco laughed.

Dominique and Silvia talked over coffee while Franco and I smoked cigarettes and looked out the window to the wet buildings and the rain.

"Dominique tells me that you write," Silvia said in English.

"Yes, I keep a journal," I said.

"What do you write about?"

"My life."

"I see. And we are in it now?"

"Yes, of course."

"Then you must make it into a movie," Franco said.

"Yes, and you will star in it with Silvia," I said.

"And, Dominique," Silvia added.

"Yes, of course and Sergio," I said.

"And you too," Franco added.

"No, no," I shook my head. "I'll only make it if Woody Allen plays my part."

Franco interpreted and Dominique and Silvia laughed.

The rain let up. It drizzled outside as we said good bye.

"Ciao." Dominique kissed Silvia, then Franco. Silvia kissed me on both cheeks and gave me a hug. Franco and I shook hands.

Dominique borrowed an umbrella from them and I held it as we walked close together. Our arms touched as she leaned into me. We walked in silence, listening to the sound of the raindrops on the umbrella.

Sergio was at his work bench restoring an old painting when we came into his studio off the plaza in Mentana. He showed me another, older painting that was in very poor condition.

"We start by first cleaning the canvas with acetone," Sergio spoke in Italian but Dominique helped me to understand. "Then apply a new base to the parts of the canvas that have holes or where the paint has been removed. I'll repaint onto the new base the part of the picture that is missing, an eye, a hand, a portion of the sky, whatever. The special paints I use do not change color so that once I match the color of the original, it will always look the same."

"For the most part it isn't the oils that get destroyed but the base behind the oils. They become brittle and crack and chip off." Sergio kicked around the disorganized studio looking for ingredients on one of the shelves. He showed me how to make the base preparation using animal fat, bone, molasses and gesso. It was an involved procedure requiring several mixing and boiling steps with two pots, an inner one for the ingredients and a larger, outer pot for the water.

I wrote down Sergio's instructions wondering why he was bothering to show me. It didn't make sense; I would never use it but I continued to write it all down and this seemed to please Sergio. He went into minute, detailed instructions. My interest seemed to impress Sergio. He lowered the wall he kept around himself and his face relaxed. He smiled.

At home that evening we sat quietly at the dinner table. Sergio had prepared a light meal of spaghetti, red wine and bread. There was tension in the air between him and Dominique and rather than talk, we all decided to go to bed early. I was brushing my teeth when a lightning bolt loudly knocked the lights out. Thunder shook the building and it began to pour outside. Sergio came down the hallway with a candle.

"Here you'll need this," he said as he placed it on the dresser in my room.

"Thank you," I said.

"Please wake me at six forty-five," Sergio said. "My alarm will be useless but your battery clock will get us up."

"Yes, okay," I agreed. "Good night."

The beam from Sergio's flashlight bounced eerily off the walls and ceilings of the hallway as he went back to Dominique.

Lightning struck the hillside outside. It sounded like World War Two. Lightning hit the apartment building next door. I lay in bed, nerves rattled.

As the storm abated, I realized that I must leave Rome soon. I was only a day or two away from making a pass at Dominique. Neither of us had said anything, but I knew she knew. I also knew that she knew it would be good between us. There was an easiness that we both recognized as the beginning of a romance. This was part of the reason why she and Sergio were fighting and that was my second reason for wanting to leave. The arguments were making me tense. My right arm hurt me all day and tonight I felt the tension in my neck.

The quartz alarm buzzed me awake at six-forty. I put my pants on and walked down the hall to knock on their bedroom door. "Okay." I heard Sergio's muffled voice inside. I went back to my bedroom to shower and dress.

We had coffee and toast, then Sergio and I went downstairs and he pointed to his car. This morning Sergio decided he needed his car in town so he drove us into Rome. While sitting in the Monday morning traffic I asked him. "How did the Dutch masters get their paintings to look like photographs?"

"They used a glazing technique," Sergio answered in Italian.

Our communications were difficult. My Italian was less than rudimentary but we persevered and Sergio patiently explained that glazing consisted of painting first in tempera, then glazing over the canvas with varnish. When the varnish dried, painting over it with oils.

"This process is then repeated but the details of the procedures are complex. The tempera must be very light for the flesh tones. Then the oil applied latter, after the varnish dries it can be made darker and darker. And you must use the best kind of tempera not the synthetic brands but the pulverized mineral temperas into which brown eggs, varnish and a little water have been added."

"Do you know the system for painting frescoes?" Sergio asked as he turned onto the main highway leading to Rome.

"I don't plan to do any frescoes," I said. I didn't want to struggle through hearing the details in Italian. The early morning pink glow from the sun warmed the earth. In the distance a thin haze hung over Rome. Sergio battled the traffic. We drove by the ancient baths, Terme di Caracalla from the 1st century. Then traveled the Apia Antica lined with splendid monuments. I imagined trumpets heralding our approach as we passed the catacombs of St. Sebastian. Then past the crumbling but dramatic remains of Circus Maxentius.

Sergio parked outside a garage at the rear of the state building for the Bureau of Art and Antiqua. He unlocked the metal garage door, rolled it up and ran inside to turn off the silent alarm, then called to me that it was okay to come in."

The strong odor of varnish and paint filled the garage. It was one large room and dozens of old paintings were stacked all about, waiting to be restored. Sergio talked me through the different restoration stages by taking me from one painting under repair to another. All the paintings were large canvases. One was seven feet by fourteen feet. At one table, I noticed a row of hand irons.

"These will be heated over wood fires and used to re-melt the paint," Sergio explained. "This re-melting of the oil paint is to correct the splitting and peeling which has occurred. The final stages are the application of the colla and a gesso base to the missing parts of the canvas. Then, repainting the picture and finally re-varnishing to seal it."

Along one wall of the garage were several murals painted on stone. These had been removed from their original walls and attached to a synthetic backing of plaster.

Other workers were arriving now and a pot of coffee was put on. Sergio introduced me to the members of his group. It didn't seem that any of them spoke English and there didn't appear to be any boss about but today I learned, an official from the restoration department was in the studio. Sergio introduced me to her. She was a pleasant, middle-aged woman who spoke quietly to the group as I explored the shop. Sergio came back after the group meeting and showed me black and white photographs of the 14th century painting that he was working on. It was seven feet by twelve feet, a depiction of the Virgin Mary and Joseph taking the baby Jesus out of Israel. The photographs showed how the canvas had been displayed in an ancient church in Napoli for hundreds of years. During World War Two the church was bombed and the painting damaged. Officials removed it from its frame and rolled it up and hid it away in the church's basement. Last month Sergio drove there and brought it back to Rome. Now he was painting in the missing parts on the canvas. He mixed his paints very quickly on a white metal board. His eye perfectly matching the color of his paints to the original on the canvas. Next to us, a woman in her mid-twenties placed the hot colla mix into a green plastic netting and suspended the net across two small wooden horses for it to cool. Two other women were working on a large canvas. They spread it flat on the floor and held it in place with stone wedges. Everything was done by hand.

"Come," Sergio gestured for me to follow him to the shop's van. I helped him load three empty garbage cans into the back of the van. When I went to get in the passenger door, I noticed a used hypodermic needle lying in the gutter.

"Heroin?" I gestured to the needle.

"Si," Sergio nodded.

"It is easy to get?"

"Si, easy and cheap. There is a processing plant here in Rome and more in Marseilles, but it is death," Sergio talked with his hands, indicated death by drawing the edge of his palm across his throat.

We drove through Rome taking the Appian Way to the suburbs. Sergio pulled into a chemical plant and purchased solvents and acetone for the studio. After the garbage cans were filled and their lids securely fastened, we traveled back on the Appian Way passing the ancient Roman aqueducts and the ruins of large villas.

When we returned to the studio a heavy smell of animal fat hung in the air. One of the woman workers was applying heated colla to the large canvas on the floor. She applied the simmering colla with a brush. The fatty oils and molasses put a resiliency back into the centuries-old canvas. Next, she used a long wooden scrub brush to gently flatten wax paper over the wet canvas.

"The next step will be to glue the canvas onto a new tailoring," she explained to me in English. "The irons will melt the two together. Tomorrow or the day after I will remove the dried wax paper, then the painting will mounted be onto a new frame. One of the studio artists will clean it and repaint it with the special restoration oil paints."

For some unknown reason, I was writing all this down into my journal. "Perhaps I can start a restoration studio in America," I said to the young lady and she interpreted for Sergio. "Only problem is, I'll have to wait a couple hundred years for our paintings to need restoration."

They laughed and I shook my head, not understanding why the Good Lord wanted me to see and learn these complicated procedures.

We left the studio at four for the drive home. It began to thunder and lightning. I listened to the raindrops hitting the thin metal roof of Sergio's ten-year old Fiat. I watched the people on the sidewalks and on the buses. They all appeared a little crazy, talking to themselves and moving too fast. Why did all Italians use their hands so much when they talked? Were there so many words in Italian that had more than one meaning and so they must use their hands and faces to provide clarity to the communications?

I spoke to Sergio in a mixture of Spanish and Italian. "I like to stay in bed on days like today," I said. "Do you think the Pope is sleeping?"

"Who, Papa? No, he's playing poker."

"With a cigar and whiskey?" I laughed.

"Yes, and an extra card up his sleeve," Sergio chuckled.

I could see that Sergio and I shared the same sense of humor; we saw things in the ridiculous. Sergio spoke no English at all nor would he try. My Italian had improved as the day progressed but we had forgotten to take the dictionary this morning and every time we were stuck in a conversation one of us would spell out the word on the car's windshield. Now at the end of the day, the windshield was completely covered with the bits and pieces of our discussions about art, history, fishing, work and money.

Tuesday morning, I sat on the couch in the living room as Dominique played soft notes on the piano. We had finished taping base lines and chords on her tape recorder for her to play back while she practiced. I felt a warmth towards her I hadn't felt in a long time. Several times I came close to reaching out and touching her. But I didn't. I couldn't come into a man's home, as a guest and then do something to hurt him. It would be wrong and I would not allow myself to do that. But my feelings for Dominique were strong. My stomach fluttered when she touched me. I recognized that the easiness between us could quickly turn to tenderness. I had to stay together enough not to make a play and then leave tomorrow before her charms overcame my will.

Outside the sky darkened, billowing storm clouds moved across the sun's path. Beams of sunlight streamed through holes in the cloud formation and hit the hillside. I went out to the balcony. A streak of sunlight hit the chateau on the far hill. I will remember these days with her. Of walking in the light drizzle on cobblestone streets, both of us listening to the sound of our shoes echoing off the old buildings. Today playing blues on the piano, both of us feeling the sound of a single note as it went through us. But she had her life; Sergio, work, a home, friends, bills and problems. My life was my travel, my painting and looking, always looking for the right one. And when she came into my life, I would have my home, my work, my friends, bills and problems.

I wanted to tell her how much I ached inside. Did she know that I trembled when we were close?

"Let's go have lunch," she said coming up behind me and touching my shoulder.

We took our coats and an umbrella and she drove us to Monte-Rotondo, up narrow alleys and streets to a very small restaurant. We sat across from each other at a table in the corner. Dominique ordered cannoli, a roast stew with potatoes and white wine.

"You are happy you are going to Barcelona?" she asked.

"No," I said softly.

I saw that my answer didn't surprise her.

"In your book, you write everything?" she asked.

"Yes," I said looking into her almond colored eyes.

"I don't need to know what you are writing."

"No?"

"No. Because I know."

"You do?"

"Yes. Before it was possible, now it is not possible. I have Sergio."

"Yes, I understand," I said. When she answered me with her eyes; I continued.

"A year ago, it wouldn't have mattered to me," I said. "I would have wanted the conquest no matter the cost; but now after the hurt I've been through...I don't want to be a part of someone else's pain. Do you understand me?"

"Yes, very well and I am happy that we both shall keep our honor," she said this softly, then smiled, still looking into my eyes.

Lord, she is beautiful. I said to myself.

We ate slowly, our eyes meeting without fear or embarrassment. Sunlight filtered through the yellow curtains and onto the tables and floor. After lunch we strolled up the street to the castle of the Baron de Orsini.

"This was the feudal castle of the Orsini family, some of whom ruled as Popes." She explained to me.

"I've read about them," I said. "They were corrupt, weren't they? They had several wives and many children even as they held the Papacy."

"Yes, many children and yes, many mistresses."

We walked up the street to the entrance of the castle. "It was built in the 1500s," Dominique explained, "and is now used as Monte-Rotondo's city hall." We went through the tall wooden entrance gate into a stone courtyard and up to the front door of the castle; then up two flights of wide, marble steps. On the second floor Dominique tried to open first one door then a second but found them both locked. She gestured for me to wait and she went back downstairs. I listened to her footsteps, thinking of our conversation at lunch. Minutes later I heard her speaking with someone as she came back up the stairs.

Dominique had found an old woman to unlock the doors. The old lady was wearing a black dress and a shabby green shawl. She smiled at me without pausing, still talking with Dominique in Italian. She unlocked a door and went in and opened the top drawer of a metal desk. She took out two large, mediaeval keys and gave them to Dominique then smiled at me as she walked past and left us alone in the castle.

Dominique and I walked through the rooms that were now used for town meetings. She unlocked a door with one of the large keys and we walked into a room whose walls were painted in frescoes. The wood ceiling, a full eight inches thick, had been carved, 3-D like and each panel painted in gold.

We walked through to an adjoining room where I was startled by the fresco on the ceiling. It was a garden scene. A bright, sunny day with nude women playing in the park. Several of the women were kissing. Three women sitting side by side, one of them playing with the other's breast.

"The world hasn't changed so much," I said. "What is it in men that creates this ultimate sex fantasy?"

"Which?" Dominique asked.

"Wanting to see women making love to women? Is it jealousy of their more sensuous bodies? Or a power trip? I don't know but here it is in the 1500s as it is today in Rome, London, Paris, New York, everywhere.

My question unanswered, Dominique unlocked another room. There was no electricity and only one small window through which daylight illuminated the ceiling but even in the dimness I could see that the walls were frescoes painted in gold, white and blue. The frescoes on the four walls combined into a vaulted, rounded ceiling.

"This is very beautiful," I said.

"It is the castle's chapel," Dominique explained. "Sergio, me and the entire group from Rome restored it this year. The walls had to be cleaned because they had covered the frescoes with plaster."

"Why would anyone do that?" I asked.

Dominique shook her head. "Mussolini announced a program to destroy all the feudal works. His men came and plastered over all the frescoes in the castle. Only the ceiling in the first room was spared. When we restored the castle in March of this year it was a fifty-year old dream come true for the town. Now we wait to get paid."

"That was six months ago. Why does it take so long to get paid?"

"There is a lack of capital and there is the bureaucracy. It's difficult for Sergio and me; always the deadlines to meet, despite all the problems to overcome in making a good restoration and then we're never sure when we'll be paid."

"It's the same everywhere, always there are problems with money," I said feeling their frustration.

We walked down the stairs and out through the stone courtyard, down the narrow streets to Dominique's faded green Fiat. She drove through the evening traffic into Rome. I looked out at the beauty of the buildings, the parks and the gardens along the way.

We picked up Sergio at his Rome work shop and he drove Dominique's car.

"We're going to Sergio's ex-wife, Dorian's house," Dominique turned to me in the back seat to explain.

"Oh," I was taken back; surprised that they would be friends with his ex-wife.

"She's an actress and lives now with director, Jesepi Blanco. Tonight, they are showing one of his plays on television and he's giving a party."

"Interesting. How long have they been married?" I asked.

"Jesepi and Dorian? Four years but they have a little six-year old boy."

I calculated in my head that the baby was born while Dorian was still married to Sergio. I didn't pursue it but wondered about the story that must go with these circumstances.

"It seems that none of the couples are married. Am I wrong?" I asked.

"No, well not exactly. Most people our age have a one ring wedding. We don't have an official paper and we don't have a church ceremony," Dominique explained.

"Why is that?" I asked.

"It's easier, this way. If you get married in church then no divorce is allowed."

"Ah, yes, I understand," I said from the back seat.

Sergio parked the car and we walked down a street of apartment houses fronting a small park. Sergio rang the doorbell and Dorian came down the stairs and opened the front door and kissed each of us on both cheeks. We followed her inside and Dominique introduced me to Jesepi.

"This is a television special Dorian and I did together four years ago," Jesipi explained to me in broken English. He was tall and thin and he had a loose vitality beneath a haggard look. "It's being re-run as a special again tonight," Jesipi explained as arriving guests rang the doorbell.

"Yes, I know, congratulations," I said.

Soon there were a dozen people gathered around an old black and white television set in the living room. I was introduced to Joseph, a Rastafarian man, the first one I had seen in Europe. Everyone settled down to watch the show.

The film was of a live evening performance outdoors in front of an ancient Roman wall. The story was difficult to follow. In fact, it was the craziest play I had ever seen. There were twenty actors who came together in different scenes to scream and shout at each other. Then every ten minutes, in the middle of the screaming, one or another of the actors walked to the side of the stage and struck a large gong with a long pole. Each time the gong was rung, the camera showed a sequence of; first, a large sunflower, then a paper moon in a black sky, then a TV camera with its lens pointed at the viewers.

This went on for an hour. Screams, shouts, cry, yell, hit, stab, moan, groan, scream, shout, hit GONG; sunflower, moon, TV camera. I couldn't believe they were entranced by the surrealism which began to nauseate me. I asked Jesepi to explain the story.

"I can't, it's too complicated," he said with a flourish of his hands. "It is my modern theater version of a very old Italian story."

I noticed five minutes later that Jesepi was explaining the story to the Rastafarian, Joseph. I felt slighted and left the living room and walked around the apartment. Standing alone on the balcony off of the living room, I smelt the aroma of dinner being cooked by the neighbors. The stars were out and it was a clear, lovely evening in Rome.

After the show and coffee and congratulations we left. We were only in the car a few blocks from Jesipi's when Sergio and Dominique began to argue. They yelled at each other then we drove in silence until Sergio stopped at his studio to pick up his own car. I went to ride with him but Sergio stopped me, "It's okay. Go with her," he said and indicated I should get back in the car with Dominique.

I got in the front passenger seat and Dominique drove; following Sergio through traffic. Neither of us said a word until we drove past the Coliseum.

"What are you fighting about?" I finally asked her.

"Hashish," Dominique said.

"Hashish? I don't understand."

"Sergio doesn't like drugs. They were smoking hashish tonight at Dorian's."

"Yes, I know, but Sergio didn't smoke any, you and I didn't smoke it. Why is he yelling at you?"

"He yells at me because I live with him and he has no one else to yell at."

"Yes, of course." I nodded. "I understand." We sat in silence again.

The evening traffic was heavy near the Coliseum. The tall, ancient arena romantically lit in yellow spotlights.

I understood very well. It was the same all over. I yelled at Mary for years. I promised myself I would never allow that to happen again.

"In Spain you will find someone," Dominique interrupted my thoughts.

"I hope."

"Yes, it will be good again for you."

We left the city and drove on the country road back to Mentana. There were tall trees on either side of the two-lane highway. The evening was pleasant, the air fresh. I felt like I was in an Italian movie again.

I packed after breakfast the next morning and said good-bye to Dominique in the hallway.

"Arreviderchi, Paul." She kissed me on both cheeks and I smiled into her eyes. Her face was sad.

"Arreviderchi, Dominique." I squeezed her hand in affection.

Sergio helped me carry the trunk downstairs. I turned back at the first landing to see her standing by the door. I smiled into her eyes and she smiled back.

Sergio drove to the train station in central Rome and walked with me through the dirty metro. He read which train went to the airport and waited with me until it came.

"Good-bye, my friend," Sergio said in broken English, his first attempt at the language he hated.

"Chaio, Sergio and grazie, molto grazie."

We shook hands and I got on the metro. On the way to the airport I reflected on my experience of Rome. It surprised me that the men did the cooking. Sergio was a very good cook and I remembered the look and taste and aroma of his pasta meals.

Life in the small towns though poor, was to be admired. The people were close, good neighbors. They appreciated the little things in life. I saw no fights or real arguments. No one lost their temper despite the fact that everyone let you know exactly how they felt about any issue, immediately and with great expression. Perhaps a bit too expressive. I hoped the Spanish people were not as animated with their hands, I had already picked up this bad habit in just ten days in Italy.

Chapter Eleven
Barcelona

As the plane flew along the coast of southern Spain, I felt a pang of home sickness. The mountains behind Barcelona came into view. Rolling hills with meadows of brown grass, green brush and Manzanita trees dotting the hillside. The plane could have been flying over Santa Cruz. I pictured the drive-up Empire Grade Road. I could imagine a fire going in the fireplace, the kids watching television and the dog lying by the door. The realization that it was over, forever, came over me again. I wanted to cry but there were no more tears, only the feeling of loss and emptiness.

As I watched the coast go by beneath us, I remembered the camping trips to Big Sur with Mary and the kids. We explored the state parks outside Salinas too. We loved to go out; roughing it for the weekend then all of us appreciating the comforts of home after two days in tents and sleeping bags.

Those were beautiful days and I ruined it. I destroyed our family over drugs and women. Why was I like this? My father and grandfather, my uncles; all my family were straight, stay at home kind of men. Why was I so bored inside when not enraptured in drugs or touching a new woman for the first time? I was raised in the age of sex, drugs and rock and roll. That might have been part of it but to be honest, I knew the real cause was inside me. I wanted adventure; thrills and the rush of drugs. I loved those experiences. This is what I've learned about the danger of drugs; ignore me at your own peril, but drugs are too good. They make all other experiences seem boring. At least for me. I go overboard, I want more then more again. The psychiatrist in Santa Cruz told me it's because I never suckled at my mother's breast or was ever kissed by my father. I was raised in a middle class, Jewish family in the 1950s; babies got bottled milk. Mothers did not breast fed their children. And men did not cuddle and kiss their sons. A hand shake and pat on the shoulder was about all you were going to get in the way of affection.

Who knows? Maybe that is part of the reason I was drawn to drug use. I really didn't need to find the reason; the only thing that mattered now was living drug free. Taking it head on; through the pain and the loneliness and the disappointments. Yes, I had failed in London when I got high on heroin. It was a shameful relapse. All I could do now was to fight the good fight and not let it happen again.

"Toughen up, buddy." I told the ten-year old inside me.

I passed through Spanish customs then went into the airport. I walked through the modern glass and chrome terminal building carrying my heavy back pack and dragging my aluminum trunk behind me. I found the underground and took the train to central Barcelona then a cab ride from the subway station. We drove through crowded downtown streets to the Boulevard de Ramblas and the Hotel Floret. The ride was a blur of newly constructed apartment buildings. Barcelona was more modern than I had expected. Using my second-grade level of Spanish, I booked a room and paid ten dollars for one night. I unpacked and showered then left the hotel and went back to the underground. I looked at my map and found which train went to the port of Barcelona and went to that platform to wait for it.

The underground was old and dirty. It smelled of urine and vomit. The subway car came and I was happy to walk back out into the bright sunshine after a short ride. The streets by the port were flowing with traffic. The buildings were seedy and in need of paint; the gutter filled with litter. On the main boulevard; whores dressed in miniskirts and wearing thick make-up stood on street corners or sat in the outdoor cafes looking for business. I walked along the boulevard searching for a restaurant. On the Calle Escudelleva I was surprised to find a clean one tucked in among the squalor. I sat at a table inside and ordered the paella. It was a full pan; enough for two people of rice filled with Octopus, vegetables, clams and two large shrimp. I devoured the meal and bottle of Spanish red wine as my thoughts turned to Mary. She would love this place and the excitement of a new city. Did she think of me when something new happened to her?

I took a bus back to the hotel, showered and slept until after dark. When I woke, I went out and walked along the Boulevard de Ramblas. I joined the thousands of people who came out of their homes each night to stroll along the wide promenade. I stopped at an outdoor cafe on the Ramblas and paid a cover charge to sit at a table where I smoked and drank alone. It had rained earlier in the evening and now the tiled sidewalk was wet and shiny. I knew how I would paint the evening scene, in a Toulouse Lautrec style. The harsh white street lights reflected on the wet pavement. The trees were lit up in strings of colored lights made brighter by the black, night sky. The expressions of the people in the café and those walking by, all frozen in the moment. Imagining how I would paint the scene got me excited. I wanted to start painting. I would do two at a time. The face of torment and this Barcelona street scene.

Beautiful Spanish women wearing high heels and dressed in fashionable clothes walked by the cafe. Some of them were alone, others were with friends and others with lovers. None of them understood my English or my Spanish.

Beat at the game, I planned tomorrow's trip. I would explore the coast west of Barcelona for a place to rent. If there was nothing, I would go back to Nice. I dreaded the French people and the language difficulties but before I left Nice for Florence, I had met a pretty woman named Muriel. She was an intern at the main hospital in Nice and she spoke good English. If I could connect with her and see her once or twice a week it would help.

The next morning, in my room on the 5th floor I counted my money out on the bed. I was running low. I would have to sell stock and I had better do it soon. I put my money belt on and went out and found a post office four blocks away. It was a plain building on a crowded, polluted, traffic jammed street. I was half suffocated from the bus and auto exhaust when I got inside and took a number from the postal clerk to make a long-distance call. Finally, it was my turn and I called Stephen but there was no answer. A wasted hour but I had no choice, I would have to try again later.

I took a bus to the train station and got on board a train traveling up the coast west towards Callella. I sat across from a man with five long fishing rods.

"You go to fish, where in Callella?" I asked him in broken Spanish.

"The fishing is best at Valascar," the man answered with a smile. "You fish?"

"Yes, I like to fish very much," I answered in my first grade Spanish. The man understood me and smiled and nodded, one fisherman to another.

"You can get off with me and I will show you," the man gestured up the tracks.

When the train stopped at Valascar, the first stop outside of Barcelona, we walked from the train station down the hill to the beach. I could see dozens of fishermen casting their lines out from the sandy beach into the surf and off the rocks of the jetty. But as I looked around, I saw new buildings everywhere. I didn't want to paint eight story, modern apartment houses. I looked up towards the hills behind Velascar, there too it was all modern buildings. I thanked the man but turned around and walked back up to the station and got on the next train headed west toward Mataro.

It was a crisp, clear day and the Mediterranean an azure blue. People sunbathed on the beaches. The train passed through the coastal towns and I got off at the ones that looked interesting. San Pol de Mar was the best of the lot. Large fishing boats lay marooned on the low tide beaches. The houses and shops were of older architecture. I liked that there were dirt streets off of the main boulevard.

At the next stop, Calella I walked around. To my disappointment it turned out to be a tourist town with German shopkeepers. When I looked inside one restaurant, I saw a big Dutchman working behind the bar. He wore a bright blue Hawaiian flowered shirt and the atmosphere seemed pleasant.

I ventured into the bar as sunlight and an ocean breeze filter in from the open door.

"There's a good catch of fresh fish with salad and potatoes for 275 pesetas," the bartender said as he handed me a menu. He was a handsome, silver haired man with big bones and tan face. His English had only a hint of a German accent.

"Okay, that's what I'll have then." I handed him back the menu without opening it.

The bartender spoke to his help in Spanish; to his friends at the end of the bar in German and to me in flawless English.

"I'm impressed," I told him.

"Why is that?" he asked me with a charismatic smile.

"You're fluent in four languages, I hardly speak English."

"Yes." The Dutchman laughed, "I speak French and Italian too but it's different in Europe. Here everyone has to know a few languages to get by."

"Not the people I've been meeting," I said and he laughed.

The Dutchman drank a glass of red wine with me and two cognacs with his friends down the bar. He asked me about my travels and laughed when I told him some of the stories. I bought a pack of cigarettes, paid my bill and walked back to the train station feeling good in the warm Spanish sun. Unexpectedly, a poor man in ragged clothes, in his mid-fifties passed me. I jumped away from him in revulsion. The man's face was covered in warts. His hands, face and arms, all had terrible warts. Were they warts or tumors? Yes, they must be tumors. He looked poor and obviously was suffering. I knew I should feel sorry for him but this was my ultimate nightmare; to be covered with bumps all over. I didn't know what this omen meant but I wanted to get away fast. Even more than snakes and rats, bumps on the face scared me bad.

In San pol de Mar I walked up narrow streets to the old Spanish church. I heard more Dutch and German spoken than Spanish. There was no market place in town. I decided against San pol de Mar and turned around and went back to the train station and sat in the waiting room. The station had old wooden benches and high wooden beamed ceilings. Green paint peeled off the stucco walls. Ten-foot-high, arched doorways framed the dramatic view of the town and sea outside. Inside, three women sat while their young children ran around in a circle in the middle of the waiting room. Sunshine streaked through the opened doors lighting the room in a bright, happy light.

I relaxed in the coolness of the light breeze coming through the doors and windows. The two children stopped spinning to study me. I smiled at them. They stared, taking in the stranger in minute detail. Ignoring their stares, I took in the view of the old town.

A train arrived and the women and two small children rushed outside to catch it. I waited for the east bound train back to Barcelona. Soon after they left, a middle-aged man came in and sat by the door. He tapped his feet and moved his hands and arms and constantly changed his position.

Everywhere it was the same. Women and children see the light but men don't even try. They're on a tight rope and though it's only imagined, it seems high enough to kill them if they slip. I knew it all too well. I was on that tight rope too.

I didn't get off at Areny's de Mar. I decided to go back to the hotel. It was time to shower, buy tickets to Sunday's bullfight and take a nap. Now that I'd seen La Costa Bravo, I knew that the Spanish explorers must have thought they were home when they first sighted northern California. The hills climbing up away from the Mediterranean looked exactly like the coast along Santa Cruz and Monterey Bay.

It was Friday night in Barcelona and the streets filled with thousands of people walking arm in arm or sitting at the outdoor cafes. The streets and parks at night were where you could meet new people but first you must speak the native tongue which I didn't. I was alone and there was an emptiness inside me that felt so big, so powerful it could be the source of the arctic winds that howled across the tundra.

I wandered through a neighborhood where a Ferris wheel and bumper cars had been set up. Bright carnival lights and loud music attracted a crowd. Colorful crape paper was strung between the buildings. Young boys played soccer with a tin can while their parents talked. Instruments and amplifiers on a stage were being tested. It was warm night. A sliver of a moon and pink lined clouds floated above the Palace de Victoria Eugenia. The young girls' vaginas twitched from the electricity in the air. The young men drank wine and smoked cigarettes, longing to touch that source of all joy.

Instead of playing Spanish fiesta music which I thought might be appropriate for a Spanish fiesta, the band played twelve bar blues. The bass player's volume was so loud that people held their hands over their ears and screamed at him. He ignored them. No one danced. The singer tried to sing but couldn't hear himself so he stopped. Then the guitar player stopped, the drummer and finally Mr. Bassman.

"Oh my God!" I said and left.

Sunday afternoon I took a bus to the bull ring. I'd been thinking about it for days. If it were brutal how could I enjoy it? But if Hemingway loved the bull fights there had to be something to it. Based on my esteem for him, today I was going to attend a real bull fight in Barcelona.

The bus stopped at the main entrance of the Plaza de Toros and I found my seat inside, twenty rows back from the sand ring. The round arena was smaller than I had imagined, the size of a little league baseball field. The audience was close and could see the expressions on the men's faces. A spectator could easily jump over the rail into the bullring. It was this intimacy that brought the audience into the drama. They could feel the power and the danger of the bulls.

At three o'clock the band on the second deck began to play. The crowd cheered and the excitement built as the parade of the toreadors, picadors, horses and entourage began. There were three toreadors for today's show. Juan Jose, Manuel Maldonado and Victor Mendes. They marched in two columns across the arena. Holding their heads with dignity, their tight costumes sparkled in the afternoon sun. After the opening ceremonies the first toreador, Juan Jose remained in the ring with three other men. The trumpets heralded the first bull's charge into the arena. He was massive and his thick muscles rippled under his black skin. He was a beautiful beast full of fury and bent on killing his antagonists. He was fresh and pranced around the ring tossing his horns in a display of his fierceness. He then stopped to look up at the crowd. He reconnoitered, saw that there is no way out, he turned to the men who faced him with long capes. He charged them. He was four or five times their size and it seemed he would tear them to shreds but then the banderillos began their work. They avoided his charge, rushed in and spiked him with their short spears. Three passes, six wounds took a little of the freshness out of him. The trumpets sounded and the picadors and their heavily padded horses entered the arena. They maneuvered their mounts near the fencing and allowed the bull to rush into the pads on the sides of the horses. They met his charge with a sharp pointed lance. The picador twisted the lance's blade into the bull's shoulder until he finally backed away and withdrew. Slowed by the slicing of his shoulder muscles, the bull stood away from the horses, blowing air, wanting no more. Vivid red blood ran from his shoulder down his black smooth skin onto the sand. The trumpets sounded and the horses left the arena as Juan Jose stepped into the ring with a short cape. He approached the panting bull and the dance began. The crowd cheered or whistled depending on whether they appreciated Juan's moves or thought him too hesitant. Finally, at some unknown cue, he went to the fence and took the sword that his assistant handed him over the rail. He tucked it into his red cape and walked back out towards the bull. As the bull charged him, Juan Jose judged the location behind the bull's head and drove the sword into his body. But to everyone's chagrin, he missed the sweet spot and the sword bent then twanged off into the air. The crowd whistled and Juan Jose retrieved it and set up again. It took him two more tries but then success. The blade had pierced the bull's lungs to the hilt. He became sick and bled from the mouth and nose then fell dead to the ground. The trumpets sounded and Juan Jose walked in triumph around the arena. There were cheers and whistles. Attendants came out and attached leather straps and metal chains to the bull's hind legs. With much cheering, the horses dragged the carcass out leaving lines of blood in the sand.

I didn't feel too good. I had been routing for the bull.

The second bull entered the ring like a king. He was pissed off and charged everyone who dared step foot from behind the wooden barriers. He didn't just go for the men's capes either; when he was half passed, instead of running through the cape, he'd turn into the Matador's body. It was very scary and the crowd could see it and shouted with fear.

On several passes he didn't even bother with the cape but charged right at the men. "Fuck that cape, I want you motherfucker."

He charged Manuel Maldonado that way. Maldonado back peddled to get out of the bull's way but he tripped. The crowd rose to their feet as one and sounded a single shout of, "Oohh!" But the bull had tripped too and before he could gore him, Maldonado was up and ran away. The bull struggled back to his feet and stood panting in the middle of the arena. Two picadors came out from behind the wooden barriers and distracted the bull with their capes. Maldonado walked away unhurt but his face was ashen. He was lucky to be alive and the crowd knew it. Now Victor Mendes came out to face the bull. He wasn't in the arena two minutes when he too went down. He stumbled awkwardly as the bull charged into him rather than passing under his cape. The bull ran right over Mendes but again he was too close to do the damage he intended. He flashed his head side to side, ripping the ground with his horns as Mendes lay under him, trampled but untouched by the horns. Mendes got away as soon as he could and limped toward the wooden barricade. We could see that he was hurt. His helpers came out and took him behind the protective barrier and he reappeared a few minutes later to a standing ovation. It was war now and clearly the bull was winning. No one could control him. Mendes took two pikes from one of the picadors and went to redeem his reputation. The bull charged, Mendes avoided his horns and bulk and was able to land both pikes. The crowd went wild, the bull turned and snorted, digging a trough with his front paw. Mendes walked away but did not turn his back on the beast.

The bull wasn't following the script and everything they tried with him barely worked. The padded horses came out and set up against the fence. The bull didn't charge them right away but maneuvered his way around so he could slam into the horse from the front! He pushed and almost, almost knocked both horse and rider to the ground. Men had to distract him away, risking their lives to move him from the panicked horses.

"Okay, this bull's won," I said to the man next to me. "Let him go. Let him live and breed him or let him fight another day." The man nodded but the crowd didn't see it that way. There was no allowance in their system to concede a bull winning.

Mendes finally drove the sword into him but even then; with a three-foot long blade inside him, the bull continued to fight. They finally killed him by severing his neck vertebrae with a knife even as the bull tried to bite them. They dragged him out of the arena with the chains and horses. The band played and we all took a break.

When the third bull came out something seemed wrong. He only half-heartedly charged the men and then stopped and stood in the center of the ring and bellowed. I couldn't tell if it was anger or fear he was expressing. He bellowed the entire time he was in the arena. It became clear that he was expressing fear, not rage.

"Why me?" he was saying. "I don't want this. Why must I die here? Mama, mama, God please, save me from this horror."

I wanted them to open the gates and let him out. It was sad to watch an animal in fear. But the Spanish didn't see it that way either. No one saved him. When they stuck the long blade into him, he walked away from the men and stood by the wall; trying to find a place to die alone. But the men wouldn't leave him be. They went up to him with capes and tried to engage him. He only sank to his knees, bellowed one last time then collapsed onto the sand. The big draft horses came out once again and men attached heavy chains to the poor beast's hind legs and pulled him through the sand, leaving a trail of blood to mark his exit.

After the last of the six bulls I walked down a flight of stairs to leave the stadium but I saw outside, in the plaza they were butchering the bulls and I stopped to watch. There was a large crowd of people, from eight-year olds to eighty-year olds watching as they worked on the last carcass. The cement was thick with blood. A man with a hose washed the blood into a drain in the middle of the plaza.

I stood on the stairway above and looked down on the crowd. As the last of the dead bulls lay on the ground several of the boys and men put their feet on his still open eyes. "Bad karma," I said to myself. It was as if they couldn't see that he too carried a spirit within him that should be honored.

The butchers skinned him, then chopped off his feet and with the use of an electric crane, lifted him up off the ground. There was a lot of blood. They chopped off the bull's massive head and threw it to the side. I watched all of these activities with a feeling of disgust. People were so cruel. It made me nauseous to watch them.

The inside of the bull was a transparent white and through it you could see the black blood and where the blood was exposed to the air, a crimson red. The bull was very clean inside. He was perfection and even in death, his body was a miracle to behold.

What kind of Supreme Being could have created that perfection then would allow it to be treated like this? I didn't understand and I wished I wasn't the one who questioned it either. Let someone else figure it out and maybe they'd tell me one day, maybe not, either way I'd be better off than having these fucking questions all the time.

The next morning, trunk and bag packed, I was ready for the trip back to Nice. My train didn't leave until 7pm so I left the trunk and bag in my room and went for a walk. I ended up in an old neighborhood with a small central plaza. I sat eating an apple on a bench and listening to classical piano music coming from one of the apartments. The music filled the air between the tall, old Spanish apartment houses. A gentle breeze blew the leaves on the trees. Children played on swings and monkey bars. Canaries sang in their cages on the balconies.

The canaries reminded me of the small birds nesting in the rafters at the bull fight. All through the fighting they chirped beautiful songs as the sun shined on the brown sand in the ring. "Heaven awaits you, brother bull. You will return to the green fields of your youth. You will spend eternity with your mother in the fields." Did they sing this for the bulls? I hoped so. For them and for me too.

Returning to the hotel the woman manager came up to my room and knocked. I opened the door and smiled but she immediately started to yell at me for having slept in the second bed last night.

"You didn't change the sheets on the first bed," I explained.

"You had five showers," she said.

"I don't understand what five showers has to do with changing the sheets? I paid each day for a room with a clean bed. Your husband told me the price of the room included the shower."

She was very animated and speaking much too fast for me to understand. I turned away, locked up the trunk and walked out without saying any more.

I felt bad. Why was I so sensitive? Why did I keep having lousy conversations with people?

The elevator was out so with the woman following behind me; asking for more money because I slept in two different beds, I walked down six floors; eight steps and turn at a landing then eight more steps and another landing. All in all, ninety-six steps. I pulled the trunk behind me, sliding it down the marble steps. A button on my shirt pooped off. The name tag on the trunk fell off. The blue bandana around my neck was wet with perspiration. I could see it clearly; this was my karma and there was only one way through it. I've handled worse. I wasn't in the Amazon being eaten alive by bugs with a three-foot tape worm in my gut. Right? So okay, I could see that this was how it had to be for me. You do something it creates waves, the waves come back to you. I did something to deserve all this. It was my karma. I just wondered how it was that other people could do worse things and still have good things come back to them? How do they throw out reverse karma? Hitler, Mary, how do they do it? I was lucky I guess, I got to see my karma bounce right back at me. Look out, BAM! Instant Karma, man. There was just no getting away from all the fun you could have on this planet.

The cab driver reminded me of the guys on the street where I grew up, relaxed, joking, nothing is serious except girls. The fare was $3, I gave him $5. I was two hours early for the train but safe, healthy and almost sane. I lugged my stuff down the block to a park, found a bench and lay back. "I'm a little beat up Ma, but I'm feeling fine."

A pretty Spanish girl walked by wearing a short denim skirt and tight blouse. She bounced.

"I could use some of that once in a while too," I explained to my guardian angel. "And more than once a month, if you please."

I watched her go by and pictured her panties and that beautiful, pink vagina. It was warm out, a mildness in the air. I looked at the faces of the people as they walked into and out of the park. The Spanish ate too much meat and fatty meat at that. You could see it in their faces, in their legs, in their torsos. They don't exercise either.

All things considered I liked Mexico more than Spain. The food was better and the people too.

I saw a middle-aged man, his middle-aged wife and their 17-year old daughter. They were German, or Swiss or something, definitely not Spanish. They sat on the bench next to mine and were passing time in the park before they caught their train. They were smiling and laughing. It was very good to see them. A perfect age to tour Europe together. When they left for the station, the father shouldered up his back pack and picked up both of their large two suitcases. The mother carried a smaller traveling bag and the daughter wore her backpack. The wife tried to get the husband to let her carry one of the suitcases but he refused, standing tall he carried it all easily. They laughed and walked off. The mother and daughter holding hands.

At the station I bought bottled water and cigarettes and left Spain with 0 pesetas, perfect. I wheeled my trunk and bag out to the tracks and passed the man, wife and daughter, the father caught my eye and smiled. "Hi," he said.

"Hello," I smiled back.

They took the train to Madrid; I rode mine back to Nice.

Chapter Twelve
Nice Again

I rode on the train eastbound out of Barcelona. Outside my window, I watched the blinking lights on a large industrial smokestack. The white smoke rose high into the night sky. I felt detached, riding in a train, alone, through Spain. A sense of fear jiggled on my nerve endings making it impossible to relax. What was happening inside? I was afraid of people. They've hurt me so many times that now I hide from them or use my anger to protect my inner self. Yet I can see myself in almost everyone I meet. I recognize myself behind our different minds. There, in their eyes, a light and common spirit.

"No one wants to harm you," I said to my reflection in the dark glass. It helped and I relaxed, some of the walls fell down and I could see clearly again.

The train arrived in Nice at 8:ooam. It was overcast outside. I wheeled my trunk out of the station and seeing that there no were taxis about, began to walk to the hotels on Le Rue de Buffa. I walked for several blocks down quiet streets but soon realized I was going in the wrong direction. I sensed my error and stopped to ask a Pepsi Cola delivery man for help.

"Excuse me," I said in rudimentary French to the young man. "Can you direct me to Le Rue de Buffa?" He gave me directions in French but seeing that I didn't understand, he put down his heavy metal cylinder and went back to the truck for a small street map. He unfolded it on top of the cylinder and showed me where I was and how I must go to arrive at Rue de Buffa, then he gave me the map.

"Merci, Monsieur," I offered him a cigarette. The driver shook his head no, it wasn't necessary.

Farther down the road an old woman stood in the doorway of a pastry shop. She smiled and said hello to me as I passed her door, "You have a heavy load," she said in French.

"Non, not too bad," I shrugged.

"Bon jour," she said.

This must be my special day. People were being easy with me. It felt good after all the hassles I'd had since arriving on the continent.

I came down the Le Rue de Buffa and found the Hotel Mimosa but decided to try the Hotel Minoan on the second landing of the same building. It was one less flight of stairs to climb with my trunk and the owners had a pretty daughter. I had seen her outside the hotel the last time I was there. I left my trunk as far out of sight as I could manage and started up the stairs but before I reached the first landing, I ran into the woman who owned Hotel Mimosa.

"How are you, Monsieur Gebhart?" she asked in English, recognizing me immediately.

"I'm fine, and you, Madame, Madame...?"

"Adie."

"Yes, Madame Adie. You remember me?"

"I remember everything. Where have you been since you left Nice?"

"Firenze, Roma and Barcelona."

"Tres bien, great travels," she said with excitement.

"Yes, but I'm tired now. Do you have a room? One person only."

"How long?"

"A week."

She stared up at the ceiling, her finger on her cheek, inventoried her available rooms, looked back at me and said, "Yes, yes we can do it."

"How much?"

"Forty francs a day."

"Last time it was 35 francs."

"But you were two then."

"No, it was 35 francs for one and 60 francs for two."

"Yes, well it is not possible now, 40 francs."

"Okay, all right, I'm too tired to deal."

We walked back down the stairs to get my trunk and backpack. I was going to stop and ask the Hotel Minoan how much their rooms were but I didn't want to start trouble.

Besides I was learning, I had run into Madame Adie on the steps, I knew that she and her husband were both nice people. Why fight it? I would pay the extra dollar a day. Then I remembered that they charged for showers. "Madame, how much for the shower?"

"Six francs."

"Six francs, oh."

"With the room and shower 45 francs."

"Okay."

"If you shower at the beach, then no extra charge."

"Sure, okay," I said. She had knocked off 20 cents but I was too tired to argue with her. I carried my trunk up the three flight of stairs to Hotel Mimosa's front door. Madame Adie went into her apartment and brought a key for me. I rolled the trunk down the carpeted hallway to my room and put my things away, changed into shorts and a Maui t-shirt and knocked on Madame's door.

"May I use the telephone?"

"For Nice?"

"Yes, local."

"The woman you saw last time?"

"Yes," I said.

"You see, I remember everything."

"You should write a novel."

"I don't write, but I remember."

"The novel is in your head?"

"Yes, in my head, that is my novel." She opened a small cabinet in the hall by her room where she kept the phone. She removed the lock from the large dial and placed the old black telephone on an antique table.

"Merci," I thanked her and called Muriel's number. No one answered.

"She's not in?" Madame asked.

"No."

"Trieste, Maybe, later," Madame was rooting for me.

"Yes, later I'll try again."

I replaced the phone onto the black receiver, enjoying the solid sound and the heaviness of the old French telephone.

"Bon jour, Madame."

"Bon jour," she smiled and closed her door.

As I drank coffee at the bar across the street, I made a list of the art supplies I would need. List in hand, I walked to an art store downtown where I purchased the oils and supplies and two canvases each 26 by 24 inches. I wanted to buy larger canvases and paint bold but my pocket book was shy and also they would be harder to get home.

Back in my room, I set up one canvas using the top of the desk by the window as an easel. I began to sketch the room and the figure of a man sitting in a chair with his arms outstretched, howling in agony at his inner torment.

In the evening I showered and roamed through Nice until I found a restaurant on a side street. Restaurant Davia had a dozen tables in the front room and behind a curtain, a Gypsy family prepared the meals in the kitchen of their apartment. Tonight's special of Bouillabaisse would have to be my last splurge.

After dinner I smoked a cigarette and finished my red wine. I had called Muriel all day but without luck. Alone now, I walked along Traverse Massena, near the beach. The stores were open and the sidewalks crowded. I couldn't bear the crowd. I had to shuck and jive to avoid rubbing shoulders with every pedestrian going past me.

I returned to my room and worked on the pencil sketch of the painting. In the morning, I began to apply the oils, painting in the walls and floor, bed and two oval windows. The cleaning lady knocked and I let her in. Moments after she finished my room she returned with Madame Adie.

"Ah, I didn't know you were a painter," Madam Adie said as I let her in. She walked past me and stood in front of the half-completed canvas.

"I have the windows open to help with the odor," I said, thinking that she was concerned with the smell from the oils.

Madame Adie took her time studying my technique. She kept her fore finger to her cheek as she went over every inch of the canvas. She turned and said something to the cleaning lady who left, but returned in a few minutes with Adie's husband, Renaldo and the handyman, Gustav. One by one each of them stood in front of the canvas and studied it. I had to laugh as I watched this French review committee considering my work. There was hardly room to stand as the double bed took up half the room and so they had to take turns bending close to the canvas. They held a continuous discussion in rapid French. Obviously, they were debating its merits and deficiencies. They hadn't seen the face yet. It was blank now but when I painted in the scream and the ugly, tormented inner suffering, they will probably think me mad.

I was happy with the drawing even though the body was out of proportion. The canvas was small but I made the head big so I could work on the expression. Actually, I did a good job getting the legs to fit, bending them under the figure but the angle was a bit strange, I had to admit that. The viewer looked down at the man's figure but straight into the room. Listen, I know it's odd but what the hell, it comes from a distorted mind, you understand. I tried to convey these complex ideas to them in my baby French as they each gave me their opinions. It was a difficult discussion but made easier from the fact that we were all smiling and I had to laugh at their facial expressions as they turned away from the canvas.

"Monsieur Gebhart, please come with me," Madame Adie said at last and I followed her; waiting first for the gang to clear my room. When they did, I locked the door and followed the Madame. At the end of the hall, near the shower room she led me up a spiraling wrought iron staircase. At the top of the stairs she unlocked the door and we walked into a large studio. The light from two large arched windows flooded into a nicely decorated apartment.

"You will stay here now. The light is much better," she said as I looked around.

"How much?" I asked.

"The same price."

"Because I'm painting?"

"Oui, because you came back here to paint."

"Merci Madame, merci beau coup."

After moving my things into the studio, I returned to Restaurant Davia for dinner. The family was eating its supper when I arrived. The husband yelled first at the wife then at the sister-in-law. I felt bad, the same shit everywhere. I left and walked around the block then returned after they had finished dinner. The husband was gone. The little two-year old was crying, falling down and crying; getting up then wailing until he collapsed again on the floor. The grandmother walked with a limp and never said a word. The wife was crossed eyed. The little boy made all the noise he wanted. It was Restaurante Davia and I figured that the little boy must be Davia. He is the experience. How many meals has he interrupted? How many polite, proper minds has he wrecked?

I drank red wine and remembered my dream from this afternoon's nap. I was a young boy in a park with green grass and trees. It was a beautiful sunny day but I was crying. Nobody knew why I was so unhappy. Everyone kept telling me to stop being so miserable, to enjoy the sunshine but I kept screaming.

They were right. Here is the sunlight. It is the constant. What we think and experience is relative and relatively unimportant as the sun will shine on. We have only so many days to enjoy it, then we're gone and the sun will shine on without us. Quite a simple truth but now I felt the sadness of it, the mortality and the wasted time I had spent on earth. I was ready to enjoy that light and share it and the wisdom it brings; the serenity but now it seemed I couldn't find a friend or a lover. It wasn't fair. Mary had the house, the kids, a cousin who loved her so much she moved from the east coast to come live with her. Mary had four, five, six boyfriends, all our old friends and I got what?

In the morning, I walked down to the post office, bought stamps then tried to reach Angela in London. The line was busy. I tried again after a cigarette, still busy so I walked to the

Hospital La Roche where Muriel told me she was interning. In the reception office there was some confusion, they thought I was trying to visit a patient. I straightened that out and they told me to go upstairs to personnel.

There was more confusion there until I said, "She's an intern." The women all smiled, "Oh, an intern!" One of them walked me across the hall to another office. The woman in this office didn't know Muriel but found her file and showed it to me.

"Oui, that's her."

They called another woman into the office who spoke a little English.

"She does not work here anymore," the young woman said. "But we'll call the university and find out where she is."

"Merci."

As she dialed the university I was captured by her black, shoulder length hair and attractive face. She was wearing skin tight, white Levi's, a loose red sweater and white high heels. She had beautiful, long, shapely legs. I wanted to talk to her but it was too difficult under the situation.

They found that Muriel was interning now with a Doctor Martine in Cannes. They wrote down his address and telephone number for me. I thanked them for all their help and walked to the post office to call Dr. Martine's office. The doctor's secretary told me Muriel was not working today. In very broken English she gave me Muriel's father's phone number and address in Cannes where she was staying.

I called and spoke with Muriel's father but as he spoke very little English we didn't get far. But he did take down my number at the hotel.

"Muriel would be back around three," he said. "Call her then".

"Yes, thank you I will."

Why had she left the hospital and moved to Cannes to live with her father? Did she break up with her fiancé?

Muriel called me at the hotel later that afternoon.

"I'm working six nights a week for Dr. Martine," she said. "My one day a week off is very busy. Perhaps I could see you next Monday or Tuesday."

"What about during the day if you are working nights?"

"I'm too tired after work. I go right to sleep but I'll be in touch."

I hung up the phone and returned to my room disappointed. Nothing ever went right and I was tired of it. I didn't know what to do now. Go back to London and the cold, rainy weather? Or back to L.A.?

I walked to the beach. The sun was going down behind a sky filled with clouds. It was 9:30 Friday morning in California. Mary would be putting on her high heels and tightest designer jeans tonight. She would shave her underarms, which she hadn't done for the past nine years living with me, put on her make-up and have her Friday night date. And I would go alone to supper.

I called Angela again in London. Her roommate answered. Angela wasn't home but the roommate took my telephone number in Nice and said she would tell her that I had called.

I stayed in my room and played solitaire. About 7pm the sky cleared and I walked to the beach. I sat on the stone wall listening to the waves lap against the large granite pebbles, I saw lavender, black and white lights in my mind, behind my forehead; shaped in long curves. That was the highlight of my day today. Of my four days in France. Of the last two weeks!

I checked the prices to Athens at a neighborhood travel agency. Airfare $270. I couldn't afford it. I couldn't even afford to go back to London. That was $46 a day and included free lodging at Caroline's. I was stuck in Nice with beautiful women who wouldn't talk to a stranger or if they did, they didn't speak English. And of course, the charming Frenchmen and the *noise;* motor scooters, buses, cars, motorcycles all with no damn mufflers. The French men all think they're formula one drivers ripping down the street, forcing pedestrians to fear for their lives.

I had to find a new restaurant too. I was going crazy with the same routine. I was going crazy anyway, no one to talk to, and nothing to do. Not enough money to leave. Then I thought of the L.A. bar scene. The L.A. pollution. The L.A. assholes. I was almost glad to be in Nice. God, all I wanted was a home in the mountains with a loving woman, good kids and the time and money to enjoy them. I had a short conversation with God; imploring Him to please do something about the situation. You're losing your best customer here.

I took the small piece of red clay shard I had taken from the Roman Forum and rubbed it in my hands as I stood on the beach. "I'm tired of thinking of her and of the past," I said out loud, near to tears. "For nineteen months that's all I've thought about. I want her out of my thoughts."

I threw the relic into the Mediterranean. Two millennium ago a Roman slave made a clay pot and it laid around for thousands of years, who knows how many Roman hands touched it. Now eighteen hundred years later I tossed it into the sea.

I went back to the hotel and slept until waking up with a start at 3:30am. I had the strangest feeling. A very, very real feeling that something had just happened or was about to happen. Something dramatic. I couldn't sleep so I got up and went to the beach as the sun was starting to come up. The wind had come up and it churned the sea into white capped waves that crashed violently and loudly into the beach. I knew immediately that it was the spirit in the clay shard that had caused the wind and heavy seas.

I lay down in a sheltered place. Around me dozens of people braved the wind to take in the sunrise. Among them was a beautiful, long legged blond. She lay ten feet away. She was topless and extremely attractive. I said hello but she looked away. I saw that it must be very difficult being a beautiful woman. I mean having men hit on you morning, noon and night. It's not our fault, ladies. This is how the Good Lord made us.

Sunday morning, I put on fresh clothes; shorts, leather sandals and white shirt and walked to the bus station. It was a warm morning and a pleasant walk through the quiet streets. The number 15 bus up Boulevard de Cinienz stopped at the Roman ruins in the foothills above Nice. I got off there as Sunday picnickers began to arrive into the park. I walked beside an ancient Roman wall near the gardens of the Monastery. I could see Nice to the south and the granite cliffs of the French Alps to the north. Across the street from the park were magnificent homes. The shade from black barked apple trees sheltered the picnicking families as they laid out their blankets and baskets. I envied them their lives and the peace they found in this safe and splendid place. Their children played. Their French poodles played. The sun was warm. I fantasized being a successful artist and writer and living in a fine villa overlooking Nice. As I fantasized an unsettled feeling came over me. Was it boredom? I wasn't sure. I had felt this same way many times before. The times we did family things. It was this same gnawing in my gut. This boredom drove me to seek something else. Why? Too many drugs? Too much violence and adventure when I was growing up? I don't know why but I could not sit and give my total existence to enjoying my children enjoying. I wanted to experience the delight too. Someday maybe I'll know how to do it. Still, I saw the serenity in these people today. They seemed to have it, at least for this Sunday afternoon and I envied them that. I sat in the park and placed myself inside them, inside their lives. I did this until I saw Noah's face in my mind. That hurt and it made me get up and begin to walk, to keep walking until my mind released me from the thoughts of my son.

Restaurant Davia again at night. Little Davia was very quiet; walking around with a blue water pistol in his mouth, not saying a word as he checked everyone out. Going up to each table and staring at the customers as they ordered their dinner or afterward when the food arrived. He took it all in. I learned that the family was Algerian, not Gypsy. The cross-eyed woman was not the wife but the sister-in-law. The younger woman was Davia's mother, in her early twenties, short and quite pretty with no makeup. A very refreshing, natural look rather than the French women who wear heavy makeup even on the beach.

Though little Davia was in a peaceful mood tonight, the crossed eyed sister-in-law was not. She argued with the grandmother. The younger sister stayed out of it. She seems used to the shouting between her mother, her sister and her husband. The husband too is quiet. He cooks and listens to his mother-in-law and sister-in-law have it out but doesn't say a word.

I slept soundly from the bottle of wine and three course meal, then awoke at 4:00am and lit a cigarette. The street was quiet until a motor scooter came down it and the rider let out a terrific scream. Not a scream of glory as you hear on the ski slopes in California,

"Yaa-Hoo! I'm alive and King!" No, it was a scream of torment. He yelled again and again. I listened to him as he went down the block. There was no other sound and I could hear him very clearly for minutes, many blocks away as he repeated the shout of torment.

"Well I'm not the only one with pain and anguish," I said. I felt good for the young man screaming his way through Nice. If I could just paint it right, there were people who would relate to the painting of my scream.

I spent the next day trying but it wasn't going well. I was too hesitant, no boldness of brush stroke or color. I admired the impressionists more and more. Manet, I read somewhere, would walk up to a canvas and paint it out in an hour. Wham, wham, wham. Not me, I was carefully, slowly applying the paint and focusing on each stroke, not liking half of them.

In the afternoon, tired of the struggle, I took a walk downtown, looking into the display windows of the different shops. Among the people on the sidewalk ahead of me I noticed a tall man with a shaved head and very thick, large ears. The man turned and looked at me. His nose looked like a bird's beak. He had no teeth and his mouth was shriveled up and his chin small and pointed.

"Oh, God no," I said. I had seen this man in a dream about three nights ago. This shaved headed man didn't speak but I knew he meant me great harm. He was evil itself. I awoke from that dream at 4:00am too, pulling myself out of slumber to escape from the evil one. Now I was seeing this face in the flesh and I knew he was Satan.

The man slowed down but I stayed behind him; refusing to let him get behind me. He stopped at a construction site and was reading a poster on the wooden fence, waiting for me to go past him. I stopped too and watched him out of the corner of my eye. He turned and looked at me again. I pretended to look into a shop's window. I waited a good five minutes, determined not to move on until the man had gone. When he finally did leave, I walked past where he had been standing. On the wall where he had stopped there was a hand written note, "Yeah right, here you saw Satan."

The thought occurred to me that evil probably did win over goodness. The story goes like this; in the beginning the Spirit of God was humming, "Oomm" to himself when out of the far reaches of the universe, or out of a black hole or from where ever such things come, the evil force arrived. There was a great struggle and the evil force won and said to the Creator, "I shall divide you into billions of pieces and not one part of you will recognize yourself in another piece. In fact, you will not recognize yourself in yourself!"

And that is life on earth. We are a part of God the Creator, and we don't recognize Him in others or even in ourselves.

I painted in the morning, fixing the howl on the face. It was a good howl and I inspected it closely as I cleaned my brushes and the plastic palette board. I was feeling satisfied with my work when later I walked to the park. It was a lovely park, no one stepped foot on the grass except the pigeons. People rented chairs to sit in as they admired the nice grass. I imagined all the people on the grass and the pigeons in the chairs.

The sun became too hot and I walked to a shady spot away from everyone except for one man who was eating his lunch. He was in his late forties, brown hair turning gray. He wore a wrinkled suit with a green tie. He had on a blue shirt. His hair was trimmed but he needed a shave. He used his pen knife to cut an apple and loaf of bread which he ate standing up, shuffling from foot to foot. I noticed that he had the biggest shoes I had ever seen. Huge brown things, not boots either but very, very large dress shoes.

Another man dressed in a fine gray suit which was not wrinkled, walked towards us but then turned at a quick 90 degrees. He walked in the new direction then turned again another 90 degrees. He did this square walk with his face turning from a frown every few moments into a big smile then back to a frown. This routine made him seem a bit strange; both to me and the man with wrinkled suit. We both had our eyes on him until he finally went away.

I liked the man in the wrinkled suit. I liked how he stopped eating to watch the other man because he saw there was something wrong with him. Our eyes met and I smiled. The man began to speak to me.

"I don't speak French," I said. "No parlez vous Francais."

"Italian?" the man asked.

"No, English."

"Polish? Yiddish?"

"No, just English."

The man shook his head and told me he spoke Italian, French, Polish and Yiddish but no English.

I smiled, "Well, what are you going to do? You know, that's the way it goes."

But the man didn't let the fact that I didn't speak French stop him. He launched into a complicated dialogue the only part of which I understood was that the man's brother was in England but that he wasn't.

"No, I can see that. You're here."

"Oui," the man said, delighted that I had gotten that concept. Encouraged, he spoke freely on many subjects.

I didn't mind him talking to me in French except that he would stop every once in a while, and look for a response, something from me to keep the conversation going. But I didn't know what we were talking about so every time the man looked at me for recognition, I would say, "I don't speak French, only English. "

"Oui," the man said and would begin talking again in French. This repeated about eight times before he finally gave up on the idiot American. He smiled at me and went about packing himself up. He had a big black garbage bag with his clothes and food. He wrapped large rubber bands around the top of the bag to keep it closed.

I pointed to his feet, "You have the biggest shoes in the world." I held my hands far apart and pointed again to his shoes.

The man laughed and told me that he had been in an auto accident. "Operation," he motioned with his finger where they had operated on his leg. He pointed to his thigh, nowhere near his feet but I guessed the orthopedic shoes helped him walk. God knows he could never fall down with them on. He could probably sleep standing up in them.

I smiled at the man. Really, I liked him. Here was a man who had everything he owned in a plastic bag with rubber bands around it, yet he wore a tie and got a haircut with what little money he had. Why? Because then he wasn't a bum. He fit into the accepted image of European society. Of course, everyone else could see that his suit was wrinkled and that he needed a shave and that he'd been sleeping in the park but he didn't have to know they knew.

Interesting fellow, a whole story right there. His life just as important as mine, as Queen Elizabeth's. Actually, we're all just a part of his story really.

I walked around the park. On one corner, sitting on the sidewalk a young man sat begging. He had taken his shirt off to show everyone that he had an extra hand growing out of his left shoulder. It was a shrunken, distorted fucking thing too. I didn't give him any money. He was young, in his twenties. Now if he had been old man with that extra hand there, I would have dropped him a franc or two but a young kid. "Come on, man, get a job and quit showing that thing in public."

That evening back at the hotel, the painting progresses, the loneliness deepens. I finished the face tonight. Looking at it I heard not a scream but a giant "Uhhh I've had it."

It was true too. I have had it! Especially with Nice. Not only did I constantly think of Mary and the kids, check the clock to see what time it was in California so I could imagine what they were doing, but then I would compare it to my day in Nice. Wake up 8:45am, dress casual, go across the street to have coffee and a pastry, smoke two cigarettes, back up to the room, floss teeth, brush teeth, shave, put on shorts, t-shirt and thongs and walk to the beach. Beach from 10am to noon, walk back to room, look at the painting, play solitaire, paint, eat lunch, nap, look at the picture, walk to get ice cream then sit in the park. Walk back to the room, look at picture, nap, wake, look at picture, dress, go to dinner, walk back to the room and look at painting. All this time my mind is holding fantasy conversations with Mary, Stephen, Mary's parents, the kids and Mary's boyfriends. All this time too the noise in Nice is unbearable. I must close the windows but it becomes too hot and I have to open them again. None of the cars, buses, trucks or scooters in Nice have mufflers and they all need new brakes very badly as they SCREEECH to stops. This mechanical deficiency is made worse by the fact that the men in Nice are the biggest asshole drivers in the world. I must be very careful crossing the street or even walking on the sidewalk as these a-holes love to get within a pubic hair of the curb, some miss and some come right up on the sidewalk and oh yes, they love to honk their horns. Not a "toot-toot" either. It's common to have a honk go on for miles! Someone would get cut off or something and they just HONNNNKKKKKKK from Nice to Cannes. I was sick of it and so "Uhhh" was exactly the right expression.

I did enjoy the man who came to clean the street at 4:45am. I lay in bed and listened to him dragging a giant hose to spray the street with. I was up anyway, it being my regular 4am dream waking, and as I lay in bed hearing the water coming hard against the pavement, "SWISH." I got up and opened the blinds. I watched him turn off the water by closing the hydrant with a large wrench. He unhooked the long grey hose, dragged it down the street, screwed it onto the next hydrant, wrenched that open and then "SWISHED" the street some more.

This man, in his mid-twenties and looking a lot like me with black wavy hair, well he really gets into his job. He doesn't just slosh the water around either, no, no, no, if there's a stubborn spot, fine, he'll stay right there spraying the water and scrubbing the spot until he's cleaned it perfectly.

I liked him. That's how I would clean that damn street too. Might as well, it's early morning, the air's clean, it's quiet, the sun's just starting to peek in, might as well let your mind drift off and think of all those things going on in your life while you wash the street. He comes several times a week and I look forward to the mornings he shows up.

Bright, bright white light through blue circles inside my head. Best sight today.

In the morning Madame Adie came up the round staircase and knocked on my door. I put on a robe and opened it. She entered carrying two flower vases.

"Bon jour, Monsieur Gebhart"

"Bon jour, Madame. Coma va?"

"Bon, merci. I have for you vases for your next picture. A still life, no? Of flowers on the table."

"Yes, thank you. I have finished this now." I pointed to the canvas still on my makeshift easel by the window. Madame Adie stood in front of it with her finger on her cheek, deciding.

"Tres bien," she finally said. "A problem with a woman?"

"Merci, yes. You understand, it was something I needed to do," I explained.

"Oui, I understand and now for the second canvas?"

"Yes, you're right," I said as I took the larger of the vases from her and placed it on the night table. "A still life of flowers," I said as I stepped back to admire it.

"No," Madame Adie said. "It is not good for you."

She removed the first vase and replaced it with the smaller one. I wanted to use the larger one because it was the prettier; maroon with gold veins and two round handles.

"No?" I asked looking at her.

"No, because what is most important in the painting?"

"Most important, well..."

"Why the flowers of course," she interrupted.

"Yes, of course the flowers."

"Oui, not the vase."

"No, but the vase is semi-important, I think..."

"No, no.," she interrupted my wayward thinking. "With this large a vase you will need very large flowers. It is no good." She showed me on the canvas that the proportions would be off.

She was right too so I choose the vase she had picked out for me and got dressed and went out to the florist shop to purchase a bouquet. I sketched the flowers and the table for most of the day. It was a difficult painting with many problems to overcome. How would I paint the reflection of the sky in the glass behind the vase? And the apartment houses across the way? Very difficult but I must learn how to do this.

I stopped at lunch to write Stephen a letter as classical music played on the radio.

"Stephen, there is a place somewhere where voices sing with harp and violins. It is not in Nice or perhaps it is, it is not in me. Or maybe they do sing in me but I don't listen close enough. I went to the zoo in Barcelona and looked at a Black Panther as he lay sleeping in his small cage. He was curled up in the back corner. He opened his eyes for a moment, sensing my presence. I looked into his eyes, beautiful green eyes, right down through the black slits into his soul light within. He blinked. Then looked away, saying to me with his expression, 'Don't pull at me.'

"I liked him. He closed his eyes again and tried to go back to sleep but I caught him twice opening his eyes to check me out.

"Perhaps I've pulled too much at you too. The one thing that sticks out most about the three months we lived together this summer was that we didn't have very much eye contact. How good it would feel to see Stephen looking into my eyes, with the warmness of his love for me right there in the room.

"The hardest thing of all is missing people you love and not being missed by them. I have been missed before. I could feel it half way around the world. I don't feel that now and there's a coldness in my life that scares me. Do I end up a wino in a little funky room with no one caring, no one sharing?

"I still have a difficult time accepting all that has happened. The kids, they don't miss my hugs? My kisses? My tenderness and caring? And Mary, no I won't even go into that.

"The painting goes well. When I paint there are times that I hear Dad's voice. We argue about how it should be done. I say, 'I want to paint big.'

Dad says; 'No, no, detail, detail. Get that little spot there.'

"It's the same kind of arguments he and I use to have over the model trains in the basement, both of us laughing at our differences. It's funny but sometimes he drives me crazy. I love you Steve."

The still life painting of flowers by a window was coming out very well. I was quite pleased with what I'd done so far. The marble top of the little table came out very nice indeed. The color was right and the paint suggested the marbling of the stone top.

Despite the success with the paintings, I grew tired of Nice. I thought of California and although I dreaded being back into the rat race, I thought soon it would be time to get an apartment and a job. I decided that I should go back to school; UCLA at nights to get my CPA certificate.

There was a man at the park today. A wino that I had seen several times before. He was at the park all day. He slept there. He had old shoes that didn't fit so he cut the entire back part off, now they flopped like slippers when he walked. But he didn't walk, he shuffled, a dead man's walk.

I had seen him several times peeing while still sitting on a bench. He didn't get up. He just pulled it out and peed. His hands have shit on them where he has wiped his ass. He eats his bread and drinks his wine with these same unwashed hands. He's on his way out. There are thousands of men like him in one borough of New York City alone. How many are there in the world?

He's gone for sure. There's no chance at all for him. His life, your life, our lives and the paths we walk and the lessons we must learn. Some are lucky, things go right for them. You see these people all over but in France they are more evident because they have this attitude that if everything isn't right in your life, like it is in theirs, that is; enough money, a good education, the right clothes, a nice home, well then you aren't human. They're snobs yes but more than that, they're killers, cold hearted murderers.

I took time off from painting to walk to Musee Jules Cheret, a museum only a ten-minute walk from Hotel Mimosa. This was once the villa of Princess Kotsobey, a Russian exile. It was as the guide said, "A magnificent villa in the Genovese style."

There were Renoirs, Sisleys and paintings by Tanoux, Alexander Montpellier and Trouillebertt. All the paintings were very large, very clear and had that light, that ancient light, yellow-gold and timeless. As I walked from room to room admiring the paintings, a woman played the harpsichord in the main ballroom. The sound floated throughout the villa, echoed off the marble floors and walls. The princess's old furniture was still there, 17th and 18th century French masterpieces. Huge, massive marble tables, hand carved dressers and chests. Statues by Rodin. It was one of the finest museums I have ever been in.

On the way home from the museum I watched several young boys play soccer in a school yard. One boy looked and acted like Noah. It was a fall afternoon. Cool, crisp air, quiet streets, kids playing. I thought of Noah and started to cry. I would never get these years back. Noah was still young enough that he would hold hands with me. That age would never come again.

I imagined being with him at his school yard.

"How's it going for you, Noah?"

"Okay."

"School alright?"

"Yeah."

"Is it hard for you without me?"

"Sometimes."

"It's hard for me too. I miss you very much."

"I miss you too, Dad."

"I won't cry, I know you're tired of seeing me cry. Just give me a hug and go back to your game and I'll watch you."

Noah didn't have it that bad. He had his friends. He was a kid and played all day long and didn't think much about what's happened. He knew Mary enjoyed her new life as she had told Stephen, she had three boyfriends; a smart one, a dumb one and one that's good looking.

I was the one who was suffering. I didn't have my children, my home or anyone. I believed, I hoped, that someday a woman would come into my life and help me get over the past. Now I had to bear the loneliness one more day and night.

After supper at Queen Burger, where punks and rockers hang out in Nice, I watched soccer with Madame Adie's husband, Renaldo. We sat in his living room on old chairs with their stuffing half gone. Renaldo played professional soccer for Italy when he was a young man and he explained some of the action in the Corsica vs Russia game. It was a 1 to 1 tie but I was bored. I don't understand the draw of watching men run up and down on a field scoring one or two times in an hour. But it was something to break the monotony. It made me think, I used to be a normal guy. I watched football games Sundays and Monday nights. I could say things to people without watching my words. I could talk to women without being nervous. I used to be normal. What happened? The break up with Mary has taken all my confidence. Still, I saw something good in that, the experience had humbled me.

Madame Adie slipped a telegram under my door as I lay in bed in the morning. It was from Stephen, "Michael, I am confused. Haven't sold car or stock. Please advise. Love Steve."

At the post office I called Stephen.

"Stephen, this is Paul."

"Hi Paul."

"Hi, Steve how's it going?

"I'm fine but I think I messed you up. I didn't sell any of your stock."

"It's okay, I'm not mad," I said. "It was like a sign to me to come home. But I don't understand, I talked to you from Spain, the call cost me... well, I thought we discussed how to do it?"

"Yeah, but the stock was going up. It's at 26 now. I didn't want to mess up."

"At 26? It was at 20 when I asked you to sell it, so you did good. But I need it now so sell a hundred shares and wire me fifteen hundred so I can get home."

"Okay, I'll call your broker in the morning."

After a sunny morning, storm clouds, black and heavy filled the afternoon sky. I went outside and sat on the marble steps in the front of the hotel. Raindrops drizzled down out of a black sky. I was worried. What if Stephen couldn't transfer the money or did it wrong. I imagined calling for a loan and everyone turning me down. "Sorry, Paul, you're always in a jam, don't bother us."

That would never happen. My mother? My sister? My brother? I might have to call Mary. I laughed at that. I could hear her screaming, "You stole the glue! You stole the glue!" Like she did last spring when I needed a drop of super glue to fix something in my apartment. We had just separated but I was at the house. I had dropped off the kids and took the super glue from my workbench in the garage. I carried it into the house in my hand, not hiding the tube in my pocket. She saw the tube and started to scream, "You stole the glue!"

"I bought the glue." I said. "I'm going to use a drop. I'll bring it back."

"You're taking things from us!"

"You're sick."

I looked up from this fantasy aware it was not here and now, only in my mind again. There was a double rainbow in the sky, clear and bright against the background of black clouds. It was another omen. I felt better. It will be okay. I walked to the post office and called my mother. My stepfather, Bernie answered.

"Bernie, this is Paul." It took a moment for Bernie to remember who Paul was.

"Paul, Paul! Where are you calling from?"

"Nice."

"Nice?"

"Yes, Nice, Bernie. I'm in Europe."

"Are you all right?"

"Yes, I'm fine. Listen, Bernie I'm having a little money problem. I need Mom to wire me six hundred dollars."

"Six hundred dollars?"

"Yes, six hundred dollars." I felt a twitch in my stomach like maybe they would refuse. My voice changed so Bernie would hear a tinge of fear in it. "Listen, Bernie this call is four dollars a minute. I'm running out of money. I need the six hundred dollars to get home."

"Okay, I'll tell Dorothy."

"Have her telex it to American Express in Nice." The phone connection was horrible. Bernie was writing down all the information but he was spelling it crazy.

"N,i,e,c?"

I visualized the money getting screwed up as they try to locate NIEC. "Bernie, it's Nice, N, I, C, E. You know in France."

"Yes, I've got it."

"Good. Look, Bernie the last franc just went down, we're going to be cut off. Bernie? Bernie?" We were cut off.

I walked back to the hotel imagining the conversation between Bernie and my mother. About an hour later I was called to the telephone by Renaldo. I rushed downstairs hoping it was Angela in London or Muriel. The long-distance operator said, "Is this, Paul?"

"Yes.

"Go ahead mam'."

"Paul, it's mother."

"Yes, I know."

"Are you okay?"

"I'm fine, how are you?"

"We're fine. What's going on?"

"Stephen was supposed to send me money to get home but things got messed up. I'm almost broke and I need money to get back to the states."

"Oh, okay. How did he mess up?"

"It's a long story."

"We were worried you were hurt or in jail."

"No, I'm fine. I just need to pay the hotel bill and get back to London to get the plane home."

"You have your plane ticket?"

"Yes."

"When are you coming home?"

"In two weeks. I'll pay you the money right back."

"How did Steve mess up the money?"

"Ma, listen this call is expensive, I'll explain everything when I get home."

"Okay, I wired the money this afternoon. They say you should have it within a day."

"Great, ma, thanks. I'm sorry I had to ask you."

"It's all right. We thought you were going to be killed by some boyfriend."

"No, really, I'm fine." I started to laugh.

My mother who usually kept a clock by the telephone when she called coast to coast was talking now like it was a local call.

"Ma, listen we gotta hang up, this call is expensive."

"Okay, I love you."

"I love you too."

"Call us when you get home."

"Yes, I will, I promise."

"Does the plane stop in New York?"

"No, it's a direct flight to Los Angeles."

"Oh, are you coming to Scott's Bar Mitzvah?"

"I don't know. I have to get a job."

"I see, but maybe?"

"Yes, a definite maybe. Ma, listen, you've got no idea how expensive this call is. We gotta get off."

"Okay, good-bye, Paul."

"Bye, Ma."

I hung up feeling good.

"My mother loves me." I said to Renaldo and Madame Adie and the cleaning lady who had all gathered around the phone.

"Oui, oui, of course," Adie said, patting me on the shoulder. "You have a problem with money?"

"Not a problem, no, not really. It's just that I don't have enough to go home.

Madame Adie translated to Renaldo. The cleaning lady followed the conversation with great interest.

I felt better. I was going home, well not home-home, but back to the U S of A. I would get a job, oh god, an apartment, more moving. I'd be back to the sick alcohol, drug, meat bars in L.A.. I felt bad again. If it didn't go well, I would move to Maui. Maui is expensive, cost you three or four thousand to move there. Yes, I know. We'll manage. It'll be fun.

"I want to go home." I heard my five-year old child say.

"That's over, Paul. It's history. "

"I want to go home now."

I visualized our home in the Santa Cruz mountains. I could feel the warmth of being in a place that felt like home. And then the hurt of the five-year-old.

"We can't go home, Paul."

"Never?"

"No, buddy, never."

The five- year old started to cry. I felt the hurt.

"Hey, listen, Paul, I promise you, I'll get you a new home. You hear me? I promise. Okay?"

"Okay."

It was a promise I meant to keep but first I needed to get a job, make some money, then find a sensitive, loving woman. I felt the time that it would take, the uphill struggle to make it all come true.

"If you need money for food," Madame Adie broke into my internal dialogue, "we can lend you a few hundred francs."

"That is very kind, Madame Adie, but no. No, I'm okay for a week or more."

It rained during the night. In the morning the sky was gray, the streets damp. I opened the windows wide then jumped back under the covers and breathed in the cool air. I felt a newness coming over me. The fresh air brought back memories of different places, different times; playing football on Saturday afternoons, ski trips, burning leaves on autumn afternoons.

I was trying to stop smoking. I could feel the poison in my throat and sinuses but even just one meal without a smoke and I felt like I was going to burst. Still the struggle to stop was better than the days of just smoking one after another without thinking. What a horrible habit. It clouded my mind and weakened my body.

To fight the nicotine fits I was eating twelve hundred pieces of black licorice a day. What was in me that fueled this neurosis?

A rainy, gray afternoon turned into a dismal dark evening. The money didn't come. I leaned out my fifth-floor window and watched an old man walking with a cane up the back alley. A white car turned up the corner, its yellow headlights throwing a shadow of the man across the wet pavement. I listened to the sound of the tires on the wet cobblestones echo quietly against the buildings. The sound of the motor hummed underneath my window, then silence as the driver turned off the engine and parked.

It's okay. I was in Nice mending a broken heart. Trying to survive the pain of a broken life; to forget a woman I still loved. Missing children I would always hunger to be near, but it was okay. In my deepest depression I told myself to feel it. Feel it, stay with it, be it, you are a story.

Thursday morning, I went to the American Express office checking for my money. It hadn't come. When I was back at the hotel Madame Adie was in the hallway.

"Not yet?" she asked.

"No and I'm beginning to worry. What if it gets lost in the system and takes three weeks to get here?"

"Not to worry," she said. "If you need money for food, I will give you some."

"I have enough for 10 days," I said. "Thank you though. You are very kind."

"It will come soon," she said. "How does the painting go?"

"Please come see the still life, it's almost finished."

We went up the spiral, black wrought iron staircase. My studio smelled of oils and turpentine despite the windows being wide open. I lit a stick of incense as Madame Adie studied my work.

"It is rough," she said still looking at it closely, "but there is a light that you've captured and the table top is tres bien. There is peace in it," she said as she turned and faced me.

"Merci Madame," I said. "I will varnish it today then make it a present for you and Renaldo. If you wish?"

"Tres bien. I will get a good frame that fits it and put it up. Of course. Merci, Paul."

My trip to American Express the next day was a home run. Both the six hundred from my mother and the fifteen hundred from Stephen were waiting for me. I felt rich! I cashed five hundred into French francs the balance into travelers checks and went to the travel agency and purchased my one-way flight to London. Then to the perfumer's shop downtown and bought three tortoise shell hairclips one for Cat, one for Angela and one for mother.

The next day I stood with packed luggage in the carpeted hallway and paid Madame Adie my overdue hotel bill and shook Renaldo's hand. Madame kissed me on both cheeks.

"We will remember you," she said.

"Yes, me too. Take care of yourselves," I said, looking both of them in the eyes and taking in their smiling, affectionate expressions.

"Yes, and you too. Au revoir, Paul. Bon voyage."

"Yes, Au revoir."

I turned and waved to her when I reached the door on the ground floor. She stood at the top of the stairs looking after me.

I took a taxi to the airport feeling excited at the thought of returning to London and being able to hold normal conversations in my mother's tongue, but sad too at leaving France. France, how would I sum it up? Such a difficult time in such a beautiful land and culture. But also, in my time here I had spewed out the howling painting and moved on to produce a pleasant still life. I felt at peace.

Chapter Thirteen
No Way Out

November 1981

It was a fine autumn day as the train from Heathrow rode on elevated tracks into London. The sky was a clear blue, the temperature warmer than Nice had been the last week. Here in London the trees had changed colors. My Air France flight arrived on time and I breezed through customs; found a pay phone and called a few hotels and made a reservation at the Gate House B&B in Earl's Court. It wasn't hard to find and I was moving right along when just blocks from the hotel the aluminum luggage cart's left wheel broke off. I dragged the trunk along with the axle loudly scrapping on the cement sidewalk. It sounded like finger nails run over a blackboard and I was getting some pretty hostile stares from the people I passed. Sorry folks, please ignore me if you can. Anyway, I rang the bell at the Gate House several times before a man came out of a back door, down the hallway and let me in. I put my trunk and bag by the door and followed him to the desk. The floors were carpeted with a beautiful red and gold carpet, Boston ferns stood on pedestals, potted in porcelain vases. A polished wooden banister led up a winding staircase.

I signed the guest book; the price was 9.5 pounds per night with a free shower but there was no lift. The man handed me a room key.

"At the top of the stairs, room eighteen."

I left my trunk in the hallway and began to climb the upstairs with my backpack and rain jacket. The man went back to his room to watch television.

Room Eighteen was on the top floor, up six flights of steps. I was sweating as I walked back down the stairs to get my trunk. It's not like he hadn't seen me struggling with it and then he gives me a room on the top floor. Sadistic?

I knocked on the door and the man appeared a bit miffed about the interruption.

"It's not that I don't like the room," I said without sarcasm, "it's quite lovely indeed. But, you see, well the trunk is a bit heavy and if you had something on a lower floor, it would make it a little less like an athletic event."

"No, that's the only vacant room," he said impatiently.

"I see. I only thought I'd ask. It's a bit much carrying the trunk up those steps."

The man nodded and closed the door to get right back to the soccer match on TV.

I picked up the trunk, heaved it onto my right shoulder and started up the stairs. On the third floor I began to talk to myself.

"I don't want sympathy. This is my exercise for the day... Ugh, for the week, possibly all I have to do this month."

On the next landing I put the trunk down, breathing hard and my shirt soaked in perspiration. After a brief rest and introspection of my life, I started off again and finally made it to my room and crashed onto the bed exhausted.

I unpacked, found my address book and went back downstairs to call Angela from the pay phone in the lobby. No one answered. I called Carol, no answer there either. Back in my room I opened the little bottle of wine from the plane. It was a nice Bordeaux. I drank it as I listened to Telemann on the BBC. Lying back on the soft bed I drifted off to sleep.

A grey Sunday morning November 1st 1981; I took the underground to the outskirts of London, past Homestead. The trains were all but empty early Sunday morning and I sat relaxed with my feet up on the next seat. Once out of central London the elevated tracks gave me the opportunity to enjoy a two-hour tour of suburban London. There are many nice neighborhoods and little towns that are technically in the city of London but not really.

The weather was still dismal later that afternoon as I toured Buckingham Palace and watched the changing of the guards. Then to South Kensington and the British Museum of Natural

History. An ornate building and very well kept. Inside dinosaurs' bones, meteors, gems and other fantastic stones including a half ton boulder of jade!

It also housed an incredible statue of Ramses II. The entryway into the Egyptian and Assyrian rooms dramatically complete with the actual gate from the ancient Assyrian capital. I saw the Rosetta stone and Egyptian jewelry and furniture made many millenniums ago.

The entry way to the Assyrian exhibition was framed by fifteen- foot tall granite lions on either side of thirty- foot high, very thick wooden doors from the palace. I *felt* the thickness, looking at the doors and their wide, decorative iron bands and hinges. There was a realness to these ancient artifacts that the modern world's plastics do not generate.

At the Gate House later that afternoon, I reached Laker Airlines and reserved a seat on the Sunday flight, November 8th a week away. Now I had to call Stephen but the post offices didn't have telephones like in France and the regular pay phones in London couldn't be used for international calls so I had to go to a main underground station to find an international pay phone.

While I waited for a telephone in the underground station at Leicester Square, a deformed man walked by, limping very badly and with one of his arms curled up across his chest. I recalled seeing a woman earlier near Buckingham Palace with one leg amputated walking on crutches. It looked very difficult to do all day long. I remembered seeing a pigeon with one broken leg as it limped around on the ground looking for food. I realized that these were signs of some sort. Could it mean I was limping around as well, emotionally? Or was it a sign that I needed to slow down?

That night I met up with Alan Lewis of the famed Guy Fawkes party. He drove us first to Jimmies Pub on Church Street, then to The Wine Pub Place in West Kensington. The stuffed lion was still in the doorway and the Scotsman, Spoon was still at the bar; obnoxious as ever and just as much fun to listen to as he had been seven weeks earlier.

Alan and I went back to Alan's flat and chewed several mushrooms that Alan had picked wild in the English countryside. He explained to me the different varieties and trusting his expertise, I imbibed. We listened to Pink Floyd and Bob Dylan as the room went into a mellow haze. I, banged my knee hard on the coffee table when I got up to leave the apartment and limped to the underground. The irony was not lost on me. I was still running away by using drugs and so still limping through life. Okay, fine; sobriety starts from this moment on.

The next afternoon I sat in Regent Park enjoying the autumn day. The trees had turned colors, the air was chilled and the sky clean blue with not a cloud or touch of haze. Brisk cold air filled my lungs. Church bells rang out every hour. That's one thing I will miss about Europe, the church bells in every town and city. I loved to hear them peal, in the morning especially. It made the new day seem special. Black handsome cabs and red double decked buses drove by. On the way back to the hotel I passed department stores decorated with Christmas lights.

On the bus ride from Regent Park I looked up and read the white lettered sign behind the driver's seat. "NO WAY OUT."

"Now that's the truth," I laughed and decided that would be the title to my next novel, "No Way Out." It would be about my return into the business world of America; money, taxes, power and uptightness. There was no way out for me. Back to L.A. and the karma comes and comes, good and bad.

My life is a story, not how I would have written it but I couldn't fight it anymore. I was supposed to be waiting in long lines at checkout stands while I study the dandruff on the shoulders of the guy in front of me. No use trying to fight it, if I wasn't waiting in this line, I would be in another one somewhere.

Back at the Bed and Breakfast, I climbed the six flights of stairs, showered and put on my blue suit. I had carried it around Europe for two months, now I was finally going to wear it two days before going home. I straightened my tie in the mirror. It felt good to be dressed up in a suit and tie. Strange too, I felt the significance of all my costumes and this made me aware of my nude body underneath; the real me hidden behind society's first wall.

I took the underground to Baker Street and walked to Carol's flat. When I arrived, the living room was crowded with people dressed in black ties, velvet jackets and women in expensive evening gowns. They were all young, upper class Brits in their early twenties. I met Gary, a tall handsome Scotsman who was very friendly and down to earth. I sat in a chair and talked and ate and drank and smoked. The room got very warm. Carol came over and sat on the arm of my chair.

"Why don't you stand up?" she asked me.

"Why?"

"It's polite and easier to talk to people."

"I'm comfortable."

She let it pass. I could see how she would like everyone in the world to behave, move, say, dress just the way her educated mind told her they ought to.

"I'm going to Oklahoma City for Christmas to see my boyfriend," she said changing the subject.

"Oklahoma? Really? Hmm, well congratulations. I'm happy for you."

She noticed that I had grimaced.

"Oh? I fancy it's as nice as Los Angeles," she said a bit defensive.

"No doubt, oil too but the people, well it isn't London high society dear."

"I don't know. I'd rather meet them than *Californians*." She said it acidly to get at me.

"Really?"

"Yes, the Californians are into astral chants, karma, natural foods and psychiatry."

"Yes, they are. I have to admit it."

"Well it's all so phony, so faddish. Don't you think?"

"Right Carol, well you should love Oklahoma City then."

"We're going to Texas anyway, to his parents' house in San Antonio."

"Oh well, San Antonio, that's more like it. I'm sure it will be quite interesting for you."

I felt uncomfortable. She was much better at this game of barbs than I was.

The party left en masse to go to Daphne's restaurant. Carol played social director and made up the seating arrangements. No free choice, no deviation whatsoever would be tolerated. She also assigned people to the cars for the ride to the restaurant.

"I want to buy cigarettes. I'll meet you there," I said as we waited at the curb.

"Why? They sell cigarettes at the restaurant," she said.

"Okay," I said. I felt like a little boy being led around.

My assigned car was driven by a young man, Peter. Peter's girlfriend was a beautiful Asian woman who spoke with a fine British accent. Somehow it seemed phony to me. She had Peter by the balls too. She told him how to do everything. He argued, but then laughed his high-pitched laugh and did it the way she told him to.

The power of pussy. She was a pussy with an attractive face. This gave Peter status among men. Who knows she might even have given him head but I was sick to my stomach as I watched and listened to them. When we arrived at the restaurant I sat at the bar and ordered a drink rather than following the party into the side room that had been put aside for Carol.

"You joining us, Gebhart?" Gary the Scotsman asked me as he came up to the bar.

"No, actually I want to leave."

"Ah come on, it won't be that bad."

"I'm bored," I said. "I have just one night left in London and I feel like doing something else."

We shook hands.

"If you ever get over to America," I said, "please get my address from Carol."

"I will. Thank you, Paul and good luck."

I left the restaurant and stopped at the Mayfair Hotel up the block. A red jacketed bellman opened the door for me.

"Where can I buy cigarettes?" I asked him.

The doorman laughed, probably at my New Jersey accent. "C'mon, I'll show you the way." He led me through the lobby, past the restaurant to the tobacco shop. He was short man, 5'4" and fat. He wore a full doorman's red uniform and hat. He filled the uniform so completely there wasn't a pleat. His round torso matched his bulbous nose. I liked him.

You see Carol, I fit better with people like this. The doorman you wouldn't ever consider talking to, caring about, thinking about. What is his life like? Yes, Carol, I'm just another doorman dear, so don't fret that I walked out on your fancy party with your fancy friends. I'm just not a decent token American.

Back at the hotel I turned on the radio took off my suit and listen to Jimi Hendrix. "Ah that's more like it. Tell'm, Jimi. Tell'm man.

Up early and to Victoria Station in a cab. The cabbie drove by Hyde Park and pointed out Albert Hall and The Albert Museum. "Built by Queen Victoria in Memorial to Albert."

"Yes, of course," I said as I soaked up the London atmosphere. "If I could have," I said to him, "I would have liked to stay here in London another year. It's the best city in Europe."

"Most Americans say that, they do. It's got lots of 'istory."

"Yes, and I love the British accent."

"Do you?"

"Yes, you speak the proper English. I guess I speak Americanese."

"Not really, at least we can understand you Americans. You speak better English than those Irish bastards."

I didn't reply to his racial slur. The cabbie, a man in his fifties, glanced into the rearview mirror, to check whether I looked Irish or not. We sat in silence to Victoria Station after that.

At the airport I checked my metal trunk and backpack and cashed a five-pound note. I had breakfast of orange juice, a scone and raspberry jam. The Duty-Free shop sold cigarettes and alcohol for twice their American price.

I bought a cassette of Pink Floyd "Relics" and a bag of fruit drops; that left me with one pence; perfect.

In London there were no commercials on television or the radio. There weren't many stations either, three for television a dozen or so FM stations and two dozen AM. There are a lot of talk shows on the radio. Their television has a lot of talk shows too.

In Paris and Nice they have fur stores in every neighborhood, coiffure shops on each block and a dog grooming store on every other block. The people have their hair done weekly and their dogs trimmed about the same.

London's Gatwick Airport. After two months of traveling through Europe, I was on my way back to the states. I was returning to Los Angeles to face the Mercedes Benz, Rolls Royce and Volkswagen class system of get ahead.

One thing though, that terrible pain from the divorce, like a knife in my gut, was finally gone after a year and a half.

I sat in the waiting area in the Laker terminal. I never did enjoy hearing a southern drawl. The sound just doesn't go smoothly through my system. Somehow it brought up feelings of racism and narrow-minded assholes who talk Jesus Christ but cannot see His spirit in all of humanity. I felt uncomfortable around southerners. Now, sitting in the lounge watching the departure board, "Laker Airway, Los Angeles Flight GK-1, departs 12:00pm Gate--Wait in Lounge" I heard the lady next to me say to her friend in a deep southern drawl, "Now NINE NINE-DEE FIVE isn't too bad a price."

Then two rows away a middle-aged man in a blue suit with no tie and a trimmed mustache was telling people across from him his opinions on Europe. I had the feeling that he must have seen too many John Wayne movies. His southern drawl was very manly. I moved and found another seat, then laughed at myself. NO Way Out, man. I would have to face all this and more. I would have to get past being uncomfortable hearing a southern accent, assholes, bullshiters, racist opinions, black snobbery and threatening behavior. I'd be in L.A., city of smog, bad water, the waste land of the west. I would have to re-enter the business world after six months of freedom. There was no way out. Well, I could go on to Turkey or India even Africa but no, Paul you still don't get it, do you. You see my karma will tag along with me wherever I go. It's time to get back and go on with my life. My fantasies of meeting the woman of my dreams in Europe wasn't meant to be. I return now to join my brother, my people, friends and strangers in the struggle to keep your soul through the slow death of America, not that it's any different anywhere else. For now, I want to feel my life through each moment, painting in oils to pass the time.

I look up at the tote board and saw that my on-time 12 noon flight has been delayed until 1:15pm. You can't run away from it, there's no way out. The world is boring and disappointing. I could smoke another pack of cigarettes or eat another pound of candy or have another drink but none of it will fill me.

I sat quietly feeling the worm of agitation gnawing inside me. There was no way out; on the train from Paris to Nice, Barcelona to Nice or Philly to New York. It comes and comes, that boredom and the sense of worthless, meaningless time. Why must I stand in all these lines? See all these faces? Hear the children cry and watch as their parents smack them. I will have to work at getting through all these unwanted moments. Meanwhile there are ten thousand skin heads walking the streets of London with white t-shirts and black pants and boots. They curse and fight, revolting against it. I did too and for too long. I took too many drugs and had too many dreams and fantasies about what life *should* be. No, it is what it is, so go ahead and drop the bomb already. Until they do, until I'm dead and laying in my coffin I'm going to welcome every day, every moment as it comes into my story. Let me feel it deeply and honestly.

Sitting here now, waiting for the plane ride back to normal, I could feel the child inside me; the scared five-year old who just wants to play and feel secure, the eleven-year-old who wants to be liked by pretty girls. All these ages I've been through, they're all there still inside me. I can see that now. I will take care of them all; not to worry guys. I know what you all need and I'm paying attention to you.

See the boring light hit the boring wall, see the boring color orange. The Assyrians are gone, the Egyptians are gone, the Greeks and Romans all gone. Their civilizations in museums, the British Museum to be exact. I looked up, an old man with a cane sat down on the seat across from me. He was skinny with thinning gray hair and baggy pants. His face was distinguished, a square jaw but narrow cheek bones. I looked at him to get the detail, the style, after all man, I was writing a book. He stared back at me, his eyes glaring. I didn't look away. The man glared harder. I went on studying the tension in his forehead and jaw, the facial language that said I was trespassing on private property.

I turned away. Why do things have to be so difficult? Why can't we look at each other and enjoy ourselves?

The old man reminded me of my grandfather, Morris. Same features and body build, same hate inside too. He disliked other people, anyone who wasn't just like him, blacks, Puerto Ricans, and you white people too. He didn't like anybody, equally.

Grandpa did all right for himself though, from rag picker to hat manufacturer. He was able to retire when he was just forty-nine years old and lived almost fifty years off of his dividends and investments. He traveled the world and told me once that the best part of traveling was coming back to America. I think he was right.

I looked at my baggage ticket and read it out of boredom. "This is not the baggage check described by Article 4 of the Warsaw Convention or the Warsaw Convention as amended by the Hague Protocol 1955."

What baggage check was it then?

Now that I knew the airlines had my best interests at heart, disavowing any responsibility for my luggage, I sat back to handle more of the inane. A tall man walked by. He had tattoos of birds and stars on his neck, part of a very large eagle showed on his chest through his unbuttoned shirt, another square, green thing was on the back of each of his hands. His blond hair was shoulder length. He had a pierced earring through his left earlobe.

I could only hope that the capitalist airline which disavowed any knowledge of my baggage didn't also put me next to tattoo-man for my twelve-hour flight back to Los Angeles.

www.ingramcontent.com/pod-product-compliance
Lightning Source LLC
Chambersburg PA
CBHW021137110726
47900CB00002B/389